Praise for Robin Maxwell's GODS OF ATLANTOS SAGA

"Robin Maxwell's Atlantos is a tremendous, exhilarating, unputdownable surprise with deep, engaging characters and a clever plot full of twists, turns and unexpected challenges. These qualities, and the sheer sustained craftsmanship of the author from first page to last, combine to make Atlantos a brilliant read. But beyond that, this unique novel offers a plausible, completely unexpected explanation of the Atlantis mystery, and with it some real food for thought for anyone interested in the secrets of humanity's forgotten past."

— Graham Hancock,
New York Times and international bestselling author of
Fingerprints of the Gods and *America Before*

"Lost civilizations. The manipulation of human evolution. Monsters, and a high-tech colony on Mars. What else can anybody ask for? Atlantos is an instant classic… a science fiction masterpiece!"

— Ronald Shusett,
writer-producer of "Alien"
"Total Recall" and "Minority Report"

"If you fancy titanic struggles of godlike beings at the dawn of history, then strap yourself in for a vivid re-imagining of one of our oldest and most mysterious legends. Maxwell has created a fantastic world so thrillingly described that the reader will want to live there for a long, long time. She's written a "Unified Field Theory" of Atlantis. I love living in the worlds she creates."

— Christopher Vogler,
international bestselling author of Hollywood textbook,
The Writers Journey: Mythic Structure for Writers

"Robin Maxwell never fails to amaze me. From a reigning queen of historical fiction, to the competitor of Shakespeare with her heartfelt novel of Romeo and Juliet, to the adrenalin-rush of Jane's beloved Tarzan, she dominates the page. Now, with Gods of Atlantos Maxwell infuses historical and science fiction with literary brilliance, creating a smashing new genre. I love these books!"

—Michelle Moran, national bestselling author of
Nefertiti and *Cleopatra's Daughter*

Praise for the Other Novels of Robin Maxwell

"Finally, an honest portrayal of the only woman of whom I have been really, really jealous. What a wonderful idea to write this book. Now I am jealous all over again!"

— Jane Goodall, for
JANE: The Woman Who Loved Tarzan

""*JANE* is a triumph. A triumph of imagination, adventure, and character. Here we have the true 'missing link' that we've always wanted. Jane's side of the story.

— Margaret George, *New York Times* bestselling author
of *Memoirs of Cleopatra*

"…respectful, exciting and disarming…Jane Goodall and Isak Dinesen would be right at home with Miss Jane Porter."

– *Kirkus Reviews*, "10 Must Read Sci-fi/Fantasy"

"History doesn't come more fascinating—or lurid— than the wife-felling reign of Henry VIII."

—*Entertainment Weekly for*
The Secret Diary of Anne Boleyn

POSEIDON
IN
LOVE

POSEIDON
IN
LOVE

THE GODS OF ATLANTOS SAGA

BOOK I

ROBIN MAXWELL

Inspired by the writings of Plato

PIPES CANYON PRESS

Published by Pipes Canyon Press P.O. Box 302
Pioneertown, CA 92268

www.RobinMaxwell-GodsOfAtlantos.com

ISBN: 978-0-9963759-3-1 (trade paperback)
ISBN: 978-0-9963759-4-8 (Kindle)
ISBN: 978-0-9963759-5-5 (ePub)

1.
Atlantis — Lost Civilizations — Poseidon — Isis — Atlas — Athena
— Plato — Solon — Xanthippe 2. Science Fiction — Space Opera —
First Contact — Historical Fiction — Prehistory 3. Ancient Astronauts
— Alternate Dimensions — Planet 9 — Grey Aliens — Giza Plateau
Sphinx, Great Pyramid 4. Neolithic Culture — Great Flood, End of
Last Ice Age — Psychedelic Mushrooms —Human Evolution

With gratitude to Plato for his dialogues,
Timaeus and Critias

BOOKS BY ROBIN MAXWELL

JANE: The Woman Who Loved Tarzan
O, Juliet
Signora da Vinci
Mademoiselle Boleyn
To the Tower Born: A Novel of the Lost Princes

The Elizabethan Quartet

The Secret Diary of Anne Boleyn
The Queen's Bastard
The Virgin Elizabeth
The Wild Irish: A Novel of Elizabeth I and the Pirate O'Malley

Written with Billie Morton

Augie Appleby's Trouble in Toyland
Augie Appleby's Wild Goose Chase

Graphic Novel

The Jungle Tales of Tarzan: Introduction

THE GODS OF ATLANTOS SAGA

Then listen, Socrates, to a tale which, though strange, is certainly true… not mere legend, but an actual fact…

– Plato, *Timaeus* 4th Century BC

Let me begin by observing first of all, that nine thousand was the sum of years which had elapsed since the war which was said to have taken place between those who dwelt outside the Pillars of Heracles and all who dwelt within them… Of the combatants on the one side, the city of Athens was reported to have been the leader and to have fought out the war; the combatants on the other side were commanded by the kings of Atlantos…

– Plato, *Critias,* 4th Century BC

ATHENS, 399 BC

PROEM

H E WATCHED XANTHIPPE place the gold coin in the center of Socrates' waxy lips. Her fingers trembled slightly, and her own lips were set tight with determination. "There, Love," she told the corpse. There's your payment for the Ferryman." She looked across her husband's white-draped body and nodded at Plato. With a sharp sniff he took the small gold tablet he had fashioned for his teacher, and arranged it above Socrates' heart.

"Of course you won't need these instructions," he told the dead man. "If anyone knows how to navigate the Underworld, to properly address the Gods there, it's you. It is just my small thanks." Plato gulped back a sob, grieving for the teacher who had lifted him out of ignorance. Who had made a man of him.

Xan smiled at Plato with tears brimming. "A favor, please" she said quietly. "Get them out of here. I don't want them near my children." She angled her eyes at a clutch of young men gathered in the corner of the courtyard. Indeed, they were staring across the garden at the widow's three little boys who huddled tearfully with their nurse. The young men stood well away from their fathers, who themselves formed a herd, like gazelles in white linen, their heavy gold bracelets proclaiming their lofty status, as if anybody could fail to recognize it. Plato understood it was

3

the sons of those men that Xan wished to disappear from this otherwise dignified funeral. Even though it had been the fathers who'd sent the boys to entrap Socrates, who were responsible for his death, Xan knew that to eject the young men would shame them more than it would their fathers.

Their fathers were shameless.

Plato smiled at the woman across from him, robed and hooded in mourning grey. People always said she was "almost pretty." Xan's lips and eyes and creamy olive skin were perfection, but her nose was thin and too long by a hair. "My pleasure," he said, and turned to his task.

Some of the young men were still gangly. Others had yet to sprout beards. Their heads were bowed in, almost touching each other. As he walked across the stones, a salacious laugh rose up from their center. *Good,* he thought, *this will make my task easier still.*

"The widow has asked that you leave her home," he said to their backs. They all turned at once, startled into silence. "Do you need me to show you to the door?" Plato asked loudly, so everyone in the courtyard could hear.

Several of the beardless faces blushed crimson.

"What if we don't want to leave?" sparred the son of Melitus, Socrates' principal accuser. The boy was as odious a creature as his father.

Plato felt his hands ball into fists. "Then I'll have to help you out."

They jeered and laughed among themselves, but they saw his dangerous resolve and decided that their fathers' silent, glaring instructions were to give up this fight. With unconvincing bravado they sauntered to the front gate held open by the old slave Zepho. He slammed the doors loudly behind them and shot his mistress a grim smile. Her shoulders sagged with perceptible relief.

Then, as if given a cue, Xan threw back her head and began

the Widow's Wail. The black-garbed crones took up the chorus, their warbling lamentation echoing around the portico.

Now the mourning could truly begin.

৵

All of the guests had gone, and the children had been put to bed. Zepho moved slowly around the courtyard tending to a trampled shrub, righting a fallen flower pot, keeping his eyes lowered when he neared the bier upon which his beloved master lay. Plato kept company with Xan on the stone bench where he had taken so many lessons from the great man. Her face was tortured and wet with tears.

"They've done it. They've gotten away with public murder."

"I know."

"Did you see them gloating?"

"Why wouldn't they gloat? They annihilated the single voice in Athens that called them what they were."

"Tell me, for what insane reasons did they seek to execute my husband?" she furiously demanded. "For failing to acknowledge the same deities that the city acknowledges? For that, he is called a 'morally abominable man' who corrupts the youth of Athens? By the Gods, his greatest crime was claiming his wisdom came from knowing he knew *nothing*!"

"He offended them. Made them look like fools. He threw their rampant greed right in their faces. Their contempt for truth and disregard for perfecting their own souls. He simply couldn't be allowed to live."

"Those boys," she said, remembering. "Monster spawn. When their turn comes they'll rule this city with equally black hearts." She laughed ruefully. "Did you see their faces at the trial when Soc suggested that his sentence should be free meals for life at the Pryaneum?"

Plato dared to look directly into her eyes. It was a bold move, but they'd been through so much in the past days. The trial. Watching as her husband downed hemlock rather than allow the State to execute him. Holding each other as the life drained out of his mortal shell. Plato could see clearly now why Socrates had loved Xan so passionately – men were not expected to value their wives except as vessels for their children – loved this woman forty years his junior, the woman he called "the hardest to get along with of all the women there are." His teacher had chosen Xanthippe for that very reason. For her audacity and argumentative spirit. Her intelligence and humor.

"By now," she said wistfully, "he'll be crossing the Styx, the Ferryman clutching his gold coin. And grinning Hades, with Persephone on his arm, is waiting on the other shore to greet him."

"He won't need my small gold tablet," Plato said. "He'll know exactly what to say."

Xan nodded and wiped at her cheek with the back of her hand. "He always knew just what to say."

It was a stifling day at the agora, the long shadow of the Acropolis stopping short of the market stalls. At the fig farmer's tent Plato worried over the green or the brown fruits till his head spun. At the vintner's he'd dallied so long at the grapes that the merchant shouted at him to stop fingering the goods and decide. He'd bought wine there as well, and across the way a portion of white goat cheese and a round of the best bread. At the fountain house he filled his water-skin, and crossing over the aqueduct – stepping clear of the slops being thrown from the windows – made for city's western wall. As he walked the muddy streets he accepted his own state of mind. He was nervous to be taking possession of his first home.

Solon's Villa.

They still called it by that name, though his uncle six times removed had been dead for one hundred and thirty years. A lawgiver, poet, and one of the Seven Sages, there was no more distinguished or revered man in Athens's history. But since Solon's death, a string of grand and great grandsons, then more and more distant relations, had inherited his house, caring little for its upkeep, leaving it in a decrepit state. Lactones, the most recent cousin to have it, had died of old age the week before, and its ownership had finally fallen to Plato's mother. At nearly thirty, he was deemed by his father as ready to head his own household. His mother had therefore graciously – if not happily, for she wasn't ready to let her youngest son go – bequeathed Solon's villa to him. His celebration of independence had been delayed by Socrates' trial and execution, and Lactones' newly-freed slaves had already gone from the house. Only one remained on the premises, on the promise that Plato would come take possession of the place as soon as Socrates was buried.

The stones of the Villa's outer wall were crumbling with mold and ivy, and the knocker was half off its hinges. He knocked as best he could on the brittle wood door and waited, his heart crashing against his ribs, till it was swung open by a round-faced eunuch. Seth the Egyptian was his name, so his mother had told him. It was easy to see he'd been rushing about. A thin film of sweat glazed his wholly unwrinkled forehead, and his words were clipped, offhanded "Come in, come in…"

"I've brought food," Plato said, feeling suddenly ridiculous.

"Good. There's no one here to wait on you. They've all gone home."

"That's fine. But you must take the time to show me the place. I was only here once when I was very small."

They walked through the courtyard, all gone to weeds, which seemed to Plato not a sad thing, but something cheerful. He enjoyed the study of living things and liked to have his hands in the dirt. He would bring the garden back to its former glory. Seth had gone ahead, slipping under the portico and in through some double doors. Plato followed him into a large, dark chamber where the servant was lighting, with a long-handled torch, the many wall sconces set high around the room's perimeter.

The chamber's illumination was a shocking sight.

The rack and ruin of the outer wall and courtyard aside, this place was intact, and well ordered, recently dusted, and crammed with curiosities. A massive Persian rug in faded red and gold covered every inch of the floor. Crossed elephant tusks hung upon one wall, and opposite was Hecaterus' famous map of the world.

"I've inherited a treasure box!" Plato exclaimed, sounding embarrassingly like a little boy. "What is all this?"

"Collected artifacts from the ten years of Old Master's travels," Seth told him.

"You mean Solon?"

Seth snorted. "Lactones was afraid of his own shadow. He never went anywhere. And the ones before him, I'm told, were less courageous than that. Lactones was altogether uncurious about the room's contents. They offended him. So he rarely came in here." Seth's face softened as he gazed around him.

He did not say, but it was clear to Plato that the servants had taken it upon themselves to care for and honor the contents of this room. Now Seth touched a tiny sarcophagus set on a miniature bier – a mummified cat by the look of it – and gazed mildly at the small gold statue of Isis and Osiris standing side by side with their arms around each other's waists. "It reminds me of home… where I'm going soon."

"Please, Seth," Plato implored, "I know you're eager to go, but will you show me the library?"

"Of course." The eunuch smiled with thin closed lips. "It's time you met Master Grae."

❦

"Truth be told," Seth began as he unlocked a door so intricately carved it was difficult to make out the entwined figures, "it was

Grae I stayed for. The others hurried away the night Lactones died. No one liked him much."

They passed in through the door. This chamber, too, was cool and well kept, but it was lit by the sun streaming in through two rectangular skylights. There were windows on two walls closed by draperies. Floor-to-ceiling on four walls were diagonal crisscrossed shelves, and protruding from each cubbyhole was a scroll. On one flat shelf were displayed many dozens of circular clay seals that looked to be Sumerian, and on another musical instruments. There were several hourglasses, as though to remind one of the importance of the passage of time. On several tables manuscripts were laid out, but it was to a large map covering a broad desk that Plato was drawn. It had been unrolled and pinned down. Troop pieces and tiny ships displayed the progress of a battle on land and sea.

"Seek the Chronicles!" came a man's voice from the library's far corner. The sun was shining down so brightly from the skylight, that the corner was wreathed in shadows.

"Master Grae!" Seth called and wove between the several tables towards the voice.

Plato followed tentatively.

"Meet your new friend, Plato," Seth added, and stepped aside.

On a large, multi-branched grapevine hanging on a chain from a ceiling beam stood a bird. An all-grey parrot with a crimson tail and crinkled white skin round its glittering black eyes.

"Hello," it said soberly.

"Hello," Plato replied.

"Have you a fig?" the bird asked politely. Then, "I want a fig!"

"As a matter of fact, I have one." Plato released his leather shoulder pack and reached inside.

"Fig!" the parrot insisted.

"Patience… patience…" Plato murmured.

"Hold the fruit away from him or he'll take your finger, too," Seth instructed.

Plato held it so far out that the grey bird was forced to lean extremely to hook it with its curved bill. Then taking the fruit in its sharp, four-toed claw, he held it up and sank its beak deep in the flesh. The tiny seeds could be heard crackling cheerfully. His face covered with shiny pink fruit meat, Master Grae took Plato's measure.

"Why is he kept locked away here?" Plato said.

"I don't know. He's always just been... 'the Library Bird.' Some say he was brought back from Solon's travels in Egypt."

"He would be unconscionably old. The Methuselah of Parrots."

He's had no lack of friends. Always the servants' favorite member of the household. And very well fed."

"I can see that."

"Seek the Chronicles!" the parrot shouted again.

"Why does he say that?" Plato asked.

"'Seek the Chronicles?' No one knows. He's always said it." Seth was seething with impatience. "Master Plato, now that you've seen the house... may I go?"

"Yes, of course! My mother is sending me servants tomorrow or the next day. I'll be fine here tonight. Plenty of food for the bird and me. Right, Master Grae? I certainly won't be lonely, will I?"

"The luck of your Gods to you," Seth said, backing from the room.

"And you yours. Safe journey home."

"More fruit!" said the bird.

⸙

He'd tried to sleep in Lactones' chamber, but even with the linens changed he felt crowded by the old man's presence. When a vision of him dying in the bed came upon him, Plato sprang up and went walking through the deserted house. The place – at least

10

when the sun went down – was adrift with shades. Plato could not be sure of their identities, as they were silent and, of course, ephemeral – coming and going as if a wisp of fog on the river. In the curiosities room they were volubly present, spirits of animals and men of tribes and distant lands. In the kitchen house, separated from the villa by a paltry kitchen garden, the lingering souls were mainly women. Here, amidst the warm spiced air there were distant echoes of clanging cookpots, the whisper of love affairs among slaves, and the bitter longing for home.

Perhaps he was just imagining things. In Plato's father's villa there were no dark corners for spirits to lurk, no silent, untended rooms. Just the bustle of a rich Athenian household. Perictione, his mother, orchestrated the days and dinner parties – gardeners, cooks, porters, and maids in a single cheerful family. Her husband, and her only remaining child at home – himself – had to be fed and dressed, sent off to meetings and lectures, and plays at the amphitheater. This goodwife's days had always been busy. Now, the loss of Plato to his own home had shaken her. The house would be quieter. More space for the specter of old age to follow her about with its niggling aches and pains and bouts of forgetfulness. So Plato was not displeased by the bevy of shades in his new home. They and the clever parrot would keep him company until the servants arrived.

It was, in fact, Master Grae's company that he craved now, in the middle of the night, and drew him to the library. First he braved the dark, rustling garden so he could steal into the kitchen house for some cheese from a cool earthen jar. He took some bread and a handful of olives. When he put more figs on a plate than he knew he would eat he began to smile, realizing he was already a slave to the bird.

In the library he lit all the sconces there were. Still, the room was dim. It was clearly a place to be enjoyed in the daytime. Master Grae was silent in his shadowy corner till Plato came to stand before him. The creature, perching with perfect balance on one foot, the other tucked into his belly feathers, opened one eye.

"I've brought you figs."

"Have you cheese?"

"Yes. I have cheese."

"I'll have cheeeeese," the bird said, drawing out the word for dramatic effect.

Plato unwrapped his breakfast and held a crumble of cheese away from the curved black beak. Master Grae ignored it, though he changed the foot he was balancing on and fluffed his wing feathers with a sharp snap.

"You're toying with me," Plato said. "You don't want cheese at all."

The bird was silent. He closed the one open eye, shutting out his company and apparently going to sleep.

That afternoon, Plato had begun a general survey of the shelves and cubbyholes. "Solon's personal library," he'd muttered with astonishment. "His library is *mine* now." These were treasures beyond imagining – scrolls and parchments, some on creamy white papyrus, some crumbling with age. On one shelf were inscriptions engraved on plates of copper, iron and bronze. On another, writings on stone, clay slabs, skins, oyster shells and bone. Orphic gold tiles from Crete shimmered in the torchlight. Wood and wax tablets looked plain besides these others. The shelves were brilliantly ordered, with a small ticket – a parchment *sillybos* – glued to the end of each scroll's winding boss, proclaiming its contents to the reader. Had Solon employed library slaves to do all this work, Plato wondered, or had he done this himself?

Everything was here. The tragedies and comedies of the great playwrights. Parchments on agriculture, medicine, astronomy, philosophy. The works of Homer. Delphic textbooks. Treaty texts and maps of the world. An entire wall was devoted to alchemy and the writings of the Thrice Great Hermes Trismegistus who had given the Egyptians their laws and alphabet. Hermetic statues, too – ones that might well have imprisoned souls of demons and angels lurking inside them. *Might one of them speak?* Plato wondered. *Engage in prophesy as the great book claimed?*

His heart had pounded as he'd moved slowly round the library that afternoon, carefully reading each *sillybi*, beginning to plan his future studies. Socrates was dead, but here before him was a head-spinning hall of scholarship. The greatest teacher of all, his very own Academy, was right at his fingertips. Many of the parchments and scrolls and tablets, he could see, were in need of translation. He would do it. It might take the rest of his life, he'd thought happily. *With this knowledge transmitted from these texts to my mind and soul, I might become a very great man!*

Now he was back here in the wee hours of the morning looking for a starting place for his studies. "How a thing ends is determined in large part by how that thing begins," Socrates used to say. The thought paralyzed him. *What if I choose wrongly? What if I start…?* All at once a vision of Xanthippe's face rose up before him. The impish smile. The curious black eyes. He must share this with her! He must…

"Seek the Chronicles!!" shrieked the parrot so loudly and suddenly that Plato's guts lurched. He turned and saw the grey bird no longer sleeping, no longer indifferent but leaning towards Plato from the lowest branch of the grape vine.

"Step up!" cried Master Grae.

"Step up?" Plato repeated, bewildered, and moved carefully towards the shadowy corner.

"Step up! Step up!"

"All right, I'm coming." He went and stood in front of the perch, eye to eye with Master Grae who shifted anxiously from foot to foot. "What do you want me to do?"

"Step up!"

"I cannot step up. I cannot…"

And with that, the parrot lifted one foot in Plato's direction.

"Ah, *you* wish to step up."

The bird's black eyes flashed dangerously.

"I don't know about this. Seth said you could take off my finger."

Then with a brief flap and a whiff of sweet parroty powder, the bird leapt off its perch and onto Plato's shoulder. He froze, seeing out the corner of his vision how close the creature, with it razor hook bill, was to his eye.

"Pentateuch Six One Five," the bird whispered into the curve of Plato's ear.

"What?"

The bird chuckled.

The bird on my shoulder just chuckled, Plato realized with a start. "You're laughing at me," he said.

"Pentateuch." This was a clear command.

"All right!" Plato looked around him. He remembered seeing a manuscript of the Five Books of the Hebrews earlier that day. *But where?*

As Plato took his first step he felt the parrot's sharp toenails pierce the shoulder of his tunic as it tried to balance. "*Pentateuch, Pentateuch,*" Plato muttered as he perused the wall of shelves, drawing a finger lightly over the cubbyholes and roll bosses, sometimes reading one of the *syllobi.* He remembered seeing the manuscript yesterday – one of the first surprises of the library. Few Greeks read the Jews' Holy Book, as it had never been translated from the Aramaic, and fewer still could read the Hebrew language. *Of course Solon was one who could,* Plato thought. He was one of the Seven Sages. A man of renown. If Solon could not read that language, who could? *Across the room – that's where the Hebrew scripture was! Not on a shelf at all.*

He spied the unspooled parchment on a long slender table, just there, and stopping to light a five-candled hand lamp, walked to it gingerly. The peculiar thought flitted across his mind that every footfall was bringing him closer to his future and fortune. But that was mad! He was a young Athenian walking across a dead man's library, carrying on his shoulder a grey bird whispering riddles in his ear.

When he – *they* – stood above the crumbling brown parchment scroll spread across the long table with its five "Books" appearing as a dense black mat of Hebrew letters, the sensation of "Destiny" grew only stronger. Now he could see that something was tucked underneath the text from end to end. He pushed the top edge of it with two fingers of each hand, and there came sliding out from beneath the parchment a new, creamy white sheet of papyrus, equally as long as the *Pentateuch* scroll.

Plato bent his head to see and realized at once that, mirroring the blocks of writing in the old testament, was here on the new papyrus *a Greek translation*! Only three of the five books had been finished. Plato read, "Genesis" "Exodus" "Leviticus." He pulled up a bench and sat, forgetting and jostling the bird so that it grabbed the shoulder of his tunic with his beak – and a bit of the skin with it – to keep from falling.

"Sorry, sorry," Plato said, offhandedly, for now he was curious. Beyond curious. He carefully slid the new papyrus all the way out and set it down flat across the top of the old parchment.

"'Six One Five' you say? 'Six One Five.'" He drew his lamp closer and sought 6:15 in the Book of Leviticus. Moving the magnifying glass over the passage, and using his finger as a pointer he read the Greek from the left. "*The priest will take a handful of the finest flour and some olive oil, together with frankincense and he will burn it on the altar as an aroma pleasing to God.*"

Plato sat back. "I don't know what this signifies," he said aloud, realizing he was telling this to the bird, but it was silent. Patient. "I think it signifies nothing. A waste of time!"

But as Plato sprang from the bench the parrot spoke.

"Six One Five. Six One *Five*."

So Plato sat again, and fixed his attention on Genesis. "If you're leading me on a fool's chase," he said aloud to no one in particular, "I will find out now." He sucked in a breath and found the passage in Solon's fresh clean alphabet characters. Was Plato imagining it? Was this portion of the manuscript darker and bolder than the rest of the document? A sign of its importance?

"Well, here it is, Master Grae. I suppose you've heard it before. *'Six One Five. When man began to multiply on the face of the land and daughters were born to them, the Sons of God saw that the Daughters of Man were fair. The Messengers were on the earth in those days, and also afterwards when the Sons of God came into the Daughters of Man, and they bore children to them. These were the mighty men who were of old. The men of renown.'*"

Plato stared at the words. They meant nothing to him – he had not yet taken up study of the Hebrew holy writings. Socrates had not taught it, and while he would one day certainly delve into the *Pentateuch*, here, now, was this puzzle, one that had dead-ended after reading a passage from a tribal manuscript sent from the past, out of the mouth of Solon's parrot. But sent to *him*? Were the Fates over-watching him even now? How could Solon have known he – Plato – would come into his library one hundred and thirty years after his death and agree to take directions from his feathered friend? Had others been so directed?

Grumbling, Plato went back to the passage. "The Sons of God…" he said aloud… "came into the Daughters of Man, and they bore children unto them." *So Hebrews, like Greeks, believed their Immortals mated with Mortals.* It was this very understanding of Demi-Gods that Socrates taught Athens' young men, and for which he had been executed by the State.

"Otis Twenty One!" the parrot sang with an eardrum rupturing sound.

"Ugh! What now?!"

"Otis Twenty One," Mr. Grae spoke more reservedly. "Twenty One. Twenty One."

"I'm assuming the *Pentateuch* again," Plato said and peered down at the text. In Genesis at 21 there was something about Abraham and Sarah having the child, Isaac. His circumcision.

"No Otis here," he said to himself, also informing the bird of it. He pulled the candle closer to the middle book of the three translated texts. "Exodus," he said.

"Otis," the parrot replied firmly. "Twenty One."

"Ah, 'Ex-*o-tis*. I see." Plato scrolled down to 21. Yes! The paragraphs numbered 21, 22 and 23 were clearly bolder than the surrounding text. "*Then Moses stretched out his hand over the sea,*" he read aloud, "*and the Lord caused the sea to go back* by a strong east wind all that night, and made the sea into dry *land, and the waters were divided. So the children of Israel went into the midst of the sea on the dry ground,* and the waters *were* a wall to them on their right hand and on their left." He stared down at the words. "A leader of the Jews named Moses took them out of Egypt," Plato said aloud, "and he parted... the Red Sea. Extraordinary. He made the sea into dry land." What kind of magic was that?

"Part the Red Sea," the bird quipped, as though his memory had been suddenly jogged. Then he became imperious, ordering Plato about. "Part the Red Sea!"

Plato felt the beak clamping on his earlobe. "All right. I'll part the Red Sea!" He looked skeptically round him at the library's four walls, the shelves and tables and maps, the two windows on every wall closed in green velvet.

He froze.

The window on the western wall was hung with two *rust red curtains* stretching from ceiling to floor – the only ones of this color in the library. Certainly, this was not Solon's "Red Sea." Or was it? The bird was silent. *Of course he was,* Plato thought with irritation, *now that he needed guidance.*

The sensation of collision with Destiny rose like a wave of nausea as he walked across the library floor. But once he stood before the curtains he felt slightly ridiculous.

Steeling himself, with two hands outstretched, Plato parted the Red Sea.

Before him, an arm's length away, was a wooden door, not

one over-tall, but wide. Its upper half was heavily carved in a labyrinthine shape with three deep circular trenches – each paired with a convex ring beside it. From the central circle in a vertical line to the bottom of the outer ring was a single deep cut sliced through all rings, high and low. A small trident with a long handle had been skillfully carved into the top right of the door, and the image of a long-stemmed mushroom graced the left. Poseidon came immediately to mind on sight of the Homeric God-King's weapon. Poseidon – Lord of the Sea and of earthquakes. He was also – if Plato was to believe his father's family – a distant ancestor of theirs. It was not something that any of them really believed. More a familial boast. Many people claimed heritage from Gods and Demi-Gods. Nobody took the claims seriously.

But what was the symbol doing here? Solon – a legitimate relative – was from his mother's family. And what of the skinny-stemmed mushroom? *Where had he seen it before?*

"Part the Red Sea," said the bird, unconvincingly. He seemed to have run out of things to say.

"Shhh. I'm thinking."

Plato closed his eyes, searching for the image of fungi that he had once seen carved into stone. But where? The image flew up behind his eyes of a great procession out of Athens. Twenty-one years of age, he walked silently among in the crowd of white-robed initiates, next to Socrates and Xanthippe.

They were pilgrims on the Road to Eleusius.

The great pillared Mystery Temple was before him, hundreds of white robes crowding in through the Sanctuary's front doors. He exchanged excited glances with his friends. The great doors loomed up before him. A glance at the pillars on either side of the doors – stone pillars carved with mushrooms!

He stood dazed in Solon's library before a carved wood door. *Mushroom and trident. A circular labyrinth. And what was this?* Below the concentric rings were five pairs of carved symbols of Aeros and two of Aphrodite. The sign of ten males. Two females.

"Are you going to tell me how to open this?" Plato said to the bird. "There's no handle. No lock. And if there is, I haven't got the key."

No answer was forthcoming.

He began to finger the door, running the tips along the high ridges and deep trenches of circles. He ran his index finger down the straight vertical gash feeling for any irregularity, any hidden clue to the door's opening. He traced around the trident. Around the mushroom. He examined the twelve male and female symbols.

Nothing. *Nothing!*

"Six. One. Five. Two. One," muttered Master Grae.

The scriptural numbers added together, Plato thought, equal 15. Combined numerologically – 6. Twice 6 was the number of male and female symbols. No. He was clutching at straws. He felt helpless. Stupid. Like a boy failing at mathematics and logic and... Perhaps it was a joke. He'd never known his uncle six times removed. Perhaps Solon took pleasure in making fools of anyone who took himself too seriously. Plato was always being accused of that. Maybe...

"Six," the bird uttered definitively.

Plato's heart nearly stopped. This was no jest. It was a true treasure hunt. Of course there was something hidden behind this door. Something that Solon wished for a worthy seeker to find.

"All right," Plato said. "6."

He took several steps back from the door. Only then did he see two additional carvings near its bottom. One – the unmistakable figure of a horse. The other, a symbol of some sort. Four lines each flowing in parallel horizontal waves. This last captured Plato's imagination. Thrust a new image into his head. A lyre plucked with its ivory plectrum. *The four waves the strings of the lyre!*

"Yes!" he whispered to himself, and walked carefully back to the grapevine. Master Grae stepped off his shoulder and back onto the lowest branch. Plato strode to the far wall where the musical instruments were arrayed on a single shelf. He took the only lyre there, so old that its gilt had worn nearly off. With a sharp sweep of his fingers he strummed the strings.

Plato startled.

Six strings.

Lyres were four-stringed and five and seven-stringed. But rarely six.

A synchronous event!

Plato was a student of these anomalies – acausal connecting coincidences. *Just as you mention the name of your long-lost uncle, here he comes strolling around the corner. You are reading the word 'tortoise' in a text, and outside your window a man walking by is uttering the word 'tortoise' at the very same moment.* Just now he'd followed a tortured path to the number 6... then been drawn across the room to a rare 6-stringed lyre.

He smiled to himself, unaccountably pleased with the moment and yet... yet he wished that Xan could be here to share it. She would know what to make of all this.

"Six!" shouted Master Grae.

"Keep your feathers on." Plato stood before the mysterious door. Of course the instructions were to play the instrument. But play what? He was not a lyrist but a player of the double-reed *aulos*. He would need to improvise. He took up the wafer-thin plectrum hanging on its ribbon from the frame and with brash determination, plucked each string – the first, the second, the third – vibrations from the last tremulously bleeding into the sound of the next – four, five – the first was fading but still audible... *six*!

And with that – all strings vibrating at once – the heavy wooden door slid downward into the floor and, with no more than a quiet *whoosh*, disappeared from sight.

Plato jumped back. The bird began screeching.

"Ah... hah... oh, oh..." He wanted to turn and be sure the

creature hadn't died of fright, but he himself was too afraid to look away for even a moment. Gathering his courage he took a step forward. What he saw before his eyes, another arm's length away was a nondescript wall.

Could it be that all this puzzlement was to show him an old stone wall? This was madness. This was... Plato glanced down. Unseen before, was a hole in the floor behind where the door had stood. A rectangular hole a little larger than the width of his shoulders. There were stairs going down.

"There are stairs going down," he said in a croaking voice to the parrot. "A stairway."

"Nothing from the bird.

Plato peered down, but there was little to see past the first step. That one – and the next one down – were lit by the library sconces. There was solid black below.

"I'm not afraid," he told Master Grae, "but I believe any further adventure here would be better enjoyed in the company of a friend." With that, Plato plucked the strings again one at a time. A moment later the door reappeared from the depths and slid back into place. Satisfied at the logic, Plato took a curtain in each hand and drew them together, like Moses at the Red Sea bringing the walls of water down on Pharaoh's army.

Xanthippe, and Plato – he with the six-stringed lyre in his hands, stood side by side before the door. She was quiet, observing the inexplicable carvings, reaching out as he had done, to touch and explore them with her fingertips. By now sun was streaming in through the library skylights making it look so commonplace that Plato had begun to wonder if he'd imagined it all.

On the way to Socrates' house he'd argued with himself about which details of the enigma to reveal to Xan, and which he should rightly allow her to experience for herself. He had shared a mystery with her once before, as Eleusian initiates. The thousands-year-old rite of spiritual passage was one that every Athenian citizen – regardless of rank – rich or poor, statesman or prostitute – was commanded by law to make, once in their lifetime. It was a pilgrimage whose sacred revelations were meant to remain secret on pain of death. Together Xan and Socrates had drunk the Eleusinian potion, so standing here today they were no strangers to ecstatic visions. If anyone was likely to understand the unfathomable, if anyone could be trusted implicitly, it was she.

He had decided that his dialogue with Master Grae – while perhaps sounding silly related verbatim – might be difficult or impossible to reproduce once Xan was in the library. So as they'd walked across the city, stopping at the agora to buy more bread and cheese and more figs, he took her on the spoken journey that had sent him back to the time of the Hebrews' origins, to their escape out of Egypt, and a magical parting of the waters. Then on to a numerological epiphany that had led to the revelation of this door of concentric circles, the trident and the mushroom.

In fact it had sounded less ridiculous than he'd feared. The Sons of God taking the Daughters of Earth as their wives recalled the Greek deities of Olympus and their marital woes with mortals. Some details varied. Fewer rapes and abductions. The inexplicable mention of "the Messengers" – whoever they were – that lived on the Earth before and after the matings and birthings took place.

That the Fates had handed him the gift of Solon's library and the door, and the intellect to decipher such a puzzle, did not seem to surprise Xan at all. Only Master Grae on his grapevine perch, fluffed and balanced on one leg sitting so still and silent, belied the veracity of Plato's account. It came down to this: if, with the plucking of the six- stringed lyre the door failed to open again, revealing the secret stairwell, he would be disgraced in the eyes of the single person in the world whose high regard he most wished to possess.

"So this is the door that that parrot led you to – through the quoting of Hebrew scripture?" Xan said, with not the faintest tinge of skepticism coloring her voice.

His heart was thumping so violently in the tomb-quiet library he was certain she could hear it. "Just listen... and watch."

Rearranging the u-shaped lyre in the crook of one arm he began to pluck the strings one by one. Midway through he knew that he had blundered. He'd plucked too quickly. By the time he'd reached the sixth string, the first had stopped its vibration.

"Wait, wait!" Plato cried, knowing the door would not be lowering. Clearly, the combined vibration of all six strings *at once* was necessary to activate the door's mechanism. Heat rose up his neck to his cheeks in a terrible flush, and he refused to meet Xan's eyes. "Let me try again." He waited for the strings to become perfectly still. But once he was sure they were he found his fingers paralyzed. He took a fortifying breath. Another and another. He had never been so painfully aware that time was *everything*. One more miss would mean the end. He would never be able to face Xan again.

He picked the strings. One Two. Three. Four. Five. Six. He was sure he could hear each one's oscillation. A moment passed, one so long he had time to die a thousand deaths...

And then the door slid quietly down and out of sight.

He felt Xan's hand reach for his. More triumphant than a humble man should be, Plato turned to face her. She was staring hard at the stone wall, her jaw having fallen slightly open. "Look down," he told her, and she did.

"A step?" she said quietly.

"At least two. I believe there's a staircase down."

"Down into what?"

He smiled. "I don't know. That's why I came for you."

She turned to face him, wonder lighting her eyes. For so long she'd known nothing but helpless fury as her family had been torn apart by the venal and corrupt men of Athens. "Soc would have loved this," she said. "A great library. A talking bird. A proper mystery…"

"A secret staircase…"

"A secret staircase," she echoed. She looked around the room and saw the five-candled lamp on the *Pentateuch* table. Together they lit the tapers, both their hands trembling so badly they could only laugh at themselves.

"Bring another," she said. "It's dark as a witch's womb down there."

He found a long-handled sconce torch and lit it on the candles, hoping that there were, indeed, sconces to be lit on their way to the Underworld.

"Are you afraid?" he asked.

"Of course I am," Xan said, but there was a smile in her black eyes. "Thank you, friend," she said, taking his hand.

"Don't thank me yet. I may have found the back way into Hades' house."

"Then perhaps," she shrugged," perhaps we shall see Socrates there."

෴

"Shall I go first?" Xan said.

"*What?*"

"I'm joking. It's your find. Of course you'll go first."

She did love to tease him. He'd just been too excited to register the jest.

"Well go on. Don't stand there gawking at me."

"Right." Plato inhaled sharply and let the breath out as a long sigh. Behind him he heard Xan do the same. With the sconce torch held near his sandals he lit the first stair down. He moved it right, then left, then above him to take the measure and material of the passageway. The stone ceiling angled at 45 degrees.

Plato took four steps down, carefully, as the rock stair was covered in an ancient slime of vegetation and dust. He stopped when he was fully belowground. What he saw stopped him. Caused him to groan aloud.

"What is it!" Xan cried. "Move down so I can follow you." Her voice was impatient.

"It's just... I'll move down. Careful. It's slippery." He took four more steps. By the untrampled film on the steps he surmised that no one had been here for a very long time. As Xan came slowly, bringing with her the additional light of her lamp, Plato put his fingers to the passage wall.

It was perfectly smooth, impeccably ground and polished like the marble in the Temple of Zeus. *How could this be?*

"Plato. Look at this."

"I am looking."

"How was this done? *Why* was it done?"

"I think we're going to find out."

"Not if you don't *move.*"

He smiled to himself. Socrates always did call his wife irascible. There was no getting away with laziness of any sort with Xan. Intellectual. Physical. Forty years her senior, Soc was never allowed to slow his pace. If he ever did – Xan reminded him – he would wither and die.

"I can't see the bottom," Plato called up to her.

"Is it like this all the way down?"

"Yes. No, *wait.*" He held the torch to the right-hand wall. Something was carved into the stone. With precision and artistry. A long line of glyphs. Not Sumerian. Not Egyptian. Not Greek.

An unknown language.

Step by careful step Plato continued down so that Xan could see the text. She was tracing the shaped glyphs with her fingers. All the teasing had gone out of her. There was awe in her abject silence. He wondered if her thoughts were skipping along the same questioning path as his own. *Of course they would be – they were both students of Socrates!* He decided the best thing to do was find the bottom. His anticipation would suffocate him if he didn't. And if he dawdled, ungodly wrath would rain down upon him from behind.

Finally at the last step – a large landing really – it seemed they were two stories below the street. Before them was a wall of the polished stone. It was carved, once again, with concentric circles. To his left was a pitch-black opening, presumably what they'd come down these secret stairs to see. He ventured into the dark and found a sconce on each wall. He lit them all with his torch, avoiding a good look at the chamber. Then went back to Xan so they could have first sight of the mystery together.

The space was small. With rough-hewn walls, it was more an alcove than a cave. Its only furnishings were two reclining couches that flanked a table along the back wall, upon which were three packages wrapped in leather. On the far right of the table was a wooden chest half the size of a man's torso. From where they stood they could see it was intricately carved.

"Will you look inside the leather packages?" Plato said. "I'll open the box." He quietly hoped that he did not need a bird's help to unlock it.

Another heaved breath… and Plato stepped into the cave. At once he felt a welcome expansion. Out of the confines of the stairwell, here was that sense of predestination again. Antiquity. But science as well. Mathematics. He thought of the six-stringed lyre and its vibrations. Xan moved past him to the table where she'd begun unwrapping the first leather package. In three strides he was standing before the wooden box. Indeed it was carved with amazing artistry, all of animals and vines and flowers. He tapped the lid with his fingernail. When he put his thumbs on the front and his fingers arrayed on its sides, the cover sprang suddenly open with a soft pop, as though any pair of human hands was the key to unlock it.

"These packages. They're books," Xan said, "stacks of parchment pages filled with text in an unreadable language. They're bound together at one side. Two volumes in the first package. Two in the second. A single one in the third. What have you got?"

Plato peered inside the box's rectangular space. One half seemed a tiny catalogue of wafer-thin glass chips, thousands of them tucked neatly into an inner case. On its other side, nestled within a soft form was a sleek dolphin-shaped artifact of metal, its material foreign to him. Harder than Chinese steel. The artifact was small. Something that would fit easily into the palm of the hand. Engraved upon it were the same four wavy lines carved into the wooden door in the library. "Look at this," he said to Xan, and she came to stand by his side.

"Go ahead. Pick it up," she goaded him. "*Do it.* Or I will."

"You're a hard woman," he said with a laugh. She had to be, he thought, to be the beloved of Socrates. A strong, flexible and curious mind. In the days when Plato was still half-formed and stuttering over an answer or logics solution, his teacher would point to his young wife. She was never shy with an opinion, and preferred answering wrongly than stammering with indecision.

With one hand Plato reached into the box and lifted out the metallic object, then dropped it back in place. It was pulsing with a low vibratory hum!

"What?" Xan cried. "Are you hurt?"

"No. Not hurt."

Without hesitation she plucked it out of its form. "It's..." she searched for the word "... alive."

"No," he countered. "Think Pythagoras. The vibration of strings. High frequency."

"It isn't music," she argued. "There's no sound."

"Let me see," Plato said, taking it from her. As he did he noticed, along its side, a row of four tiny, perfectly rounded apertures like little portholes, and two slightly larger ones on one end. He regarded them closely, then closed his eyes to go within. Here he would find inspiration.

Xan was silent, likely searching for answers herself. Nothing was coming to him. A blank slate had risen in his mind. Nothing had prepared him for this. Except… He opened his eyes and smiled at Xan. She was lost in contemplation. "Watch this," he said. As he had with the wooden box, Plato placed his four fingers along the tiny side windows and his thumbs upon the two at the end. "It's flute-like. It feels…"

Without warning a narrow shaft of red light shot from the device, striking the stone floor… excavating a precise and slender tunnel in the rock! Xan shrieked, and he would have, too, but he refused to appear cowardly again, and held on stubbornly.

"Perhaps we should stop," she said, catching her breath. "I… I'm the mother of Socrates' sons. I cannot risk making them orphans."

"No. Of course. Uh… wait. Please. Let me try again. Different… points of contact." While the finger placement was random, Plato did not repeat the previous setting. But as they watched like two wide-eyed children, one of the volumes in the sights of the device began to slowly lift off the table."

"Impossible!" she cried.

"No. Possible. Possible. We're seeing this, Xan. It's happening." He was staring in wonder at the apparatus.

"Put the thing down!"

He removed his fingers from the portholes. But hesitating, he surreptitiously reset his fingers. The book began to spin.

"Plato, *stop!*" Xan snatched the leather-bound volume out of the air and clutched it to her breast. "You don't know what you're doing."

"How else will we learn what it's capable of?" There was real fear in her eyes. "Maybe you're right," he said. "Maybe you should leave."

"Not on your life!" She glared at him defiantly and nodded towards the device. "Again."

He had to smile at the fearless, ungovernable girl that his teacher had chosen for his wife. Plato reset his fingers, and the two of them dug in their heels for the next effect. But nothing in Heaven, Earth or the Underworld prepared them for what came next.

A phantasm with the size and shape of a man slowly materialized before them, standing in a brilliant rectangle of light!

Xan froze in place, moaning in terror. Plato was no less immobilized and felt his lips flapping wordlessly together. Finally he – the responsible party for this horrific apparition before them – clutched Xan to him. Her face was buried in Plato's shoulder, but one eye – he was sure of it – must be fixed on the specter.

It had taken full form – an old man in a short, wrapped skirt and a simple T-shaped shirt with short sleeves. Fat rows of red and green beadwork rounded the neck. His feet were bare. *Egyptian style.* Plato was sure. And yet, when the vision opened its mouth and spoke, it was in familiar Greek.

"I am Solon. If you are seeing me here and now you have come through the hurdles. Met a feathered friend of mine. Proven intellect. Curiosity. Courage. You have activated the device you hold in your hand. The 'hub.'" He smiled to himself. "You will be wondering why we are here."

"An Eleusinian vision?" Xan said in a hoarse whisper.

"No. We've drunk no potion. Sought no initiation. Perhaps it's a waking dream."

The image wavered then, in and out of solidity, threatening to dissolve.

"No!" Xan shouted. "Don't go!"

"He can't hear you," Plato said, equally desperate.

But a moment later the phantom reasserted its integrity and once again Solon – one hundred and thirty years dead – was standing before them.

"If I'm to make sense of this," the old man began, "I must tell you about my journey to Egypt, to the land of Pharaohs. The tale I returned with from the Nile Delta is greater than all the stories of Greece, Israel and Persia combined. The sheer wonder of it, of

ROBIN MAXWELL

the device, allows me to speak to you like this – *magically* – across time and space. And you've seen the invisible seeds of all life on our planet tucked inside the metal ark." Solon walked about in the rectangle of light, as though gathering his thoughts. "I had gone into Egypt to speak of war and Greek mercenaries with the Pharaoh Amasis, but I'd stopped to pay my respects to the priests Sonchis and Psenophis in Sais at the Temple of Neith. It was they who took me aside and read to me from the double pillars in the Temple's Holy of Holies. It was their mission, they told me, to find a worthy Greek to tell this story – the tale of Poseidon and Athens, the two brothers and their families, two magnificent cities, their dazzling rise and dreadful fall.

"They mocked me, these priests, for the pride I owned for my ancient Athene heritage. 'O Solon, Solon,' Sonchis chided me, 'you and your people are *children*. Even the oldest men among you are nothing but infants.' We were, he told me, deluded into thinking our culture was an ancient one. But we were nothing of the sort. The truth was, all of our Athene histories, all of our civilizations had, time and again, been obliterated by the agencies of fire and water, so that each time a Greek history might be told or written down, it was drowned or lost in conflagration. Only Egypt, her stone pyramids and monuments – by dint of their placement above the Nile floodwaters – were safe from destruction. Only the people of that great river were spared from having to begin their histories over and over again.

"But once I'd been thoroughly chastened these priests were eager to tell me the story written on the two columns. It was of a time called 'Zep Tepi,' which meant in their language, 'The First Time,' a primordial age when the original Gods and Goddesses lived in our world and mated with mortal men and women. 'A time before Poseidon was your God,' they said, 'before Isis was ours.' It was a record written in stone of our beloved Athens, and that rival city known as Atlantos. How and why such enlightened civilizations went to war with each other, and the terrible

30

catastrophe that overwhelmed them shortly thereafter. They spoke of the survivors of the last and greatest deluge that had drowned every coast of the world. It was, they insisted, 'a true history' that extended back more than nine thousand years."

"Nine thousand?" Plato heard Xan mutter disbelievingly. "Nine *thousand?*"

Solon laughed ruefully. "I didn't believe the Sais priests at first – their tales of gods who were mortals and men who were godlike. Of earthly dynasties and feuding city-states. The stories were too wild. The characters too many. Incomprehensible science. But then Psenophis pointed to a single row of glyphs on one of the pillars. Glyphs that spoke of 'five great books' – the *Chronicles of Giza.* In the gravest of tones they said that what was written on their temple pillars was only the broadest of knowledge. These volumes were the true repositories of the world's history. No one had ever found them. No one had even looked. The oldest books in the world, he revealed, were hidden away in a 'Hall of Records' between the paws of a stone lion. The priests of Sais had been ridiculed by their Pharaohs for daring to tell a story that styled any civilization older or more magnificent than Egypt's. So they were told to hold their tongues and let sleeping dogs lie.

"Well, I listened respectfully but feigned indifference. This was no more than a clever myth, engagingly told. I made sure they never knew how haunted I'd become. How the story gnawed at me night and day. I wanted to find these books. Needed to find them. When I'd gone from Sais I quietly sailed upriver on the Nile and began to search among the riverside monuments seeking a certain stone lion. There were many – some in pairs guarding temple doors, others in long rows leading to a kingly palace. The Nile peoples looked unkindly at tomb raiders, but this was not my purpose. I cared nothing for mummies or jewel-encrusted coffins, and part of me celebrated my dismal failure. I'd nearly given up my quest and had turned back around to continue my travels. But then, at the Great Pyramid of Cheops, I stopped to explore the mysterious chambers, and I overheard two men whispering about the 'River Lion' long buried in the sands of time, and its excavation about to begin.

"So I put aside my fine linen robes and donned a workman's loincloth. All day long I sweated and toiled with the crews uncovering the massive head and neck of the stone beast. But where there should have been a mane and leonine snout, there was a headdress and the face of a pharaoh. Still I persisted digging, for the body was certainly that of a great cat. At night I stole back to the site, examining every seam, every crack in the rock-face. No one was looking for a way inside. Then one night, in the newly excavated rump of the statue I did find a door, and a long-forgotten passage…" Solon's eyes grew misty, remembering. "I found the books. A treasure more valuable than all the gold in existence – the written stories of early Earth, and the means to read its language." Solon looked down at his feet shamefacedly. "I stole the *Chronicles* and the ark with its seeds of life, and the 'phaetronic frequency modulator' that you hold in your hand – the key to unlock the pages. I brought them home with me to Athens."

These were the volumes on the table behind them! Plato felt Xan trembling at his side, gawking at the apparition of Solon in front of them.

"This 'device' that shoots fire. That defies the laws of nature. That allows a dead man to show himself as living, and speak to us, is… Godly magic," she said.

"No," Plato said. "Science. The 'incomprehensible science' that Solon spoke of."

Xan was desperately trying to reason things out. "This science… makes men into gods."

Together they gazed at Solon, who was moving away from the rectangle of light. They saw now it was the floor beneath the library's skylight!

"Look at that," Xan said. "He mastered their science. Does that make him a god?"

"Perhaps it makes this…" he gestured to the device, "… a 'Godmaker.'"

Now they watched as Solon walked to the grapevine and gave his shoulder to a spectral Master Grae who was only too happy to hop aboard. Together they crossed the library and sat at the *Pentateuch* table, now displaying not the Hebrew text, but the five *Chronicles of Giza*. Solon ever so carefully placed a volume before him. Then he took the dolphin-shaped device in his hand and directed it to the page. He looked out at Plato and Xan. "Yes," he said. "I'm going to read you the translation. Giza, author of the books, was a friend of everyone. They spoke freely to him of their lives and loves, triumphs and follies. They gave him permission to write everything down.

"Today I give you a gift incomparable – the gift of *true history*. Not convenient history. Nor comfortable truth. There is much you will not understand. Nonsensical words – 'technos' 'Vibrus' 'phaeton.' There are flying ships. Floating boulders. Men on the moon. A god and a mortal giving birth to *five sets of twin sons*! Brothers who went to war with each other and the planet itself. You'll hear of the heavenly dance of stars and planets. Rogue comets. Collisions. Consequences. The insane orbit of our sister world named 'Terres' and a chance impact that sent it spinning off to the depths of an unforgiving dark. Do you fear the Underworld? I say, fear the black hell of space, and unknown dimensions that lay beyond a fragile curtain invisible to the eye. Monsters. Inhuman creatures. This is a tale of the Gods who are not gods at all. I think they meant well, yet evil followed them everywhere they went. They believed themselves brilliant, but stupidly turned the world on its head. It all sounds mad, I know. Yet you have no choice but to trust the Egyptian priests. To trust me."

Solon's eyes grew wistful. "I came home and tried to tell this story. No one would listen to me. They thought I had lost my senses. Gone senile. Maybe they will listen to you. Maybe not. I fear the men of Athens are lost in willful ignorance, making the same blunders again and again, blind to all remedies. But nevermind that." He gestured to the reclining couches, addressing his listeners. "You will want to make yourselves comfortable... whomever you are."

Plato, shaking his head, incredulous to be following instructions given by a ghostly vision, helped Xan to her couch, then laid himself down, stretching out his legs.

"Now you will listen to a story which, though strange, is certainly true," Solon intoned. "Not mere legend, but an actual fact. Let me repeat that *nine thousand* was the sum of years which had elapsed since the Great War and the cataclysms that followed. Of the combatants on the one side were the people of Athens, and on the other the kings of Atlantos." He chuckled, correcting himself. "But of course, the terrible war to end all wars is the *end* of this tale. To understand how a story ends, we must, of course, begin at the beginning."

Xan and Plato were silent, still and utterly breathless when Solon, greatest of the Seven Sages and Plato's uncle six times removed, lowered his head to the first *Chronicle of Giza* and began to read.

THE BROTHERS RA

Origins

SleepPhase

POSEIDON COULD HEAR his brother weeping broken-heartedly and his mother's soft voice soothing the little boy's misery. Great sobs racked Athens's tiny frame, echoing under the great oval "eye" on the Atlas City SleepPhase Dome. Their father – coming their way through regimented row-after-row of sleeping pods in the cavernous stadium – was the picture of Terresian perfection. He was tall, angular and grey-haired with dull alabaster skin, back held rigidly. His expression was entirely divorced from emotion as he greeted fellow Federation men. Once he'd left them all behind, moving closer now, he scowled with embarrassment hearing his son's loud weeping.

Athens had always been a child of untoward emotions. Rages, tantrums, paroxysms of delight, unrestrained laughter. And fears. His fears were the worst of the impulses so frowned upon in their society. From his earliest days Athens had lacked all reserve or restraints, all moderation. And yet, Poseidon mused as he ran his hand over PM-Pod 74.888 – the narrow tubular chamber in which he would endure the first hibernation of his life – this was precisely and paradoxically the reason that people adored his younger brother. Athens would, of course, grow out of such unfortunate traits, such evolutionarily ancient behaviors. They were, in an adult, unacceptable in their culture. Dangerous. Certainly requiring modification.

But in a four-year-old boy, especially one as physically beautiful and innately charming as Athens, the traits were tolerated. In the privacy of their home the boisterous, jolly child was an entertainment, a ray of sunlight in the waning years of the ever-darkening solar cycle. Each of them – his mother, father, himself – hoped that when they awoke from their long sleep Athens would have shed those qualities and grown into a proper Terresian man.

Still, now he wept as though his heart was breaking.

Mother, leaning over his pod, was making promises as she wiped his tears with the hem of her garment's loose sleeve. Her mahogany skin radiated warmth even in the artificial light, silver hair flowed long, her words, expression and posture exuding unabashed comfort.

"You will enjoy your sleep, I promise you," she said as she wiped her younger son's tears with the hem of her garment's loose sleeve. "You will dream wonderful dreams."

"I don't want to sleep!" Athens wailed. "What if the *bad* dreams come?"

"They cannot come, child. This is not ordinary sleep, not at all the same as when I put you into bed at home. You're safe in your pod. No one *ever* has bad dreams in SleepPhase. You must trust me, Athens." She tilted his face up to hers and held his eyes. "Do you trust me?"

His nod was small, a single tilt of the chin, and his lips were pursed tight. But Athens's eyes were dry.

She grinned then. "When you wake you'll be all grown up. Your brother and your father will have hair sprouting all over them. Above their lips, on their chins and their heads."

"No they won't!" Athens was giggling now.

"Oh yes they will. Their hair will be so long it will fill up their pods. We'll have to dig through it all to find their faces."

Athens gave a small shriek of delight.

She had not said that their finger and toenails would be long and curled, Poseidon thought, as this might incite memories of Athens's many nightmares. In the extended sleep Terresian bodily functions were drastically slowed, micronomically close to death. But as their hibernation was so severely extended – nearly the length of a Terresian "year," some growth did take place. Athens, as their mother had told him, would awake as a young man. Poseidon, himself a young man today, would emerge fully matured. His parents would age perhaps a decade. And their protein bio-locations – hair and nails – to the sleep engineers' chagrin, continued to grow unchecked throughout the long dark solar cycle, ten thousand years longer than those of the inner planets' orbits.

Terresian technos was marvelous. It was, however, imperfect.

Their mother smiled and pulled her cheered little son to her breast. Poseidon found himself squirming uncomfortably to see this display of affection in a public area. At home her embraces – while frowned upon by their father – were welcomed by both boys. Manya had always been different from other mothers in this way. It had been the family's small secret. Poseidon had overheard his father chastising his mate, inferring that her over-affectionate ministrations somehow contributed to their younger son's intemperance. And now in the Sleep Stadium with the entire populace of Atlas City gathered for the most solemn public event of their culture, his mother and brother were displaying for all to see the most unsuitable of emotions.

Poseidon was grateful that decorum had been restored by the time his father joined the family on the 7000-row of pods.

"It's time, Manya," he said. "Shall I help you in?"

"No, I can manage." She gazed steadily into his eyes. "We've already said our goodnights." And more quietly, "Be gentle with the boys." Then she climbed into her pod.

Ammon Ra went first to Athens and bent low. Poseidon could

hear nothing of their exchange, but he did see his brother's small hand reaching up to touch their father's face… and the man pulling away before the fingers could make contact.

When finally he approached Poseidon's pod Ammon Ra's expression showed not a single trace of sentimentality. "Your first SleepPhase," was all he said to his firstborn.

"Yes, Father. I'm looking forward to it."

"Use the time wisely. Have you some problems to solve?"

"I do. The generalized displacement ratios of glaxin hydroxalide. A new simulation protocol for bio-stem endrites. And equivalencies for the inverted macro-vibrus paradox."

"Good. I'll see you in the morning." With a brief pat on his son's cheek his father turned and climbed into the pod next to his.

Poseidon did the same, positioning his body into its warm enfolding fiber-cushion. He knew that as soon as the lid closed and locked – as would all 92,785 of the others in the dome at the same instant – a narcotizing frequency would activate and lull him to sleep. The temperature would begin to drop slowly, then precipitously, till crytonic stasis had been attained.

He allowed his eyes to close. '*I'll see you in the morning*'. Were these passionless words all that Poseidon would have to remember before his thousands-year sleep? *No*, he decided. *I will remember my mother, her fragrant embrace, a kiss on each of his cheeks and the smile that had warmed him to the core.*

'*Sweet dreams, my son,*' she'd crooned. '*Sweet dreams.*'

AEROS

Fourth Planet from the Sun

10,000 years later

ONE

"SIR, MARS IS gone."

Mars missing? At least that was what Poseidon thought he'd heard inside his helmet. It made no sense. His focus was as strong and steady as the 15-foot diameter red phaetronic cold-beam now boring down into the Aerosean mantle, rock vaporizing beneath him and his crew. In their climate suits they were hovering near the beam two miles underground.

The column of light blinked off suddenly at Poseidon's command, leaving the crew in pitch black aside from their helmet torches.

"Give me a minute, Cyphus" Poseidon said. He needed to compose himself. The blistering attack by Chronus in front of the 4-man crew moments ago in the close confines of this dangerous mission had rattled him as much as his own wavering certainty about finding the titanum vein. With the Federation Energy drill rig hovering a hundred feet above the circular borehole, they were finally, after four years, at Site 62. Four years that Poseidon had been begging for a chance to prove himself right. Time was running out to find the vein of titanum ore.

Enough to power their technos. Enough to keep their world alive.

"Let's go again," he directed Chronus who had nothing but argument in his eyes.

"I don't think..."

"Just do it."

With withering defiance the geologist tapped instructions into his wrist hub to reactivate the drill rig.

The blood red energy column blazed to life at the phaetron's most potent vibral calibrate, boring into the excavation with staggering force. Around them the mantle itself shuddered, and Poseidon felt suddenly queasy. *Rape* came to mind – an abomination that no longer troubled the people of their world. Like violence. Greed. Anger. Lust. All were relics of the distant past. He was being foolish.

You could not rape a planet.

Below them the rock gouged from the Aerosean crust was pulverized, then vibrated and vaporized out of existence. Perhaps above them a fine reddish mist would be drifting above the lip of the borehole.

Thirty seconds of the boring felt like an eternity.

"Let's have a look," Poseidon ordered as the beam blinked off again. He and the team descended further into the hollow core. A 3-Dimensional diffracted facsimile of the rock wall appeared before them, the stratum showing multi-colored rock and sediment.

"Here, between the vitrium and the granite," Poseidon said to Chronus, pointing to a thin brown seam.

"Yes, it's titanum ore," Chronus said, "And it's three *microns* thick."

"There's more here." Poseidon's words were unconvincing, even to his own ears. "We need to drill deeper."

"Sir!" Cyphus's voice in his ear was insistent. "Commander Mars is *missing*."

Poseidon brought up Cyphus's image on the inside of his faceplate and gave "Security One" his full attention. He could see that his friend, normally composed under the most chaotic situations, was unsettled. Too important to keep to himself, Poseidon shared Cyphus's projection with the other crewmen.

"How can he be missing?"

"Commander Mars was last seen on Mile 7 Beach when he separated from the rest of the patrol to explore on his own."

Everyone had quieted to listen to Cyphus.

"Wonderful," Chronus said. "Fourteen hours before our launch window closes."

Poseidon addressed Cyphus with a calm he hoped would annoy Chronus. "Take a search party out. We're staying here. Continuing the drill. We're very close."

"You're dreaming," Chronus insisted. The 'Mars Motherload' on Aeros is a fantasy."

Poseidon felt gorge rising in his throat. Chronus's old refrain. Doubt and mistrust sown into the minds of everyone on the mission. Even his friend and mentor, Elgin Mars.

"Your coordinates don't square with anyone's data but your own," Chronus said. "No significant deposits found anywhere on this planet in four years. Let's just find Mars and go home."

"I'm Second in Command, Chronus. It's my call. Cyphus…"

"Yes, *Sir*," he snapped with military gravity.

"Find him."

Security One blinked out of view.

I love this man, Poseidon thought. He could always count on Cyphus to have his back. Poseidon turned to Chronus. He wanted to shout at him. Shout the obvious. *If we don't locate a great vein of titanum ore in the next fourteen hours it won't matter if we make it home or not. The only means to power our technos dies. Our home planet, what's left of our glorious civilization barely existing under energy domes, dies. We all bloody die!*

"Again!" Poseidon said, pure stubbornness hardening his voice. With his own wrist hub he re-established the coordinates deeper into the unyielding hole that he'd never once despaired of till this moment.

The red beam blinked on again.

❧

Mile 7 Beach was one of those places that tugged at the heart, even ones as coolly Terresian as his was. It was enough, thought Cyphus, that the viewscape was a gorgeous tumble of soft red boulders, huge broad-boughed fern trees and an actual moving ocean – something no one on the home planet had seen for hundreds of thousands of years. But this shoreline of the Aerosean Sea was a broad expanse of pink sand that glittered jewel-like in the sun. He stood spellbound at the sight, gaping really. But then Tybo, Chief of the mission's FirstLine Scouting Team, was striding toward him, his blue uniform worksuit torn in several places, as though he'd been scraping among the rocks.

"Cyphus," Tybo said, uttering only the one word before swiveling back towards the rocky escarpment and Scouting Team's shuttle, now heavily landed in the sand – an ore-preserving protocol they were all using now. They couldn't afford to waste a single pellet, a single tron of titanum. Not if they hoped to see home again.

Two of the scouts milled somberly around their craft, and the Borehole 7 Site. The rest were down at the shoreline engaging with the strange and delightful Aerosean creatures who'd stolen everyone's hearts on this mission. The "solies" sprawled out at the waterline enjoying the caresses of the crewmen. They were creatures of both land and sea. A silky grey-furred coat over a sleek-body with a single back flipper. And two muscular front appendages that ended with almost human "hands." The huge black eyes and slender snouts, whiskers and a thick beard-like fringe under their chins created a sweet, almost comical expression.

"We've looked everywhere," Tybo said, his palms raised in a gesture of futility. Terresians were unused to this kind of uncertainty. They'd experienced nothing out of the ordinary on the Mission thus far, aside from the horrifying prospect of returning home emptyhanded.

"I know. We'll make one more sweep." Cyphus had his eye on a high, rocky palisade that curved around the half-circular inlet and started for a narrow walk-through in the boulders to what he presumed was the next cove over.

"He said he had to come back one last time." Tybo trailed after Cyphus, distraught. "He was sure there was something here. He wasn't himself. Said he needed to talk to one of them…" He gestured to the solies. One of animals had flopped over on its back to let a crewman rub its belly. "They were the only ones who were unaware of the disgrace he'd be facing at home."

Cyphus beckoned to his team to follow him.

"We looked there," Tybo moaned. "We've looked *everywhere*."

"We'll just look again," Cyphus said, putting a hand on Tybo's arm.

❧

The Aeros Mission – Elgin Mars's celebrated expedition to confirm a massive vein of titanum on a distant planet in their solar system – had become Terres' last hope for survival. In the phaetron drill's red glow down in the borehole Poseidon recalled the last time they had taken in the sight of the Aerosean land and seascape. Side by side in the shuttle hovering five hundred feet above the planet's surface they gazed out the window at the pink sand beach on the coast of Aeros's central continent. To the east was a vast ocean, to the west lay an entire landmass covered in a single species of giant tree fern – a mono-forest – the only vegetation that had yet evolved on the fourth planet from the sun. Poseidon steadfastly believed in the man – his mentor and professor at the Academy – and his elusive ore, even as the years on this primeval planet so far from home wore on and on and nothing was found. Tempers had flared. Not just Chronus's. Everyone suffered nightmares of societal collapse – the single advanced species in their solar system annihilated for want of some chunks

47

of dull brown stone. Here in this interminable isolation the crew felt the weight of the whole world on their shoulders.

They were a hairsbreadth away from catastrophe.

They'd drilled incessantly in Commander Mars's chosen boreholes, and only in these last hours, when all hope was gone, had he consented to Poseidon's alternative site. It was little more than instinct that had led him to 62. No one else dared challenge the august and supremely dogged head of the mission. The coordinates had been at odds with Mars's analysis. Poseidon had heard the whispers – *He was no Elgin Mars.*

Yet he'd been certain titanum was here. As certain as he'd been about anything in his life. A sense in his long limbs that tingled when he'd stood on the Aerosean soil *in this place.* A human divining rod.

But 62 was failing him. Failing them all. And now Mars was missing.

"It's here," Poseidon whispered to himself, hovering with Chronus and the team in this intractable borehole in the red glow of the phaetronic beam.

And then, almost imperceptibly, the glow an arms-length away grew brighter.

He stiffened. Realized no one else had noticed. Maybe he'd imagined it.

It happened again.

"Chronus…" he began.

But Chronus had seen. "Sir?" he intoned warily.

"Hold steady," Poseidon told him, unsure if the order was judicious or utter folly. Phaetronic technos was virtually foolproof, as were their climate suits. But they were two and a half miles underground.

Poseidon tapped his wrist control to shut the beam down but suddenly the phaetron was unresponsive to the command. Then another incremental change in intensity.

"Everyone, full comm with me. We're getting out of here," he told the crew, his voice unwavering as his mind raced.

Normally the four-foot space carved out between the active beam and the borehole wall was sufficient for safe and easy passage up and down. Now it felt claustrophobic, with not a micron for mistakes. He wished to shoot upwards at speed. Get his men as far as possible from the malfunctioning drill beam, but this was impossible. Instead, with arms tightly held to his sides, his propulsion module set to what felt like a crawl, he led the crew upward in single file.

A thousand feet up Poseidon's heart crashed into his ribs as a tiny rogue beam escaped sideways, shooting out in front of his eyes, causing a small poof of dust to explode in the borehole wall near his head. He adjusted propulsion speed. *They had to get out…*

Without warning the beam's color shifted again, this time quite obviously from red to amber. He heard groans of alarm from the men below him.

"Hug the wall! We need to hurry." Poseidon told them, unsure if the change in color also reflected a change in the beam's thermals.

They were making good time. Not five hundred feet to the borehole's lip when he heard Talent cry out.

"Report!" Poseidon commanded. "Talent. What's happened?"

"A spark – my thigh's burning!"

"Can you keep up?"

"Yes," Talent answered, his voice pained but determined.

"Almost there!" Poseidon shouted, but he could see that the amber beam was growing lighter, to a pale yellow. And the heat on his back coming through the climate suit assured him it was *hot* yellow. Now he could see a faint light above him – the lip! It was still out of reach. *Bloody stars, are we all going to die in a hole on Aeros?*

A final burst of speed, his helmet scraping against the basalt wall, and they were there. First one out, Poseidon reached down and pulled Chronus up and out, and the three others. The Drill Ship hovering above the borehole shooting down the ever-lightening beam itself seemed unstable, wobbly. Its crew of three was just now evacuating. They propelled towards the hovering shuttle two hundred feet away at the same level. Its portal had opened for them already where a gentle blue tractor beam awaited.

"Go!" Poseidon commanded and watched as three of his men shot skyward to the base of the shuttle. Talent was on one knee, agonized, clutching his thigh where a large hole had burned through his climate suit. "I've got you," Poseidon said, attaching them by a short tether, then encircling Talent's waist with one arm.

They were the last into the tractor beam. As they were pulled upward into the shuttle Poseidon looked back to see the drill beam burst into pure white incandescence. What had been a controlled, focused red beacon had grown volatile, unstable and growing exponentially into a spinning vortex, its energy sparking wildly past its boundaries.

The crew stood at the window staring in stupefaction at a sight none of them had ever witnessed – a phaetronic device completely out of control.

The drill rig itself was glowing white-hot and vibrating uncontrollably.

"Shields!! Now!!" Poseidon shouted.

Chronus threw the controls. An invisible vibrational bulwark engulfed the shuttle an instant before the drill rig exploded, erupting and fracturing outwards in all directions. The blast super-shot the shuttle far out over the ocean, its shield hull holding structural integrity, but dashing the crew to the floor, into walls and consoles.

Once it had stabilized Poseidon dragged himself to his feet and scanned the beach. Chunks of the rig were arrayed around the bore hole like the petals of a flower on the sand, and the great white-hot column of phaetronic energy, without benefit of the drill ship, continued its violent gouging into the Aerosean mantle.

❦

The rocky cove was a solie haven. A breeding ground for the overly sociable animals. Two hundred females sunbathed and groomed one another while their pups suckled. There were sand fights and lumbering races into the surf. Juvenile males crashed chest-to-chest in practice for mating.

It was paradise.

Cyphus followed Mars's footprints to the edge of the squirming solie huddle but they were lost in the disturbed sand. There was no sign of accident or violence. No blood. And his BioScan of the herd showed no vibral spikes within the past six hours.

"Spread out," Cyphus called to his team. "Anything out of the ordinary. *Anything!*"

The word wasn't out of his mouth when, without warning the clutch of solies froze. Adult heads rose to alarmed attention, then swiveled all in the same direction. A moment later the mass of animals on the beach scattered in panic, galumphing awkwardly across the sand diving into the waves.

Only then did the ground under the team's feet begin to shudder.

The vibration grew more violent. Some boulders from the bluff above them tumbled down in slow motion, allowing the men to hasten from harm's way.

As quickly as it had begun the quake ceased. Cyphus's head count found everyone unharmed.

"Damn planet," muttered Tybo.

Unseen on the high bluff above them a long red-orange gash had torn open. It oozed molten lava slowly popping large magma bubbles and began spreading to the north. Beyond the now deserted solie paradise and past the next rock cove the gash angled suddenly, coming down from the bluff, tearing through the soft sand and into the sea, throwing up a hissing cloud of steam.

No one in the search party had seen it. They resumed their search.

❦

Cyphus returned to 62 to find a scene of chaos and celebration. The drill rig was utterly destroyed and the shuttle was parked on the ground. The crew was outside it, reclining in the sand knocking back cup after cup of jog. Clinking toasts. Back slapping! Cyphus spotted Chronus refilling his cup.

"What's happened?"

"I'm eating my words." He took a hefty slug of the fermented brew. "*Drinking* them!" He looked across the beach to Poseidon. "He was right. We found it. The Mars Motherlode. It's right under our feet. It stretches a tenth of the way around the planet! Nearly killed us all, but…" He called to the pilot. "More jog!"

Cyphus caught Poseidon's eye. He looked relieved enough to weep. In fact his eyes were twinkling with happy tears. He grinned at Cyphus, but the smile faded and Cyphus realized that his own expression held tragedy. Everything quieted. A hand about to clap a shoulder dropped heavily to the officer's side. The clinking cups were suddenly an embarrassment.

No one had to be told that Mars had not been found.

❦

Out the window the spectacular Aerosean land and seascape receded as the craft rose into the atmosphere. The crew once again lifted goblets in a toast. But this was a somber celebration.

"To Mars," Poseidon said.

"Mars," the crew intoned.

"And to the beauty of Aeros," Cyphus added, to everyone's surprise.

All but Poseidon glanced skeptically at Cyphus. *Love of place* was not a typical Terresian sentiment. It was the smallest of smiles that Poseidon directed at his friend. "To the beauty… and gifts of Aeros."

Despite the very real loss of their commander, the relief and quiet self-satisfaction among the men was palpable.

"Here's to a quick trip home," Chronus added.

The men raised their goblets again, drinking heartily.

"More jog so we can drink to that again!" Delos cried.

The pilot refilled everyone's cups with green liquid, but before another toast could be call Poseidon said, quite unexpectedly, "The return mission to begin mining Aeros should happen immediately."

Chronus looked up. "What? Before the next SleepPhase?"

Delos leaned forward into the middle of the table. "There's not enough time to mount such a massive operation. You're talking five thousand colonists and a transport large enough to carry them."

"They've already begun work on the transport," Poseidon answered. "It can be stepped up."

"Not in time to have them settle, build the colony and dig the mine before Terres leaves HelioArc," Chronus argued.

"They'll need to send the first shipment of ore back to Terres as well," Poseidon added, almost a challenge.

Everyone laughed derisively.

Chronus said, "It's ludicrous."

"What's the hurry?" the pilot asked. "Certainly we're low on pellets, but it's more than sufficient to get us through another LongOrbit."

"We need to plan for the worst," Poseidon insisted. "What if the sleep pods fail in mid-circuit? What if the dome ruptures and we're down to the dregs?"

"Then we wake people up and they'll deal with it," Chronus answered.

Poseidon looked around the table at his crew. "Why take the chance? Surely five thousand hardy adventurers will relish the idea of a new life on a splendid planet, water all around them, natural air to breathe."

"I'd come back!" Cyphus cried.

Chronus was growing surly. "I don't see the rush."

"I'll take it further," Poseidon persisted. "I think the new Gaian mission should be launched as well. If we find ourselves in real trouble we'll need to emigrate off world."

"You're mad!" said Delos. "The entire population sent to Gaia?"

"It's a spectacular planet," Poseidon answered.

"Filled with monstrous carnivores and hideous microbes," Chronus, said, losing patience with his new commander, "and a population of primitives no better than apes."

"Hence the Gaian expedition," said Poseidon. "Dr. Horus has her protocols in order. A few short generations should render the Gaians…"

"The *Gaians*." Chronus snorted derisively.

"…should render the aboriginals fit companions for us," Poseidon finished.

"Pour that man another drink!" the pilot cried.

"Or put him to sleep!" Delos added.

Poseidon laughed good-naturedly.

Cyphus leaned into the center of the table. "I know his problem. He's been dreaming about the lovely Doctor Horus. She's addling his brain."

Poseidon squirmed visibly at the truth of this. "All right, all right. No more about off-world expeditions. Just the Long Orbit Sleep."

"That's better. Stop worrying, Commander. Start celebrating."

We found titanum!" the pilot said. "A *lot* of it. We're not all going to die a horrible death!"

"I will drink to that!" Poseidon said.

All goblets were raised and clinked.

Apocalypse averted.

ঔ

Four miles above the rookery, the last of the shuttles and DrillUnits were disappearing into the OffWorld Transport. On the beach below one solie mother was remembering the strange land animals who'd come to their shores. Though ugly, with four too-long flippers that would be useless appendages in the water, they were somehow familiar. Companionable. And though the tall creatures were not aware, a rude sort of communication had occurred between them.

But now they had gone.

She suddenly missed her pup – he'd wandered away some time back after a long, slow suckle. Now she could see him following a colorful hard-shell pincher along the cove's stony wall. She could see something moving behind his plump little form. Like a thin flap of dried seaweed trapped between rocks, caught and waving in the breeze. She watched it closely. No, not seaweed.

A piece of the flimsy blue skin that had covered the tall creatures' appendages.

The solie cub was head-down, having to run now to catch the red pincher before it escaped into the waves. He did not feel the shadow above him so much as smell the stink of something rotten all around him. The heavily muscled tentacle – when it lifted the little body high in the air – waved with a weird grace that had all the mothers and cubs barking and bellowing in frenzied confusion. But when the writhing cub was finally conveyed to the giant's razor-toothed maw, the only sound on the whole length of the pink sand beach was the solie's pitiful high-pitched squeals.

TERRES

Tenth Planet from the Sun

10 Years Later

TWO

HOME WAS A dark planet.

The OffWorld Transport tracked the equator of Terres low enough so that its undercarriage lights illuminated its rocky mantle, with no atmosphere to distort it. The black sky touched the ground here, night and day. Far, far in the distance a pinprick of light did nothing to distinguish itself as the planet's sun, Helios. They coursed above Terresian continents. Endless deserts. Desiccated rivers. Desolate plateaus. Ancient lava flows reached their brittle fingers thousands of miles in all directions. Even its volcanoes were cold and dead. Terres was a ghost planet shrouded in unremitting darkness.

Poseidon glanced at the faces of the crew. Not long out of MicroSleepPhase, they were largely expressionless. Terresian reserve permitted nothing but gratitude for return to this sorry world of theirs. When the LaunchDome appeared below them, a swollen blister of light in the spreading dark, merciful amnesia descended. Aerosean beaches and the endless sea were all forgotten.

Landed and debriefed at the LaunchDome, a short train ride through the pitch black night sped the crew, largely silent in anticipation, towards the vast Contour Dome. Encapsulated within the greatest protective field of phaetronic energy on Terres, the bubble that sheathed and protected all that was left of life from the darkness and death of deep space, was "Atlas Environs" and hundreds of square miles surrounding it. The City, outlying burbs, farms and orchards. Glorified hills they called mountains. The PseudoSun rising and setting in a semblance of day and night. Manufactured atmosphere.

As they approached the membrane of the Dome they quietly observed boxy shuttle pods and their crews in propulsion suits repairing small tears in the force field. The train slowed as it breached the Ingress Portal and exploded into the city itself. It was daytime, and Poseidon was cheered to see the beautifully laid out grid of elegant public buildings, modest residential neighborhoods checkered with greenways and parks. They passed the beloved Arboretum housing all that was left of the planet's rare ancient vegetal species. The Museums of Arts and Sciences. The Atlas City Theater Complex. The sprawling campus of the Xenophon ScienTechnos Academy with its School of Architecture "Pyramidium," and the famous stone obelisk gracing the Genomics Department. At the edge of the campus rose the SleepPhase Stadium. From ground-level you could not see the immense "closed eye" etched into its domed roof. Everyone knew it was there, a symbol of the safety and preciousness of the hibernation that kept the population alive during the near-endless Long Orbit.

Sleek hovercars navigated the city skies, but the streets and parks and public plazas were peopled with Terresians going about their peaceful lives. Some heads turned at the sight of the train coming into Federation Square. Most people knew the Aerosean crew had returned, but few were yet aware of the triumph they'd brought home with them.

Poseidon saw the Federation Commissioners waiting in the Square. To the man, they were bristling with elation. *They* knew the mission's outcome. They were bursting with accomplishment. As the train glided to a full stop, Poseidon stood and shared a smile with Cyphus.

They were home. Mission accomplished.

⤪

The three Physics Men lived and breathed their science. Each, like most Terresians, was a WombBaby. This particular trio whose laboratory was tucked in a basement of the Xenophon ScienTechnic Academy, overlooked one another's most annoying habits. Completed each other's thoughts. Laughed rarely, but at the same things. For good reason. They shared a single essential purpose – the science of matter.

Now, inside the bell chamber, Clax, Monas and Enoc watched two empty pedestals within it. Standing close to the glass wall, their breath fogged it in three ragged patches.

"Come on. Come on!" Enoc said through gritted teeth. His patience ran the shortest of the three of them.

"It shouldn't be taking this long," said Monas. Even his easy, sensible demeanor was wearing thin with this waiting.

Clax's exterior calm was belied by his drumming fingers on the transparent wall. "No, no. We're well within range…"

There. There! Molecule-by-molecule, something began to materialize on the right-hand pedestal. Between the three of them, hardly a breath escaped their lips.

"Please, please…" Clax moaned.

It had the shape of a small, furry mouse-like creature, but as it coalesced, they could see its composition was more red than brown. Once fully formed… the poor bloodied creature was mutilated beyond recognition. Four legs sticking out of its spine, guts outside the body. No head.

"Wait!" Enoc cried, his eyes swiveling left. On that pedestal, just a head appeared, the tiny mouth opening and closing piteously.

"Ugh." Monas wasted no time filling the chamber with a mist that took the mangled thing out of its misery.

"Let's go again," Enoc said.

"No. No more today!" said Monas. "The poor creature."

"Our LiveBio protocols are eating up our pellet quotas," Clax admonished them. "If we use much more, Admin will cut off our supply."

"Of course they won't!" Enoc spat. "The price of progress is titanum. End of story."

Monas grabbed a little satchel from a shelf. "We have to go. We'll be late."

Clax heaved a sigh. "You go on. I'm staying here."

"Not a chance," Monas said. "If you want that steady stream of ore from Federation, we have to make a show at their silly ceremony. Clax!"

The Physics Man was still fixed blindly on the pedestals. "I was sure we had it this time. What did we do wrong?"

"In five thousand years of scientechnos, no one has gotten translocation of living tissue right," Enoc argued.

"We'll get it next time," Monas insisted, going back and tugging at Clax's arm. He wrenched it away. "We'll get it next time," he said gently.

⋘

Standing at the front of the massive welcoming crowd at Federation Energy Square, Professor Talya Horus cocked an ear to the phaetronic hiss high overhead. She was a woman of great, if chilly, loveliness, with a rod-straight back and a steely gaze, as tightly wound as her sleekly knotted blonde hair. *Another breach in the dome's field*, she thought. Sunlight – if one could call it that – illuminated the day. She could see the actual tear in the synthetic blue sky and illusory cloud formations right through to the black of sunless space that enveloped Terres. It would be thousands of years before the first of Helios's faint rays fell on their planet.

In other times, she thought, such a breach would have been

an emergency, an ugly reminder of the trouble they'd all been in. The conservative men at Fed Energy would have flown into crisis mode, calling for the start of titanium rationing. The loudmouths would shout them down, insist that their new technos – in various stages of development – would, with sufficient investment, render titanium dependence obsolete.

But the success of the Aerosean explorations had changed everything.

And Poseidon had come home a hero.

He sat with the others from the Aeros Mission on the stage, with Senior Commissioners Elo Denys and Emmet Praxis, while his father – High Commissioner Ammon Ra – stood at the podium, droning on. She found herself thinking that Poseidon Ra was the ideal man. Physically striking with a stunning intellect. Disciplined yet adventuresome. She wondered how long she should wait to broach the subject of their breeding together.

"...so in order that Elgin Mars's foresight and ultimate sacrifice never be forgotten," Ammon said, "we hereby dedicate a whole *world* in his name."

The High Commissioner tapped into his wrist hub and there, next to the podium, a metallic statue of a planet uncloaked, spinning in all its anti-gravitational and phaetronic glory, with "living" continents, oceans and clouds moving around it. "The planet Aeros... now 'Mars.'" he announced. "This magnificent creation has been graciously gifted to Atlas City by its most distinguished Master Artisan... Micah." Master Artisan... Micah." The tall, barrel-chested red-haired bear of a man came forward to stand beside his technological masterpiece, accepting the audience's polite applause with a theatrical bow.

Talya squirmed. Micah was a buffoon. Ridiculously confident without a shred of reserve. Every sexual advance he'd ever made towards her had been sternly rebuffed, but he tried repeatedly, as though he'd forgotten the last attempt as well as the rebuff.

"Now let me introduce Arlan Chronus," Ammon went on, "Geological Engineer of the... 'Mars Mission.'"

As Chronus came to the podium Ammon stepped down into the audience and joined an older, dark-skinned woman standing in the front row. Talya recognised her as Poseidon's biological mother. Manya was her name. In her simple fabric sheath, with a long flowing silver ponytail and unabashed warmth emanating from both posture and expression, there was something primal about her, and to Talya's taste vaguely unsettling. Though the couple stood shoulder-to-shoulder, they were separated by a small but boundless gap, he holding himself rigidly away from his wife. It was clear there was nothing between them. No fire. Not the merest spark of affection.

Chronus took his place at the podium and stared out happily at the great assembly. "It's not often that a man likes to be proven wrong," he began. "But in the case of my professional disagreement with Elgin Mars and my esteemed colleague, Poseidon Ra, I couldn't be more delighted. Fourteen hours before our launch window closed..."

Talya saw a minor commotion down the front row from where she stood. Those young Physics Men, the ones who'd recently made a name for themselves with a groundbreaking protocol they'd named "DreamCapture," arrived noisily. It was a clever diversion, she thought, and was all the rage, particularly with Atlas City's Dome Engineers and Academy students, always hunting for another harmless thrill. She hadn't decided yet what to think of it. Dreaming was a practical pastime for Terresians. So much could be accomplished in the hallowed state. It seemed somehow wrong to use it purely for entertainment.

Now she spotted Athens in the crowd. He was scanning the audience, lingering momentarily on the face and figure of every pretty girl in sight. It was said of Poseidon's brother that he had been blessed – or cursed – with the personality of five men. He was wearing that famous smile of his, the one that caused the easily-moved to feel unaccountably happy. He was admittedly handsome. Full of natural masculine grace. She knew that for Athens, who grudgingly harbored both great and petty jealousies towards his brother, the adulation showered upon Poseidon this day and in the days to come would be next to unbearable.

Bloody stars, he was coming her way! She fought back her annoyance. While Athens exuded tremendous charm, Talya mainly found his chatter inane. And the way he was leering at her now he was probably picturing her in his bed writhing under him, groaning with pleasure.

Then he was at her shoulder.

"You have a new fissure," she said without looking up.

"Energy is already aware. Crews are on their way."

"Nice to know such things are no longer catastrophes."

"Thanks to my brother?"

Talya saw his eyes wander from her face to her throat. Perhaps, she thought with irritation, even lower. She was certain he knew this would annoy her, and did it all the same. Athens was the kind of man who believed those close to him would always disappoint him, so – without fail – he disappointed them first.

On the podium Chronus was drawing his thoughts to a close. "…so let me introduce my colleague and – without hyperbole – the salvation of Terres…Poseidon Ra!"

The audience showed the greatest approbation that they were able – polite clapping and even a few cheers. Poseidon, at his most reserved and humble, took his place at the podium. He looked, she thought, distinctly embarrassed by the acclaim. He easily quieted the audience with a raised hand.

"Elgin Mars was my friend. My teacher. Without Elgin, we'd be here today staring out at a desolate future. His vision of plenty – scorned by many of you – was so tough and tenacious that he pushed and argued until enough of you gave up and let him imagine… *the unimaginable* – enough titanum to give us freedom from worry or harm. To give us life rather than a cold, hard death – and a tragically extinct civilization. From the beginning, I believed in his dream of unlimited ore on Aeros. He'd shown me the numbers and geography, and they were solid. Convincing. Convincing so long as you allowed yourself a bit of optimism. Elgin was rich in optimism. It was something I learned from him. But while I believed in his Aerosean titanum, we did disagree slightly – only about which borehole to drill."

"Quite an accomplishment," Talya whispered to Athens, never taking her eyes off Poseidon.

"Not unexpected," Athens said. "He always attracts the greatest good fortune. Though being the savior of our world is a stunning accomplishment, even for him."

She turned briefly to Athens, looking surprised.

"I'm perfectly capable of being kind."

"About your brother?"

"Yes."

"No you're not."

"Well, I'm happy we're not all going to die. And that's his doing." He regarded her cynical stare. "No? Not brotherly enough?"

She refused to let her annoyance show, so turned her gaze to Ammon and Manya Ra. "They must be pleased."

"Our mother is."

"I regret that we got to 62 so late," Poseidon continued from the podium. "Just a few hours sooner and Elgin Mars would be standing here today, enjoying some well-earned accolades. I think he would have taken the greatest pleasure in saying 'I told you so,' knowing that you were all happy that you'd been so utterly wrong."

The crowd erupted into applause and Poseidon, almost embarrassingly relieved, stepped down off the stage. He went directly to his mother and father. Ammon Ra nodded with cool approval, but his mother drew her son into a warm, proud hug.

Next to her, Athens stiffened, unable to watch the affection given. He looked up instead, then tapping his wrist hub affected the need to check in with his DomeTech crew about the fissure. *He is so transparent*, she was thinking when Poseidon slipped his arm around her waist, startling her, and stiffened slightly at his over-demonstrativeness, perhaps the only one of his traits that rattled her.

"That was appropriately and sickeningly humble," Athens told his brother.

Poseidon accepted this with a sanguine smile. Nothing Athens said surprised him.

"The speech was fine," Talya said. "Don't listen to him."

"Fine? *Fine?*" Athens taunted. "Dr. Horus, the extravagance of your praise!"

"All I needed to hear," Poseidon said.

Talya turned to Athens. "You know, you're an animal."

"And the two of you are entirely bloodless creatures."

Ignoring him, Poseidon turned to her, determined to finally have the reunion so rudely co-opted by his annoying brother.

"Welcome back," she said.

He kissed her cheek. "You're the most beautiful thing I've seen in years."

"In historical times, wars would have been fought over our Talya," Athens interjected.

"How fortunate we are that such stupidity has been bred out of us," she said, perhaps a bit too pointedly.

But Athens was, if anything, thick-skinned, and his eyes had already begun wandering to a female student who gazed at him adoringly. He excused himself and steered through the crowd towards her, flashing one of his dazzling smiles.

Talya felt that moment of discomfort, being with Poseidon in public. Their pairing was still relatively new. She wondered if everyone was watching them.

"When we were gone I found myself thinking about you – the last time we…"

"What a waste of valuable time," she murmured.

Poseidon chuckled.

"Are you laughing at me?"

"I imagine you're laughing at me," he said.

"You *are* overly sentimental."

"Guilty." He leaned over and whispered. "Come home with me…?"

"I thought you'd never ask."

⁋

The Xenophon ScienTechnos Academy was beloved by all. Every Atlas citizen alive, and those long dead, had studied here when they'd come of age. Education was universal, unquestioned and uniformly excellent. Its campus, populated by some of the planet's most ancient trees, was built around a grassy quad surrounded by the graceful architecture of its lecture halls, libraries and laboratories. Students were as drawn to the sports stadium as the classrooms.

Inside the soaring astrolarium, otherwise known by its shape as The Pyramidium, Samos Korbell was holding his audience enraptured. He was famous for his voice, celebrated as much as an orator as an astrophysicist. The opening lecture of his First-Year program always drew so many of his past students and faculty that all classes but his were cancelled this morning on campus. The Pyramidium was a magisterial space of acoustical perfection, and its soaring ceiling allowed for vast celestial light shows. Korbell at the podium was spotlighted to one side of a central stage that he shared with a 3-dimensional diffraction projector.

At the moment it displayed their solar system – four inner planets in their orbits, and the five outer bodies. Terres, at the Aphelion of its long elliptical orbit, was nowhere to be seen.

Poseidon and his mother sat side by side in the topmost seating of the theater. Today her silver hair was woven with large, artful metallic baubles. It never failed to amaze him how naturally elegant and comfortable she was in her own skin. She leaned into his ear and whispered, "Korbell does have a flair for the dramatic."

"Like you."

"It was my *job*," Manya said, unable to suppress a smile.

He saw her gazing around at the audience, wistfully, he thought. She had been the greatest thespian of her day. The stage had been her home. And Korbell had famously been her first lover.

"You all recognize this," the professor said, waving his arm above his head. Our Solar System as it is today. 'Hermos' and 'Aphrodise' closest to the sun. 'Gaia' next, and 'Aeros' – what we now know as 'Mars.' We head for the outer reaches of our solar system. The gaseous orange giant, Zeus and its seventy remarkable moons. You all know what comes next in the planetary succession – the many-ringed beauty, Kronos. But she is still far, far in the distance. Four hundred million miles past Zeus… Wait! What is this coming?" Korbell called playfully to the audience.

Out of the black reaches of space, on an orbital plane unlike any of the others, came hurtling an immense rocky planet slicing evenly between the two orbits of Zeus and Chronos.

"Terres!" the audience responded gleefully, like a classroom of clever schoolchildren.

"Of course," Korbell agreed. "We all learn our home planet's position in the solar system in our primary classes. "What we learn today is the significance of Terres's placement and it's long… *exceedingly* long 'Eccentric Orbit.' Watch now!"

The diffracted Terres, finished with the inner arc of its orbit, was propelled from the solar system's heart and back out in the depths of space.

"There she goes. Watch her. Flying farther and farther away – past Ouranos, past Radon and Pluton – on that killingly long circuit from the light and heat of our sun Helios and the companionship of her sister planets." He shook his head sadly. "No fault of her own."

The stadium was silenced as they watched their beleaguered home growing smaller and smaller till it once again disappeared from sight.

"This is what you must know as you begin your ScienTechnical studies here at Academy," Korbell continued, "Our civilization, our technos, our history and our Fate are all defined by one single circumstance – *the unconscionably long orbit of Terres*. We are forced to adapt, squeeze every aspect of our living, learning, arts, OffWorld explorations and progress into the portion of our "year" that the planet is bathed in natural sunlight – the one hundred and two years before leaving the 'Inner Circuit" of the sun... and returning to universal night." Korbell brought his hands together in front of him. He seemed to be gathering his energies in order to begin the most critical moment of his lecture.

"Collision is Destiny," he intoned and grew silent. He stayed silent for so long a moment that everyone began to squirm. "That is why today we must understand the collisions that impacted the most ancient version of our Solar System."

Overhead there was a subtle rearrangement in the projection of the four planets closest to the sun as the others remained in place.

"As you can see, Hermos and Aphrodise are in their expected orbits, closest to Helios. And there..." Korbell paused for dramatic effect, "...there is the third planet from the sun, not Gaia, but *'Tiamat!'*" He spoke the name with such fervor, such mystery, that even faculty and older students who had heard the lecture before were brought to the edge of their seats.

Now Korbell looked out over the audience in its tiered seating along two of the angled walls of the Pyramidion. His eyes finally came to rest on Poseidon and Manya. He smiled wryly. "How honored we are to be graced here today by the presence of the one and only... Manya!"

There were murmurs of approval and some heartfelt applause.

Poseidon could see Korbell's eyes moist and glittering from

where he sat, and absorbed how the pleasure of such adulation warmed his mother, even though it had been two Long Orbits since she'd performed onstage. Then the professor's expression grew mischievous.

"And sitting next to our beloved thespian is her son, the single man on the planet I would consider sharing the podium with to present "The Great Fracture."

Taken by surprise, Poseidon felt his face redden and he quickly tapped at his wrist to regulate the embarrassing flush.

"Many of you know him. I take that back. "You *all* know him now. He's new to his role as the savior of Terres, but he was once a lowly professor like me."

The audience chuckled and all eyes swiveled to fix Poseidon in their sights, hoping to measure his response to Korbell's gentle kidding.

"You see I'm not the only one qualified to lecture on those collisions, the day that sealed our civilization's Destiny. Terres's most distinguished geologist, Poseidon Ra, gives the story a distinctive *terrestrial* flavor, while my tale focuses on the celestial 'rogues' – comets, asteroids, wandering moons and even small planetoids – that come speeding in from the far reaches of the cosmos to do their damage. To change form, spark fire, create virgin terra firma... and foment Destiny. What do you say?"

Poseidon realized that the last had been directed to him. A question. "Yes, of course I'll join you, Professor." Poseidon stood and descended the central steps and came to the center platform of the Pyramidion. He and Korbell dipped heads in mutual respect.

The audience stirred with anticipation.

"Let's make it a good show," Korbell whispered to him.

Poseidon laughed. Then he turned to the eager eyes before him. "For the moment, let's forget the outer planets – Mars, Zeus, Chronos and beyond. For now focus on the third planet. "Here..." Poseidon paused and intoned with utter gravitas "...is

Tiamet." As he gazed above him the planet, nearly the size of Zeus, further enlarged and enhanced till it virtually filled the upper reaches of the astrolarium. In this way students could see details of Tiamet's vast oceans, its continents alive with forests, mountains and deserts, erupting volcanoes and shifting continents.

"By virtue of her placement – not so close and not too far from Helios, she was provided sufficient light and heat to ferment the oceans into a rich biological stew. Tiamet teemed with strange primitive life in her seas. Within her waters lay greatness. Endless possibilities of life."

"And then the day of reckoning!" Korbell boomed.

The most reserved among them, Poseidon thought, *will be moved by the enormity of his next words, always suffused with power and passion._*

"What can be said about the death of a world? One so gargantuan in proportion… so miraculously fecund? It is what we call 'The Great Fracture.' We must remember to celebrate this disaster," Poseidon continued, "for without Tiamet's destruction we would – none of us – be sitting here today having this lecture. We would, rather, be swimming in her salty soup," he added with a touch of levity, "with a population of armor-plated monsters."

The laughter shuddering through the audience was muted, uncomfortable. But neither Poseidon nor Korbell needed further words for the teaching. Up above them, Tiamet had shrunk slightly so the whole dazzling array of the solar system's planets, moons and rings was again visible. And suddenly as everyone watched in horrible fascination, a massive comet the size of a small planet, streaming white and gaseous, raced into the solar system past the outer orbs, clipped one of the Marsean moons, and slammed into Tiamet with unconscionable force and velocity. You could hear the groaning of the first-year students as they witnessed the collision, gaping spellbound at the breaking asunder of the once mighty world.

It ripped apart, separating at the seams, its molten core, rocky mantle and atmosphere chaotically roiling and re-coalescing into something new. One giant fragment shattered into billions of burnt shards of stone that, in a slow-motion dance, reassembled themselves into a ring of asteroid-sized rocks flying within the original path of Tiamet.

"This is what we know as "The Rocky Belt," Korbell interjected now.

A second part – sucking into itself both oceans and landmasses – reformed, then propelled itself into a new stable orbit between Aphrodise and Mars. "This," Poseidon added, "became the *new* third planet from the Sun – what we know as 'Gaia.'"

"The final fragment," Korbell went on, "also coalesced land and sea into a solid orb. This, as you all know, would become our home planet, Terres. Her orbit, somewhat less stable than Gaia's, found its place between Zeus and Chronos. But our story is not yet finished." He paused, allowing questions to gather in the dark. "Remember the moon of Mars that was dealt a glancing blow by the incoming comet? That moon's wobble, in time, gave way to an orbital shift, and that to a complete expulsion from Marsean gravity."

There was hardly a breath to be heard in the darkness as, above them in the upper astrolarium, Mars's vagrant moon careened through space on a collision course with the new planet Terres. "While the blow was far less destructive than the comet had been to Tiamet," Korbell continued, "it was sizable enough to destabilize its orbit and set it on an altogether different 'plane.' Worse, it began an inexorable arc over the millennia, farther and farther into the black reaches of space in an unnaturally long elliptical path."

"Ten thousand Gaian orbits to every one of Terres's," Poseidon added. "Today Terres is lost in the blackness of space five billion light-years past Pluton, without the sun's life-giving rays for most of its… year."

"So we have witnessed those collisions and a deathlike fate.

And yet here we sit today, the most advanced civilization in the solar system. We have somehow evolved – as the creatures on our sister planet, Gaia, did in reasonable parallel – from primordial soup to primates. But here is the difference between us – *more collisions* afflicted Gaia, many asteroids knocked out of The Belt just as we were migrating out of the danger zone. Her evolution was set back millions of years, stunted, as ours progressed apace. In further lectures we'll be discussing how Terresian primitives dealt with the dying of the planet's surface to emerge as a *civilization*, one that was eventually capable of developing 'Phaetron Technos.'"

The Solar System dissolved and instead, large glowing words **"The Vibrus"** now hung emblazoned above the central platform. Poseidon, seeing that his presence was no longer needed, quietly left the podium.

"It is the principle that all matter and energy, at their most basic levels, are nothing more than vibrational frequencies. This," Korbell told the room, "and our ability to harness and modulate the Vibrus, became the key that unlocked the very universe! It utterly transformed our world. The miracle of 'Phaetron Technos' – now these two words were projected above the central platform – allows our planet's remaining living environment, as well as its people, to survive Terres's long dark circuit under our Contour Dome. So…" Korbell said, taking a moment to pause and choose his next image.

"Here it comes," Clax said quietly to Monas. "The "Triad of Terresian Scientechnos.'"

"I don't know if I can bear it," Enoc said.

"Let's not be rude," Monas argued.

"…let's have a look at 'the Triad of Terresian Scientechnos,'" said Korbell. "Firstly, 'Genomic Sciences.'"

THREE

ATHENS AND HIS three-man unit floating in their propulsion suits – Deacon, Darius, and Harmonan – hovered above the vast Contour Dome. Encapsulated within the greatest protective field of phaetronic energy on Terres, the bubble sheathed and protected all that was left of life from the darkness and death of deep space. The City's manufactured atmosphere, when whole and functional, its phaetronic bubble cloaking Atlas Environs, was invisible. The projection of sky and weather inside it was seamless, whether a cloud-dappled afternoon under a warm NearSun, or a nighttime thunderstorm with righteous spectacles of harmless lightning. And there, dotted round the outside of those hundreds of miles of energy sheathing, working inside or outside his solo shuttlepod, was his DomeTech army – numbering 99 in total – repairing small tears in the force field.

He and his unit were working above Central City. It was daytime inside. Far below the people going about their peaceful lives in streets and public plazas appeared, from up this high, as tiny insects, and the closed "Eye" of the SleepPhase Dome was clearly visible.

The four of them worked near each other. There was friendly helmet-comm banter about women and too much jog – when when without warning a hole the size of a man's body ripped open beneath Darius, blasting out a high-speed volume of inter-dome propellant and detritus… cleanly slicing away half of his body.

There was a sickening lurch in Athens's gut at the sight… and a singular instinct kicking in at the same moment. Or was it his training? Everything happened fast. The three of them flew for their shuttles. Made it inside. He'd just closed the hatch behind himself when it happened.

A massive rupture, hundreds of feet across, blew through the Dome's energy fabric. Its network became suddenly visible, crazing and sizzling at its raw edges. It began unweaving itself even further from the rupture site, growing its damage all the way out to the seam of its dodecahedral angle. Once there it began its destruction on the second of the twelve sides.

It was moving fast.

Watching for the most visible crazing, the near-crew began containing the lateral damage and anticipated the next walls failing. He had commed the wider crew from around the entire Dome, calling them to the site. All at once the entire 3-dimensional dodec spiderweb briefly flared-up… then collapsed.

What was left in its place was cold and black, an immense 12-angled spherical bite taken out of the clouded blue sky.

Then each of the 12 contiguous "sides" began feasting upon its neighbor.

Athens watched now as the larger fleet of repair pods came racing in from their sectors towards the fast-disintegrating energy shield. He remembered the first orders he'd commed the full crew – "Compartmental failure – exponential. Set 7.2.4. Maximize…" He hoped his voice sounded calm and steady. Steadier than his heart, which seemed to be adding an extra beat every few moments.

He had countless walls to repair and 97 crewmen to govern.

In the Central City, people were looking up in confusion as a 12-sided chunk of blue sky turned black, an occasional star winking through, pinpricks of light darting nimbly at the edges of the damage. In the moment when the dark patch expanded suddenly and aggressively – fizzling out into several directions at once – everyone began to run. They knew how to find shelter. Some hesitated, as though measuring and choosing the closest escape route.

But not for long. People grabbed anyone close to them, an arm or hand or shoulder, herding as many as they could towards the giant arched doors concealed in the walls of public buildings that were now automatically gliding open to receive them.

In the sink of space above them all the pods were working the damaged perimeters. Monstrous and dynamic as the damage was, the repair was already beginning. A discharge of fine phaetronic webbing streamed across the breach from every pod, assembling a new energy field, one wall of the network surging to meet the next.

Then, with no warning, a projectile from above – a tiny stone pellet, a meteorite, a bit of space junk – shot diagonally across the blackness. The once-intact Contour Dome would have stopped the thing, bouncing it back out into space or frying it on contact, but the little superheated rock racing at miles-per-second pierced the fragile new webbing the pilots had not yet completed.

The damage was instantly apparent. The newly woven energy shield crumbled like tissue and disappeared entirely. Worse, the projectile tore through the last layers of weakened but still-intact atmospheric dodecahedrons and into Terresian soil at the east perimeter of Atlas Environs, delivering the blackness right down to the planet's surface.

Everywhere this "space" touched – a building, a tree, a person – froze solid. And the gash was spreading. The icy night began to engulf the better part of the Academy campus, adjacent residential streets and parklands, moving into Central City, heading towards the SleepPhase Dome. Above, the pods were propelling a continuous stream of phaetronic webbing into the gaping "lower wound."

❧

Looking out the window of Talya's second-floor lab that morning past the Obelisk the sky had all at once become checkered ominously with blue and black. On the Quad, people were sprinting towards the gaping mouth of the rarely-used shelter. Overhead, the black was descending quickly. Some part of her realized this was an emergency, but panic was an alien emotion.

She collided with Poseidon just outside her lab. He'd come to rescue her. *What a strange, primeval notion,* she thought.

The hallway was crowded with students pouring out the doors – young, frenzied, falling one on top of another. Poseidon shouted orders at everyone, stopping the panic, forcing them to move quickly down the stairs two-by-two.

She and Poseidon exploded into the catastrophe, his arm cradling her shoulder. Together, wordlessly, they ran for the shelter. But the freezing dark had reached the Academy campus. She chanced a look behind and saw it encroaching, frosting the quad lawn into a field of sharp icicles, solidifying a thousand-year-old tree and whitening the leaves that fell down like glass shards from the branches.

They saw, as well as heard, the hundred-foot-tall stone Obelisk cracking as it froze solid. Sharp pops and creaking, and then an awful groaning sound.

They turned. Saw the impossible.

He grabbed her waist and tore away as the sound of the falling tower became a thunderous roar. It shattered into a million pieces of stone, some of them ripping into the flesh of their backs and legs. The pain was sharp, intense, but there was no time to self-anesthetize. Students were racing in through an arched doorway to a lighted chamber. She and Poseidon, bloodied but whole, ran behind them.

Blackness had fallen outside the doorway just as a transparent

ShieldWall materialized between the airless dark and the lighted space. But in the final moment a straggler captured in mid-stride by the shield, found her face, chest and outstretched arms inside the shelter, the rest of her body trapped without. As her eyes bulged and face stiffened into a silent scream the posterior parts froze solid, crazed and disintegrated into a sickening pile of pink chipped ice.

❦

In his pod Athens heard Deacon shouting, "It's not holding!" and his own insistent, "It is!" shouted with more confidence than he truly felt. "It *is* holding. Don't let up!" The other 97 crewmen were, in fact, making headway in re-weaving a patch on the larger gouged-out holes. "Give it everything," Athens called urgently, and the small team had obeyed, restoring the energy net below them.

But the freeze was relentless.

It was overtaking the eastern end of the SleepPhase Stadium. Half of the etched eye on its curved roof frosted over. A few moments more and the dome would collapse. *All is lost,* Athens thought, feeling bile rising in his throat. *The city destroyed on my watch.*

And then all at once it stopped.

The woven web closed its circuit, the sectional walls holding steady. Shield failure ceased expansion and the giant void stabilized.

Athens gulped his first conscious breath since the emergency, sweat pouring down into his eyes. With no further orders to give, silence filled his pod and those of the other 97. The seconds grew to a minute, then two and three. It was not until the glowing phaetronic web had congealed into its "solid" colorless energy shield – albeit with a giant bite hollowed out of it – that Athens began to hear echoing through the repair fleet comm, wild whoops of triumph, and his name – like a song – shouted over and over and over again.

୶

Poseidon had called a special meeting of the Fed Energy commissioners. Athens was staring out the conference room window at the "sky," usually pristine blue. After the Dome accident it had become a sickening patchwork of blue and black starry space. Dozens of his repair pods were flying around trying to rebuild the larger energy shell and the shattered city beneath it.

At one end of the long table with Poseidon was their father, High Commissioner Ammon Ra, and equally insufferable Sub Commissioners Denys and Praxis. Athens was doing his best to tune them out. Truly, they made his head explode. Talya was halfway down the table, sitting so straight it looked like a rod had been stuck up her rectum. They were all a bit shock-eyed, everyone's gaze darting out the window at their brush with the end of the world.

Athens had never heard his mild-mannered brother speak so forcefully.

"We've got to start the mining operation on Mars. Now," he asserted. "Make sure that first shipment of ore gets back here and processed, *before* the next Long Orbit Sleep. We can't afford to wait. We need to dispatch the Gaian expedition, too." If for any reason the Marsean mission failed, Poseidon reasoned, they'd need Gaia for relocation of the entire Terresian population. Doctor Horus had all her genomic protocols in order, he assured the commissioners, and was ready to go. The fate of their civilization depended on launching both missions as soon as the two vehicles could be built.

When the quibbling at the far end of the table became too much to bear, Athens leaned back, folded his arms across his chest and began slowly undressing Talya Horus in his mind.

She was nearly naked when he noticed that Sub Commissioner Denys's face had turned an alarming shade of red. He was looking up at Poseidon as though he'd been stabbed.

"You can't mean that!"

"I can and I do," he heard his brother say with irritating calm. *Oh, how he loathed the sound of that voice.*

"I have no interest in governing the Mars Colony," Poseidon finished.

With that, the meeting exploded into a barrage of objections. "No one knows Marsean geology better than you do," Denys insisted.

"The colony will be permanent," Poseidon went on composedly, as if he had not just thrown a dead, rotting animal on the conference table. "Five thousand Terresians who know nothing about physical labor will be forced to work productively in dirty, dangerous conditions for an extended period. It's critical that they be kept happy. They'll need congenial leadership, someone who will keep their spirits high." He looked around the table defiantly. "That's why I'm recommending my brother for the post." Then he turned and fixed his mild gaze on Athens.

Everyone's heads swiveled his way. They were dumbfounded.

It was an ambush. Athens felt his face flush. His heart pounded wildly. *Governor of the Marsean mining colony?* He was a DomeTech Supervisor! His bloody brother! Why had Poseidon sprung this on him with no warning?

Before he'd been able to object, a verbal brawl broke out around the table. Insults began flying. Their father was true to form. Demeaning. Contemptuous. The others piled on. He was unqualified, too young, too volatile – a "hothead."

They were all still grumbling when Poseidon silenced the room with an unaccustomed raised voice, "I'm amazed! Look out the window. My brother just saved our Dome from catastrophic collapse! For years he's been responsible for the very air we breathe, maintenance of our PseudoSun. He already holds the lives of every one of us in his hands. On Mars we'll make sure he has the best support possible. He'll learn on the job. But we cannot send someone to lead an off-world colony who's simply practical. What's needed is… genius." He glared at the commissioners and smiled coolly at their father. "If you insist on rewarding me for finding titanum, you'll grant me Gaia. And if you're looking for an inspired nomination for Mars, look no further than my brother."

FOUR

T HE BULLET TRAIN slowed to a stop in front of the Launch Dome. Poseidon made his way inside the energy blister and across its expansive floor, gazing with considerable awe at the two space vehicles being readied for dispatch.

Their construction had been the most extensive building project in Terresian history.

The Colonial Transport – a black trapezoid the size of a small city, and its silvery sister craft *Atlantos Discus* – had been built on the spot. No one liked thinking about the mountain of TitanumCarbonite alloys that had been processed in its foundry's phaetronic blast furnace for the project. How the project had depleted the planet's already dwindling titanum stores to a frightening degree.

But what other choice did they have?

The Marsean vein needed mining and shipping back to Terres if there was to be any future at all. So it didn't matter in the scheme of things that the Transport was not much more than a hulking freighter.

The *Atlantos* was something else altogether.

Created by Micah, the massive mothership meant to house Poseidon's ScienTechnos crew was a slim, sleek, silvery disc, elegant in proportion and design and as classically beautiful as its brother was relentlessly functional. This vessel's form was enhanced by function – stark, refined and exquisitely advanced.

Poseidon was surprised to see his father here, speaking with Athens not far from the snaking line of colonists boarding the Transport. Not pleasantly surprised, he thought. Ammon Ra's presence rarely improved any circumstance and often subverted them. Far more forbidding and indifferent than the classic Terresian male. Manya believed genomic restructuring had gone too far with Ammon's generation. Poseidon often wondered why so wonderful and greathearted a woman as she was had not only mated, but stayed with such a man. As if he'd conjured her with his thoughts, Poseidon spotted his mother standing alone, staring at the Transport wistfully. As he came to her side she gave him her cheek to kiss.

"It is beautiful in its way," Manya said. "The savior of our planet."

"You're referring to your younger son, I assume?"

She smiled and he placed his long arms around her and held her close for a moment longer than was seemly for any Terresian.

"I know. I smell good," she whispered. "You always say that."

Their eyes fell on Athens and Ammon across the way.

"I shudder to think what Father's final words will be to his son."

"Don't worry," she said. "Athens is stronger than you think."

"Why are you being so nice to me?" he asked his father. Ammon had never had any patience for his younger son or what he called the boy's "disordered Vibrus." Athens looked across the dome floor and saw Poseidon standing close to his mother. "Ah, you've been threatened."

Ammon refused to answer.

"Come on, tell me. What's her threat?"

"That she'll leave me."

Athens barked a laugh. "Why hasn't she left you already?"

"I don't know, and honestly I don't care. Just as long as she doesn't." Now Ammon glanced at Manya and Poseidon. "It's easy enough to pretend civility from a distance," Ammon said.

"True," Athens agreed, perhaps a bit too quickly.

"I've never been uncivil to you," Ammon remonstrated.

"Merely inhuman."

"No need to be unpleasant."

"I may not be your favorite son," Athens said, flashing a feigned smile at his father. "But I am your *remarkable* son. You know Poseidon's a terrible bore. Just like you are."

Ammon slicked back his handsomely greying hair with the flat of his hand, and pretended to smile back at his son. "When will you learn that you can't hurt my feelings?"

"She's looking now," Athens whispered. "Pretend to hug me."

His father did what he was told, oblivious to Athens's generous gesture, so that when they separated Ammon murmured, "About Mars…"

"I won't ruin it," Athens finished for him, finally annoyed. "Give me that much credit, will you?" He gazed disgustedly at this heartless excuse for a man, glad that it would be the last time he would ever have to see that icy expression, those steely eyes. "Goodbye, Father," he said, turning on his heels to go. "Don't bother to call."

≪

Manya pushed out of Athens's embrace and gazed at her sons. She noticed a bruised look on Athens's face as he glanced in every direction but his father's.

"He's an old fool," she said. "He doesn't deserve you."

"He's harmless to me."

The three of them turned their attention to the thousands

of men and women waiting in lines four-across to board the Transport, nervous laughs and genuine smiles. And there was Samos Korbell speaking congenially with the trio of young Physics Men as their experimental bell was loaded aboard one of the freighter's cargo holds.

Their gaze swiveled across the way to the *Atlantos* then, in all its stylish glory, Zalen welcoming a select crew aboard his amazing vessel. Talya, carrying a small satchel, stepped up to him and put out a graceful hand. Poseidon could see admiration in the Captain's eyes. Even Talya's stiff formality could not hide her gorgeousness.

"Look at the two of you," Manya said, bringing her attention back to her boys. "I'm so proud. Your glorious adventures..."

"I have to go, Mother," Athens said.

"I know," she said with a firm smile.

Manya cradled him to her, the beautiful son she would never hold in her arms again. Poseidon stepped away, leaving them a private moment. His brother clutched her tightly as she wept. Then refusing to meet Poseidon's eye, he hurried away.

Finally she collected herself as she turned to Poseidon, wiping at her wet face. "And you. You I will live to see again."

"I'll back before SleepPhase." He looked, suddenly shy. "Tell me, Mother, what do you think of Talya Horus?"

"You're a grown man. Why ask me?" Manya cocked her head. "She's very beautiful. Brilliant. She couldn't be a more perfect Terresian woman."

"But?"

"Does she move you?"

"I don't know what you're asking."

"Do you dream of her?"

"I don't think so. Does that matter?"

"Perhaps not." She laughed softly. "I hope you find what you're looking for on Gaia."

"What am I looking for?" he asked, truly baffled.

"You'll tell me if you found it when you come home. I hope it's wonderful. I hope it surprises you."

"If it surprises me half as much as you do, Mother, I will hold myself a very lucky man."

SPACE

FIVE

ERE IN A place of universal night, all was timeless. Silent. Cold. If a breath could be inhaled, one would know the odor of burnt rock. Gaia – loveliest of all planets – was not far off. From here it showed as a small, perfect bluish disc, while Mars, reflecting the sun's glare, was a distant speck of light. The two vessels running on parallel courses toward the center of the solar system – like the brothers who commanded them – could not have been more mismatched. The Colonial Transport was a huge lumbering thing never even given a name, an unlovely but efficient mover of goods and restless immigrants necessary to permanently populate the New Marsean Mining Colony. The *Atlantos*, a gleaming silver disc as classically beautiful as the Transport was relentlessly functional would – with its small, elite exploratory team headed for Gaia – in several years time return to their home planet, Terres.

The slumbering brothers Ra, encased in their sleeping pods as all the travelers had been for seven years, were people who loved their dreams. Seven years now, with new worlds shimmering in wait…

Poseidon saw his beautiful, grey-eyed mother, Manya bend
down into his pod, her fragrant embrace, a kiss on each of

his cheeks, and the smile that had warmed him to the core.

"Sweet dreams, darling boy," she'd crooned. "Sweet dreams."

"Poseidon…Poseidon…" he could hear a man's voice from afar. In his hibernation chamber he slowly raised his hand to his chin and felt the tough stubble of a beard. He forced his lids apart and looked up to see Cyphus standing beside the pod. It was he who'd called him out of his slumber.

"I was dreaming about dreaming," Poseidon uttered groggily. "My first SleepPhase."

Cyphus helped Poseidon from the pod and handed him a robe. Seeing his friend now caused a strange warmth to blossom in his chest and evoked a deep, relieved sigh to escape him. Cyphus was the only person in the world, aside from his mother, who was unfailingly loyal, unfalteringly kind.

"The others are up. They're gathering in the Library at 2-and-a half," Cyphus offered.

"Talya?"

Cyphus shot him a cheeky smile. "You were the first one she asked for."

Poseidon took his first steps in seven years, crossing his elegantly appointed private quarters, catching sight of himself in a mirror. The grey eyes that matched his mother's.

Cyphus watched him examining the shadow of a beard on his pale brown chin. "Leave it," he said. "You can afford to be grubby one day in your life."

"She'll hate it."

"Yes, she will."

Poseidon drew closer to the mirror. Thought about Talya. Thought about rubbing his face on her milk white neck. Decided in that moment to keep the stubble. He walked to a broad expanse of windows under his dining table and stared out at the Colonial Transport.

"It'll be all right," Cyphus told him. "Athens is happy with his command, ugly ship and all."

"My brother is never happy."

"Maybe those ReGenomic protocols he had before we left…"

"I'm not sure he actually went through with them."

"He's going to be fine," Cyphus insisted.

⁓

"Bloody stars, woman! Slow down!" Athens could see nothing through the thick curtain of pale hair whipping his face and chest, obscuring his eyes. But he didn't need to see. Sensation was all there was. The blonde was straddling him, riding him, tossing her head and groaning with pleasure. She was totally in control. She's was going to come, and could barely get the words out. "Can't…slow down.

Can't…"

"Horus…" he said, glimpsing the exquisite line of her jaw, the tensed lips, the sheen on her forehead. But then, in a baffling gesture she put a long-fingered hand on one of his shoulders and began to shake it. "Horus, stop…" It was breaking the rhythm of the ride. Ruining the mounting sensations… "

No, wait," he begged.

It was only when Horus's face above him began to transmute, reshape itself into another face altogether — a kind-eyed but less-than-lovely olive-skinned woman with close-cropped hair and a high-necked crew uniform — that Athens knew he'd been dreaming.

He opened his eyes and, indeed, it was Persus Elrah shaking him awake. The walls of the hibernation chamber felt awful, confining. He sat up abruptly, his eyes gaining focus, only to see his ugly, strictly utilitarian sleeping quarters. *At least they're private*, he thought, a small perquisite for being the Marsean

Governor. His heart was suddenly pounding, so he took some calming breaths and resisted lashing out at Persus. In fact he gave her a sweet, sleepy smile.

"We've already got a few fires to put out," she said. "And Vice Governor Pra…"

"Persus, don't! Don't utter that name while I'm trying to wake up."

She smiled indulgently. "There's a good-sized breach in the outer hull of Section 47, but not to worry…"

"Triple hull."

"Very good, Governor," she said in a teacherly tone.

"See, I remember everything you say."

She rolled her eyes.

"Occasionally something slips my mind when we've had a few."

"We need to keep our heads straight now," she told him.

He gazed at her fondly. "But they were fun, those nights. You and me and the finest Terresian jog."

"No more fun, Sir. Five thousand colonists are depending on you."

He rose naked from the hibernation chamber and felt her eyes on him. Saw her look away quickly.

"You'd better bathe," she said.

"That bad?"

Smiling to herself, she moved to the door. "There's a problem with two of the medical diffractors, and with everyone waking at once there are bound to be dozens of emergencies. I'll meet you at MedLab."

"Persus…"

"Sir?"

"Find us a nice bottle for later," he said with that special charm he knew was unnecessary with Persus. "Just one. We'll need it. It's going to be a long day."

❧

My own little kingdom, thought Athens as he walked through one of the transport's large common rooms teeming with cheerful colonists. It was gratifying to see how they greeted their Governor with warm, friendly smiles. Nearly every young woman gazed at Athens with what could only be described as blatant invitation. There was an unmistakable spirit of celebration for their coming adventure and he, Athens, symbolized their glorious future.

The mission was already proving a balm to the wound that had always afflicted him. His father's neglect. *No,* he thought. *Call it what it was. Mental torture.* Since his waking he had enjoyed a new buoyancy, a certainly that he and his colonists would live in great contentment on Mars. Even the notion of manual labor in the titanum mines didn't appear to blunt their enthusiasm.

It had always grated on Athens, first to be thought the inferior younger brother, then to be forced to live in the shadow of their planet's savior. But things were different now. Here were all the colonists. A future. A whole new start.

They were to be bold pioneers on a sunlit planet. It made him smile.

❧

Poseidon turned his eyes to Doctor Talya Horus standing close at his side on the floor of the expansive Shuttle Bay. Even in everyday coveralls she took his breath away. This being a celebration night – the end of Flight Hibernation – she'd dressed for the occasion, putting on a simple sheath that turned her sharpest angles into sleek curves. Not three hours before they'd been together in bed, and she thought it made him squirm when she juxtaposed her collegial and carnal selves before him. It might have in the past, but since his waking this time a new aspect of his psyche had revealed itself. Funny, he didn't remember reprogramming himself before leaving Terres, but during his long sleep it had self-generated and gestated – a new looseness in him. A propensity to follow instinct over reason. To feel an increased range of sensations without use of his enhancer. It was slippery and mysterious. He liked the new trait but kept news of it to himself. Talya's pale blue-ice eyes that remained opened during the sex act to observe and assess her partner's climax had never registered the change in him, but then they'd only been sexualizing for a short time before the expedition. For now he would keep it to himself.

Still, gazing out the Shuttle Bay's window as a boxy shuttle pod – a vehicle just as unsightly as its mothership – crossed the dark distance from the Transport, Poseidon found himself unnaturally aroused by the thought of Doctor Talya Horus in his bed. He snaked a discrete hand around her waist.

Not discrete enough.

"Not here," she whispered sharply under her breath.

"No one is watching," Poseidon replied just as quietly.

"Not. Here." She leveled him with a cool smile. "Later."

The bay doors slid open and Athens's pod glided noiselessly in and set down amidst the half dozen 30-foot diameter discoid shuttles. They were pretty miniatures of the *Atlantos*.

"Please let him be of good cheer," Poseidon said.

"Why shouldn't he be? He's Governor of the new Marsean colony with hardly a single qualification to speak of... besides a guilty brother."

"He's got Vice Governor Praxis...and Officer Elrah to back him up," Poseidon suggested.

"He's probably spent all seven years of his cryogenesis pseudosexualizing with hundreds of pretty young women."

"Not everyone uses the time for serious SleepWork like you," he said.

"You do. That's why I like you," she said, perhaps the warmest words she was capable of giving.

The moment the port doors closed, pressure and gasses

stabilized. Athens emerged from the pod and was instantly thronged by the *Atlantos's* crew who'd come to the bay floor to greet him. He was followed out of the shuttle by Persus. With her meticulous gaze she was observing every detail. Watching as he moved among the flight crew with effortless charm.

"She's really something," Talya told Poseidon. "That woman's going to save his life."

He searched his brother's face. It seemed unnaturally peaceful. Though Athens hid it well, he had been since childhood, awash in fears. And fear was the foremost of the human impulses so frowned upon in their society. Perhaps Persus would, in fact, become his savior.

Athens caught sight of Poseidon and flashed one of his winning smiles.

"This bodes well," Poseidon observed.

"He was smiling at *me*," Talya said.

Indeed, when Athens came walking towards them it was her his gaze was fixed on. "You're a sight for sore eyes," he said. He reached out to embrace her, but pulled back with a smile and a theatrical flourish instead. He turned to Poseidon.

"Was your waking comfortable?" Poseidon asked.

"A bit bumpy coming out. You don't look any worse for the wear."

"That might be the nicest thing you've ever said to me."

"Don't get used to it," Athens said, craning his neck to find Persus.

"Where's Vice Governor Praxis?" Poseidon inquired. "Ooooh, I think I forgot to invite him."

"Be careful, Athens," Talya said. "He has Fed's ear."

"And how many millions of miles are we from that august council?" Athens asked rhetorically Poseidon conceded with a nod. Happy with his small triumph, Athens took Talya's arm and walked off with her. Poseidon waited for Persus to catch up.

There was no getting around it, Poseidon thought as the four of them made their way to his quarters. The massive mothership meant to house his elite ScienTechnos crew, was as elegant in proportion and design and as classically beautiful as his brother's Transport was relentlessly functional.

Walking behind his brother he noticed that Athens kept his eyes focused entirely on Talya, refusing to linger on the finer details of the *Atlantos.* He seemed determined not to let the habitual rampant jealousy get the better of him. There would be no complaining that his ship was built in a style Athens derided as 'Early Hideous.'

"He seems well," Poseidon suggested to Persus.

"Better than he ever was at Dome Tech. He had a good sleep."

"Don't let him bully you."

She laughed at that. "He knows better."

What a relief, Poseidon thought. *A whole new start for Athens. Perhaps a whole new kinship with my brother.*

The Physics Men, themselves just released from their sleep pods and a bit rumpled – stood in their laboratory at the Colonial Transport's wide window, thoughtfully regarding the grey metallic sphere hovering between them several feet off the ground. Clax, Monas and Enoc exchanged a silent look.

"What are you waiting for!?" Enoc said.

Clax tapped his wrist hub and the metallic orb burst into phosphorescent white light.

"Yes!" Monas cried.

Enoc, checking his hub, announced, "Translocate probe 6.8 clix at 3.77 tron."

The sphere blinked suddenly out of sight between them, but

at the same instant reappeared on the other side of the glass. It hung there in space, glowing steadily. There was nothing to be said at this stage, but their heads bobbed in silent unison. They had been experimenting with translocation of matter since their graduation from the Academy. Their work had been astonishingly successful except for – and it made them furious – the transit of organic matter from place to place. But that was child's play. Today – *or should they say tonight?* – they were on the verge of breaching the "Membrane" between two dimensions!

Clax initiated another TransLoc, and the probe popped out of sight, reappearing 700 clix away in the space between the two vessels. Enoc chewed his lip. When Monas nodded, he sent the spheroid farther still. It hung there glowing bright white.

Tension rose between them suddenly.

"We shouldn't," Monas said.

"Of course we should," Enoc argued. "We're millions of miles from anywhere." He skewered Clax with his glare. "*Say something.*"

But Clax was silent, biting his thumbnail.

"Come *on*," Enoc pressed.

"It's childish to just do something the moment no one's watching," Clax said.

"No it's not," Enoc persisted. "Out here we don't have to worry about tearing a hole in the Atlas Contour Dome and killing every living thing in the environs."

"We don't actually know what effect ripping open a Dimensional Boundary Membrane will have," Clax said.

"That is because we've never *attempted* it before!" Enoc lost all patience then. "What have we been shredding our brains over since Korbell's lectures?"

"This," Clax admitted.

"This," Monas agreed.

"Then let's *do* it," Enoc demanded.

"We don't even know if we can breach the Membrane," Monas said with a petulant whine, but the other two were not listening.

Clax tapped tentatively into his wrist hub. "6.8 tron," he announced.

"Not enough," Enoc chided. "We need serious Vibrus. Magnitude Vibrus."

"7.2." Clax said, bumping up the frequency. "Not...*enough*."

Enoc was losing patience.

"We're already .75 above 'drill and kill,'" Monas argued.

"There's nothing out there to drill or kill!" Enoc cried. "Just do it!"

Clax complied, excited now, tapping in the tron sequence. They waited, all eyes fixed on the glowing white probe. Nothing happened.

"Bloody thing," Enoc growled.

Clax tapped determinately at his wrist again.

Still nothing.

And then... the probe... winked silently out of sight.

The three of them crushed against the window and scanned the blackness around them.

The thing was gone.

"Is she transmitting?!" Enoc nearly choked on his words.

Clax switched on a diffractor image between them. "This should be it," he said. "This should be...the other side."

It was solid black. No Terresian vessels. No Gaia in the distance. No stars. No galaxies. Nothing.

"That's it?" Enoc asked. "That's what she's seeing?"

Clax said nothing.

"Are you sure she's transmitting?" Enoc snapped.

"Yes, I'm sure!"

Enoc pounded the console with his fist. "Our first transdimensional leap and there's nothing there?"

"But we did it." Clax's voice was unconvincing.

"And how," Enoc questioned angrily, "will we ever *prove* what we did?

Clax pounded his head with the heel of his hand. "It makes no sense."

"Bring her back," Enoc ordered. "Now."

Clax nodded, then fiddled with his hub. The three of them stared out the window 7.2 clix. Nothing reappeared.

Nothing.

⋞

It couldn't have been a more congenial dinner, Poseidon thought, with he, Talya, Athens, Persus, Cyphus, and Samos Korbell. They sat at the table beside the large picture window in Poseidon's quarters – larger, and designed more elegantly than he had asked for. The Colonial Transport glided along outside a distance away. Athens was still behaving himself – he'd thankfully kept a check on his jog con- sumption. The mood was positively buoyant, the conversation sparkling.

Korbell was leaving aside science for more congenial talk.

"Any good dreams?" he asked.

"A recurring one, just as I woke up today," Poseidon said. I'd just laid down in my first Full-Orbit SleepPhase at the Stadium. I was fourteen and very serious."

"I remember that." Athens interjected. "I was six, lying in the next pod over, crying and terrified," "I'd never seen the entire population of Terres under one roof before. In nightgowns."

"Will you let me tell it?" Poseidon said.

"No!" Athens cried. "You'll only tell your side." He grinned charmingly. Everyone was used to humoring him. Everyone but Talya. "Our mother was promising I'd enjoy ten thousand years of hibernation, but she'd already scared me silly with visions of men in the SleepPhase Stadium waking up with hair so long it would fill up their pods and we'd need to dig through it all to find their faces..."

"Quiet! This is my dream," Poseidon said. "Yes, our mother was there. She was leaning over my chamber. What I remember every time is her sweet smile, that long silver hair, how she wore it loose around her shoulders." He smiled, remembering. "It was brushing my face, and she was kissing both my cheeks, whispering..."

"*I* remember how she smelled," Athens interrupted. "It was a particular scent, like she'd just come in from her garden."

"Sentimental wallow!" Talya said, exasperated. "I've always suspected your mother was the real culprit with you two. A parental retrogression. Far too much physical affection doesn't do anybody any favors. You're a couple of mutants. You could both do with some serious re-calibration."

"I'll tell you my dream," Athens said, leaning in, elbows on the table. "I'm floating on my back in the warm salty Marsean Sea. I want to keep floating, but I'm dying to bury my toes in that fine pink sand at the shore."

"About to become a reality, Sir," Persus interjected.

He smiled at her. "Our great adventure."

"None of you are ever going to work!" Talya cried with mock despair. "There'll be no one to man the mines."

"Precisely," Athens agreed, and everyone laughed.

"I'll make sure he works," said a straight-faced Persus, "or it'll be me who never has a day at the beach."

"And you, Doctor Horus?" Athens said, pouring himself another goblet of jog, looking across the table at Talya. "What's in that ice box of a brain?"

She smiled a small maddening smile. "I don't share my dreams with anybody. Truthfully, I was thinking about my Protocols."

"What a surprise!" Athens said. "You probably think about your bloody Protocols while you're..." He shot Poseidon a lascivious smile.

"Not just any Protocols," Talya continued, ignoring Athens. "These are critical. And not executed lightly. 'Terminations' are performed on those chromosomal groups deemed 'counter-biotic' to the overall Breeding Program. I won't know till we arrive which will subvert the preferred populations. Some have been essential, some simply fascinating to track for hundreds of thousands of years. Some of the offshoots and mutations have proven the strongest and most resilient. The truth is, we've gone two full Terresians orbits without intervention. Like it or not, some groups – the flawed and unnecessary – will simply have to end. These are my Protocols. Federation-endorsed. Don't look at me like that, Poseidon."

"Like you're an extinction machine?" Athens interjected with a jovial grin.

"Because that's exactly what you're going to be."

"Not really. I'll be collecting and storing 'materials' from all terminated groups. If we ever need them down the line, we can re-gestate. There really is no logic in allowing small brain-to-body ratio populations to continue breeding."

"Consider yourself educated, Brother," Poseidon said. "Admit defeat."

"I yield to your authority," Athens said with sudden sincerity and expansiveness, and lifted his cup to Talya. "To a brilliant Gaian Breeding Program." Athens filled everyone's goblets. "To the Gaian Expedition… and to Marsean deviants!"

They all laughed.

Then Athens looked directly at Poseidon. "I never would have dreamed Mars for myself. But my brother dreamed it for me."

Poseidon was unsure if he'd heard correctly. *Athens was toasting him!*

He raised his goblet. "To Poseidon!"

"To Poseidon!" Cyphus cried.

Everyone happily raised theirs as well, and began to speak his name, "Posei…"

The word caught in their throats. Out the window a thousand clix away a large tear ripped open the star-studded sky. Its jagged edges were brilliant white, and the space behind the bizarre opening glowed a deep purple. Stranger still were glimpses of galaxies visible in impossible shapes never seen in their own – straight lines stretching into infinity, full circles, parallelograms.

No one moved.

৵

The Physics Men gaped in triumphant wonder at the long-dreamt-of portal through the elusive Dimensional Membrane, now – unbelievably – connecting their universe to another, until-now-undiscovered and unique cosmos. One that had not shown up on the probe's transmission.

And, too, they were missing their probe.

None of them had uttered a sound since the breach had broken open. All three were madly punching at their wrist hubs, trying to locate the errant device.

Finally Enoc spoke. "Where is it?"

It's there…I think…just cloaked," Clax offered.

"Or gone. Far away. Many universes away," Monas said.

With speed that took them all by surprise, the glowing white sphere came streaking from the torn Membrane, aiming for the space between the two vessels.

Cheers were ripped from the trio's throats, but died suddenly when a squadron of small amber plasma orbs came chasing out after the probe.

"Bring her in!" Enoc shouted. "Now!"

"No! We can't!" Clax barked. "What if they follow her back here?"

Enoc tracked the movement with his eyes. "It's all right. Look."

One by one the orange energy spheres were hurtling past

their presumed target, zooming in a single direction with zero course corrections.

"They're missing everything," Monas said. "They're missing the probe and the vess…"

"No!" Enoc cried, and clutched Clax's arm.

They could see now that one of the amber spheres on the outside edge of the squadron was dead on course for the *Atlantos*.

᪥

The glowing amber spheres were moving toward them at so great a speed that no one at Poseidon's table had the presence of mind to act, or cry out, or even brace for impact before one of the orbs came crashing through the ship's hull just beyond the window frame.

But no impact came.

Instead the sphere – not solid but pure energy – sped across Poseidon's quarters and missed the diners by less than an arm's length. Instantly it disappeared through the opposite wall into the body of the ship with no material damage to anything surrounding it.

But relief was short-lived.

The craft shuddered violently, as if shaken by a great hand, and all magno-electric systems ground to a halt. Then anti-gravity failed, and everything and everyone – gasping in fright – was tossed weightlessly into the air. Worse, the lights died, and they hung there helplessly, quietly groaning. Now the true damage became apparent. During its trajectory through the Atlantos, the orb had crippled the vessel's core matrix. But the terror was cut short as emergency back-up engaged and a ghoulish green light suffused the chamber. Gravity resumed. Objects clattered to the floor and everyone found their footing.

"Let's go," Poseidon ordered them.

"Follow me," Cyphus ordered them. Out in the corridor crew

members clustered in the hallways. "The Shuttle Bay!" he called, hurrying them before him down the corridor toward the central elevator hub…but stopped short as they reached it.

The elevator beam was crackling with dangerous blue energy. Cyphus changed course, everyone following. Poseidon kept Talya near as they scrambled down ladders two flights to the Shuttle Bay, only to find the *Atlantos* crafts dead and techs milling around helplessly.

Zalen found Poseidon among the incoming crew. "The Core has been neutralized," he said.

"*Neutralized?* That's impossible. What could…?"

"Propulsion, life support – down," Zalen continued, insistent, assured. "Our shuttles. Athens's transport pod as well." He called out to everyone, "Is anyone's hub working?"

"I've got something," Athens said. Poseidon saw the faintest flicker inside his brother's wrist, and heard a static-plagued voice emanating from the thing.

"Conn with your Captain," Zalen told him. "Tell him we're nearing zero propulsion. He's got to slow the Transport down. Stay close."

Poseidon could see his crew rubbing their chests. Oxygen had thinned. A current of panic was running close to the surface. "Zalen, Cyphus," he called loudly, curbing his turbulent thoughts. "Help everyone into their life support suits."

There were sounds of rustling in the dark as one hundred and seventy-five terrified men and women donned the emergency garments they'd been assured they would never have to wear.

Then the lights died again. A collective gasp shook the pitch-black bay.

"Let's get these doors open," Zalen said.

Zalen and Cyphus manually cranked the Shuttle Port doors open. But when they finally rolled wide a terrible sight greeted everyone. *There was that horrifying rip in-between two dimensions.* And the Transport was nowhere in sight. It had sped off ahead.

"It's all right!" Poseidon called out to the crew. "They're coming back."

"We'll get everyone over there," said Athens, excitement thrumming in his voice. Even as a child he'd made a challenge of danger.

Talya was at Poseidon's side. "We're not going out there…" she whispered to him.

A collective gasp echoed through the bay as the Transport came back into view. Its welcome glare of lights illuminated the space between the two ships.

Into his hub Athens barked, "Prepare to receive entire crew of the *Atlantos*…What?" Athens put the hub to his ear. "No, we have no shuttles, and I can't be sure that any of ours won't decommission if you bring them too close to this ship!" He seemed to devise the plan as he spoke. "String a tether between the vessels… a tether!"

"I know you're all frightened," Poseidon announced, his voice echoing in the cavernous shuttle port. "But there's no need to be. We're going out there together. We'll be firmly attached to a blenium cable stretched between our two vessels. We'll keep our heads, and we'll all be across in no time." He hoped his message to the crew sounded confident and commanding. He knew that beyond the immediate illuminated zone between the two vessels was the vast expanse of lifeless space and that terrifying rip in the Membrane.

All he could think – but did not dare say aloud – was, *Luck to us all. We are out into the void.*

⚶

Before terror could fully seize them the crew found themselves strung along a cable between the two ships, like jewels on some fantastical necklace. Athens and Zalen, in two of the few propulsion suits onboard, had gone across first, and now dozens of colonists in life support suits were floating out to assist in the rescue. One by one the *Atlantos* crew was pulled aboard the ship.

Talya had insisted on staying close to Poseidon, though he'd been last to leave the stricken vessel. Now hanging in the vacuum side-by-side he calmly assured her that the heavy clip holding them to the tether was foolproof, that there was no way she could break free and float off to her death in deep space. A moment later he heard her speaking to the man hooked to the cable a good way in front of her – it was Korbell – telling him not to worry, that everything was under control.

When she turned back to him, Poseidon detected a hint of a smile through the faceplate.

He looked away. There, in his propulsion suit, was Cyphus, moving from person to person, checking their connectors to the blenium cable. He was always good in an emergency. He began pushing their crew into the Colonial Transport's door. It wouldn't be long before all of them were safe.

It was then Poseidon felt a shock wave behind him. He turned back to the *Atlantos*. The sight took his breath away. It was incomprehensible.

What he saw was the end of the Gaian Expedition.

∽

Everything was happening at once in the Transport Shuttle Port. Persus could see Vice Governor Emmet Praxis, rude and imperious, supervising the rescue pods' egress out into the night. She knelt before a suited-up Athens, tightening his boot. Clax, Monas and Enoc, meanwhile, stood nearby at embarrassed attention. None of them were able to meet Athens's or her eye.

"There are protocols for those trials," she said with barely controlled fury.

Clax looked down at his feet. "Enoc wrote them," he said.

"There's such a thing as chain of command," she snapped, unwilling to let up just yet.

"We're very sorry," Monas said quietly.

"No we're not," Enoc objected. "We saw inside another universe!"

"Brilliant …about your Membrane," Persus said. "Pivotal. But can we please arrive on Mars intact?"

"No real harm done," Athens said with a sly smile. "Now had it been *our* vessel disabled…"

Persus gave him a withering glare as the Physics Men shared a congratulatory smile. She said to the three, "Go! Make sure it doesn't happen again."

They were glad to slip out from under Persus's rebukes and shuffled out of the shuttle bay. She looked up to see Athens smiling at her.

"What would I do without you?" he said.

"Fall apart."

"I said that while drunk."

"Are you sure you don't want me to come with you?" she asked.

"I wish you would." He raised his voice then, so the room could hear. So Praxis could hear. "But someone with half a brain needs to stay onboard."

Praxis registered the insult with a terrible smile to Persus. She could see retribution behind the Vice Governor's eyes. The "young idiot" who'd become his superior would pay for his arrogance. Perhaps not today. But with so much malice roiling behind Praxis's eyes, retribution would certainly come.

Now an adjutant was whispering in Praxis's ear. The Vice Governor straightened, then turned to the pilots in the port. "There's just been an explosion aboard *The Atlantos*," he said. "It appears the titanum storage hold has been breached."

"Get these doors open!" Athens cried.

They rolled apart.

In the lower body of the sleek silver mothership a gaping wound was spewing a steady torrent of what might appear as detritus but was, in fact, the very lifeblood of the *Atlantos*. Titanum pellets of every size and shape. Tiny beads. Propulsion bricks. Discs meant to be stacked one upon another to replace spent units in the Central Core.

"Everybody, out there!" Athens called to the pilots. "Lycan and Bursus – use your tractor beams and make a full sweep. We need to recapture as much of the ore as we can." Persus was sure that in this moment Athens wished he'd had his brilliant DomeTech crew here. He'd asked that they be assigned to Mars, but the Atlas City Dome could not be left unprotected.

Now she dared look out at the dimensional tear beyond the two ships, the strange purple universe on the far side of the membrane, and appealed to the Fates, *or whatever they were*, to desist from sending more of those bloody amber orbs through the gap while their men were out there.

"Grantus and Anitor, you come with me," Athens directed." We'll re-conn on the ship's breach. See if we can start sealing it. Everyone else, help the *Atlantos* crew inside."

Persus felt her gut roiling.

As the PodTech closed Athens into the shuttle with a metallic *thunk*, she felt the sound deep in her chest. *Heart Vibrus,* she thought. *He and I resonate.* She watched the pods float, one by one out the bay door into space. A moment ago… she'd been comforted knowing the *Atlantos* crew was being pulled aboard by colonial rescue parties. A moment ago… Athens had said, "Someone needs to stay on board." What he had not said – *If something happens to me… I trust you to take the helm.*

If something happens to Athens… Persus thought. She could not end the sentence. The very idea felt like cold fingers squeezing her brain. She shook it away. *Nothing is going to happen to you, my love. Not on my watch.*

❧

It was at times like these that Athens came alive. Solo at the controls, he swept the pod out into the night, deftly avoiding the rescue parties strung between the two vessels on the tether like jewels on a giant necklace. He came abreast of Lycan and Bursus who'd begun throwing their yellow tractor beam in a wide net around the escaped pellets, hauling a good many of them in. Then he ran a scan of the ore.

"Bloody stars!" Athens cried as the results flashed before him. "They're all neutralized! Like the Core. Leave them," he told his pilots. Go help with the rescue operation."

He set his sights on the repair crew working the breach in the *Atlantos's* hull and began crossing the divide between the ships. *Disaster piled upon disaster*, he thought with irritation. *Would they even make it to Mars?*

Without warning another squadron of amber plasma spheres streaked by Athens's shuttle. Once again, their trajectory was precise, uni-directional and indiscriminate but as he watched, two of the orbs clipped the blenium tether, slicing it in two places. It left the *Atlantos* escapees dangling on their cable from the Colonial Transport, and the last three unlucky crewmen severed completely from the rest. A force – akin to a tailwind – whipped the trio along in the sphere's wake for long enough that, to Athens's horror, they disappeared out of sight.

❧

The three were free-floating in space. Talya, Poseidon and Korbell, tumbled head-over-foot, plunging deeper into the black void, getting tangled in their length of tether. The sight of their receding ships was awful, but Poseidon forcibly stifled his fear. "Suit, stabilize," he said. The verbal command righted Poseidon's body. Hand-over-hand he began reeling Talya towards him. She was first into his grasp. He'd never before seen such naked terror in a person's eyes. But there was no time to comfort her now. Korbell was still out there.

He felt panic rising, but logic welled up to defy it. Someone would have seen them torn away from the tether. Someone was coming to rescue them.

❧

Athens's controlled adventure had taken a sudden and desperate turn.

He would not allow tragedy to overtake his expedition before it had even begun! His thoughts shifted instantly to contain the circumstance. He quickly located the separated trio's coordinates, overrode the pod to manual control and shot out after them. He careened up and over what was left of the long human chain, hardly giving these escapees a thought. This group would be rescued. It took only moments to regain visual contact with the three castaway crewmembers. On this course he would intersect within the minute.

And then – with nightmarish velocity – another clutch of plasma orbs came screaming towards the shuttle and were gone before Athens had time to startle.

But not all of them had missed the pod.

One was inside. With him.

There before his faceplate was one of the spheres. It hung perfectly still, unwavering. A dull torpor seized Athens before he could act. He was paralyzed. Stupefied. His eyes, while functional, were fixed on what was before him.

His rescue of the marooned trio: *forgotten.*

He could feel something now. A light, radiating pressure rolling evenly from the top of his head down. *A scan,* he thought dully. *Right through the pressure suit. I'm being scanned.* As the targeted beam encompassed each organ, he felt a faint pulsing zrrrrr… zrrrrr. Heart. Stomach. Liver zrrrrr…zrrrrr. Intestines. Lower. *No, not there. Please.* Helpless panic rose as the pulsing reached his manhood.

Don't worry, said a bland voice in his head. *He was not hearing it through his ears.* His mouth twitched as he tried to object. It was all the protest allowed him. But now came a change in the amber orb. *Dissolving,* thought Athens. *Disappearing. It's going away!* Relief flooded his brain. *Soon he would be freed of this presence. Soon, as soon as this* thing *had gone…*

But no. In the orb's place something else had materialized. *WHAT ARE YOU?!!!* he wordlessly shrieked. *No, no, no, WHAT ARE YOU!!!!!!!!* A disembodied head of nearly colorless flesh hung before him, inches away from his face. The creature's mouth, a lipless gash, did not move when it spoke. Its two slit nostrils did seem to flutter slightly. The bulbous black eyes gleamed with what Athens thought with revulsion was interest.

Entity. Beast. Monstrosity.

Its mouth did not move, but the voice was clear inside Athens's head. The voice. *It was Talya's voice.* Liquid. Crooning. Seductive. *Do you like it this way? Slower? Faster? Mmmmmm…* The vibration tingled between his legs. *No. No. Not this, please.* Pleasure mounted quickly, so quickly. He was hard before he knew it. Rock hard. *Stop this. Leave me alone…ahhh…ahhhh. No, oh no, please no!* The monster's loathsome face, Talya's voice. *Oh, you do* like it this way. *Let me just…* Acute, searing ravishment. *Reaching, reaching…*

His climax cry shook the pod and in that moment the thing, the frightful creature blinked…out…of…existence. It was gone, nothing but the pod's controls before his eyes. But there was no relief to be had. None needed.

For all memory of orb…and the beast was gone.
Erased.

He sucked in a full breath and exhaled heartily. He could see out the window that the strange dimensional tear through which those amber spheres had come crashing – one of them had disabled the *Atlantos* – was finally zippering closed.

Good.

He looked for the unlucky *Atlantos* crewmen, now only a trio of white dots far in the distance. *Well, about to get lucky,* he thought cheerfully. About to get saved. He had them in his sights. He took manual control and reset the pod's trajectory.

✍

"We're going to reel him in," Poseidon told Talya. Together they tugged on the length of tether.

It was then they saw the shuttle pod carefully closing in on them. Talya's relieved sigh was almost a gasp.

"Keep pulling," Poseidon said to her. The pod was close now. "Talya, look!"

She turned her helmeted head and saw it was Athens at the controls. He had begun deploying the craft's gripping arms as it deftly maneuvered close to them.

"Almost, Korbell," she told him.

"I've got it from here, Horus," Athens said into her helmet.

The metallic arms gently encircled Talya first as Poseidon continued hauling Korbell in. He was within a dozen feet of the shuttle when a single rogue energy sphere sped out of nowhere. It smashed through Korbell's midsection and was instantly gone. His body spasmed violently, then he fell limp inside the suit.

Inside the pod Talya and Poseidon were shaken but unharmed. In silent trepidation they removed Korbell's helmet, its faceplate glazed into opaqueness.

All that remained of the man was a pile of crumbled bones encased in a bag of seared skin.

SIX

AS ATHENS, WITH Poseidon and Talya in tow, passed through into the mess hall, Persus caught them up from behind. The woman was a miracle. She was at her best in a crisis. *How did I ever live without her?* But now, Athens saw, she was as somber as he'd ever seen her. She spoke directly to Poseidon.

"Repairs on the *Atlantos* are going to be extensive, Sir. I'm sure your brother told you that all the titanum stores expelled into space are worthless. They're still taking stock of what's left in the storage hold. Captain Zalen's working with our best tech people closing up the hull. For now the Transport can tow her, and work can continue on route."

Poseidon, always alert and ready, stood even taller.

"Life support is a relatively quick fix," Persus continued, "but rebuilding the Core is a problem. Without propulsion on line before the Gaia Intersect we'll have to ferry her down to the surface with our pods."

"Thank you, Persus," Poseidon said. "Let Captain Zalen know I'll be back over when I'm through here."

"Sir…" she said, and strode away.

"What now?" Athens said. "There's not even enough left to get you to Gaia."

"Or get us back home," Poseidon said, his eyes fixed on an arbitrary point on the bulkhead in front of him.

Athens could see he was already running figures in his head. "We can't spare any of our stores," he said. "You know that."

Poseidon nodded silently.

"We'll have to tow you down to the surface." He was thinking ahead. "Once we're up and running on Mars we'll come back... make a delivery..."

"That will take years. We'll miss our escape window," Talya said, not bothering to hide her alarm.

"You could fly the shuttles back to Terres instead," Athens said. "We can spare enough ore for that. If you leave now."

His brother turned his attention out the window and across the gap between vessels, gazing at the *Atlantos*. Talya came to stand beside him. The irony was stunning. Seven years before, Poseidon had come home from the exploratory mining mission a hero. Elgin Mars had had a planet named after him. Terresians were still celebrating when Atlas City experienced its worst dome failure in history. The collapse had taken out half of the metropolis, nearly ending everything in a heartbeat. But Athens and his DomeTech crews had flown in and flawlessly done their jobs. They'd snatched Atlas Environs back from oblivion. That was when Poseidon had decided to take charge of their planet's future.

To Lead.

Now seven years later, here they stood. Poseidon's mission in jeopardy. His own intact.

"Tow us down to Gaia," Poseidon said.

"It's risky."

"We're not turning back now."

"If that's what you want."

Poseidon took him by the arm and led him away from the window. He spoke softly, calmly. "Listen Athens... there's something you need to know about the Aeros Expedition." He was finding it hard to get the words out. "Elgin Mars went missing shortly before we returned to Terres."

"What are you saying? There was an accident. He died of his injuries."

"It wasn't like that. There was no accident. A search party was sent out to look for him while I drilled at 62."

"But his body was brought back. What was left of it."

"That was a lie. There was no body. We left…" Poseidon sighed heavily. "We left Aeros without Mars. When we got back, the Commissioners were told the truth, but no one else."

"What happened to him?"

"We don't know. After the drill rig exploded…"

"Hold on. No one was ever told about an explosion. Did he die in…?"

"No, no. The beam – a focused drill column – was gouging through the mantle and it…escaped its boundaries…"

"What does that mean? Those beams don't 'escape their boundaries.'"

"We don't understand what happened, but… a phaetronic device went entirely out of control before it exploded. It's a miracle no one was killed."

"But Mars…if it wasn't…?"

Poseidon shook his head. "The planet swallowed him up."

"That's mysterious, coming from you." Athens gaped at his brother. "So you left Aeros without Elgin Mars?"

"We had no choice. We'd run out of time."

It felt good to wheedle. Old habits died hard. "That means the New Aeros Colony should rightly have been named 'Poseidon,' not 'Mars.'"

"Don't…" But Poseidon didn't finish. He had never learned the art of threatening.

"Quite a story, Brother."

"It wasn't meant to entertain you. It's your planet now. Every person on this Transport looks up to you, depends on you. You're all making this incredible sacrifice – never going home again, so you can save our glorious civilization. And after today…"

*After today…*Athens thought. *It had been amazing. Brilliant. Yet…it had been…strange. Unsettling.*

"You need to take a good look at yourself," Poseidon said. "You're not the person Father thinks you are. You're a bloody hero. Don't forget it."

Athens squirmed at the compliment. "Let's get over to Physics Section. Those idiots nearly turned the universe inside out."

❦

They found Persus with the young trio huddled around a grey burnished metal probe, hovering in place at chest level looking no worse for the wear after its inter-dimensional adventure. They were arguing with each other as if no one else was there.

"You're certain?" Clax said, running a diagnostic over the sphere with his hub.

"Not entirely," Monas said.

Enoc glared at them both. "It breached the Membrane! We all saw it disappear." He fixed Clax in his gaze. "Didn't we?!"

"But there's no data from the other side," Monas complained. "Nothing recorded. Even the unique galactic structures we saw with our eyes behind the tear. Our rules of physics apparently don't apply there. We have zero confirmation. The probe came back to us exactly as it was before launch."

"What we can say with some certainty," Clax said, finally turning to acknowledge Athens's group, "is that the amber plasma orbs that emerged from the tear were 'Inter-Dimensional Energy Phenomena.' IDEPs."

"We've seen nothing remotely like them occurring naturally on Terres," Persus insisted.

"Or reported on Mars, or Gaia on previous expeditions," said Poseidon.

"Perhaps a type of ball lightening?" Talya suggested. "Such a thing has been observed on Gaia."

"Gaia has an *atmosphere*, Doctor Horus," Clax corrected her. "This occurred in a vacuum."

Clax called up a diffracted replay of the tearing Membrane, the probe's emergence from it, and the first barrage of amber orbs. "You can see here they moved with precise, straightforward mono-directionality."

Monas added, "Which is why we suspect there was no intelligence moving them."

Athens listened carefully to the report, aware of its importance, nodding his understanding of the strange phenomenon that had ripped through his brother's ship. That had ended Korbell's life. Perhaps this was why he was strangely uneasy. Felt a crawling sensation under the skin of his arms.

Felt, surprisingly, an unwelcome twitch in his groin.

Clax stopped the playback and pointed to the large cluster of IDEPs on the probe's tail. "The orbs appeared to be chasing the probe when they breached the Membrane," he said, "but none of them ever collided with the probe. If it was the target, we assume it would have been intercepted."

"But at least one of them impacted the *Atlantos*," Poseidon reminded them. "The one we witnessed in my quarters. Damaged the Core. And a delayed reaction that caused the titanum hold to explode from the inside out."

"And neutralized most of your ore," Monas added.

Clax started the playback again. The orange spheres moved like a large squadron of fighters. Only one of them on the far edge of the squadron was on course to intercept the Atlantos. They all watched in silence as it did.

"Judging by its trajectory, all the damage was done by a single orb."

"We believe this impact was random," Enoc said.

Clax continued. "As was the severing of the tether in two

places. Ninety-eight per cent of the orbs never connected with any solid object. Except the *Atlantos*."

"And Korbell," Poseidon added.

The Physics Men shuffled uncomfortably.

"A tragedy that the professor didn't live to see what we did," Enoc said.

"Let me understand…" This was Poseidon. "You're saying those collisions were bad luck. Statistically insignificant."

They all watched as the orbs continued past the two vessels and disappeared in their precise, straightforward mono-directionality into the depths of space.

"We can playback the other swarms if you like," Clax offered.

Athens found himself fidgeting nervously. Hairs at the back of his neck stiffened.

"There's nothing we'd like better than to find an alien intelligence on the far side of a Multiverse Boundary," Monas said with uncommon enthusiasm.

"One," Enoc added, "that *we* successfully breached…"

"Simply because we haven't yet experienced such contact," Clax said, "no one disputes intelligent life here and everywhere in the…"

"Persus," Athens interrupted, feeling his skin begin to crawl, "have you found our guests places to sleep?"

"I have."

Summarily dismissed, the thick-skinned Physics Men continued arguing among themselves.

"Why don't you take Talya and my brother to their rooms?" Athens said to Persus.

Talya smiled slyly at Poseidon. "We'll only need one," she said.

⤚

Finally they were safe and alone, in small and spare but private accommodations. Talya thought that Poseidon, even with an ugly stubble on his cheeks and chin, looked as attractive as he'd ever been.

"Danger excites you, doesn't it?" he said.

"You're mocking me," she said, taking off her earbobs, placing them on the metal shelf that served as a bed table.

"I'm not. And no, it doesn't."

He came around behind her and pulled at the pins that held her hair, and the coil unfurled, falling around her shoulders. He kissed the back of her neck.

"And I'm not mocking you."

She unbuttoned her sheath, allowing it to drop to the floor and held her naked body inches away from his as she tapped the enhancer controls at her wrist hub.

"Could we...?" Poseidon said softly, and placed his own hand over hers to stay it. "Let's do without."

"Why would we want to do that?"

"We don't need 'enhancing.'"

She turned and gave him a sharp look. "I prefer a richer experience," and completed the sexual programming at her wrist. She fixed him with her eyes. "Are you having doubts about us?"

"No, I simply want it all to be perfect for you. I just thought..."

She kissed him lightly on the lips to silence him, then unfastened his shirt at the shoulder. "It will be. It always is. Here, let me." She turned Poseidon's right hand palm-up and began lightly tapping the hub controls at his wrist, eyeing him suspiciously. "You're becoming something of a primitive, Poseidon." She let go of his arm.

When he pulled her to him he was rock-hard. How quickly the enhancer function had worked! There was real desire in his eyes, but she saw that all tenderness, all sentimentality had fallen away. This would be sex for sex's sake.

She pulled him down between her naked thighs.

"Perfect," she said.

ROBIN MAXWELL

❦

Athens had gone back to the Commons Room for a further dose of adulation. The colonists were plying him with jog, women vying for a single smile, a kind word, his smallest mote of attention. Even the men were fawning, playing over his heroic rescue of his brother and Talya Horus. They toasted him again and again. Yet he felt none of their joviality or the warmth of the drink. Only a cold, hollow feeling in his chest. Finally he excused himself, pulling out of the arms of a luscious young woman who had whispered the most salacious invitation he had ever heard in his life, and made his way back to his quarters.

Persus was leaning up against the bulkhead wall when he got there, holding a jug of their favorite beverage and smiling guilelessly. "This deserves a celebration, Sir."

"You can stop calling me Sir, you know."

"I don't think so," she said, more serious than teasing.

The door slid open and he stepped inside. He hesitated and turned back to her. She was about to follow him in. "I'm sorry, Persus. I'm not...I don't know what I..."

"No, no *I'm* sorry. You're exhausted. How stupid of me. Get in there and rest." She held up the jug, already halfway down the corridor, calling back to him, "We'll share this tomorrow."

Collapsing on his bed he rubbed and rubbed his face with both hands, raked his fingers through his hair. *I should feel better than this!* He pulled the covers over himself. *That cold feeling again. Like outer space in his lungs.* And...no...he was *hard.* Erect! *You're going mad,* he thought. *Insane. Not possible. Not now. This is your moment. Your chance. You saved your bloody brother's life! Calm down,* he commanded himself. *Remember how you got here. This was no mistake. You earned this. No mistake.*

But as soon as he closed his eyes he imagined Talya and Poseidon disappearing into the crew quarters together. *He could see her moving slowly, sensuously under his brother's body.* This was wrong. He knew it. But he felt strangely, almost sickeningly aroused. Back on Terres, at civic functions and at Federation Council meetings he had studied her carefully, but it had only been imagining. It was not until Poseidon's return from Mars that Athens's compulsion with Doctor Horus had grown overwhelming. All the time Poseidon had been gone Athens had been content to play with his thoughts of her. He'd made do with programmable dreams.

But then his brother had come home a hero.

Even Talya's frigid reserve melted under the universal gratitude that bordered on worship felt by every living Terresian. All the celebrations, speeches to the gathered masses, the statues erected. Their world's future existence was assured by the persistence and courage on "Mars," at Site 62 of the man Athens had for so long loathed above all others.

What was it that he always hated? That was the thing. There really was nothing to despise. Poseidon was neither smug nor arrogant. He was kind. He enjoyed a laugh. He loved their mother and detested their father with as much vehemence as Athens did.

It's been envy all along. The thought struck him like a blade through his heart. How pitiful he'd been to harbor such a feeling for his brother. Maybe Poseidon was right about him. Maybe he'd earned this extraordinary governmental posting.

Maybe, he thought, *I just needed a little reminding.*

The Colonial Transport's Library was nowhere near as grand as the *Atlantos's*. But once Athens was slouched in a viewing chair, a full dome diffracted image of the night sky above his head, he became entirely lost in the vision. It was the time he and his DomeTech crew saved their city.

He recalled the orders he'd barked out, the instincts born of training and persistent practice. He played it to the end and again heard the whoops of triumph when the breach closed, and his name shouted over and over again by his crews.

By the time the re-play was finished Athens was sitting bolt upright in the Library's viewing chair. He found himself grinning, his cheeks burning with ... something... it was pride. He *was* a hero. He had saved their city, their civilization, every bit as much as Poseidon and his Aerosean excavation had. He was off to govern an exuberant colony on an exquisite sunlit planet. He would never have to see his father – that heartless excuse for a man with his icy expression, those awful steely eyes – ever again. He deserved this posting. Deserved every wonderful thing that could come to him. Dignity. Respect. And all the adoring women who would come crawling into his bed.

He threw back his head and laughed. Life on Mars was going to be a dream come true!

SEVEN

I T WAS GOOD to be back in the *Atlantos*. In her laboratory. The loss of Korbell had been unfortunate, thought Talya. Shocking, in fact. Life on Terres, until the Contour Dome failure, had been placid, unerringly pleasant. This off-world mission was proving more troubling than she'd expected.

Gazing at the face of the adult female subject suspended upright in the Genomic Preservation Chambers provided Talya with a sense of normalcy. Calm. The adult male and the juvenile male hanging in suspension never held her interest as intently as the female did. The skeleton and musculature were all in place, even if the limb bones were thick, and the legs bowed, the muscles anything but refined and sculpted, as they were in the Terresian anatomy. But the facial features were so coarse as to make her wince at the sight of the specimen. The protruding brow ridges made the female look monstrous, and the hair – so much of it – was wild and matted. The hairline around the face crept down low on the forehead and into the hollow of her cheeks. The irises of her eyes, open and staring through the pale pink gel, were muddy brown, a color rarely seen on Terres anymore. Blue, green, grey were the norm.

"Is the female *Pithekos gaiensis* a woman...or an animal?" Talya said aloud, AutoAssist recording her words. "How many

Terresian gene pairs must a creature share to be deemed human? The *Pithekos* brain - ironically - is larger than our own. But those hands…" She stared at the thick digits with palms like leather. They were reminiscent of the great apes that had come before, lower on the evolutionary ladder. "…look as though they could rip raw meat from the bones of a fresh kill." She paused to reflect on earlier data. "While the last Gaian expedition observed primitive linguistics and the rudiments of religion and consciousness, the species *Pithekos gaianesis* has been engineered for extinction. Only a minimum population should be evident when our expedition arrives. Protocol for remnant individuals is – after collection of full specimens and chromosomal materials – 'termination.'"

Talya turned her attention to another cylinder, this one housing a male *Sapiens gaiensis*. A large, well-muscled and slightly more hairy "modern man," the specimen was big and primal and somehow frightening. If shaved, combed and dressed as a Terresian, this species would easily pass for one. But here, with his prodigious manhood floating before him in the pink liquid, he was tamed.

"*Sapiens gaiensis* – the principal objective of the imminent Gaian Mission," she continued. "My curiosity is intense. How far forward have previous modifications taken the creatures in their evolutionary process in the intervening years? Before our interference, millions of their years ago, they were hardy, fur-covered, knuckle-dragging apes. They've experienced tremendous evolutionary advances in cognition and intelligence, tool and artifact-making skills. Of course, the breed still lacks Terresian genomic and cultural refinements. My protocols will redress these omissions – 'Take the savage out of the beast.'"

Her eyes fell on the male's genitals. She suffered a moment of chagrin, but safe in the privacy of her laboratory, she reprogrammed her wrist hub. All at once an old diffracted image of Poseidon appeared before her. He was teaching to a full classroom of students at the Academy. She magnified his face and regarded it carefully. Then over his image she superimposed a Duel Helix, Poseidon's own molecular structure and instructions. She studied it carefully.

"He's proven more than fit. Outstanding really. His mind and character are stellar. Heroic, even." When the Dome breach had happened – the day the sky had fallen – he'd come for her in her Academy laboratory. To rescue her.

As Talya decoupled from her thoughts she found herself clutching the edge of a counter, her heart rate uncharacteristically elevated. A moment later, to counteract the annoying autonomic response, she programmed a small calming adjustment at her wrist – feeling it take effect immediately – and refocused her purpose, magnifying a single one of Poseidon's nucleic acid sequences on the projection in front of her. "With the exception of his annoying trait of over-demonstrativeness," she continued aloud, gratified her voice was again cool and unruffled, "he is quite the perfect man. I have some concerns that subject shares this geno-sequencing with sibling, Athens Ra."

She called up a second double helix and superimposed it over Poseidon's.

"Look more closely into this sibling's profile," she reminded herself. "Was Athens ever re-calibrated when he was a boy?" Then added, "Initiate impact and modification, referencing Poseidon's sperm and my own corresponding genomes. Is he dominant for these inconvenient traits? A latent strain? What about our off-spring? Would he agree to modification?"

She wiped the genomic analysis and magnified his face, the eyes in particular.

"A mutant sequence or two should prove inconsequential and..." Talya checked herself. *Ridiculous, sentimental rumination!* Feeling suddenly foolish, she wiped Poseidon's image altogether, straightened her spine and set her mind to something sensible. "Euros, Afros, Australos. All homes of primordial human species. With the last Gaian Expedition aborted we'll be seeing 20,000 years and countless generations – undocumented. Who knows what will be found?"

"Prime Staff to the Library," AudioAssist reminded her." "On my way," Talya said.

⌘

Poseidon stood, a solitary man, in the circular, domed magnificence of the *Atlantos* Library, relieved for the restored life-support systems and grateful for the small fleet of Transport shuttle pods towing the still-crippled vessel the last few million miles to Gaia. He gazed at the multi-dimensional image at the Library's center, a blue and green orb with clouds swirling above it, suspended in the pitch blackness of space.

How many times had he watched and studied the diffractal called "Gaia Approach?" It must be hundreds. But now, perhaps knowing he was days away from setting foot on the planet for the first time, he was stunned, speechless at the heart-stopping immensity, and its beauty – both seen and unseen. Beneath the crust its molten core roiled with oozing red magma, the warm seas teemed with unfathomable species. The continents thundered with hooved herds. Endless forests blanketed vast plains and mountains alike. Skies were blackened by great dancing clouds of winged creatures.

With the actual globe before his eyes spinning in slow majesty on its invisible axis, Helios bathing one half in light, the other half shadow-bound and awaiting its moment in the sun, Poseidon knew that nothing – neither his studies, his previous explorations, nor his discovery of titanum – could have prepared him for this moment.

Poseidon heard the Library door whoosh open and low chatter as Chronus and his new field study partner, Climate Science Officer Ennis Ables, entered side by side. Silently they flanked Poseidon and stood speechless at the sight.

128

"They say nothing can prepare you for the real thing," said Poseidon.

Chronus was wide-eyed. "To think home once looked like this…"

Others began filing in, talking among themselves. Biology Chief Leones and Captain Zalen. Cyphus and Talya. She was centered and professional, and Poseidon saw nothing of the highly sexualized bed partner of the last few weeks aboard the Colonial Transport. Korbell's absence was a conspicuous void, but they were Terresians after all, and largely unperturbable, so no mention was made of him. Then, once everyone set their focus on the Gaia diffractor image, silence fell as their individual calculations began.

"Nominations for headquartering?" Poseidon asked. He nodded to Zalen who, with a few touches, magnified Gaia so that it towered above their heads, rotating on its axis. Details invisible from a distance were now revealed.

"Central North Platos," Chronus suggested in his next breath.

The two great continents stacked at a slight diagonal and linked by a narrow isthmus, had never been the focus of previous Terresian expeditions. There'd been far too much to study elsewhere, in Afros and Australos. Now Chronus pointed to the northernmost continent of the two. Most of it was sheathed in white, from one coast to the other.

"Until 1,000 years ago," Chronus explained, "the landmass was covered by a miles-thick ice sheet. Then…a comet impact – or asteroid, we're not certain which – directly impacted the ice. Caused catastrophic flooding. Changes to coastlines and land bridges, and permanent sea-level rise planet-wide. The event sent all but the equatorial regions back into another ice epoch – one that most of the planet is enduring even now. North Platos is a fascinating continent. That's my choice."

"Absolutely not," Ables objected. We need a *temperate* climate for Headquarters."

Leones said, "I say Afros. Unparalleled for bio-diverse flora and fauna."

The diffracted planet had rotated on its axis and the massive Afrosean continent was visible. With a touch of his finger to the image, Gaia halted its spin. They were all aware of the "Great Rift" in the northeast.

"Amazing you can see it from space," Leones added. "Plenty of seismic interest there," he said to Chronus, as if to convince him of his choice.

"Can we take a look at the new South Asyan Island?" Talya suggested.

This startled Poseidon. Till this moment she hadn't spoken of her preferences to him. But knowing Talya she had come prepared. She stepped forward and herself spun the globe, tracking east from Afros across what previous researchers had named the "Indus Ocean" to the southernmost aspect of Southeast Asya – a small continent-sized island.

"A thousand years ago this landmass..." she pointed Asya, then to the island, "...was joined to this one." She acknowledged Chronus. "Remarkable – your comet's effect halfway around the world. Once a peninsula, now separated by hundreds of miles of ocean."

Activating magnification they descended quickly over the immense island, a lush patchwork of mountains, forests, rivers and plateaus. Tracking from west to east they soared over the north-south-bisecting "Central Range" of seven volcanic peaks, now apparently dormant. Further magnification and tracking all the way to the mid-eastern coast found them zeroing in on a settlement of mud huts. It appeared peaceful and prosperous, with industrious tribespeople and happy children at work and play. Fishermen paddled hollowed out canoes and women worked among nets on the beach. A hunting party was just now returning with a large hoofed animal hanging on a pole.

"I'm projecting the greatest diversity of advanced *Sapiens* tribes anywhere on the planet," Talya said. "They fish *and* they hunt. This is ground zero for our genome protocols. I can always go abroad for my *Pithekos* studies."

She glanced up to see everyone reeling at her autocratic tone. Poseidon was amused that nothing deterred her. "The last two Gaian explorations were called off," she said. "That's twenty thousand years of evolution without scrutiny and management. Whole generations, countless mutations have gone undocumented."

"Fed has charged Doctor Horus with bringing all those protocols up to speed," Poseidon added in support, and for that she graced him with a brief nod.

"Honestly," she said, "isn't species reprogramming the reason we continue to come to Gaia at all?"

"No!" Chronus and Ables cried in unison.

"The planet's a seismic wonder," Chronus argued.

"And a massive climate laboratory," Ables insisted.

"You seem to think your work takes precedence over every other discipline," Chronus accused her.

"It *does*," she said, unflinching in her certainty.

Ables and Chronus bristled while she held Poseidon in her steely, insistent gaze. "I say we headquarter on the new South Asyan island – "Atlantos." She bared a narrow band of teeth in a smile. "Or are we calling it a continent?"

GAIA

EIGHT

NIGHT WAS FALLING and the *Atlantos*, perched on its five retractable legs, gleamed in the sunset's light. A dozen pods – those that had towed the mothership to the ground – prepared for departure to the Colonial Transport, now hovering several miles overhead. The brothers stood looking out across Gaia's landscape –the broad central plain, an immense range of jagged mountains serrating the eastern horizon.

"You know I envy you, Athens."

"Nonsense. Look at this place," he said, sweeping his arm before him. "It's breathtaking. Mars has precisely one species of land vegetation and a featureless ocean." *There was something odd about Poseidon these days. Nothing Athens could pinpoint.*

"True. But my stay here is short," said Poseidon. "We'll have only begun to enjoy it before we have to leave for home."

"Trade with me then," Athens teased. "You take my post on Mars with twenty-five hundred nubile girls panting after their hero, and I'll stay here in paradise with the lovely Talya. That's fair."

Poseidon laughed aloud.

Athens looked away, scanning the landscape for a hint of the curious affinity he sensed between Poseidon and this world. As though they shared a frequency. A Vibrus. Athens fixed his eyes on his brother. His features seemed somehow more defined, and a kind of energy radiated – no *pulsed* – around his body. Was it merely the quality of light on the planet, he wondered. Or was Gaia playing tricks on his own mind?

"Are you all right?" Athens said impulsively.

Poseidon straightened, looking suddenly uncomfortable. "I'm fine."

"You're more than fine. Something's changed," Athens insisted. "What is it?"

"Nothing has changed. I'm who I've always been. Your aggravating brother."

"Poseidon," Athens continued in a tone that sounded, even to his own ears, remarkably affectionate, "thank you for Mars."

"There was no one more qualified than you."

"We both know that's a lie. It was a brotherly gesture, a peace-offering."

"I may have wanted peace between us, but not at the expense of Terres."

Athens embraced him impetuously and felt the embrace returned. It was, he realized, the first in their adult life. As children Poseidon had learned physical affection from their mother, and had tried hugging his little brother many times, but Athens had wanted nothing to do with them.

Abruptly, feeling moisture gathering at the corners of his eyes, Athens turned away, calling behind him, "We'll talk," and strode off to his waiting shuttle.

He piloted through the pale blue atmosphere towards the darkening sky and the others pods, and beyond to the glittering lights of the Transport. As one by one they were swallowed up by the gargantuan black box, Athens allowed himself a final thought of his strangely transformed brother and the third planet from the sun…before snapping his attention inward.

The colonists awaited, and Mars. His own adventure was about to begin.

NINE

FIRST DAWN ON a new world.

Poseidon rose earlier than the rest, dressing in the dark to hasten from the confines of the *Atlantos*, now humming subsonically with the Vibrus of thousands of life support machines, those that the technos crew had managed to make operational. At the craft's hub he stepped into the center of the exterior blue beam elevator. At the lowest level of the craft, a round door slid open under his feet and the beam shot through thin air to Gaia's surface.

He stepped out into what was left of the night, a wide band of stars still winking in the west, a diffuse, promising glow to the east. The moment he exited the elevator beam he felt himself overcome by an avalanche of sensations. The moist breeze that ruffled his hair had brought with it smells of rich, dew-dampened topsoil, a strong vegetal fragrance gathered, he guessed, from the profuse forest canopy nearby, the pungent scent of a distant herd – odors foreign to his senses, but all vaguely and mysteriously familiar. By habit he moved to switch on the enhancer function of his wrist hub, but thought suddenly with a jolt of surprise that it was unnecessary. And suddenly he was remembering his mother. The last time he'd seen her.

"I hope you find what you're looking for on Gaia," she'd said.

"What am I looking for?" he'd asked, truly baffled.

"You'll tell me if you found it when you come home. I hope it's wonderful. I hope it surprises you."

And suddenly Poseidon was back in the present, standing alone on the surface of a majestic planet. *Here it is,* he thought, *the first surprise…*

Even before the tiny startling point of sun made its appearance on the horizon, the eastern sky filled with streaky, haphazard clouds of brilliant orange. As each second passed everything around him began turning a sharp, deep unimaginable blue. He had seen sunrises before. First dawn after the endless Terresian hibernation was cause for celebration. But nothing, he thought, walking quickly to be gone from the vessel's suddenly unnatural shapes and surfaces and burnished metal, *nothing* had prepared him for this. He knew in his scientist's mind that what he was seeing was merely a coalescence of the weather conditions and upper atmosphere causing cloud formations, enriched by splendid life forms. Still he was dazzled. Over-awed. Even bewildered.

Then the sun burst over the horizon in an explosion of phosphorescent yellow in the full spectacle of Gaian dawn. To the east was a vast grassy plain. Underfoot was loamy soil sprouting a cover of large pale flowers with insects buzzing round them like planets orbiting a miniature sun. Standing in place he turned in a full circle, feeding on these visions, growing fat on the feast of beauty. In the silence, without the enhancer, he could hear blood pounding in his ears, feel a sweet tingling the whole length of his limbs, and a warmth spreading outward from his chest that rivaled the heat bathing his body from Helios. Breath escaped him in a long deep sigh, and suddenly he realized with as much certainty as incredulity that he had traveled nine-hundred-and-forty-million miles through the vast reaches of space to find himself, inexplicably, home.

TEN

HERE AT THE mountain's pinnacle, the planet's tallest peak, Poseidon and Cyphus stood side-by-side in silent reveling. Of course they had trained for such a climb in the snow simulator – on this very mountain in the Indus Range. On the real ascent, one that had taken a full month, their personal vibral shields had protected their bodies from extremes of temperature, atmosphere and noxious vapors. Their enhancers had provided all the extra strength and endurance needed to protect them from nature's furies so that the climbing, while strenuous, was neither dangerous nor exhausting. But here, now, having claimed the peak, the mind-shattering vistas as the cloud flotillas parted below them, they were giddy, omnipotent. Simply speechless.

Poseidon considered his less-than-emotive companion. Friend since school days. Cyphus, who – unlike Poseidon's own highest orders of education in Planetary Sciences – had tracked in the Body Arts and Guardian Forces. He was as fit a physical specimen as any Terresian alive. Logic-driven but instinct-rich, fearless and bold, in Cyphus Poseidon had found a perfect exploration partner. A man who'd made clear, with neither sentiment nor wordy declaration, that he would gladly lay down his own life to save Poseidon's.

And here Cyphus was beside him on the mountaintop, both of them silenced in awe of the spectacle.

In their travels on Gaia they had dived in their shuttle to the lowest spot on the planet – a trench to the east of the Atlan Continent, clocked pressure a thousand times that of the surface. Observed worms the size of a small building and vents spewing poison gas that became the feast of a billion small crustates, marveling at the absurdity of such life forms. They had watched herds of millions – hooved creatures – migrating across endless tracts of Afrosean plains, and flocks of broad-winged, round-beaked birds on their thousands miles-long mysterious navigations at altitudes so lofty there was barely oxygen to breathe. They had indulged every sensory fiber in their bodies, floating in a warm salty sea of crystal blue, lolling on a fine sand beach, turning their eyes inland to wonder at so lush and fragrant a jungle shore.

The Great Spire Mountains of Asya had baffled them. *How could such a landscape even exist?* Poseidon carefully recreated, then recorded the slow and steady erosive chemical geology that had shaped the needle-like towers of sandstone. While he measured, Cyphus scanned the tree-topped spires for falling boulders, nagging at Poseidon to finish his work. The danger – even with a sharp eye and the hub's power – was simply too great.

But it was finally the climb from the Indus Foothills to the summit at the top of the world that had turned the pair of them inside out. The verdant forested canyons and gushing melt-ice rivers. The rumblings of the mountain and the small avalanche that had buried them in dozens of feet of powder. Their hubs' heat blasters had carved out a neat diagonal tunnel from their snow tomb to the surface, and they'd emerged from their underworld celebrating the glories of phaetron technos, feeling invincible.

Still nothing had been said as the last rays of sun were setting the mountain ablaze. As if rock itself had been set afire. This was Cyphus's limit. His thunderstruck groan projecting out before and below them echoed unexpectedly and vastly, and the sound of it wrenched a laugh from them both. These were not quite words, but the silence was ended. Their smiles affirmed what they both knew.

Two friends had struck out in simple exploration… and they'd fallen in love with a planet.

✦

Every evening the two of them decided on the safest… or most spectacular setting to secure the shuttle. It was a game they played, measuring risk against pleasure. To balance their vehicle on the precipice of an eastern-facing rocky ledge was dangerous, but it insured they would wake to a heart-stopping Erthan sunrise.

Much as he enjoyed Cyphus's company, Poseidon took special pleasure in the time he spent in his personal privacy dome. Reclining now in his bunk with the opaque, sound-secure virbral shield separating them, Cyphus was only an arm's reach away but completely oblivious to Talya's diffractor visit inside with him.

The last time they'd commed this way she'd been troubled by her findings at the extreme southern edge of the Atlan continent – a population of child-sized *sapiens*. Different from the Afrosean pygmy tribe an earlier expedition had discovered, Talya's find had been fully formed adults with reasonably good brain-to-body ratios, possessing two separate heavy brow ridges like *Pithekos*, and huge feet. There was no record from previous expeditions of their existence.

'Lost data?' Poseidon had suggested, but Talya dismissed the idea that such an exceptional and noteworthy offshoot of the species had fallen through the cracks of her predecessor's records. 'From which line did they originate?' she'd repeated several times during her report to him. It irritated her beyond measure to be scientifically baffled. She disliked mysteries, and these miniature humans were an unwelcome enigma. When it came to the ultimate conundrum of overall human origins – how the species had emerged on both Terres and Gaia, but at different rates of evolution – she was strained to the furthest limits of her patience.

Today, however, Talya was in fine spirits. Her fieldwork had taken her to the eastern coast of the Atlan continent, standing amidst a honey-skinned tribe at the water's edge – the one she had shown them on the phaetronic globe during Gaia Approach. Fish were being hauled to the shore in nets. Handsome, dark-haired men, women and children prepared the catch for smoking on wooden racks.

"They call themselves the Shore People," Talya began. "They've begun exploiting their proximity to the sea, harvesting edibles from the shore, as well as constructing simple vessels that take them to reefs and nearby islands where larger sea animals can be caught. No navigation as yet. She stood close to an embarrassingly virile young man, long dark hair flowing around his shoulders as he single-handedly hauled a heavy wooden canoe onto shore. His sweat-slick muscles rippled in the sun. He appeared altogether unaware of her presence.

"This is the male subject I mentioned. 2287," she told Poseidon. "He's called Boah."

"What would he say if he knew what was standing over his shoulder?"

"He'd likely fall on his knees, sobbing. He'd think 'Great Mother' had come down to rain punishment on him for cutting the fish tail off before the head. This tribe – *all* tribes I've visited so far – are fraught with superstition."

"Your favorite evolutionary trait."

"I do wish they'd grow out of it a bit faster."

"Look how long it took us on Terres." He saw she was unconvinced. "You don't have to equate magical thinking with ignorance, you know."

"Well, I do," she said.

"So you remained cloaked for the entire period of your study?" he said, feeling himself suddenly annoyed at her rigidity.

"In light of my predecessor's disastrous experience," she said, "I decided I shouldn't reveal myself to the tribe."

"The Goddess Talya," Poseidon teased.

But she was in no mood for levity. "Our incorporation into tribal myths is an unacceptable contamination of the test sample. Don't you agree?"

"We've been tampering with the species at the most profound levels possible for millennia," he argued. "A few small additions to the local cosmology seems a rather minor contamination to me."

"I wouldn't let your colleagues hear you say that."

"So when do I see this "missing link" specimen?" Poseidon asked.

Talya turned inland and walked towards a rocky palisade and climbed some well-worn steps in the stone to the village fifty feet above the beach.

"She really is our best hope for this wretched species," Talya said.

In the privacy of his bubble, Poseidon quietly magnified Talya's buttocks and gazed at the sight with admiration. *At least one part of her was soft.*

"In general the *Sapiens* species is substantially more advanced than we expected. We anticipated any number of evolutionary strides since the interventions of our last expedition. I was particularly pleased to see the short, once-yearly female estrus cycle replaced by a monthly period of fertility. It's the reason we've seen such an explosion in the population."

"Brain capacity has increased?" he asked.

"Generally, though not in size… but complexity. Some of the small wandering tribes we saw on the last expedition have settled into stationary villages like this one. There's rudimentary mining – flint for weapons, ocher for ceremonial use."

Poseidon followed Talya as she walked through the cluster of sunbaked mud and thatch huts, shadowing more industrious shore villagers at work. They tended cook fires; knapped a long piece of obsidian into a spear tip; artfully decorated gourds. Children came chasing after one another, knocking over a fish rack. A wolf mother sunned herself lazily, watching her pups play.

Talya approached a hut at the edge of the village where, lying by its door, was a large adult wolf. Sensing something near it that it could not see, it sat up, sniffing and growling with menace.

Talya opened the flap door and entered the birthing hut. Half a dozen Shorewomen were gathered around a pregnant young woman on the ground in the throes of labor. A midwife, with her back to door, knelt between the pregnant woman's thighs, her head bowed. Her long-muscled arms were ringed with tattoos.

Poseidon could now see glimpses of the midwife's face – tawny skin, brown eyes, high rounded cheekbones, a perfect chin.

"Subject 4251," Talya said. "Seventeen Gaian years old. She's physically and genomically sound. Factoring in obvious cultural liabilities and rudimentary language, her reasoning, logic and learning factors are roughly equal to our own. While the general population is slightly more advanced than expected, this particular female's cognitive skills are superior."

Poseidon found himself staring at the image of the midwife. He quietly magnified her face and he saw that her expression was intent, intelligent. When the laboring woman shrieked, 4521's face creased with empathy. But her will was steady as she slowly coaxed the child out of the birth canal.

"Can we assume that she's a natural, if statistically rare, mutation of the species?" Talya nodded in the affirmative. "She seems well integrated in the village."

"In ways. But she is considered something of an oddity. When she was still a girl she single-handedly domesticated wolves and brought them into the village. It caused a good deal of strife at first. Now the animals are not only accepted, but an integral aspect of the hunt. When she was fourteen, subject became the tribal healer. She uses medicinal plant substances she concocts herself. She's present at every birth. Devises simple tools,

weapons, instruments. Her problem-solving abilities are superb."
Talya could see that her report had captured Poseidon's imagination. "Are you all right?" she asked.

"Go on," he said, shrugging off the question.

"For 4521 – like every tribesperson – each object, plant and
animal is imbued with a particular spirit, but they're all part of this
"Great Mother" cosmology. Like so many of the planet's mamma-
lian species, these people are highly territorial — and they'll fight
to the death to protect their food supplies and families."

Now before them, subject 4251 successfully delivered the
infant and placed it on her mother's breast to suckle. She pulled
a stone blade from her waist and skillfully cut the umbilical.

"Of course this means the natural aggression of their primate
ancestors has begun escalating," Talya continued. "And with the
growing population, the tribes will be coming into contact with
each other more frequently, so I'm going to recommend in my
final report that during the next mission we initiate GRP."

At this, Poseidon felt a knot tighten in his belly.

The Genomic Restructuring Program, to which all humans on
the home planet were subject, was a protocol whereby the particular brain chemistry which produced aggressive and murderous
behavior in their species had been bred nearly into extinction.
During their long evolution the Terresians – not unlike the
Gaian primitives – had made bloodshed a way of life. Greed,
sexual jealousy, even differences in religious beliefs led to slaughter on a frightening scale. But natural evolution of consciousness
and advances in phaetron technos – particularly the science of
genomics – brought with it the discovery of a specific genome
which, when excised from the basic helial structure, eradicated
the impulse to fight. It had been a revolution unparalleled in
Terresian history. With each succeeding generation children grew
up to be non-aggressive adults. War and crime ceased to exist
except in the occasional mutation. Religious conflicts, once a
common catalyst for great wars, no longer precipitated hostilities.

Some believed the previous Gaian interventions with the primitives were already excessive – that Terresians ought simply to be *observers* of their twin planet's development, and careful about tampering with an extraordinarily pure lesson in the evolutionary process of a closely related species. But Poseidon was not one of them. He'd always been among the majority of Terresians who were satisfied with their existence no longer plagued by violence, and believed it their duty to guide the Gaian primitives to a more peaceful planet. *Now he was questioning it.* Too deeply lost in thought, with glazed eyes he finally looked up to find Talya staring at him with annoyance.

"The males and females have adopted monogamy," she told him pointedly, "though there is a period of youthful sexualizing with random partners before the final mate is selected."

"And 4521? Has she chosen a mate... or random sexual partners?"

Talya exited the hut and Poseidon reluctantly followed. "Happily for our purposes, neither. While she's considered a person of stature within the tribe, no man has dared approach her sexually. There is one young male of approximately her age, subject 2287... they grew up together. It's expected that they'll eventually mate."

Talya had just projected near the hut wall an InsertImage of the virile young man on the beach when Poseidon looked down to see that his hands had, without him knowing it, clenched into fists. In the next moment the midwife walked out of the hut carrying a leather pouch. Instantly, the wolf came to its feet and accepted a brief head rub before following its mistress away. Poseidon could not take his eyes off the young woman – tall and lovely with long, but shapely limbs. Her dark hair fell on strong, finely sculpted shoulders that flanked high rounded breasts under the skins she was wearing.

"What's her name?" He was trying not to gawk at 4521.

"Her *name?*"

"Surely she has a name."

"Cleatah," Talya snapped. "Child of Luna and Evenor."

With that, Talya de-materialized the entire diffractor presentation. Poseidon was startled to find himself alone in his privacy bubble with Talya, whose tone had gone suddenly sharp.

"I'm leaving tomorrow. There are clusters of promising subjects in some of the southwestern settlements. Hopefully some suitable sperm donors for the study before we harvest the female's..." she smiled sarcastically "...Cleatah's ovum." She fixed Poseidon with her icy blue eyes. "Have you missed me?"

He laughed. "You never care if I miss you."

"Well I do now."

With that he was drawn right back into her frigid web. And yet... something besides Talya had aroused him. "Take off your clothes," he ordered her.

"What?"

"Take them off."

"Right here?"

"Nobody can see you."

"I know, but.."

"Move into the light. I want to see the sun on your breasts."

"This is mad."

Poseidon pulled off his sleep shirt. Altogether naked, he watched Talya – surrounded by tribesmen and women – undoing her jumpsuit and letting it fall to the sandy ground.

"Synchronize with me," he said.

"Yes, Sir."

They both punched into their wrist hubs the program for "enhanced coupling." Then he gestured for her to straddle him. He could see she was aroused and pleasantly appalled. There inside his privacy bubble Talya lowered herself onto him. As she began to move, her image overlapped and blurred into his corporeal body. But their synced, linked sexual protocols did allow for a decent semblance of long-distant coitus.

"Turn it up," he said, gesturing to her hub controls.

"What's got into you?"

He didn't answer, but she obeyed. He moved sinuously under her image, and he heard her utter a long, low moan.

"What's got into *you*?" he growled.

ELEVEN

BOAH WAS THE most vigorous of the men hauling in the log boat. The others were old men, their arms, though stringy, were still taut and strong. They all grinned slyly, knowing they were letting Boah do their work. But what was youth for, if not making an old man's labors easier? Boah showed them his teeth to make them laugh. They were all in on the joke.

When the boat scraped ashore Boah wasted no time unloading the haul. Fletter and stomat in the nets, and a slew of flying fish that had jumped in their boat and were lying still on the floor of it. Marak, the oldest fisherman – knew just where to row to and when to land the biggest catch of them. He would smile toothlessly and call them a "flock" like birds in great numbers were called. Boah liked the flurry of fish in the air. It made his heart race to see them explode from the water, some hitting the wooden hull, some flying straight up, others crashing into the men's chests or heads, making them all curse and laugh. They were small. You had to eat five or six to fill your stomach.

The others had already dragged the net catch across the sand to the women waiting on the shore, many of them young, with babies on their teats, for cleaning fish was a young woman's job. Boah sighed with satisfaction thinking that Cleatah was not a fish cleaner. Not a mother with a baby sucking on her chest.

He would rather be the one sucking on her chest. He grunted a laugh.

Loth elbowed him. "You thinking about her, are you?"

The others heard.

"Who?" Boah said, teasing. Everybody knew who he thought about night and day.

"Your woman," Marat said.

"Not my woman yet."

With his hips, Elkon made the movement of mating, and they all laughed again.

Boah walked to the back of the boat and lifted the prized kokea swirling shell in both his hands. It was the largest he'd ever seen, and finding it in the shallow reef today had brought hoots of envy from the other fishermen.

"You better watch out," Marat said. "I'll come in and steal it from you while you sleep."

"You better steal it now because Boah is taking it to his woman," Loth said.

Boah felt his face redden. *How did these old men know what was in his heart? What was pushing between his legs at the thought of Cleatah?*

"We were young once," Loth added, answering without being asked. "She'll like it, the swirl shell."

"She'll like what's inside it more," Elkon said. "The ink in its sack heals burns."

"After she drains the sack I'll cook the kokea meat for her. Till it's crispy and the oil drips yellow."

Boah strode away, ignoring the calls behind him insisting he help stow the boat. But he shot them a grin and made a rude punch of his fist which they all chuckled at. Their payment for Boah's teasing.

He ran up the stone stairs to the lower village and made for the outskirts where the new-made men lived, two to a hut. Alhar was not there. He'd gone with the hunters to the plateau to collect a buron or two. So Boah sat in front of his flap door, glad for the shade of the spreading yew, and began to work at the kokea shell. It was easy to forget that deep inside hid a living thing, so lovely was its hard, bright colored house. The smooth flange where the prettiest colors were was soft and smooth, the way he imagined the inside of Cleatah's thighs would be.

Get the kokea body out, he told himself sternly. *Think too hard about Cleatah's thigh, or breast or…* Boah grabbed his blade and plunged it into the shell opening. He'd speared the slimy creature just right, killing it so that it slid easily out of the shell. He threw it in the bowl of water near his ankle and now began the pleasurable part – the cleaning with a pounded bark pad, and then a soaked sea sponge. The colors of a setting sun were flecked with black, matching the tips of the spoked spirals of the shell.

Cleatah would be impressed. He was sure of it.

Some young boys chasing by knocked over the bowl as they passed and sent the kokea body sprawling into the sand. He shouted his annoyance at the boys, but they were already gone back to the center of the village. Boah put the sandy creature back in the empty bowl and kept polishing.

It wasn't long ago that he'd been a rowdy boy himself, annoying every adult he saw. His manhood hunt was only a year past. He was glad that was behind him. He'd always been a good hunter, even in his youth, but you never knew what surprises the ritual hunt would bring. It might foil you with no game showing themselves, too many missed spear shots, or an injury. You might need to repeat the hunt. Humiliation. Manhood denied for another moon. But Boah had done well. Brought down a loresk with his second throw, and a red-feather quillet – an unexpected surprise.

That night at the central fire all the women were admiring the fleshy loresk, skewering it on a branch to hang over the fire. Two more women carefully harvested the feathers of the quillet, keeping the tail and wings intact. They would make a handsome headdress for him, unless he chose to gift it to one of the elders, not a bad thing for a newly made Shoreman to do. You never knew when a favor might be needed in return. If his father had been alive, Boah would have gifted the plumage to him.

The women had brought the cleaned wings to Boah and draped one around each shoulder. Everyone looked up from their food bowls and smiled, enjoying the female humor.

The wings were pretty spread like that, Boah thought.

Then he looked up and saw Cleatah watching him from across the fire. It wasn't so much a smile on her face so much as a question. He jutted his chin in her direction. She tucked her fingers into her armpits and flapped her wings. She always liked a joke, *Cleatah*. They'd been friends since they'd started to walk, and she always found a way to make Boah giggle. He was not as clever as she, and his jokes never as good as hers. But he pleased her. He knew that. She was not unhappy that they would one day life-mate.

Till then she teased him. Gave him no easy way to touch her *that way*. She was slippery as that kokea. *Still too young,* she would bark at him to make him withdraw a probing hand. But she wasn't so young, really. Other girls of her age had mated. Some had babies. Some children running around the village paths.

Suddenly in the light of the central fire he'd felt himself harden under his skins. Just thinking about her. His cheeks burned and he ventured a look in her direction. *She had seen his excitement!* He'd torn the red wings from his shoulder and stomped from the fire, unable to hide his shame.

By the time he'd returned the loresk was on the spit and beginning to sizzle. Spirits were high. Boah – a well-liked father-less boy – had become a man that day, and now they would feast to celebrate it.

But when Boah looked around the rows of villagers sur-rounding the central fire, Cleatah was not among them. He had disgraced himself with her. Boah sat heavily near the fire between Marah and Loth and drank some kav.

Then soft fingers tapped his shoulder. He'd turned behind him to see Cleatah smiling down at him, clutching a bunch of dried flowers. He knew they meant something good. Something that pleased her. Something only she understood. He would ask her the next time they were alone. Then Loth had moved aside to make room next to Boah for his woman.

Today was that day.

Cleatah had promised him many times she would take him with her on one of her mysterious journeys onto the Great Plateau to collect her medicines. This time he would bring her a beautiful gift, the swirl shell. Something in return for the flowers she had given him at his manhood feast. She would be his life-mate one day. She would tease him and make him smile. She would like the hardness between his thighs. They would make children together.

But now as he crossed the village center and hurried to the south path up to the Great Plateau Boah only hoped Cleatah would look favorably upon the kokea spiral shell.

There she was, up ahead. She was nearly at the top.

It was a long, steep climb up the path to reach the Great Plateau above the village, but this day Cleatah hardly felt it at all in her legs or chest. As always, Sheeva bounded ahead, her scout and guardian. The name she had given the wolf was, in fact, the word for guardian, and in their years together they had become the closest and most trusted of companions. Now that her mother and father were dead she had grown content being left to herself as long as she had the company of her wolf.

"Cleatah!" It was Boah's voice calling from below, and now she could hear his heavy breathing getting closer and closer. He had followed her up the path.

"Why are you following me?" she asked him once he'd reached her, and kept on climbing.

"You said you would let me come with you."

"Not today."

"You say that every time."

She felt his warm hand on her waist and twisted out of his grasp. "Not *today*."

Sheeva came bounding back to her side and bared her teeth at him, though halfheartedly. She liked Boah. Two of her pups lived with him in the new made men's village. But the wolf knew Cleatah had no wish for Boah's company today.

"I brought you this," he said, and held out the largest and most beautiful swirl shell she had ever seen.

It would be hurtful for her to refuse it, but it would take up so much room in her medicine sack. And today, of all days, she did not wish his company.

"It's beautiful," she said, taking the shell in her hand. She ran her fingers along the smooth orange flange, then admired the black tips of the spiral. "I'll make a place at Great Mother's altar for it. Would you..." she hesitated, looking for words that would not crush his heart. They would be life-mates one day. "...take it down to my hut. Go inside. You choose the spot for it." As she handed back the shell she watched his face. Saw the disappointment, then his understanding of the honor she had bestowed. Before he could say another thing she turned. Sheeva had already run ahead. Cleatah trotted after her, never looking back.

She and the wolf climbed until they reached the plateau, cut by rivers and smaller streams, each one bordered by thick patches of forest. From this height she was also blessed with sight of the far mountains they called Krakatoh, and the Great Sea, its horizon unimaginably distant. Since earliest childhood she had roamed these fertile flatlands with her mother Luna – the Shore People's healer – in search of the plants the woman had used in her treatments. Everything grew abundantly in the grassy meadows and along the rich wooded riverbanks, and the waterways teemed with life.

Luna had instructed her daughter where to discover brushweed – used for stomach cramps – and golum, which together with the hard berries of the junip, relieved the swelling of joints. She had learned which willow branches were best to make splints for a broken bone, and how to find the orange mushroom that, ground into a mash, made the best poultice to draw poison from a festering wound. Her mother had shown her how to test each plant by taste – the tiniest nibble would tell the girl if it was fresh, ripe or fermented, and which was most potent. And of course she learned the signs that told if a plant would sicken or kill.

The recent coming of the great herds onto the plateau had changed the tribe's lives forever. She could remember how, in the short time since her childhood, the weather had also shifted. Longer droughts had driven many different animals that had once roamed the inland plains to the rivers near the Great Sea... and her home.

The mighty herds of hooved creatures had trampled much of the vegetation, destroying many of the plants her mother had depended upon. While the men celebrated the bountiful hunting grounds, never coming home empty handed, Luna had despaired. When a child died for want of a medicine that no longer grew, her mother had cursed the buron, refusing any longer to honor their animal spirits – they who had taken from her so many tools of her calling.

Though not yet a woman, Cleatah had been old enough to venture out on her own. She'd become the sole gatherer of whatever healing plants were still to be found. She enjoyed ranging far over the Great Plateau but she was always careful of her safety. She knew that a mistake in the presence of such large and numerous animals could mean terrible injury or even death. She learned to search out the medicines where the herds had not found them. Then she fashioned sturdy barriers from large fallen branches and built little untouchable gardens of the valuable plants on rocky ledges where the cattle could not graze on or trample.

Leaving the village this day she followed the worn path leading to the closest stream she called White Waters. She took notice of those plants that were in perfect readiness for picking – one, like the yellow fern that she would pluck on the way home for freshness – and others, like the sunwort which had already dropped its seeds and could be gathered now.

The path took her through a recently grazed field, Sheeva ranging ahead, her nose down in the grasses, scouting for poisonous vipers. She knew by the shape and content of the large droppings that it had been a herd of antelers, and whispered a low curse, knowing that she would find no spirit mushrooms in this particular dung.

It never failed that gazing out over this lush meadow reminded her of a special day, soon after her first blood, when she had discovered the mushrooms. It had rained all of the previous night. The days following such showers were always the most pleasant and favorable for finding and collecting medicines. She roamed in many places, but on that day she chose to visit the most distant meadow. She had observed that the buron herds had left it three days before. The grasses always revived after a downpour and now new, tender shoots were springing up everywhere. She had stopped to switch her gathering sack from one shoulder to the other when her eyes fell on a large pile of dung, steaming as the moisture was drawn out of it by the morning sun.

Poking out of the dropping was a delicate, long-stemmed mushroom. Her eye was trained for spotting such things, but she had never before encountered such a plant. She knelt to look at it more closely and suddenly saw that all the piles of droppings nearby sprouted the same mushrooms. She had picked one carefully, and turning it in her fingers looked at it closely. It was red-capped with many white spots scattered upon it. She saw none of the signs that it was poisonous. *Surely a small nibble*

– the way I had been taught to test plants – could not hurt me, she thought. She could compare the taste and effect on her tongue and lips with the other mushrooms she *did* know.

She had bitten off the edge of the cap. The taste was earthy and slightly bitter, reminding her of the great, red-capped, white-dotted fungi that grew in the softened bark of fallen trees. There were no signals of danger so she had taken bite after bite of the cap and ate downward into the stem. She thought of how proud she would be to bring home a plant that her mother had never before seen. Together they would see if the mushroom had uses as medicine.

Then all at once she had felt a tightness in her throat. She became alarmed. She knew how angry her mother would be if she made herself sick, or how aggrieved if she died. *How stupid I've been!* She thought she should walk home quickly, but as she stood she saw that everything around her had changed.

No, on second look it was the same meadow she had visited a hundred times, still trampled and littered with cattle dung. But now the insects – the flies covering the dung – seemed to be singing, singing the praises of the delicious meal they were enjoying. She giggled at the strangeness of the thought, but truly she could hear their voices. *The flies were fattening themselves up on the droppings, preparing themselves to be happily sacrificed to the flock of red-throated fly-catchers that had arrived in the meadow and were swooping down to snap up the insects in mid-flight with their pointy black beaks. The movements of the birds were precise and perfectly timed. And the red of their necks – had she ever seen such a color as beautiful? Yes, color! Everything,* everything *was vibrant, shimmeringly beautiful. The pale fresh green of new grass was the loveliest thing she had ever seen. The edge of a single blade of grass seemed sharp enough to draw blood from her finger, and its top-heavy tip swayed a green dance in the breeze.*

The tightness in Cleatah's throat was forgotten. Her mother was forgotten. The mushrooms forgotten. She felt she was walking above the ground, her head pleasantly hollow, eyes seeing with the keenest sight. She explored the meadow for hours, hearing the voices of every living thing. Even rocks spoke to her, and the streams. The beauty of the world several times made her weep, but the weeping would turn in the next moment to laughter – watching insects working atop an ant hill, or the dance of a butterfly, which she would herself attempt to copy. While she danced she felt light as the butterfly and almost as lovely.

She did not remember gathering dozens of the mushrooms, nor the journey home. Her mother was not there, so she had sat herself down in the family hut. Better not wander through the village as she was. Finally the magic of the mushroom had begun to leave her, and Cleatah had spent the time waiting for her mother's return, trying to find words to tell her of her blissful communion with the world.

When Luna returned, all her daughter's attempts to describe it were fruitless. Luna had shrieked at Cleatah – eating a mushroom growing from a pile of cursed cattle dung! Had she lost her mind? No, her mother said, she had no interest in studying it. And her father had better not hear the silly stories of songs of flies, and plants speaking to her in the "green language." These were nothing like the spirits their tribe believed resided in Great Mother's domain – in creatures and rocks, the wind and the water. Cleatah was not to go near the mushrooms again. Ever!

But of course she did. Again and again. The mushroom, which she soon understood was as sacred a plant as any known to her tribe, became as much a teacher of the world as her mother had been. On her gathering expeditions, when she was sure to be alone, she would eat the mushroom. Then, holding a medicine plant in her hand, she would listen while it spoke to her of its qualities. In this way she learned a new use for it, or how it could be mixed with another plant to increase its strength. With "mushroom sight" she watched a flock of birds pecking at the brittle rock cliffs above the river and discovered the healing properties of the mineral imbedded there. She found useful essences in sea plants and even insect venoms. The workings of her own body became clear to her, and then the bodies of others. She understood the cycle of a woman's bleeding and the flow of breath in and out of the chest. She saw, like no other man or woman in her tribe, a strange new world that lived side-by-side with the old one. Soon her mother was unable to answer her daughter's questions. Cleatah no longer asked them.

Words began to come into her head. Words for the new sights and sounds and smells and thoughts. Her head was *filled* with words, and songs that the tribe would sing in celebration, or a mother to put her child to sleep. The people were grateful for all these gifts, yet they had become fearful of her. They left her alone, thought her strange. No one, not even her mother, dreamed these gifts had arisen from the eating of a mushroom that grew in the steaming dung of the wild herds.

This was her secret – *Ka*, which meant "the other place." And now, as Sheeva and she entered the shaded forest leading to White Waters, she would find the soft red ground fruit and journey there again.

TWELVE

CYPHUS WAS PACKING up his things as Poseidon brought the exploratory craft down over the Atlantos Operations Base in the center of the expansive Western Grasslands. On his display, the mothership, perched high on its legs, and two shuttles showed as "cloaked," a precaution necessary to hide themselves from the occasional nomadic tribe wandering this otherwise deserted section of the continent.

As they descended, the *Atlantos* – now in its final stages of repair – came more clearly into view. Rooted to the spot, Poseidon felt the breath go out of him. As though his eyes had opened for the first time, he could see that the ship, with its neatly functional form and smooth metallic symmetry, was no more than a blight upon the Gaian landscape, completely anti-thetical to its surroundings, an affront to the rolling meadow. It was, he thought, like a cold blade lying on the belly of a beautiful woman. Perhaps it should be buried underground.

He stopped himself. *Bloody stars, I'm thinking in metaphors! Bury the ship? The crew will think I'm insane.* Maybe he *was* losing his mind. Lately he'd been entertaining a madly subversive idea: how wonderful it would be to ignore the Planetary Escape Timetable and miss the scheduled window from Gaia's orbit back to Terres. He would never say it out loud, but the truth was, he didn't want to go back. He wanted to live here forever.

Even this silent admission rocked Poseidon on his feet. Frightened him. There was no time for such erratic self-indulgences. He had to get his head straight. And under no circumstances could anyone know these strange turns his mind was taking.

Anyone.

He stepped out of the blue elevator beam and strode down the Library Corridor. It seemed like every person he passed was relaxed and smiling at him. He heard, "Welcome back, Sir," a dozen times before he was halfway down the hall. Yet all he could think was that the ship stank. *Dead air*, he thought grimly. *I'm breathing dead air.* He fought back the urge to choke and tried not to grimace at the next crewman who greeted him. He thought he saw a trace of alarm mirrored back at him.

Were his emotions so apparent in his expression? Quickly Poseidon twisted his face into the semblance of a smile. He could not meet Chronus and Ables this way! He'd go back to his quarters. Reschedule. He turned on his heels and moved back towards the elevator, all the time trying to quiet his rapid breathing, his racing heart. When no one was looking he disappeared into a small alcove. Quickly he set his hub to the 'chemistry-balancing'. The jolt of moderating Vibrus surged into him, but it barely slowed his heartbeat and breath. His nerves were still jangled when the comm from Zalen came through.

"Yes, Captain," he said, attempting a steady calm.

"I need you in the Shuttle Bay."

"Be right there." *Pull yourself together*, Poseidon ordered himself. He tried to shake away the thoughts, the desires, *raptures* threatening to swamp his rational self. He straightened his posture and forcibly composed his features.

He stepped out into the corridor and strode for the elevator.

THIRTEEN

*S*HEEVA WAS WAITING *for Cleatah when she pushed through the hut door. As they moved through the village she shared greetings with the seated circle of women carving gourds, squatting down to admire their work. The wolf sat on its haunches just outside the circle, waiting patiently, always keeping one eye on her mistress.*

Poseidon came upright in his bed, reprogramming the diffractor for a better view of the midwife's face. He was watching her with a secret pleasure as intense as it was ill-advised. Eager for more, he brought up another study in which Cleatah climbed a steep path cut into the rocky palisade leading to the plateau above the village. Poseidon found himself gratified when she shooed away Subject 2278's rather innocuous advances. Like a hungry man, Poseidon called up yet another study. In this, Cleatah knelt at the ocean's edge, fashioning a shell-cutting tool.

He sat unmoving, utterly transfixed as he watched her every move.

"Poseidon…"

He nearly came off the bed at Talya's voice, with guilt and relief flooding him almost immediately. *It was only a comm on his wrist hub.* He never took his eyes from the girl as he spoke. "When did you get back?"

"Late last night."

He watched as Cleatah raised a corner of her vest to clean the shell off.

"Shall I come to you?" Talya asked.

Cleatah's pink-nippled breast was revealed beneath the fur.

"No!" he barked, then quickly composed himself. "Not yet. I have a report that needs…" He found himself magnifying the girl's dewy cheek.

"You're distracted tonight."

"Right," he said.

"Do I have your permission to visit the tribes to the north and west when I go back out?" Talya said. "I'm hoping to find suitable male sperm donors for the control study before we harvest the female's…" She corrected herself with the mildest touch of sarcasm, "*Cleatah's* ovum."

It startled and embarrassed him to hear the name spoken aloud. "Of course you have. Breakfast tomorrow?"

"No," she said, mildly annoyed. "I'll see you at Morning Status."

"Good. Good," Poseidon said, clicking off the comm. Forgetting everything.

Everything but the girl.

FOURTEEN

"WE'LL BE TACKLING the Central Range to the east of here first," Cyphus announced to the team heads gathered around the Library table.

"We've been from pole to pole but we haven't explored the seismic matrix right under our feet," Poseidon added. "This continent is intensely volatile. Cyphus and I have been lucky so far." He addressed Ables. "We'll be doing core sampling in the glacial ice for you."

"Good. Get me some vegetal samples as well. The oldest trees you can find."

Poseidon could feel Talya's eyes boring into him. He kept his expression level, mild.

"After that," Cyphus said, "we'll proceed across the eastern plateau to the central coast."

"Your purpose?" Talya's voice was a scalpel.

Poseidon remained cool, holding her eye. "I'll be looking at the Shore Tribe."

"That data's already been collected."

"There's more I'd like to know."

"Then I'll join you," she said.

"It's more important that you adhere to the Sperm Collection

Protocol on the west and south coasts," he told her. "We'll need the broadest possible sampling of the population."

Her fingers tapped restlessly on the table. Poseidon envisioned her trying to rip out his eyes. He managed a bland smile. Then he stood and gazed around at his crew. "That's it, then. Cyphus?"

"Yes, Sir."

"Tomorrow. We'll get an early start." He felt Talya's eyes boring into him, but refused to meet her gaze. Something was overtaking him. Something he did not understand.

"I hope you find it," he heard his mother say.

༺

The sun glinting off the curves of the *Atlantos* and its shuttle disc lent an air of celebration to the send-off. Talya had been glaringly absent. As he'd boarded the shuttle with Cyphus, turning for a final wave, a phrase that had repeated itself a hundred times inside his head in the past week reasserted itself once more. *I should be going alone.*

But once exploring, as the lush Atlan continent spread out before them Poseidon was glad for the company. The two of them drank in one thrilling sight after another. The tawny, long-fanged felidae cats. Wooly, ivory-tusked creatures twelve feet high that roamed the endless inland plain in herds, tenderly minding their young, feasting on the plentiful grasses and wallowing in muddy watering holes. A great thundering waterfall that held a constant rainbow in its midst. Long-necked scarlet birds in so enormous a flock that when they took flight the sky became a flaming, sunless sunset. There were brilliantly hued trees which would, in a surprising explosion, be shorn of its "foliage" as fifty thousand delicate, large-winged insects blossomed into a fantastical cloud.

Following a dry riverbed between the sheer walls of red granite, Cyphus and he uncovered the perfectly preserved fossil remains of a monstrous reptilian creature that had lived two hundred million Gaian years before. Volcanism had produced many wonders as well – chasms, crystal caves and vast expanses of soil so fertile the variety of plant species were uncountable. Cloud formations – non-existent on water-starved Terres – were particularly dazzling. Sometimes Poseidon would find a private place, lie on his back and simply watch as the majestic flotillas passed him by.

But it was the massive, mid-continental mountain range that had beckoned Poseidon most seductively and mysteriously from the start of the journey, looming larger and more imposing the closer they came. Gathered storm clouds crowned the conical peaks on most afternoons, though the seven volcanoes themselves had been serene during their slow approach, not a single lazy tendril of smoke rising from any of their snowcapped tops. Before they'd set out he had studied the range in great detail – aerial maps and geologic surveys that showed the peaks and jagged pinnacles, each neatly numbered. This morning the shuttle had landed at their base. He and Cyphus stared up at the mountains.

"They should have names, not numbers," Poseidon said.

"What should have names, Sir?"

"Each of the mountains." He had never before been prone to such flights of fancy. "Don't you see faces and figures in the rock? There!" He pointed toward the saw-toothed foothills. "I see the distinct profile of a man lying on his back. Big nose. Long neck. There…a snake swallowing the world whole. And there – the throne of a gargantuan king."

"Those two symmetrical mounds there?" Cyphus said, finally joining the game. "The ones standing apart from the others? A woman's breasts."

"You sound like my brother."

They laughed.

Poseidon stared in silence at the tallest of the peaks with

its graceful, white-draped slopes. "That one is Manya," he said quietly.

"Your mother?"

"See," said Poseidon, "her shoulders are draped in a cape of snow."

"Aauugh!"

"You don't see that?"

Cyphus was laughing. "I don't see that. No." He started away, muttering, "Your *mother*…Don't you go soft on me now."

❦

They climbed the foothills, Cyphus scouting ahead with his hub and his wits, insisting on caution, Poseidon reporting and recording everything. They moved through a grove of venerable old trees intermixed with jagged boulders which, long ago, had surely been tossed like pebbles from Manya's fiery mouth. Numerous sinewy caves snaked far back into the mountains, and every one they passed beckoned mysteriously to Poseidon.

Cyphus noticed the longing gazes. "Explore every one and we'll miss making the summit before nightfall," he threatened.

They emerged onto Manya's summit in blazing sunshine, a gently sloped field of blinding white snow. From here they stared eastward across the endless plateau all the way to the horizon. At this altitude the continent's edge was visible, as well as a slice of the glittering sea beyond. Directly below was Manya's eastern slope, the top third covered by a thick blanket of snow, and a massive glacier flowing down between two smaller, tree and boulder-strewn mountains at her base. Despite the snow and ice all around them the noonday sun was warm on their faces, and it was a pleasure to stop and gather the ice core samples for Ables. They worked in amiable silence.

Then the ground began to shake.

"I'll call the shuttle," Cyphus said, tapping the order into his hub.

A sharp jolt beneath them brought them to their feet.

"Let's move," Cyphus said. "We're too exposed here. We'll wait for the shuttle down there."

They moved out onto the eastern slope.

Gaia, Poseidon suddenly realized, *has cast a spell on me.* He saw now how the mild weather, the extraordinary grandeur of the surroundings had wrongly caused him to perceive the planet as benign.

This is a dangerous world, he sternly reminded himself.

The eastern slope was steeper than the one they'd traversed on the ascent, so to prevent an out-of-control tumble they were forced to tread with maddening care in the sometimes ankle-deep, sometimes hip-deep snow. Several times sharp tremors caused them to lose their footing, and they would slide tens of feet out of control, sometimes finding themselves buried over their heads in the fine, cold powder.

"Stay calm. Keep moving!" Cyphus barked.

Poseidon struggled for only a moment with exhaustion and a gripping pain in his legs before programming himself with enhanced strength, but the truth was they had nowhere on the mountain to shelter.

Just as they reached the end of the snowline a great double boom sounded. The slopes below were a huge patchwork of boulders and trees, with the glacier nestled between them. Footing was slippery on so steep an incline, peppered as it was with small rocks and gnarled roots. As they bounded down the slope Poseidon wondered if he had ever been so perceptibly connected with his body, his feet somehow finding the perfect spot to land, the precise angle at which to strike it, correct weight allotted to toe, ball and heel. *If I were not fleeing in terror for my life*, he thought, *I might be enjoying this exercise.* A sudden violent tremor flung him off his feet and into the air. When his body began falling, the slope's angle rolled and tumbled him like a stone, down and down in the company of all that was, like himself, unrooted to the earth. He came to rest at the base of a huge boulder, bruised and bloodied but alive. He scanned the slope for Cyphus. He was staggering towards him from fifty feet away.

The phaetron had signaled the shuttle. They would be safe in a matter of moments. Poseidon watched as the craft cleared the summit, hovering momentarily above it to relocate its ground crew and lock their positions for rescue.

Then Manya erupted. A monstrous fountain of molten fire shot skyward, with horrifying velocity, a thousand feet in the air, engulfing the shuttle entirely. It exploded with a violence that matched the mountain's fury, hurling globs of red lava and burning metal projectiles in every direction, starting fires in the trees where they fell. Their body shields repelled the worst of it as they ran futility for non-existent cover.

Poseidon, stunned at the sheer ferocity of nature, reeled at the loss of their vessel.

But then the eruption's true legacy revealed itself.

The infernal heat had melted the mountain's enormous cape of snow. It was now a seething wall of water heading straight at them. Gathering what strength they still possessed, the two men bolted for the closest standing tree. They grasped and clung, climbing as fast as their battered limbs would take them, calling encouragement to each other as they went.

Halfway to the top the wave struck, the force of it uprooting the tree as if it was a sapling. It, and dozens of small boulders nearby, joined the flood that scoured the steep slope in a raging tide.

Choking water from mouth and lungs Poseidon clung more dead than alive to the tree, riding the torrent on the branched raft, submerged and grappling desperately among the limbs to find one above the waterline. The harrowing ride ended suddenly as the pile of debris washed up against a tall outcropping of rocks. The tree crashed to a halt, rocks and other trees battering it, crushing its thick branches like twigs. He cowered in a sturdy crotch while the last of the flood washed over him, spent itself and finally slowed to a few muddy rivulets. Then his eyes fell on Cyphus hanging motionless from a limb above. Poseidon tried to call out to him, but his lungs were still choked with water, and all that came out was violent coughing. Finally there was movement. Cyphus's head turned and his weary eyes met his. *Thank the stars*, he thought. *We are both alive.* Then from above began the sounds of crashing and shrieking so loud that he feared looking up to see what new terror now descended upon them.

The glacier, pulverized into great, razor-edged shards and massive chunks of ice, tumbled and crashed down the mountainside toward the dam of rocks and trees where Cyphus and he still clung. There was hardly time to think.

He looked down at his wrist hub blinking in healthy sequence. He extended his arm and pointed it at the first ice boulder heading straight for their perch. The 'neutralize' function vaporized the projectile moments before it would have slammed into them. Cyphus, even had he been armed, was too badly injured to protect himself. Now, as the barrage came fast and furious, it was all a matter of aim. Poseidon swiveled left, right, center, one flying iceberg close behind another. A trio of them side-by-side. Once, he missed and was forced to duck as the ice rock came racing overhead, cleanly slicing away the limbs a mere foot above him.

Then came a terrible sound – a low, earthshaking rumble as the great grandmother – the very heart of the glacier, seventy feet thick – came sliding slowly, inexorably toward them. The phaetron, aimed at the monster, worked... but too slowly. *Too slowly!* Pieces were disappearing under the device's beam but there was more mass than could be dealt with. It was coming – what was left of the glacier's heart – and as it came crashing blue-white through the broken limbs, Poseidon wondered briefly what it would feel like to die.

How long it was before he regained consciousness was unclear, but the phaetron – still set to vaporize – had melted a substantial hole in his icy tomb. He opened his eyes but they were awash with blood. His legs were completely trapped in heavy packed ice. He tried to move his arms but found himself instead scream-ing with pain. A bone was fractured. Several bones. *Is my back broken?* he wondered. *My spine crushed?* He tried moving his feet and shouted with relief when they responded one at a time. He concentrated his effort and focused his will. He knew he must have the use of one arm, one hand if he was to survive. He tried the right one but found it fully outstretched at shoulder height crushed between a branch and a boulder – the source of the most excruciating pain. His left arm, which until this moment he'd not felt at all, was suddenly discovered pinned behind his back as the prickle of returning sensation replaced complete numbness. Slowly and carefully, arching his body to make room for move-ment, he slid the arm out to his side. Once freed the strained shoulder objected mightily at being returned to its natural posi-tion with a searing bolt of pain that brought tears to his eyes. But the hand was free now, function returning.

By the time he was confident enough to try to activate the phaetron he felt cold fingers of confusion muddling his brain. He could not tell if it was the head injury or the onset of shock. *I will close my eyes for just a moment, a moment…*

The sun was beginning to set when he opened them again. His body was very, very cold. Throbbing pain in his right arm had woken him – perhaps, he thought, saved his life. He knew he must act decisively if he was to survive. With what strength was left he brought his right hand before his eyes and saw it had already turned a bluish-grey. He examined his head with his left hand and found a small but severe crushing injury to the temple which, he assumed, had caused his unconsciousness. He knew he must treat the head wound first, before attending to the shattered arm, before beginning his escape from this icy tomb, before losing consciousness again.

In his present condition it was difficult to remember the phaetron function and procedure for healing. *But I must*, he blearily thought. *I cannot let myself die out here*. In the fading light he programmed the hub as best as memory served and held it, tremblingly, over the head wound. For a long moment he felt nothing but the cold skin of his wrist against his forehead. Then slowly heat and a mild tingling signaled that the healing had begun.

As he waited for relief the ice around him began to melt. He took measure of the small cavity that had been hollowed out. In fact a substantial melt hole had opened below him. In the fading light his eyes settled on a dark shape. *A boulder trapped in the tree limbs*, he told himself. *Oddly shaped. Perhaps an animal caught up in the flood. No. Not an animal.* With painful effort he shifted his body for a better look. But dread swept over him like a cold wave, and he closed his eyes. *Not an animal. Not an animal.* His thoughts had begun to clear but in fact he wished for oblivion. He twisted his head and look down between his splayed legs.

There was Cyphus, his body crushed and pulverized by the ice. His head and neck sheared completely off his shoulders.

An animal cry echoed off the rocky canyon, piercing Poseidon's head. He felt it keenly in the still unmended tissue in his skull. It went on and on, this agonized wailing. It took him a while, but finally he knew the voice was his own.

Later, battered and weak, he stood over what remained of his dearest friend. Still addled, he struggled to find the proper setting, but once he had programmed the deconstruct function and leveled it on Cyphus's body he looked away as it did its work. When nothing remained, Poseidon fell to his knees and quietly wept.

※

It was dark when he dragged himself to his feet and his way illuminated by the glow of his hub he limped towards the rock wall, climbing a way up the eastern slope, locating the deepest cave that he and Cyphus had ventured into.

Here he collapsed into a painful heap.

It was hours before he could bear to program a protective pod around himself, an energy couch and a constant emersion of healing frequencies to bathe his body and brain. He lay in the dark, pathetic and self-pityingly. When he finally switched on his hub to make his report, his voice was raspy and weak.

"I searched for the shuttle but there was nothing left of it. Just the spouting column of magma that took it. What a grave mistake in judgement – lulled into trusting our safety on this planet. Gaia may appear benign, but there's danger everywhere. Not simply the wild beasts or the violent weather, but the ground under my feet. Though I know the emotion to be ridiculous, I feel as though I have been betrayed, nearly murdered by a beloved friend. My stupidity caused the death…" His mouth quivered and he pulled himself together barely enough to continue. *"I was born with more good sense than this. I see now these passions are non-essential. Irrational. Deadly. There is a spouting column of magma – smaller now – and an endless river of lava flowing down the eastern slope of Manya, disappearing back into a great crack in the earth at the base of the mountain. The planet's blood returning from where it came.*

It was all he could manage. He laid back, more despondent than exhausted, and slept.

※

Zalen stood before him in the cave, the weak signal causing the image to waver.

"I see no reason to abort my mission," Poseidon insisted.

"Because you're 'fine?'"

Poseidon had no argument for the well-intentioned sarcasm.

"Let us at least bring you in for a week or two. Get your strength back."

"Not necessary."

Zalen regarded him with a piercing gaze.

"Honestly," Poseidon said, feeling like the liar and fool that he was. "Honestly."

⤚

A grassy plain. The woman Cleatah walked ahead of him, her hips swaying sensually under her pelts, the hair flowing around her naked shoulders, her hand trailing along the tops of the tall grasses. When she turned her head behind to talk to him he could see the curve of her cheek, her chin. She spoke in a language he didn't understand. Then she laughed, a warm, throaty sound. His arms reached out to her body.

Poseidon came awake with a jolt, the scent of woman he had never met, strong in his nostrils. *So much for Terresian rationality,* he thought.

MARS COLONY

FIFTEEN

THE THRILL WAS nearly unbearable. In his whole life, Athens had never felt so vibrantly alive. Racing helmeted head-first under the surface of the warm Marsean Sea, his arms and legs gripped the muscular front fins and sleek body of an adult solie. Racing at breakneck speed next to Leanya on the back of her "mount," they hurtled between canyons of glorious living reefs populated with myriad and spectacular aquatic species.

"Take us home," he heard Leanya say to her creature. They were answered inside their helmets in a language of complicated clicks and nearly human groans.

"To Halcyon Beach," she added.

Instantly, and in perfect synchrony, the solies' course corrected and with their riders hanging on tight, sped back to shore.

They exploded out of the waves and came to a graceful landing on a broad beach of pink sand. Athens and Leanya ripped off their soft helmets and flopped down beside the silky grey-furred animals. They rolled onto their backs and stretched out their flippers that more resembled elbowed arms with five-fingered hands, hoping for a belly rub. The humans happily obliged.

Behind them, nestled in the jungled cliffs overlooking the shore, were hundreds of lovely homes. Even now several giant phaetronic constructors was building one more, materializing its walls, struts and ceilings out of thin air. Beautiful as the homes were, Athens thought, the real treasure here was the beach and the luxury of a friendly and abundant ocean. Water was life. The colonists had fallen instantly and completely in love with their existence by the sea. It startled him how quickly Terres had become a distant, mildly repugnant memory.

Leanya – *bloody stars she was luscious!* – was whispering something in her solie's ear as she pulled down the top of her watersuit. He looked beyond her to the beach where colonists sunbathed and romped in the waves with more of the creatures. He watched as a mother placed her three-year-old boy on the back of a large female and strapped him into a "solie saddle" girdling the animal's torso.

"Not too far out," Athens heard the mother say to the animal who nodded its head, then headed out into the shallows with the giggling child. "Izzy!" she called after it. The solie turned his head back at the sound of its name. "Fifteen minutes!"

Leanya sat up and grew serious. She looked deep into her solie's eyes. After a moment it replied to her silent comm in its clicking language. "Good," Leanya said out loud, "Come back tomorrow. Same time."

The creature nodded its head vigorously.

Athens smiled and extended his palm to his solie's front flipper – a crude fingered "hand" with a rudimentary opposable thumb, and they pressed flesh before the two creatures, in perfect unison, slithered away and dove into the surf.

Leanya was already reporting into her hub as Athens pulled her to her feet. "Cerebral Telepath 1742. Response to simple silent commands improving. Increase complexity. Explore human reception." She smiled prettily at him. "Imagine an animal who's smarter than we are," she said to him.

"That's your job, not mine," he said, and together they headed to the glass house perched on the jungle-festooned cliff above the beach.

❧

Leanya was the first one naked. Standing behind him she tugged his watersuit down to his ankles, then rose and circled his waist with slowly wandering hands.

"Not now," he said.

"You don't have to go to work."

He turned to face her. "I do," he insisted, despite her pouty gaze, and walked through the doorway to the sky-lit polished basalt shower.

She followed him in. "I like the old Athens. More fun."

"Too bad," he said, but his face was already cracking into a smile.

"You can be a little late," she said, slowly lathering his chest.

"Maybe," he said, moving her hands lower, "Maybe a little."

❧

Athens's shuttle descended into the central square of the Federation Mining and Industrial Center, a sprawling basalt complex carved out of the giant tree fern forest a short way inland from the colony's coastal residences. It was all about enterprise here. Prosperity and commerce. Offices, manufacturing, transport, mining.

He strode across the black stone plaza, greeting everyone with his famous smile, gratified that the smiles returned were respectful and genuine. Planted like a large rooted tree at the center of the square, assessing his newest creation and speaking intently into his hub, stood Micah. Terres' most distinguished master artisan was a tall, barrel-chested red-haired bear of a man. The piece *was* impressive, Athens thought. A Kinetic Metal Sculpture of their solar system made all of shiny titanum metal spheres.

The man had outdone himself this time.

Around a huge Helios the familiar planets of "Hermes" "Aphrodite" "Gaia" "Mars" "Zeus" "Kronos" "Ouranos" "Radon" and "Pluton" flew in their roughly circular orbits. A large sphere that clearly depicted Terres was just now sailing away from the statue's central "Sun" and far away on its ridiculously long elliptical outer orbit.

Athens came and stood silently with his friend, waiting for its return.

"Bring it in 6.75 degrees," Micah ordered into his hub. A moment later the Terres Sphere came flying into the inner circuit and stopped in mid-air. "Move Gaia 2.16 distal." Now the Gaia Sphere shifted slightly in its orbit.

"Leave it to you," Athens finally said.

Micah turned to him. "You like it?" he said, gazing up at his creation.

"The tragedy of the Terresian orbit forged from the very substance that will rescue the planet," Athens observed.

"Is the irony too obvious?"

"The people will adore it," Athens said.

"Come to the studio later. I've asked a few people over for a private viewing – a new piece – and dinner."

"Should I bring Leanya?" Athens said as he headed away across the plaza.

"I wouldn't," Micah called after him with a smile that was more of a leer.

Athens headed towards Fed Headquarters, the tallest of the buildings in the complex, but stopped first at the construction hangar. Its massive doors were wide open and inside was housed his personal project – a fleet of shuttles, nearly completed – to replace the hideous ones they had been saddled with by the Terres Federation. These were not unlike the *Atlantos* shuttles, but with the exteriors designed by Micah, were even sleeker and more elegant in proportions than Poseidon's.

"You're gawking," he heard at his elbow. The physicist, Joya, had approached him from behind, silent as a cat. He turned to see her. She was a sensational woman, physically magnificent, with a cool-blooded nature and intellectual prowess. An engineering genius, she had single-handedly invented the internal components of the mini-discus crafts. At the moment she was sharing Micah's bed.

"I love them," Athens said, turning back to the shuttles.

"Of course you love them. They're more beautiful than anything your brother has."

"Am I really that transparent?"

"Absolutely."

"I think Mars has a new hero of phaetron technos."

"Kind of you to say."

"Will you be there tonight?" Athens said.

"Of course."

"Maybe he'll let me 'borrow you' for a while.

"He's not the one you have to ask," she said, looking stern. "Has he told why he wants you to come?"

"A private showing."

"Call it a new commission. He's finished with the shuttle. He wants something big."

"How big?"

"A monument. A pyramid. I don't know. But very expensive. Ask him." She gazed into Athens's eyes. "Am I worth a monument?"

He resisted the urge to reach out and caress her breast. "We'll see," he said.

❧

Athens stood at the top floor window of his offices looking down at the busy plaza. The metallic Solar System planets whizzed through the air, glinting in the sun.

"The Governor's got his hands full today," he heard Persus say behind him, "so it would be helpful if you got straight to the point about…" She hesitated… "the waste substance of several billion billion microbial creatures."

Athens turned to see the short, unpleasant looking man grimacing, fiddling with his wrist hub. "What's so important," the man said, "is the nature of the substance itself, and the location of the microbes in relation to the titanum mine."

Athens was becoming impatient. "If it's going to complicate the mining operation in any way, just avoid it. We have one mission on Mars – stockpiling ore and sending it home."

"I'm sure Chief Geologist Goldius knows that better than anyone, Governor," Persus said.

"You need to see the substance for yourself," Goldius insisted.

"You want us to go and view a big pile of excrement," Athens said.

"Ah!" The geologist had finally gotten his wrist hub to work. "Let me show you something, Governor."

A diffracted image suddenly appeared in the space between the three of them. Hundreds of five-inch long, oval shaped creatures undulated amidst a crystalline matrix. "The 'Goldius Organisms'– as we refer to them," he said, "have been magnified here 10,000 times. They live nearly five miles beneath the planet's surface at a temperature of one hundred and thirty degrees. Look here," he said, pointing to a budlike structure at one end of the animal. "You can see it ingesting the mineral substance surrounding it – its only food." Indeed, the enlargement was so detailed, and the creature's body so transparent, that a pale greyish substance could be seen entering through an orifice in the bud – a mouth of sorts – and its progress through the simple digestive system was actually visible to the observers.

Athens was trying not to roll his eyes.

"Have you any samples of the ore?" inquired Persus.

"You're not impressed," Goldius said. "You will be."

Athens, Persus and Goldius were flying above the new colony. There was a lot to admire. Giant tree ferns blanketed nearly every inch of the land, and pretty little satellite towns already dotted the shoreline as far as the eye could see. No one, it became clear shortly after their arrival on Mars, had any intention of building their homes anywhere but near the water. There were perhaps a dozen small villages to be found inland, but they were invariably on the shores of one of the many Marsean lakes. There would have been plenty of space to clear fields for growing food, but no one was remotely interested in outdoor agriculture, so everything was cultivated in vast covered grow-houses tended by machine. Though beneath the great fern forests the landscape was nearly as flat as Terres was, the lush greenery, the sun rising every morning, and the presence of water made Mars a truly exotic world.

It was only a short distance to the enormous titanum mine, processing plant and laboratories that sprawled for miles. It employed more than eighty percent of the Terresian colonists and operated every hour of every day of the year. This, thought Athens, was the center of his world and locus of his waxing influence.

Once landed he and Persus followed Goldius into his laboratory, a large but unimpressive workspace to a wall of shelving. A smooth slab of a unique, burnished yellow substance several feet long lay on one shelf, and on others were geometric shapes – spheres, pyramids, squares, rectangles made of the stuff.

"The deposit has apparently been building up for 2.8 billion Marsean years, Governor," said Goldius. "There've been some very busy little microbes down there. Our sensors indicate that the vein is almost as long – if narrower – than the seam of titanium. And that, as you know, extends a substantial distance around the planet."

All right," said Athens, unable to tear his eyes from the lustrous array of magnificence spread out before him. "You have my undivided attention. Now show me what the problem is."

The titanum mine, a miracle of Terresian architechnos, resembled an enormous hive of robotic, web-spinning insects. On three sides the cavern rose to a height of nearly two-hundred feet, where row-atop-row of individual cells cut into the wall of solid ore. In the center of the brightly illuminated cave rose a great metallic column whose multiple purposes depended upon the functions of a massive phaetron mounted within it. From each of the cave wall cells streamed chunks of newly mined titanum, suspended in mid-air within a yellow tractor beam – the threads of the web – and were pulled into openings on the central column. The collected ore was then sucked into a thick blue elevator beam and transported up to the Marsean surface where finally it was carted off for processing.

At the mouth of each cell in the mine hung a smaller phaetronic device, sprouting six spindly legs, which allowed the insect-looking thing to creep about, directing its narrow red beam in through the orifice to gouge the ore from the rock wall. Inside, a team of four miners lifted the chunks as fast as they fell, heaving them into the tractor beam, heading – with many hundreds of such ore-laden beams – to the central column. Men, too, rode the yellow beams back and forth between their cells and the central core, waving to one another as they passed. As the mining progressed forward, cell walls would be broken down by the six-legged phaetrons, and new ones carved out. Used-up cells on the side walls were simply abandoned. In this way the mining progressed laterally through the core of Mars.

Inside the central column there was a second elevator beam paralleling the upward flow of ore. This one carried workers into the depths of the Marsean lithosphere. Athens rode this beam down with Goldius and Persus, watching with an odd sense of gratification the continuous upward-bound stream of titanum. There was the Terresian air of industriousness to the place. Though it was tedious work it was clean, efficient and safe. The undistinguished grey-brown rock promised continuing life to an entire planet, and Athens was proud of the flawless operation that provided it.

They had reached the lowest level Athens had previously visited – the floor of the cavern. But now the elevator was descending even deeper into the Marsean crust. Athens, Goldius and Persus stepped out into a sweltering, dimly lit chamber which lay directly below the titanum mine. It was perhaps a quarter as wide as the cave above it, and roughly hewn from the surrounding rock. Only the most rudimentary excavation activity, with miners using hand tools alone, was underway. The small crew of shirtless workers, their bodies glistening with sweat, chipped almost tentatively at the walls.

The miners greeted their governor with genuine pleasantness and, as usual, this warmed Athens's heart. But he was fired with curiosity about the yellow ore and impatient to see it in its raw state. In the shadowy cavern he could see nothing.

"This is an unauthorized operation, Governor," said Goldius. "Very few personnel are aware of these activities, and everyone working down here has been sworn to secrecy."

"Good, good," Athens muttered impatiently. "Why don't you show us this vein you've discovered."

"Yes Sir." The geologist nodded to the foreman and the cavern was flooded with light.

The effect was mind-exploding.

The cave was completely illuminated with glittering yellow luminosity, as though the sun was afire in the walls all around them. Rather than jagged veins interspersed with the common ore it fed upon, the uneven walls appeared to have been thickly coated with a layer of the gorgeous substance.

Athens actually groaned with the sight of it and found himself speechless. Even the unflappable Persus was gazing around with childlike wonder. Her look was so nakedly awestruck that he laughed aloud.

Athens turned to the scientist. "Where are these famous 'organisms?'"

"They lie beneath the layer of gold," he answered.

"*Gold*?" repeated Persus.

The scientist seemed suddenly embarrassed. "It's what the miners have begun calling the substance, Sir. We can change the name if you like…"

"No, no, it's your discovery. We'll call it 'gold.'"

"I hope it's all right that I haven't alerted Vice Governor Praxis yet."

Athens turned to Persus, his expression serious. "What do you think, Persus? Good call?"

"Excellent call, Goldius. You get us the numbers for the extra workers needed and equipment requisitions for a separate extraction operation and processing facility, and the Governor will handle Fed Energy himself."

"Now what's the problem you spoke of?" Athens said.

"Preliminary reports indicate that for the microbes to continue metabolizing the ore, the temperature must remain at a level that is quite uncomfortable to the human organism."

"All right. Put some men on designing a comfortable working garment," instructed Persus.

"Secondly, none of the phaetronic frequencies we've already established can be employed to separate the gold from the microbial layer without damage," said Goldius.

"Damage to the gold or to the microbes?" probed Athens.

"Both, for the moment, so we're having to work by hand. It's extremely tedious work, and there's so much we still don't understand."

"You'll begin a series of studies to find solutions. Immediately. And Goldius…"

"Sir?"

"For the time being, until I can determine the importance of this… 'gold' on the systems and priorities already in place, continue to restrict information to the general public. Do you think these men have kept silent so far?"

"I have no doubt of it. The stories and rumors would have been rampant all over the colony by now if they hadn't."

"That's surprising," said Athens.

"Not really. I've made the reward for their silence utterly irresistible."

"How so?" asked Athens.

"I'm paying them…in gold."

GAIA

SIXTEEN

POSEIDON TOOK A single step from the shadow of the cave and winced at the glaring sun, feeling like a big-eyed rock lizard. Just a few seconds worth of solar glare burned his cheeks and forehead, and he quick-stepped back into the cavern's cool dark.

Stupid, he thought. *Still not thinking straight. Phaetronic DermaScreen is a must for fair Terresian skin. And CornealShield. How could I forget? Will I ever feel safe on this planet again?* He steeled himself. *Just walk out of this cave and proceed with my field mission.*

One single step. But it was harder than he thought.

Regrets are out there. Visions of a dead friend. A whole colony placed in Athens's hands at my insistence. If only I'd been a better brother to Athens. Had protected him from Father's malicious neglect. Too consumed with myself to care, to counteract fatherly scorn with brotherly love. But what did any Terresian know of filial responsibility? It was freakish to have two invested parents. Unheard of to have a brother or sister of the same pairing. And what of Talya? Had she been a mistake, too?

STOP!

He took the step into a glaring sun. DermaScreen CornealSheild in place. He felt strong. Pain free. Another step.

And another. He walked out onto Manya's eastern slope. Snow had fallen since he'd taken refuge in the cave. It sat heavily on the branches of downed trees and piles of broken boulders. Melted away were the patches of ice above the broad lava flows, still warm beneath their jagged black crusts. Utterly humbled, he moved across and down the landscape with Terresian discipline and embarrassing caution. He employed his phaetron frequently to scan and survey each step – what lay underfoot, around and above him.

Be brave, he commanded himself.

This night, second day out, when he activated the small safety dome around him he found he was able to concentrate. Ready to work. A vibral map of the Atlan continent was spread out before him on his energy table. He summoned his chair and sitting back, threw up a diffracted image of hunters, a small band of them, stalking one of their antlered four-footed ungulates through a woodland. He leaned forward to study their keen-eyed tracking, stealthy approach, and their precise spear tosses. Then the kill. How intently they knelt round the carcass! Took the heart of the beast and in primitive ceremony ate the raw flesh.

He called up the east coast's Shore Village next, a pleasant scene of tribesmen launching a tree trunk canoe from the shore into the surf. Tribespeople came to see them off, shouting and laughing. Then the woman Cleatah walked into the frame. He startled at the sight of her. Leaned in further to observe her more closely. He sat back. Then with godly restraint he shifted to another scene in the upper village where men in a circle chattered amiably as they fashioned their spear tips.

Excellent!

Poseidon magnified the men's work, the tools for flaking spear tips. But his eyes were drawn curiously to one man's pelt vest, beautifully crafted, its front closing of sinew and shell. He magnified once again, and found himself staring at the finely cut muscles of a hunter's upper arm. A bracelet tattoo. A mat of long tangled hair.

Suddenly irritated, he swiped away the image. Stepped outside the energy shell. Regarded its brilliant glow attracting battalions of moths, and shut it down as well. All at once he was there alone in a meadow, the cool dark of a moonless night surrounding him. He dared look up, stunned to be here in outer space unprotected. Alone. Without the protection of technos. He sat down heavily. Crossed his legs like the tribesmen had done. A natural pose to be sure. The grass beneath him was a soft cushion. He leaned back on his elbows. Threw his head back. Closed his eyes and experienced the living silence.

No! Beware the seduction.

He sat up. Stood. Summoned his dome. Lit the light. Called up his bed and laid down. He stayed motionless for a while in the cheerful pod. Remembering the Shore Men. The fur vest, the *tat tat tat* of the rock tools on obsidian. Poseidon smiled as a thought took him. With a wave of his hand he turned off the lights. Through the transparent shield, the stars were bright. He was safe. He was cradled in ultimate technos. Nothing to be ashamed of. *Yet here in the safety and comfort of an invisible bed, Poseidon Ra could still look up and see the stars.*

Shirtless, he sprinted across the plateau, his skin burnished a sunburnt tan. He ran up to a rocky escarpment, heaving boulders in his arms, panting as he climbed the incline.

Talya is correct. There's no benefit to introducing one's self to the tribe as a godlike being. Too much data will be unattainable. Yet there are limitations to remaining cloaked with invisibility and denying all interaction with the people. My solution is unconventional at best, and will likely invite scorn.

In a forest he climbed tall into gnarled branches of trees. Stark naked, he exploded from a large herd of antlered ungulates grazing in a meadow. His hair had grown long and his chin was host to a bushy new beard. *I believe the transformation is as much a state of mind as it is of body, and a constant reliance on technos will be confusing.*

He stood at the door of his safety dome looking westward at a sunset sky, the volcanic peaks of the Central Range, remembering their treachery. Then with a few taps at his wrist, the energy pod flickered momentarily...and disappeared. *At night my muscles complain, but I've determined not to use the phaetron's soothing effects, as I know the unpleasant experience will harden my mind as well as my body.*

He was fast asleep on the hard ground, when the vision of a snake slithering across his ankles shocked him to his feet. Poseidon looked down and saw the flesh and blood creature wriggling away into the shadows. *I will use the phaetron thoughtfully and sparingly.*

He sat, unconsciously swatting insects from his legs, watching the image of male subject 2278 striking a block of obsidian with a granite hammer stone. He picked up his own tools and began to imitate the movements. *I know I must learn to hunt, and hunt well if I want to earn the respect of the tribe. If I fail at this I can never hope to be accepted as one of their number. I'll have no chance of gaining close access to the woman I seek to examine.*

He practiced obsessively, throwing the spear he'd fashioned at chosen targets – a bush, a rock – but he failed and failed and failed. Instead he ran. He was good at that. His muscles hardened. Grew more finely cut. His long wild hair flew out behind him. Oblivious, he'd grown beautiful, graceful and strong.

≼

Now he stood at the edge of the forest, stock-still, armed with his spear, facing the thicket of trees as if it was an opposing army. *It is the day I have been dreading for so long. I must learn to hunt. Small animals and large. All the edible creatures of Gaia...of "Erthe." They are a source of food and pelts. I cannot walk unclothed into the village. If I fail in this final test I have no hope of serious acceptance into the tribe.*

Remembering the hunts he had studied, Poseidon went stalking, slow and crouched into the underbrush, his weapon poised above his shoulder. A hare nibbled intently on a low shrub. He raised his spear. Aimed, hardly breathing. Loosed the spear. Missed. The hare scampered away. *Hare. Wild pig. Giant rat. They evade me. My humiliation is complete. For the first time in my life, I'm growing hungry.*

Poseidon gazed longingly at the white-striped antelere grazing on the leaves of a gum tree. He steadied himself. Closed his eyes and took a single calming breath. Then opened them and sent his spear flying. *Miraculous!* The spear buried itself in the animal's neck. Yet it sprang away. Injured, it ran faster by several times than Poseidon. A proper chase. Over fallen logs. Down stream beds. Out onto the plain, *far* out onto the plain. *Stamina holding. My training bearing fruit. Is the creature slowing, its strength draining away?* The antelere collapsed, and Poseidon stood gasping, arms at his sides staring with disbelief. He walked the final distance, expecting any moment that his downed prey would spring to its feet and bound away.

When finally he knelt above it, it was not yet dead. He pulled an obsidian hand axe from his sling, and holding the antelere's head in one hand, cut its slender throat, feeling every fiber of the sinews and muscles as he sliced, warm blood running down his fingers.

By the light of his campfire, fighting revulsion, Poseidon skinned the beast and later, with gore-covered hands, cut a long strip of meat off its bone. He skewered it on a thin stick and thrust it into the fire, then sat watching morosely as its flesh bubbled and browned. It was only then, smelling the aroma of the roasting meat, that his primitive olfasenses registered the smallest hint of pleasure. Much as he regretted the admission, he found the smell good. *Indeed, delectable.* He tore the meat off the stick and steeling himself, put a bit of it into his mouth. Chewing slowly, he swallowed. It was more than endurable. Pleasurable even, so he took a larger piece and devoured that as well.

And with that, his innards rebelled. Poseidon vomited profusely, disgustingly, and even when the offending stuff was long gone from his stomach he continued retching.

He lay on the ground all night, feverish, his guts cramping, cursing himself. His plan to pass himself off as a primitive seemed ridiculous now. He gazed longingly at his wrist hub, then punched in a healing protocol, but canceled it before it could take effect.

Dawn broke on Poseidon, ragged and sore. But he was proud. *I am a hunter,* he said to the stars.

❧

Poseidon sat back from the river's edge, speaking into his hub, poking at a scab on his leg that had nearly healed, feeling the strange desire to pick it off. *If Zalen could only see me now,* he thought as he said, "No need to worry. I'm healthy. Even a bit stronger than I was."

"Doctor Horus wants to cut the southwest study short," Zalen said.

Poseidon glanced down at his forearm where he'd inscribed a simple bracelet tattoo, one that he'd copied from one of the inland tribes, deciding that he would add another above it. Just past his foot, a thick brown-skinned constrictor was slithering past. Slowly, carefully he grabbed his spear and stood. "Negative. Tell her the GRP Protocol is crucial. All the western tribes should be included."

"She's complaining about your stat-comm blackout," Zalen said.

"Not my problem, Captain." Poseidon watched the snake moving quickly away. He took aim and threw the spear, effortlessly impaling his prey. "Not yours either."

✥

Poseidon trotted effortlessly at a pace across the vast plain. His limbs stuck through the holes of an antelere tunic and trousers. On his feet – hare pelt fur boots. His tools and weapons, hung from shoulder and waist on slings and carriers. *After repeated failures I finally relented and using the phaetron, made my fur and leather garments softly pliable. And I've stopped bathing. No longer does my body odor interest biting insects, and my natural "fragrance" allows me to move closer in among the animal population. This makes hunting easier. I am almost ready.*

SEVENTEEN

H
E ARRIVED ON the coast of the Eastern Sea, and found himself as spellbound as he had been on his first sight of the Marsean ocean. Behind him was a range of low, rocky outcroppings, and on the plain between the sea and the rocks he spotted a grazing herd of magnificent, four-legged, proud headed creatures he remembered as "horse."

He lingered there for several days to watch the beasts which numbered more than forty, with most of the females tending skinny-legged but otherwise perfectly formed young. He hid himself in the tall grass to witness a birth, and was dumbfounded by the speed with which the newborn climbed to its feet and took its place among the herd. He relented, and filled his phaetron's memory bank with copious data regarding the horses, sensing it was valuable. That this creature might be of some use to the primitives at a later date. Honestly, he felt a tug in his chest as he watched the horses thunder in their numbers across the grasslands.

But it was time for him to leave them.

Poseidon walked south toward the edge of the great plateau and the steep cliffs of the land mass's eastern coast – his destination. From his vantage point on the headlands he could look down and see the Shore Village. Located on a "ledge" of land – a narrow ridge perhaps fifty feet above the beach was the settlement – huts of mud and straw – and villagers working in their terraced gardens. Some of their canoes lay untended on the shore below.

He recalled for the hundredth time his pretense – a solitary traveler from a distant village, all of his clan slaughtered in a raid – and repeated several of the phrases of a rudimentary language common to several tribes, among them the Shore People. Any blunders he made he'd ascribe to differences in local dialect. He stood from his perch and heaved a long and hopeful sigh.

It was time to move.

❧

He tramped along the headlands searching for the least precarious route down to the beach north of the village. He assumed his most robust posture, making sure his tools and weapons were slung around his body in keeping with Talya's images of a primitive tribesman. He hoped his appearance and odor were appropriately unkempt.

Thus he made his way south along the coast.

Up ahead he could see several women with small children, all engaged in gathering sea animals from the shore in nets. Once he was close enough for the women to recognize that he was not one of their own he stopped, stood in place and opened his palms toward them to show he held no weapons. One of the children made a dash at him but was caught up by one of the women. They were now standing and staring openly at him with moderate alarm. One woman broke from the group, and herding the children before her climbed the diagonal steps up to the village.

Poseidon stayed where he was, trying to remain dignified and non-threatening with smiles and waves. It was not long before a grim looking delegation – a knot of five men armed with stone tipped spears and clubs – appeared and approached him directly. He could see several other groups fanning out along the village's

199

perimeters and either end of the beach, clearly meant to determine if he was alone or had come with others for an ambush.

Heart pounding, Poseidon stood his ground, open-handed but attempting to exude manly strength and fearlessness. He remained silent while they talked among themselves and waited – as custom demanded in such a situation – for them to initiate communication.

Finally the leader, a tall, well-muscled man of middling years, stepped forward and stood chest-to-chest, eye-to-eye with Poseidon, facing down the "stranger." He held the tribesman's gaze and consciously slowed his breathing so that he might appear far calmer than he actually felt. The stand-off seemed to last an eternity, the Shoreman's muscles tensing, Poseidon's fingers poised to throw up a phaetronic shield around himself if attacked. Finally the leader drew several sharp sniffs and screwed up his face in a grimace. A word or two was spoken to the group and suddenly they were all laughing. Indeed, laughing at Poseidon. He realized the reason.

I smell unpleasant to them, and a joke about my hygiene has been made at my expense! He was unsure if it was appropriate to laugh along with the delegation, but the situation *was* amusing, so he joined in. Poseidon's laughter did not stimulate any aggression. In fact it made everyone laugh harder. Feeling more confident he sniffed the pit of his arm, then made a terrible face. They all roared.

By this time many more of the tribespeople had gathered, wondering at the commotion on the beach. Poseidon drew a breath and tapped his chest. "*Eng sa Poseidon*," he said loudly. The laughter ceased. "Poseidon," he repeated, and with a questioning gesture requested the leader identify himself.

"*Eng sa Brannan*," he said, and turned to the delegation.

One by one they called out their names.

"*Eng sa Heydra*," said the oldest man.

"*Elkon*."

Then Poseidon saw the virile young man from Talya's report, #2287, step forward. "*Boah*," he forcefully announced.

Suddenly from behind Boah the fifth tribesman stepped out with an adult brown wolf at his side, the hackles spiked high along the back of its neck. But this was no man the wolf was protecting. She was tall, nearly as tall as Poseidon, and she was as lovely as a Terresian year was long. The dark hair fell in soft curls on her sculpted shoulders flanking high, rounded breasts under the skins she wore. Her complexion gleamed with youth, and the gaze of her rich brown eyes was sharp and confident. The limbs were long, muscles full but shapely.

"*Eng sa Cleatah*," she said.

Poseidon faltered. Suddenly confronting the very individual he had traveled the continent to see was itself startling, but the look and presence of the woman – despite his earlier viewing of her – was astonishing. He forced himself to tear his eyes away from her, as such interest in a female would be thought highly suspect, even aggressive. And the wolf had never taken his eyes from the stranger.

As the people crowded round to accompany Poseidon up the stone stairs to the village he noticed about them an almost complete absence of rank body odor. Many appeared freshly washed. Talya had failed to mention this inclination of the Shore People towards cleanliness, but her omission had happily provided him with a natural and humorous introduction to the tribe.

He'd carefully studied Talya's images of the village environs and artifacts, but in the same way a phaetronic image of a forest or a mountain range never imparted the true impact of the place itself, the mud and thatch enclave on this broad ledge of the plateau was far more fascinating than its three-dimensional portrayal. As Poseidon came into the village surrounded by his welcoming party the sun was bright, bleaching the varied earth tones to a homogenous pale tan. Yet there was a mysterious quality here, and beauty to be found in the simplest and most unexpected places. A basket that sat outside the door of a hut was woven with intricate artfulness out of four subtly different colors of reed. An obsidian spear tip flashing momentarily in the sunlight hinted at artistry. The murmur of the villagers' voices as they had their first sight of the stranger sounded strangely melodic. Wolf mothers lay sunning themselves lazily, watching their pups rough-and-tumble in play. And the people themselves – this was the most astonishing of all – the people were beautiful to his eyes. Primitively dressed as they were, rugged and tan and rough, they all – every man, woman and child – exuded vitality. A healthy fire shone in their eyes.

When everyone had gathered, a man from the welcoming party who had called himself Boah, began to speak. He was the youngest of the four males, and powerfully built. Poseidon now recognized him from Talya's data as #2287, a young hunter of the tribe, his status recently elevated by a success during a daring and dangerous kill. He was the man who'd begun showing sexual interest in Cleatah.

Boah had been chosen by the elders to introduce the stranger to his people. It had been an interesting choice, Poseidon reasoned, as he himself would in the coming months be tested as a hunter, would seek status in the male hierarchy of the tribe, and most certainly come into conflict and competition with the man who was even now presenting him to this society. Poseidon's grasp of the language was still imperfect, but when the people broke into gales of laughter, he understood that Boah had poked fun at this malodorous stranger. Poseidon grinned, feeling foolish but unaccountably happy.

EIGHTEEN

CLIMBING UP TO the Great Plateau above the village, Sheeva bounding ahead of her, Cleatah was lost in thoughts of the stranger. That morning on their way to the plateau she had stopped to stand in the shade of Jandor's hut and watch the seated circle of men carving arrow shafts, her eyes falling upon Poseidon among them. His head was down, and he worked with his flint knife on a hard wood branch.

This stranger carries within him a secret, as I do, she'd thought. Poseidon looked as the other men did, but something was different. She liked the way he looked, though could not say why. He was no taller than the other men, and not as brawny. He was more clumsy with his body than the males of the tribe, and could not dance. But he worked very well with his hands, was able to weave the slenderest threads of the lota plant into fine netting used to harvest brill from the sea. She had secretly watched him one day as he had examined the muscle inside a small, double-shelled sea creature. No one beside herself looked that closely or for that long at so common an object. In many small ways Poseidon was very ignorant. Maybe the customs of his people and his language being different from her own could explain this.

His story was a sad one. His inland people had been slaughtered by a hostile neighboring tribe while he and a small party were hunting. Not a man, woman or child had been left alive in the village. It had been decided by the survivors that they must go in search of new families and friends, but that they would be more acceptable to a tribe if they were one man alone. That was why he had come by himself to the Shore Village.

Poseidon would smile and joke when the others did. He was kind to children and never stared too long at a woman, unless she was very old. But he seemed to take no real pleasure in his food, nor celebration in the blessings of the bounty. He had refused to eat of the sweetest white flesh of Cleatah's favorite long-tailed shellfish, claiming his tribe did not eat animals from the sea. She would watch him at a feast after a large kill, and though he had eaten his share, and even chewed on a second piece that was offered by one of his hunting companions, she could see strangeness in his eyes. A feeling with no name. Was it disgust? Of course that made no sense. He was a man like any other.

Still, she was sure he carried a secret.

Poseidon had looked up from his carving and saw Cleatah looking at him. His eyes stayed fixed on her and paid no attention to Sheeva pacing impatiently at her feet. She saw that he was studying her face the way she herself would examine the inside of a flower. Lamarak, sitting next to Poseidon, had poked him with his elbow and gestured to the bowl of pitch. Poseidon looked quickly away from her, grabbed the pitch bowl and handed it to Lamarak. *Too quickly, as if he did not wish to be caught,* she thought. The stranger with his secret was interested in her.

She spent much time thinking of Poseidon as well.

Cleatah had moved out of the shadows to pass directly by the circle of men before going on her way. They each called out their usual pleasant but reserved greetings. Now that her mother and father were dead no one strayed too close to her, for her differentness made them uneasy. Much as she liked being left to herself, now she found the stranger's curiosity warming. *Poseidon.* Different, like she was. Hiding a secret.

She would make it her business to discover what that secret was.

NINETEEN

HE'D THROWN OPEN the hide that covered the door of his hut – a small but private place Poseidon had been given on the far edge of the village. The sky was an ominous grey, and only a feeble light illuminated his bed of skins. He couldn't shake the state of gloom he was feeling.

It was, he reminded himself, the day of the hunt, something he'd dreaded for months.

He'd had little time for close observation of the woman, Cleatah, and no luck increasing his worth among the tribesmen, a circumstance that would make his approach to her possible. His hunting skills had been adequate enough to deflect suspicion, but he continued to blunder in small ways and manners, sometimes causing great hilarity, especially among the women. Today he would hunt with the men again, and he found himself dreading it. He still found no perceptible good in the act of taking an animal's life.

And Boah had continued to challenge him at every turn. Poseidon walked a fine line in this competition, and he could not afford to make an enemy of him. But failing to best Boah would ruin any chance of improving his status in the tribe. Boah regularly showed sexual interest in Cleatah, though it appeared that she'd gently but firmly rejected his advances. Poseidon was still convinced that she was observing himself with as much interest, and secrecy, as he was her. She appeared to be everything that Talya described, and more, respected by all and a natural leader of men as well as women. Her presence was powerful.

Just yesterday he'd been waiting to be given his meal portion and became aware of someone standing behind him. Without seeing the person, he knew it was Cleatah. He'd recognized her identity by her unusual scent – the smell of skin and hair baked by the sun, and flavored with a rich sweet spice – a fragrance only she bore. *Perhaps it's what she washes with,* he thought. He'd followed her one day to where one of the rivers met the sea and watched as she'd taken a brown root from her sack, smashed it against the rocks and adding water, made a white lather from it. With this she washed her long dark hair...*and her body...*

He caught himself in this unscientific musing, then stood, reminding himself of his purpose – to distinguish himself in the next several days in order to accelerate this study.

He dressed in hide trousers, tunic and knee-high boots, then began to strap on the tools and weapons he would need for the hunt.

"Poseidon!" It was Boah outside his door. His rival had recently built a small hut close by. With several other unmated men and their wolves setting up camps in the area, it was becoming known as the stags' village. Poseidon found himself bemused to be thought of in such a way. "Better hurry," called Boah, "or they'll leave without you."

"If only they would," Poseidon whispered to himself, then strode out the door into the gloomy morning.

⁊

The hunt had proven frustrating. While his stamina had held up admirably on the day-long tracking of the buron herd, when the prey had been singled out, the wolves harassing it till it was worn down, and the long-handled spears hurled on the run at the fleeing beast, his weapon had missed by an embarrassingly large margin. Heydra's and Elkon's spears had found their mark, but Boah's spear had pierced the buron's neck and was proclaimed, with much backslapping, the killing blow. Now the men in the hunting party – the wolves in a barely controlled blood frenzy – were arguing loudly about whether to take down a second buron, or simply return to the village with their kill. Wretched with disappointment, Poseidon moved away into the bush to relieve himself.

The wild thing was suddenly upon him, and before he had time to think, he was fighting for his life. The beast had sprung from behind and knocked him to the ground before he saw it was a man – red-eyed and snarling, spitting flecks of white foam from his terrible mouth. And ungodly strong! They rolled and grappled and grunted – the foul stench of the creature's breath nauseating. But as the thing began to claw at his eyes, some force – an instinct so ancient as to be primeval – welled up from the depths of him, and all that was civilized fell away, supplanted by a vicious will to survive.

Despite his strength the wildman was strangely clumsy, and once Poseidon felt the power surging in his limbs he sought to flip the man on his back. He'd almost succeeded when a knee rammed into his groin. He screamed and levitated in agony, falling back down and curling into a ball. The man sprang, but Poseidon rolled, leaving his attacker sprawled face-down in the dirt. Rallying, he leapt on the man's back, grabbing him from behind. The man struggled, writhed, bucked and with inhuman strength turned, coming up with a rock in hand that swung in an arc toward Poseidon's head. He stopped it a moment before it met its mark. The rock dropped to the ground, and Poseidon's fisted hands pummeled the man's face.

By now the hunters had found the fight and stood in a circle around them, screaming for Poseidon's victory. A terrible waking nightmare, he could hear their shouts, the wolves growling, feel the pain still throbbing between his legs, see the hideous, snarling creature pinned under him… The man's hands suddenly clamped around Poseidon's throat, all fury, seething hatred. The grip was vice-like and in moments he was fighting for breath. His hands found his attacker's neck, thumbs on the windpipe. He knew in that moment he not only had to kill this man, he *wanted* to kill him.

He fought for consciousness as the man squeezed harder, but saw his advantage was position. He was on top – his body's weight behind his fingers. Suddenly inspired, he rocked far back, then forward with momentum – and with a force that surprised him – began crushing the man's throat. The fingers around his own neck began to relax as the man's thrashing increased. The face slowly turned from brilliant red to blue, the mouth open in a silent scream, the foam drying on the parched, bleeding lips. Then with a soft, sickening crack under his thumbs he felt the man's body fall limp. But he did not let go his grip, just kept pressing and pressing and pressing. It was finally the odor of release from the dead man's bowels that brought Poseidon to his senses.

Still, it took four men to pull him off the body.

He was vaguely aware of the hunters' excited hugs, laughter, backslapping. But when several of them began examining the corpse he felt the powerful instinct that had surged through his body to save his life begin to drain out of him. His knees jellied and he staggered away so the hunters would not see him retching.

He had killed a man – killed another human being. Dressed in the skins of animals, long wild hair and beard… *What is becoming of me?* he wondered miserably. *What have I done?* He would never ever tell another person, or even record into his phaetron what he'd felt as he'd choked the life out of the poor creature who had attacked him.

It was determined by a set of telltale teeth marks festering on the man's arm that he had been bitten by an animal which carried a dreadful sickness. Once bitten, a person – no matter how healthy, no matter what medicines were given – died a gruesome, raving death. In their tribe such a person was put out of his misery before the excruciating pain began, before the madness set in, before the foaming at the mouth turned him into a monster that children ran screaming from. Once the discovery of the illness had been made Poseidon was solemnly examined to see if he had been bitten by the man, and all breathed easier when he was found to be bruised and scraped but clean of teeth marks. Before beginning the trek back the men piled dead leaves and branches on the body and set it on fire, not wishing their wolves or scavenging animals to feed on the sick man's flesh and themselves be poisoned.

In celebration of their new hunter's triumph – which though unspoken was seen as a kind of initiation – the men had decided to hunt for a second buron. They now therefore staggered cheerfully under the weight of two carcasses and were forced to stop more frequently than usual to rest. He dreaded these respites, for then he had time to think. Under the strain of shouldering the heavy pole all he could do was breathe and concentrate on putting one foot before the other without stumbling. But when he stopped he could suddenly recall the fetid stench of his attacker's breath, the fear that animated his limbs, and the violent power which had overwhelmed the civilized man he believed himself to be.

He had studied the Erthan animals, and only one fought the same of their species to the death. *Human beings*. Occasionally the lower *Pithekos* might murder another, and even devour a helpless infant. But all same-species battles – usually over territory or a female – ended long before death. One individual was driven away leaving the winner dominant. No other species fought and killed in anger. Certainly no Terresian in his right mind...

He knew he must banish all such thoughts before the hunting

party returned to the village. He had defended himself against a mindless, raging creature – hardly a man. *The choice was kill or be killed, and I simply chose survival.* He decided that if he repeated the phrase again and again he would come to believe it, but was uncertain if he could muster the air of celebration that his fellow hunters were exhibiting. It was right and natural in their way of thinking that for Poseidon to have survived unscathed he must have been blessed by many benevolent spirits. Thanks and rejoicing for his life would certainly flavor their homecoming feast.

Somehow he would have to live with himself.

TWENTY

GREAT MOTHER IS *blessing our celebration this night,* Cleatah thought as she watched the raucous firelight gathering. Children were shrieking with glee and chasing each other on the outer fringes of the village. The women had cooked half a buron, and she had provided special flavorful plants ground into sea salt to season it. The men were all gathered around Poseidon, urging him to recount once again his heroic fight to the death. He smiled as he spoke, but it did not seem to her that the smile was true. A man of her tribe who had saved his own life with such bravery and accomplishment would have been basking in glory, dancing round the bonfire, drinking great quantities of kav, perhaps taking a woman to his bed.

But Poseidon only pretended joy. She was sure of it. Now Elkon had taken up the story for the newcomer, demonstrating the final moments of the battle – Poseidon's hands around his opponent's throat, strangling him. In the flickering light, though no one else saw – for they all watched Elkon – Poseidon's smile was frozen unnaturally on his face. *He is a strange man,* she thought, *with more differentness than what comes from a distant tribe's customs.* Boah, too, looked stiff. His face was a rigid grimace.

With a great whoop the retelling ended, and the men returned to their family groups as the feast was served. She could see that several tribesmen invited Poseidon to their circles, but when the crowd dispersed he stood alone. She moved quickly to his side and with a few swift gestures settled herself beside him to eat the meal. He seemed surprised, though not displeased. Always before when they had been near each other he had had little to say and turned his eyes away, out of respect. But tonight Poseidon was an important man, no longer a stranger to the village. His stature had grown from that one brave act. He had earned the men's respect and the right to talk with the women if he chose to. And she had made sure it was to her this night that he would be speaking.

A bowl piled high with steaming meat and mush made from a mealy garden root was placed in front of Poseidon. He turned to her and saw that she had not yet been served. Without speaking he slid his bowl in front of her. She stiffened, looking around to see if any villager had noticed, but thankfully no one had. Despite his victory today, and increased stature among the men, what he had just done was a serious mistake in manners: a man did not serve a woman first unless he meant to mate with her. She was sure it was Poseidon's ignorance of such things. Carefully she slid the bowl back in front of him, just before the server returned, bringing another bowl and laying it down before her.

"Did I blunder?" Poseidon whispered after the server moved on.

"Not unless you wish to take me to your bed." She spoke quietly and directly, but hoped he could hear the smile in her voice.

Poseidon grunted in reply, cleared his throat noisily, then crammed a piece of meat in his mouth and began chewing. She did the same and so, side by side, they ate in silence for several minutes. Finally she spoke.

"How is it your skin is so soft?"

"My skin?"

She turned and saw Poseidon staring down at his bare arm with so bewildered a look that she almost laughed. A moment later he sagged with what seemed like relief, finally understanding the question.

"My skin." He patted the front of his fur tunic. Then another look of confusion crossed his face. "My skin..." he repeated stupidly. "Soft..."

"How did you dress it?" she prompted. "What did you use? I have never seen a pelt so pliable."

"I...I..."

Was it possible he was blushing, she wondered, or was it the firelight?

"It was a gift," he finally blurted. "From my sister. She was a master tanner before...before..."

"I am sorry, "Cleatah said quietly, placing a hand on Poseidon's arm. "It hurts you to speak of your family."

"No, no," he said. "I can speak of them. They rest in Erthe's bosom, cradled by the Great Mother, no longer in pain."

"No longer in pain," she said, repeating the familiar blessing. So there *were* some rituals the two tribes shared. "What was your sister's name?"

He paused again, though for longer than seemly, then answered. "Talya."

"May the Spirit bless the memory of Talya," Cleatah echoed.

Now their eyes met and held steady, but this time it was she who turned her gaze away. She had glimpsed something beyond her understanding. A knowing that defied all of Poseidon's ignorant ways. *This* was his secret, she realized all at once. He was hiding a part of his mind! She suddenly wished she could look through his eyes into his spirit having partaken of the sacred mushroom. Surely he would be unable to hide from the clarity of vision that the mushroom provided.

All at once the thin, high sound of a reed flute pierced her mind and brought her back to the night, the feast and the mysterious man beside her. The villagers were swaying with pleasure as the tones filled their senses with delight.

She smiled, then whispered to Poseidon, "Do you like the sounds that Sanson's instrument makes?"

"I do. I have never heard anything like it before. We played only drums in my village."

"As we did here…until I made the instrument Sanson plays."

"You *made* the instrument?"

She struggled for the right words. "I found it. It is a simple reed. I was gathering medicine by the river. I heard the wind flowing through a piece of dried reed. I picked it up. There were holes rotted through in three places. I put my mouth on one end and blew. I put my fingers over the holes and different noises came out. I brought it back to the village and showed my cousin Sanson, and he learned to make these beautiful sounds."

"You *invented* the instrument," Poseidon said.

"Invented?"

"As you invent medicinal uses for the plants you pick."

"Is this a word used in your village?" she asked, perplexed. "We have no such word here."

"Yes, it is a word my tribe uses. Ones who 'invent' are important people. The most important people."

Now it was her turn to blush. It was a relief when the servers began to clear the feast away. This man was not what he seemed to be. And as she had sought to peer into his spirit to understand him better, now she knew for certain that Poseidon was gazing into hers. *What if he learns my secret? All my secrets?* she thought but did not say.

And just as suddenly, she knew that nothing in the world would make her happier.

TWENTY-ONE

THE SHORE PEOPLE gathered once every year to hunt the wild bull. It was a new custom, celebrating the recent coming of the great herds onto the tribal hunting grounds. They had always killed small animals to supplement their food from the sea, but the arrival of hoards of buron, kassel and antelere had meant great abundance for everyone. The men had had to adapt to hunting larger animals, the tool and weapons-making revised, and the women learned to cook the tougher flesh. No one except Luna had complained – she had lost her medicines that grew in the hunting grounds.

This day Poseidon joined the people in their trek up the path behind the village to the Great Plateau. It was a joyful occasion, and no one seemed to mind hauling the quantities of wood, cooking utensils and musical instruments they would need to make camp and prepare for the feast at day's end. As soon as everyone had assembled at the chosen site, the tribe's twelve strongest hunters – he was not among them – had been blessed by the elders. Then armed only with staves and nooses, they set out to locate the buron herd. Their first task would be to cull from it a single, long-horned bull and drive it back to camp.

But before they'd taken their leave he was witness to a very public courtship display. Boah had made certain he was standing in front of Cleatah as he prepared himself for the hunt. He never took his eyes off her as he rubbed onto his muscular chest, arms and thighs the nut oil that guaranteed strength, and tied on necklaces and bracelets of tiny shells worn by all the hunters on such a day for luck. Poseidon observed Cleatah's reaction to this open display of sexuality and noted that while she did not avert her eyes from Boah altogether – for that would have signaled a humiliating insult – she never quite met his smoldering gaze.

Now the hunters had gone, and he and the remaining villagers began preparing for their return with the bull. A large ring was delineated with cut wooden stakes and skins hung on them. Into this the bellowing, stamping animal would be driven. It was explained to him that with all the villagers watching from the sidelines, several of the most agile boys, dressed in gaudy costumes, would join the hunters in the ring, tumbling and shouting in wild antics to distract the bull while the hunters attempted to slip their nooses around the beast's neck and all four feet. Once subdued it would not be killed outright, but tethered to four tall stakes. Only after the sun set behind the distant western mountains would the animal be ritually slaughtered as the Shore People invoked the Great Mother's blessings. The sacrifice would then be celebrated with a bonfire, music, dance and prayer in thanks for her bounty.

It wasn't until he was pounding one of the stakes for the bull ring into the ground that he recognized his feeling of satisfaction and relief that Cleatah had rebuked Boah's seduction. But this admission troubled him. *Why should it matter that a tribesman pursued this woman?* Surely Talya's egg harvesting – if Cleatah was finally chosen for the genomic procedure – could proceed even if she was mated with the young man.

A second unsettling thought rattled Poseidon's mind. What right did the Terresians have to tamper with these people at all? *They were human beings*, he had come to realize in the months he had lived among them. *Really no different than Terresians.* He wasn't certain when he had ceased thinking of them solely as test subjects.

He had been slowly and subtly increasing his contact with Cleatah, and he had to admit that she charmed him. Her intelligence was beyond question, but it was the easy way she dealt with him – confidently, as an equal, and with a gentle teasing about his clumsy ways – that most endeared her to him. It was wonderful to be treated as other men were. It had become tiresome being a Terresian hero. *Cleatah, beautiful Cleatah...* He stopped his hammering, suddenly shaken by the outrageous and inappropriate sentiments. He threw himself back into the task at hand and forcibly banished all renegade thoughts.

The makeshift shelters had been erected and decorated, the wood piled high for the bonfire, the ring and four-pole bull tether completed. Everyone was waiting with good-humored impatience for the thrilling moment when the bull, pursued by the hunters, would come racing across the plain and the spectacle would begin. Before they had appeared, however, thunder began rumbling, and all could see storm clouds gathered in the distance, and forked lightning striking the ground in numerous places.

As they worked the people talked about the distant storm, some of them wishing for the badly needed rain, others happy that the downpour was moving away and would not drench their celebration. No one realized until too late that the thunderous noise that slowly grew in intensity and never seemed to end was not, in fact, coming from the storm. By the time they felt the ground vibrating under their feet and saw the great cloud of dust moving in their direction, the first of the stampeding horses were upon them.

Chaos was instantaneous – shrieks and cries of pain and terror as the moving wall of wild beasts tore through the makeshift encampment. Had the horses been able to gallop past unhindered, the episode – damaging as it was – would have ended as quickly as it began. But the animals – confused by obstacles and panicking people – scattered, sending the rampage in every direction. In a frenzy they trampled cooking hearths, flattened tent poles. They reared in wild-eyed fury at the men that were stabbing at them with spears. Tribesmen shouted and waved their arms, anything to scare the animals away from the women, children and helpless elders.

Battling dust and fury Poseidon grabbed whomever he could, pushing them into larger groups, encouraging them to cling together. The bigger the human island, the more the horses avoided them. He grabbed and pushed, sidestepped panicked animals. He found himself searching desperately for sight of Cleatah. *Where was she!* He stumbled over a woman's mangled body. *Was it Cleatah?* Screams of horses, people, collapsing tents. Dust. Blood.

A child stood crying…standing in the path of an oncoming beast. No! Poseidon dashed for the boy, crossing the horse's path to tackle the child a moment before the animal thundered past, sheltering the tiny body from the barrage of pebbles thrown up from its hooves.

He lifted his head from the curled figure of the child. It was over. Dust was beginning to settle. Moans and anguished cries could be heard from all parts of the camp. He released the boy and within seconds his father, Dyon, was beside them. He embraced Poseidon in tearful thanks, then lifted the boy in his arms and moved away in a daze. He stood then and began searching for Cleatah. Many villagers were injured, several appeared dead. *Where was she?*

Suddenly he stopped, feet rooted to the ground, his eyes drawn to the bullring. It had, unbelievably, been left intact during the stampede and a single horse had been trapped inside. Unable to find its way out again it now trotted round and round within the enclosure, snorting furiously, tossing its head, searching for the disappeared herd. Poseidon could not tear his gaze from the sight of the proud-headed beast so confined, its movements controlled by the ring's perimeter, its gait slowed and regulated.

Suddenly he saw, as if in a vision, *the future* illuminated before his eyes. A design began to unfold. In the next moment his vision was shattered as the trapped horse took sudden flight, leaping over the top of the ring and galloping away to his freedom. Poseidon watched it disappear in a cloud of dust...

Then he saw her – Cleatah. She stood, stunned and rigid but apparently unhurt. Sheeva, too, was unscathed but yapped about her legs in frantic confusion. He saw her reach down to calm the wolf at the very moment their eyes met. A wave of the profoundest emotion swept over him, through him. At the same moment, they heard the piteous cries of a woman. The elderly Ilato was lying in a swirl of dust. With the wolf trailing at her feet Cleatah went and knelt beside her.

As he hurried to assist a pair of bloodied tribesmen he wondered how, in so short a space of time, his perfectly ordered life of ScienTechnos and reason had come to this antithetical turning. *Was it a new faculty he had acquired? An acknowledgement of instinct, impulse, intuition, a dexterity of mind.* If so, he decided, it was a most glorious gift.

He opened his heart and accepted it.

From where she knelt tending the injured elder, Cleatah recalled the moment just before she and Poseidon had found each another in the wreckage of the corral. He had been staring with what she perceived – strange as it seemed – as *longing* at the last of the creatures that had destroyed their temporary village. She tried, but could not imagine what he had been thinking.

She called one of the boys, told him to fetch her some willow branches for splints, but as she turned her attention back to Ilato's broken arm – willing herself not to search the grounds for the reassuring sight of Poseidon – she finally admitted to herself her fascination, her longing for this impenetrable stranger. She vowed silently that nothing in the world would keep her from knowing him.

≈

When the hunters and wolves returned, they found the ceremonial village in shambles, the women weeping for the dead. And they had come empty-handed, unable to find the buron herd, as though it had vanished from the plateau altogether. The two tragedies together were seen as a terrible omen, yet no one knew what offense they had committed against Great Mother to exact so serious a punishment from her.

But there was no doubt they had committed a serious offense.

TWENTY-TWO

FOR WEEKS AFTERWARDS the elders sat together day and night, only emerging from their meeting for the burials of the dead. It was a solemn time for all. Children were forbidden to play and the women, normally jovial and talkative as they went about their daily chores, were largely silent. The men, every one of them, believed they had suffered a loss of their masculine powers. They had been helpless against the horses and unsuccessful as hunters. As the days went on it had become impossible for them to even look each other in the eye.

Poseidon was quiet and appeared to be brooding much as the other men were. But his mind was afire as he sought a graceful excuse to absent himself from the village and carry out his plan. On the first full moon after the terrible events he made his way to the elders' compound and humbly asked for admittance.

"I wish to leave the village for a short while," he told them. "There are rituals I need to perform at this time."

"What rituals?" demanded Elkon irritably. He was the youngest of the group, only recently having been admitted to the circle and still unsure of himself.

"It is a ceremony for the dead – the ancestors of my own tribe. But of course I will include the Shore People in my prayers. I would stay here and perform the rituals, but I am afraid I might offend someone with my ways which are… different."

"How long will you go for...if we give you leave?" asked Heydra. He was said to be one of the tribe's oldest men, but he had a sweet round face almost free of wrinkles.

Poseidon hesitated. He had no way of knowing how long he would need to accomplish his goals. This might be his only opportunity to go, but he could not be sure if he would be welcomed back if he stayed away too long.

"I will return by the half moon," he told them.

"That is a long time for rituals," Elkon said, more than a little suspicious.

Poseidon turned his palms upward in silent supplication. Further explanation would only complicate things.

The elders argued among themselves for a while longer, Elkon poking sullenly at the fire with a long stick, Brannan never taking his eyes from Poseidon, as though he was trying to pierce the outer shell that hid the stranger's secrets.

"Let him go," said Heydra finally. "Poseidon has shown himself a worthy man. We should respect his rituals."

"He should be taking part in *our* rituals," said Elkon, "if he wants to be part of this tribe."

"He saved the child's life with no thought for his own safety," argued Brannan. "I say let him go, but for one quarter of the moon's cycle."

At last a consensus was reached and Poseidon was given leave to go.

"You will come back to us in seven days then," Brannan said.

"You honor me with your trust," Poseidon replied, feeling strangely humbled before these primitive people. "This is my home now. I will return in seven days."

He searched for Cleatah, wishing to see her before his departure, but she was nowhere to be found. And though his stature had been increased further since the day of the stampede, he nevertheless felt uncomfortable asking anyone of her whereabouts.

TWENTY-THREE

SHE COULD NOT be found because she had returned alone to the plateau in search of the mushroom. The dead had been buried, but despite the many prayers and properly made offerings, the Shore People were suffering. *What had they done to deserve such punishment from Great Mother?* Cleatah wondered. In such times she found wisdom in the mushroom, so she'd woken before dawn and set out for the plateau.

She thought to seek Poseidon out and tell him of her plans, but hesitated for so long she abandoned the thought. He, more than the tribe's miseries, filled her mind as she made the climb, feeling the sun's first heat on her back, and set out across the plain towards the forest.

Now having eaten several of the caps she sat beside the river in utter stillness, silently calling to herself the visions and the words to give them shape. *She saw the great buron herd grazing on the distant plain. Their movements were languid and the grasses, lush and greener than she had ever seen them, swayed in rolling waves. As the enormous bellowing bull moved among the cows with their large liquid eyes, their heads turned slowly, slowly in his direction. 'No punishment,' came the words on the wind, the words as a chant. 'No punishment...' The herd was intact, the sacred bull still within the tribe's grasp. There had been no punishment intended by the spirit of Erthe. The bull lowered his head and began to feast on a stand of sacred mushrooms. His handsome head and powerful shoulders began to soften and melt, becoming the face of Poseidon, clean-shaven as Cleatah had never seen him before. It was a strong and beautiful face, the shapely lips moving, speaking her name – "Cleatah, Cleatah" – speaking her name with love. And all at once she was weeping, for the future was bright, full of promise and joy. Then the clouds swirled and parted, and there on a sunny shore she saw herself reclining, draped only in silvery seaweed, hundreds of little children at her feet, some bathing in the water, some playing in the sand. And they were all her children, beautiful children – girls and boys – and their eyes were grey.*

Their eyes were sparkling grey...

TWENTY-FOUR

USING HIS PHAETRON it had taken Poseidon no time at all to locate the herd of wild horses. They had moved north along the coastal plateau and stopped to graze near the low rocky mountain ridge where he'd seen them before. Climbing to the highest point he was delighted to find almost exactly the pattern of rocks necessary to begin his endeavor. A semi-circular stone canyon had been naturally carved in the range, and now using several of the hub's functions he split, moved and levitated several boulders to finish enclosing the circle, all but a narrow-necked opening at the front of it.

Satisfied with his work he descended from the ridge and sat hidden in the tall grasses quietly replaying previously recorded data on the herd. He watched them with renewed interest and a certain respect, having experienced the deadliest aspect of these magnificent beasts. He knew what he wished to accomplish – *to ride on the back of a horse* – something that had never been done by any man before him. He realized, however, that he had planned only the first step: separating one of the animals from the herd and guiding it into the stone canyon.

The canyon was an approximation of the bullring in which he had seen the single horse trotting round and round, and had been inspiration for what might be the most foolhardy act of his life. He whispered into his hub, "*The problem I face – one that worked steadily on my mind as I traveled to this place – is whether to use the technos at my disposal in my capturing and taming of the horse, or to use my knowledge, wits and physical strength alone. I realize that if I cannot manage without the aid of ultra science, the exercise will be of no use to the Shore People. However, my time is limited. I fear if I overstay my absence from the village I will lose the advantage I have recently gained. More importantly, I cannot afford to scare the herd away with what will surely be my clumsy attempts at separating one of these beasts from the others. I think I must therefore use the phaetron, though I will use it as sparingly as possible.*"

Carefully and slowly, Poseidon stepped out of the long grasses and revealed himself to the herd. Many heads were raised from their grazing, and several of the females with young ones nudged them in the opposite direction. There was some whinnying and snorting and pawing of the ground. In all, however, they seemed unperturbed and not particularly prone to aggression towards him.

In his observations he had singled out the horse he wished to use for his experiment – a youngish female, not terribly large, white with brown spots, her shaggy mane and tail solid white. She seemed spirited but not especially bold or skittish. A graceful whorl on her forehead appealed to Poseidon, and he thought the animal especially pretty. He named her Arrow. Though she grazed on the outskirts of the herd nearest him and close to a mature female – likely her mother – it appeared that Arrow had recently separated from the mare, for the elder horse was now suckling a new foal.

With a final tinge of regret that it was necessary, he set the phaetron on a mild 'narcotizing' setting and widened the beam to encompass the entire herd. At once the horses' heads that were not lowered in grazing dropped into the position of sleep. Several babies who had not yet learned the art of sleeping on their feet collapsed to the ground and rested in that position. Having no experience using this procedure in such an unusual circumstance, he could not be sure if the animal he wished to cull would become too lethargic to manipulate, and whether once Arrow was removed from the beam's influence he would be able to control her movements at all.

As he approached, he recalled a scene he had observed being played out again and again within the world of the horse – mothers training their young in the art of socialization and hierarchy. It was done with the posture and angling of her body in relation to her offspring, with eyes insistent and directing, silently instructing the student in the correct behavior, and banishing the animal when it disobeyed.

He was close to the herd now, and despite the phaetron's control of them his heart began to pound in fear. The sight of the horses and the almost overpowering smell of them reminded him of the awesome power they wielded, the deadly danger they presented. Now shifting the beam from a wide setting to a full circumference including himself for safety, he moved inside the herd's outer perimeter, just behind where Arrow stood.

In her semi-stupor she was not much alarmed by his approach. When he began the slow, careful process of separating and herding her away from the others – moving her in the direction of the canyon – she did not resist.

She walked ahead of him through the long neck leading into the rock ring.

He hesitated before beginning the next phase, apprehensive about switching off the narcotizing function. Though out of range of the herd he could not know how Arrow would react to finding herself confined in the circular enclosure with a human being. But it was imperative that he release the narcotizing beam just now, as the phaetron had to be used to close off the mouth of the canyon so that Arrow could not make a dash for freedom.

Quickly, for the narcosis began to dissipate immediately, he reset the phaetron frequency and aimed it at a massive boulder near the neck of the canyon. The rock began to move slowly to cover the enclosure. Careful as he was, the sound of stone shrieking against stone brought the horse to its senses. She was suddenly altogether conscious of her unusual surroundings and confinement, and the strange creature imprisoned with her.

Arrow trotted as far away from him as she could, but found that the ring – any way she moved about in it – somehow brought her back to the man. To stay out of harm's way he stood at the center of the ring. Arrow's trot increased in speed and became a panicked gallop. Distressed and wild-eyed as the horse was, he saw only her beauty, the rippling muscles of her flank, deep chest heaving, the glorious mane flying.

And suddenly his fear ceased.

It was merely a matter of time, he told himself, before he and the horse would be joined. He stood very still and looked into Arrow's terrified eyes as she came round with every circle, like a planet revolving about its sun. Again and again she came, Poseidon's calm deepening. *He would wait an eternity to gain this animal's trust.* Her pace slowed perceptibly and finally, in exhaustion, she stopped, her tongue loose, licking her lips. He noticed her inside ear cocked toward the middle of the ring where he stood. Man and beast stared at each other with curious intensity.

Then a small rockslide spooked the horse and she bolted. He remained still. Arrow made another orbit and came around so that she fell under his gaze again. It was time to employ the technique he had observed in mother horses to elicit desired behavior from their offspring. Averting his eyes from Arrow, he took a small step towards the animal. She remained still. Another step closer, this time positioning his shoulders at a forty-five degree angle to her. The moment he did this she moved a step closer to him. His heart nearly stopped.

It had worked.

Then without warning Arrow charged him and with only a glancing blow knocked him backwards onto his rump. He had to laugh at himself, for her defiant eyes clearly said, "You seek to control me, stranger. Now I will control you."

Aware that he could ill afford to appear so weak for too long he sprang to his feet. He took several more definitive steps in Arrow's direction, angling his shoulders in the opposition direction. This time she appeared ready to bolt. He realized he had forgotten the eyes. Another step, this time with his eyes averted. She moved in concordance, then waited, he imagined, poised for his next maneuver.

It became a dance, he clearly in the lead, the partners straying closer and closer together. Sometimes it felt like a game, but one of the greatest import. Always, it felt as though the man and horse in the same ring were the only two creatures in the wide world. They were less than ten paces apart, and Arrow seemed skittish. This time after his angled step toward her he crouched down and looked away altogether, in a gesture of subordination. A few moments later he could feel the horse above him. She was sniffing his head and neck. *Had she lost all fear of him?* Very, very slowly he rose to standing, less than an arm's length away from her. He was not sure whether first to touch her forehead, her nose, her neck…

But before he knew what had happened she'd taken the decision from his hands – stretched out her neck and pushed at his shoulder with her nose. He gasped delightedly. He reached out for her, but his movement was too quick and she backed away, retreating to the outer perimeter of the ring and making several circuits before she slowed and stopped.

"Forgive me, Arrow," he said aloud. The sound of his voice did not appear to frighten her, so he began to vocalize as he approached her, words and nonsensical sounds as well, but all in the most soothing tones. They were an arm's length apart. As he stood contemplating his next move the horse nudged him again, he was sure in a teasing manner.

Knowing he was losing the day he reached out his hand and grabbed ahold of Arrow's thick mane. She pulled back her head but not out of his grasp and regarded him with one eye, waiting for his next move. It was this very move, however, that had haunted his thoughts from the moment he had seen the horse in the bullring and envisioned himself riding on its back.

How should he propel himself up there? This was the crucial question. He was strong, but he lacked leverage, and he did not know how much pressure he could place on the mane to pull himself up. And would such a bold and invasive action terrify the horse completely? The day was dying and there was anticipation of some great climax to this long dance. He knew he must move decisively and do so quickly, but found himself ambivalent about what he should next do.

He argued with himself. Since the closing of the canyon's neck with his phaetron he had proceeded within the boundaries of the natural world, and the results had been miraculous. The horse had begun to trust him. But did he trust himself? Did he really trust the natural world, naked of his technos? The last time he had done so – while in the volcanic range – it had nearly cost him his life. He must act sensibly. He needed to mount the horse and do it quickly. In the fading light he therefore again set the phaetron to the narcotizing frequency and directed it toward Arrow. She sagged at once, her head drooping nearly to the ground. Instantly he felt a pang of regret, a keen sense that he had betrayed her. But there was no time to lose.

He grabbed Arrow's mane with both hands and with a push catapulted his body to her onto her back. With a few adjustments to his posture he found himself astride her! He sighed with relief and wonder, but he had no time for self-congratulation. "May the spirit of Erthe protect me," he whispered and switched off the hub's narcotizing frequency.

All of Arrow's muscles instantly tightened beneath him. She lifted her head, suddenly aware of the strange weight on her back. Slowly she turned and saw the man atop her. He hardly breathed as Arrow shifted carefully on her feet. He was ecstatic. She had accepted him! The slow building of trust between them had…

Poseidon suddenly found himself flying through the air. He

landed with a thump on his back and saw, to his horror, the furiously rearing horse poised above him. He rolled sideways just as Arrow's hooves came crashing down. He jumped to his feet and found himself facing the horse, now dancing in agitation, her angry eyes flashing. Summoning self-control he used his most soothing voice, whispering nonsensical words, clicks and kisses. "Whoa, whoa, shhh girl, shhh. Arrow, Arrow, beautiful girl…

The horse slowly calmed. Did he dare touch her, try to mount her again? He must. He stretched out his arm and carefully stroked her nose. She did not flinch, seemed to remember the moments of trust before the betrayal. He moved closer, grew bolder, stroked her neck and shoulders with more pressure, more assurance. Was he imagining it? Was the horse enjoying the intimacy, or at least the sensations?

Nearly all the light had gone from the sky now. Poseidon was weary from the struggle and felt the horse was weary, too. Now was the moment. Without hesitation he grabbed Arrow's mane and with all his strength swung himself up onto her back. She did not move but stood solid as he clumsily adjusted himself in the seat of living muscle and bone.

He sat as quiet and still on Arrow as he was able, the night coming up around the newly coupled pair. As the moments passed without struggle, and his breathing slowed, the accomplishment of the deed began to dawn as something more magnificent than words could describe. His gratitude for the beast swelled and threatened to burst his heart. He leaned down and laid his cheek upon her sleek, powerful neck.

"Bless you Arrow," he whispered, overcome by an alien emotion that cracked his voice and brought stinging tears to his eyes. "Bless you my friend, sweet Arrow." He smiled in the dark and spoke as much to himself as the horse when he said, "The rest will be much, much easier."

If the following days were not precisely easier, they were filled with startling discoveries about the communion of men and horses, and many successes. Confined together in the ring he and Arrow worked, learned, ate and finally played together. As the bond of trust deepened, anything and everything became possible. He found that he needed a method of guiding the horse's movements. A leather thong around Arrow's neck was useless. The same thong around her forehead irritated her. The idea of placing it in her mouth at first seemed cruel, but finally worked if manipulated gently.

They walked, trotted, galloped. Poseidon took dozens of spills; the horse gazing down at him with what he began to think was amusement. He became adept at pulling himself up by her mane and seating himself in one graceful move. And the pain in his thighs caused by the constant use of previously unused muscles for gripping her sides – excruciating for the first few days – finally began to lessen.

It was time to leave for the village, and Poseidon was apprehensive. The herd had moved on, he having scared them off with a barrage of light beams radiating from his phaetron. Though this eliminated the risk of Arrow wishing to rejoin her family, he could not know how she would behave outside the confines of the rock ring. With no small regret at leaving behind the private marvel of the previous days, he levitated the large boulder at the neck of the canyon and sitting proud on the back of his horse, rode out into the world.

Free from all confines, Arrow stopped of her own accord and gazed around with some confusion. Where was the herd? She stubbornly refused to move when he gave her the signal they had devised for that action – a gentle heel in her side. She became agitated and danced on the spot. Her ears were upright, listening for her family, nostrils flared, searching for their scent. Poseidon held his seat as she threw her head up and down, blowing and snorting. Then he leaned down and began murmuring comfortable words in her ear to say that *he* was her family now.

In this way man and horse remained for some time, he allowing her to mourn for her loss, her agitation by degrees lessening, and her body regaining its natural balance. Finally, without prodding, Arrow began to walk. Poseidon's heart swelled, for not only had she apparently accepted her strange future, but she had with some unfathomable instinct or unspoken communication with the man on her back, begun walking in the precise direction that would take them home.

TWENTY-FIVE

WHAT SHE WAS seeing was not possible. Squatting in the sand with a group of children, teaching them how to extract the dye sack from an eight-tentacled sea creature, Cleatah had glanced up briefly and caught sight of a dark speck far in the distance, moving towards them along the northern beach. She squinted at the speck with confusion, for it appeared much larger than it should have, had it been a man approaching at that distance. The children stopped their lesson, looking up at her – she had gotten to her feet and was staring in silence down the long stretch of beach.

She only became alarmed when the strange shape reached the fallen boulder. It was still far off, but she knew how big a man should appear at that distance, and this was not a man approaching. Neither was it a known beast – too tall for a buron, the largest known animal.

"Go," she said to the children. "Up to the village. Tell your parents to come down to the beach. Hurry!"

The children scrambled away and up the footpath, leaving Cleatah alone and trembling at the black shape that was coming slowly but steady towards her. Nothing about the thing made sense. Clearly it was living, an animal of some sort, but nothing she had ever seen before. And while it did not appear to be attacking, she could not be sure that it would not do so when it caught sight of her.

She was glad when the first of the villagers began clamoring down the beach steps, surrounding her and plying her with questions, then staring down the strip of sand as they followed her outstretched arm and pointing finger. Men who had rushed down to the beach without their weapons called frantically to others who were still descending to bring spears. Many spears.

The figure was becoming clearer now, though what the villagers saw made no sense to them. Cleatah could feel that even the bravest of hunters were stifling their terror, for this beast was unknown to them and it was horrible to behold.

Above, it was a man, and below a horse.

What terrible god ruled this creature? All the men had gathered, spears at the ready, into a protective mass, facing the northern beach. Still it came, with a blessed slowness, apparently lacking aggression, but many villagers were no doubt remembering the recent carnage caused by horses at the bull camp.

Then suddenly its posture changed. It seemed to be dancing excitedly in place, and the creature revealed itself to be more fearsome than before. It had two heads! That of a man *and* a horse. It turned and bucked and suddenly, as in a nightmare vision it rose up on two legs, its front legs pawing at the sky. A woman screamed and all at once the men, infused with the courage of the kill, spears poised for the throw, charged the horse-man, shouting their most fearsome war cry.

On first sight of the gathered mass of villagers Arrow had panicked. It had taken all of Poseidon's strength and calm assurances to steady her. But now the men, shrieking to the heavens, were running at them, weapons raised, and he could feel the horse beneath him ready to bolt.

He began to shout. "It is Poseidon! I am Poseidon, your friend!!" He could make out some faces, but they were coming very fast. "Kalar! Boah! It is not a beast, but your friend Poseidon!!"

Several spears had already been loosed and they flew swiftly with precise aim. Poseidon ducked to narrowly avoid the first, maneuvered the terrified Arrow to avoid the next two. But the sound of his voice had so startled and confused the onrushing hunters that several had stopped in their tracks. He continued his vocalizing, calling out men's names the moment he recognized their faces. They all slowed, lowered their weapons and were staring incredulously at "Poseidon" straddling the back of a horse! Some of them shouted angrily at him, others fell to their knees overcome. The women had begun slowly to approach, curiosity overcoming their fear.

Poseidon who had managed, somehow, to calm Arrow, continued to speak in soothing tones to the villagers who could still not believe their eyes and even less, their ears.

"Poseidon?" It was Cleatah's voice. Tentative, fearful. It occurred to him that he had never before this moment known her to show fear.

"Cleatah," he said evenly, "Come closer. I will not harm you. It is your friend, Poseidon. I am merely sitting on the back of a horse. And this horse will not harm you either."

She moved forward slowly, ignoring Boah who tried to stay her.

"How do I know it is really Poseidon, and not some man-beast from the spirit world?" she asked apprehensively.

"This way," he replied, and in a single, much practiced movement, dismounted, landing gracefully on his two feet.

There were more shouts and gasps, but now as many in delight as in terror. Cleatah had come close, very carefully, having never been so near to a horse, and not altogether believing that the man who had just separated himself from it was Poseidon. She reached out and touched him quickly, pulling her hand back, and found human flesh beneath her fingers. She touched him again, this time grasping the muscle of his forearm. Finally satisfied, her face broke out into a smile and she turned to the villagers.

"It *is* Poseidon." The onlookers were not yet convinced. "It is Poseidon, I tell you!" Cleatah turned and looked over her shoulder at Arrow, who had calmed even further. "And he has brought us…" she hesitated, hardly believing her own words, "…a very… great…gift."

⤷

"I wish to take a party of men to gather the herd of wild horses," Poseidon announced as he sat at the community hearth. The Shore People had not fully recovered from their first sight of him riding on the back of one of the beasts. "When they have been captured I will give you my knowledge of them. I will teach you how to ride on their backs, as I do."

There was no sound at all for a space of time, save the buzzing of night insects and the whimper of a child before being put to the breast. Then like a fire erupting in a blaze of sparks, everyone was talking at once, shouting.

"It is impossible," Elkon insisted. "How can men take control of such huge animals?"

"We have already seen one man do such a thing," offered Heydra.

"I say no." It was Elkon again. "Men will surely be injured or killed."

Poseidon remained silent, allowing the arguments to swirl around him. Someone dumped more wood on the fire, and everyone settled in to listen, or participate in the debate. Children slept in their mothers' laps. Elders scratched at their chins.

"Think," said Boah, "We could become a tribe of 'horse-men'."

"That is a bad idea," said the old woman Ilato, whose arm had been broken in the stampede. "I think Great Mother would punish us for even thinking such thoughts."

"Why would she do that?" reasoned Brannan. "The horse is her creature and we are her creatures. If Poseidon has managed to subdue this animal, perhaps Great Mother means for us to ride upon their backs."

Now Boah stood, as if to drive home the importance of his words. "We *must* have the horses." Demonstrating true courage, he had been the first tribesman that afternoon on the beach to accept Poseidon's frightening invitation to mount Arrow. It had only taken Boah a moment to comprehend the power of partnership with the mighty beast. Even his bristling competitiveness with the newcomer and Poseidon's increasing status within the tribe were nothing compared to the lure of the horse.

Elkon waved his arm at Poseidon. "You left the village on false pretenses!" he cried irritably. "You cannot be trusted!"

"Be sensible, Elkon," said Heydra, far too old to ride himself, but intrigued by the idea of the horses. "If Poseidon had told us his purpose we would never have given him leave to go."

Poseidon looked around the campfire trying to catch a glimpse of Cleatah, but she was nowhere to be found. It disturbed him that she took no part in so important a debate, and if he was honest with himself he would admit he simply missed her presence.

He rose. "I'm going to bed," he announced evenly. "I mean to sleep well, for I'm leaving at dawn for the Great Plateau. Anyone who wishes to join me should carry with him five days' food, and at least one torch. The wolves must be left at home."

All were silent as Poseidon left the campfire's circle of light and disappeared into the moonless dark beyond it. The moment he was gone the voice of the tribe exploded once again into spirited cacophony, a tumultuous song that continued unabated deep into the night.

TWENTY-SIX

THE DAWN WAS shrouded in a thick fog from the sea, so that when Poseidon mounted his horse and rode to the edge of the village the men that had assembled to accompany him were ghostlike, their voices muted in the half-light of day. All the previous night he had contemplated the position he should take on this adventure – either as an equal comrade leading his horse on foot, which would strengthen the male bonds, or on horseback with the others walking – the group's unequivocal leader. He had finally, for better or worse, decided to stand as leader. He would ride to assert his position and to control a potentially dangerous exercise.

He therefore walked his horse slowly enough for the group – which he guessed numbered about fifty – to keep up on foot. The men were reserved, perhaps fearful of what lay ahead as they trekked north along the coast and climbed up onto the plateau, the fog only dissolving once the sun reached its noonday zenith. Occasionally a man would come forward, shyly, to speak with him, perhaps ask a question about the plan, or to study the beast that would – spirits willing – be in the tribe's control in a few day's time.

When the shadows were long and the rocky outcroppings glowed mellow in the setting sun he saw the moving cloud of

dust on the distant plain that he knew to be the wild herd –
moving toward their usual night's resting place. He dismounted
and gathered the men around him. They were not at all tired
from the journey. Rather, they were thrumming with excitement
and anticipation. He'd not yet seen all their faces, and now he
addressed each one by name, welcoming and thanking him for
joining the hunt. Banda, Uru, Slane, Boah. Then he stopped,
startled.

He was staring into Cleatah's brown eyes.

He found it suddenly hard to think clearly. He had never
expected her to come but she had, and none of the men were
opposed. The last thing he wanted to do was put this woman in
danger, but to insult her now would be a mistake. He must take
his chances.

"I have never seen you hunt before."

"This is not the same," she said evenly. "This is for the horses."
And with great seriousness added, "You will be glad I came."

Later, when night had overtaken the great plain Poseidon, on
foot and still as stone, composed himself as best he could. Arrow
was tied to a tree upwind of the herd. He would not ride her in
the roundup, he had decided, unsure how she might react in the
herd's presence, so soon after her separation from them. He knew
he was endangering these men, and the woman so precious to the
Terresian expedition. He'd promised them the capture of a herd
of wild horses and knowledge of their taming and riding – a skill
that he had only recently acquired himself. If he failed he would
lose whatever stature he'd already attained.

For many reasons he had decided against using his phaetron
in this endeavor, except in the most extreme emergency. It was
vital that the tribesmen learn to control the horses using their
natural skills alone. The capture itself was certainly dangerous,

but he believed it attainable. He tasted the cooling night air, the merest hint of fog, which would surely roll in some time before dawn. They must move now. The plan would be foiled by the thick fog.

Poseidon lit his torch. And with a magic both grand and primitive the plain was illuminated. What he saw before him was this: holding each torch aloft was one tribesman, more than fifty in all, forming a great circle around the herd. The horses, startled by so unthinkable a phenomenon, were paralyzed, their eyes reflecting the blaze of lights. Straight ahead, across the plain from Poseidon, was the thin-necked canyon and its rock ring in which he had cornered Arrow only two weeks before. Though he could not see her at her designated position, he knew that at the mouth of that canyon Cleatah waited for the moment the herded horses would thunder past before throwing the heavy net he had fashioned, across the canyon's neck to imprison them. It was as good a solution as he could conceive, Poseidon thought, to give the woman an important job, but one that kept her largely out of harm's way.

Flaring out to his left was one curved line of torchmen. Six hundred feet behind them lay the eastern coast of the continent – the sea cliff with its rocky shore below. To his right was the other half-circle of light, and the wide plateau stretching out for hundreds of miles behind it.

The animals stamped and snorted nervously in a tight cluster.

With a silent prayer Poseidon signaled the men to close the circle. Stealth and slowness of motion were of utmost importance. No sudden or jerking movements… and complete silence. They must avoid the animals' panic at all costs and move them, in small increments, in the direction of the box canyon by closing in on them.

It was working smoothly, he thought. Just as he had planned it. He had counted on the element of surprise, the horses being encircled by the light – to keep them controlled. One false move would be disastrous. He had learned that his own horse responded to fear by fleeing in the opposite direction from what frightened her. Now the animals were walking, warily but calmly towards the only area of darkness – the mouth of the box canyon.

Then it happened. A man halfway down the circle on the right stumbled, and with a loud involuntary cry let go his torch which flew straight out from him into the circle of horses.

The response was instantaneous – *stampede in the opposite direction*!

The plan collapsed disastrously into chaos, and in moments the horses were racing towards the east – the sea cliffs and the jagged rocks below them! The once careful line of men were frantically scrambling to avoid the oncoming herd. Horrible shrieks from the broken line of men told Poseidon the stampede had claimed human victims. Into the jumble of flickering torchlight he aimed his phaetron, but stopped short of activating it. He realized that if he triggered the narcotizing function, men as well as animals would be disabled by its beam, perhaps causing more casualties.

Instead he raced to Arrow and leapt on her back, spurring her towards the cliff edge with a wild prayer that he might somehow reach it first and turn the beasts from their deadly course.

But he was too far away, even on horseback.

The animals were galloping madly for the dark abyss, everyone watching helplessly, Poseidon closing the distance, but not fast enough. A few moments more and the horses would find nothing but air under their hooves. They would scream in terror, fall and die writhing on the razor points of stone below.

Then two torches burst brilliantly to light at the cliff's edge. They were being waved frantically, and a human voice was raised in a wild shriek meant to ward off the stampede. The sudden light and sound frightened the horses. Stopped them dead in their tracks. Now Poseidon could see the torchbearer.

It was Cleatah!

She lunged forcefully at the confused herd, waving the flaming torches and shouting unintelligible noises. The horses, desperate to be rid of this fire-breathing, shrieking dragon, ran in the opposite direction – away from cliff's edge.

The tribesmen finally comprehended what they were seeing, and moving in pure instinct as one body regrouped to assist the woman. They gathered the herd with their torches, ever closer to the rocky foothills, tighter and tighter into a long single file. At breakneck speed and with a thunderous echo they galloped through the stone neck and into the canyon. All of them. Every horse. At the last moment the net was flung across the gap, and suddenly it was done.

It took some time for the men to realize their success.

From his position Poseidon could hear the whoops and victorious shouts. But there was no time for celebration. He raced to the two fallen men. One was dead, mangled beyond recognition. The other, Boah, lay groaning even in his semi-consciousness. Hiding the phaetron's tiny blinking lights from any curious eyes, Poseidon worked quickly in the dark before the men now approaching reached them. He repositioned the leg with the blessed device and mended it, bone, blood vessels, nerves and sinews.

More than half the men now surrounded their fallen comrades. Boah was lifted gently and carried to the protection of the foothills where a camp was already being set. Others knelt around the body of the dead man – discovered to be Uru – closing his eyes and offering up a ritual blessing. Already two biers were being fashioned to carry each of the fallen back to the village.

A lone figure at the cliff edge drew Poseidon's eye. It was Cleatah, a torch burning at her feet lighting her figure – a strange illusion with the thick bank of fog bearing down behind her like a great wave. Riding slowly towards her he found himself savoring the sight of this woman, a tightness in his throat and a hardening beneath his tunic announcing unexpected desire.

She turned and smiled at him with quiet triumph. Silently he reached down with one arm sweeping her up behind him on his horse, and she wrapped her slender, muscled arms around his waist. In this way she rode with him back to the firelight of the makeshift camp, as though this place so warm and close – both guarded and guardian – was the right and natural order of things.

Nothing had prepared him for such a woman and nothing, for Poseidon, would ever be the same.

MARS COLONY

Gold

TWENTY-SEVEN

SEEING HIS FATHER in front of him caused Athens's gut to twist in a sharp knot. He thought he was prepared to see Ammon Ra sitting at the end of the Federation Energy conference table flanked by Denys and Critias, but the moment his father had opened his sanctimonious mouth Athens felt the urge to flee. He, Persus and Praxis were at the Mars Fed "other end of the table" separated by 740,000,000 miles making their second report on their mining efforts.

Calm yourself, Athens told himself, *you have the upper hand here.*

Praxis projected onto the center of the table a small fleet of angular black ore transport vessels that were – it was hard to believe – even uglier than the ship that had brought the colonists to Mars. "Two of them are nearly filled," Praxis reported. "As soon as we're given the trajectory and timing, we'll launch and get them off to you."

"We're ready and eager to receive them," Critias said. "We've just about completed the rebuilding of the SleepPhase Dome and replaced the damaged pods."

"How many of the crew will be needed to travel back to Mars?" Denys asked.

"All of them," Athens said, attempting to stifle a smile.

"They'll all be coming back here." He did not say, *There's not a single man or woman who has any desire to stay on Terres, climb into a pod and lay down for a LongOrbit sleep when they can return to paradise.*

"We received your report on this new ore that Goldius discovered under the mining operation," Ammon said. "It has uses?" he asked.

"It's pretty to look at," Denys added.

"Truly, that's as far as it goes. Baubles. Trinkets," Athens told them.

The door whooshed open and Rufus Golde – he had shortened his long unwieldy name – hurried in. Athens turned his back on the men at the other end of the table and gestured for the geologist, who had recently discovered flamboyance, to remove his gold ear clips and the long length of gilded fabric he wore wrapped around his pudgy neck before he sat down with them. Athens turned back.

"Here he is, Terres's true savior. He's getting titanium out of the ground at an astonishing rate, and he oversees the processing into ready-to-use pellets as well."

The Fed Energy men greeted Golde respectfully as he took his place next to Athens.

"I was just telling the commissioners that your newest find has been a small but quite pleasant distraction for the colonists. Not a lot of excitement around here, but we really are all right. We enjoy our beach houses, the seaside. Our little solies."

"Those ridiculous looking creatures," Ammon Ra scoffed.

"You wouldn't understand, Father. You have to have something called 'feelings' to appreciate them."

The response was a smug shake of the head, but Athens felt suddenly immune to his father's cruelty.

"So, will you send us some samples of this 'gold' in the shipment?" Denys asked.

"Of course," Golde said. "We won't be able to send much.

It's coming out of the ground reluctantly. The conditions in the lower mine make for slow going."

Praxis was squirming in his chair. The Vice Governor opened his mouth to speak, but Persus broke in, "So that's all we've got for you today. We'll get back to you on the delivery coordinates."

Calling some parting encouragement, Denys and Critias waved goodbye and rose from their seats.

Athens gazed mildly at his father. "How's my mother?"

With a dismissive wave he stood from the table. "Oh, still going on and on about building a new theater. Nothing wrong with the old one." Without another word to his son he shut down the transmission.

Athens and his team sat quietly at the long table. Praxis opened his mouth to speak, Athens sure it was to object.

It was Persus that silenced him. "You want this as much as we do, Vice Governor. If you disapprove, I suggest you let the commissioners know immediately."

"And plan to be on one of the ore transports when they go," Athens added.

Golde was re-wrapping the gilt-threaded scarf round and round his neck. He looked down at Praxis's hands. He picked one of them up. There was a gaudy gold ring on every other finger.

"Hmph!" Golde scoffed.

TWENTY-EIGHT

FORMATIONS OF SILVERY shuttle discs swooping in elegant maneuvers above Rufus Golde Plaza, all of them tailing long gilded banners and weaving intricate multi-colored vapor designs in the sky were the first sight colonists would have of the celebration going on below. The place was already shoulder-to-shoulder with revelers in the square and the hangar where the shuttles normally moored, its massive doors wide open for the mingling crowds inside.

It was the first "Gold of the Gods Day" in Marsean history but, Persus thought, slicing through the crowd on her own, judging from the crush of people who'd already arrived, it would not be the last. She was certain that every person alive on Mars was already here...or on their way. Vibral music was blaring around them, a world away from the gentle tones provided by living musicians that graced much smaller gatherings on Terres. And every single person – man, woman and child here today – was flaunting their proudest gold possessions. Jewelry and clothing shot through with the metallic yellow threads. Entire bodies burnished with gold powder. Gilded hair in outlandish styles, beards, eyebrows and lashes were everywhere. Clothing hid golden pubic bushes.

Persus had herself decided on a subtler look. The ankle-length black "shaper" gown – it was the only dress she owned –smoothed out the lumps and bumps in her middle and too-heavy thighs, and its simplicity showed off to perfection the gift that Athens had given her – a large brooch of two sleek-bodied solies, designed by Micah himself. She wore it over her heart. Persus found herself touching it frequently to remind herself of Athens's affection. He'd never given her a gift before. She liked to imagine the conversation he'd had with the artisan in choosing it. "*For a special woman in my life,*" he might have said. *I desire the others. But Persus – I need her. I cannot function without her. I…*" She felt herself blushing at her own hubris. She had no business indulging in such fantasies.

Then she heard his laugh. It was loud and raucous and utterly unique. She headed for the sound on the far side of the hangar, catching snatches of conversations around her as she went. Three women comparing their gold piercings – upper lip, nipple, and a patch of tiny gilded threads woven through the skin of a cheek hollow.

"Synth gold is everywhere!" Persus heard a man complain.

"Not if you have this," said his friend, proudly shoving his wrist hub before the man's face. "It's new. A protocol to detect forgeries."

"Check this for me," the man said nervously, thrusting his forearm out. A thick gold bracelet encircled it. "I traded away half my furniture for it." Hovering the wrist device over the ornament elicited a mild three-tone ring. "Furniture well-spent," his friend said with a smile. "You need to get one of these," he added, tapping his hub.

Further on, a large group of colonists was huddled, arguing about the outrage that had occurred recently. It was the talk of the colony. An artist had fetched an enormous price for a "solid gold" soup tureen that was revealed instead be only gold-plated, a thin veneer at that. The buyer had learned the true nature of his purchase, and annoyance had turned to fury when the artist refused to make good on the deceit. Worse, he'd failed to show any remorse for his actions. The victim was calling publicly for the artist to be punished for the "crime," and it had even come to blows. Persus could hear voices raised, but the squabble had no real coherence. Crime and punishment, and especially violence were concepts utterly foreign to modern Terresians, relegated to ancient history, barely studied anymore.

"What if deceptions like this become more common?" one man demanded angrily.

"If the artifact is beautiful enough," his female companion suggested, "I'm not sure I'd care."

Several of them shouted indignantly at her.

Persus walked on. An entire corner of the hangar had been set aside for artisans to show off their golden artifacts – statuary, vases, dishes, goblets, furniture, draperies. Micah's stall was the largest and most prominent of all. She saw him holding up an ornate face mask to an interested colonist and heard him explaining it was styled after one found in the Atlas City History Museum, a design of Terres's most ancient tribe. Micah caught sight of her as she passed. He looked pleased to see her wearing the brooch, and she clutched it proudly before moving by.

Another group of colonists was joking about the new, rather heated competition for jobs in the "lower mine." They were few and far between because, though the work mining gold was indisputably grueling, no one already employed there wished to relinquish his or her position there because "wages" – a new concept to the people – were paid in raw gold ore. Somehow, despite the preponderance of it, Rufus Golde had devised a payment scale for the miners, as well as a growing stockpile of it – "supply and demand" – so that the metallic excrement of billions of microscopic creatures had become precious, expensive, and the desire for it obsessive. *Gold had become desired beyond all reason,* Persus thought, *the source of mass addiction…*

There was Athens's laugh again! She found herself drawn to

the sound, physically excited by it. It irked her to admit it, but there was no one on the whole planet that possessed a fraction of the Governor's appeal. If he wouldn't take her to bed, she would just make do with spending endless hours on the job with him.

She could see now the little circle that had gathered around him. Golde, Praxis, Leanya among them. Just now, Persus realized with a sinking heart, Athens was draping a fabulous golden neckpiece around a black-haired beauty's throat and shoulders. Dangling baubles lay prettily in the cleft between her breasts. Persus's hand flew to her solie brooch, and she considered for a moment turning and walking away from a humiliation only she would comprehend. *Stop it!* She commanded herself. *Don't be ridiculous.* She took a breath. Then another, then insinuated herself into Athens's circle.

"Persus!" he cried on seeing her. "How lovely you look," he lied, though he somehow managed such sincerity in his voice that she thought for a moment he might have convinced the others that she was something more than short and graceless and plain. He thankfully did not reveal that the modest solie brooch was his present to her. He was kind that way. They both knew – perhaps everyone in the colony knew – she wanted him desperately, but he not her, but the deception of mere friendship the two of them played for others allowed her to keep her dignity and a very real place in his heart. "We were just discussing Rufus's notion for a gold 'currency.' Coins that can be exchanged for goods and services. And gold artifacts," he added with a smile.

"Quite an antiquated concept," she observed. "Precious metals to trade with. If I remember my history correctly, it caused all manner of misery on societies. Wars even." She skewered the geologist with her eyes. "A 'Gold of the *Gods* Day?' Was that your idea as well? By the stars…" she softened her words with a mischievous grin, "You've gone wholly archaic on us."

"They love it," he said, patting back the flared lapels of his golden knee-length jacket. "Of course 'gods' are preposterous, but it had a nice ring to it. And the currency idea is catching fire. I've heard women are thinking of selling their ovum for the coin. Men their sperm. Funny, they were never that valuable before, but anything provably 'natural' is becoming a valued commodity."

"Maybe I'll sell my hair," Leanya said, her teasing eyes fixed on Athens.

"How much would a kidney fetch?" Praxis asked.

"Who'd want *your* kidney?" Athens said, but it came out more sourly than he'd meant it, so added, "Everyone knows synthetic organs are more durable than real ones."

"You're missing the point, Sir," Golde told Athens. "What people will want to spend their coin on is the 'elemental,' 'authentic.' That which cannot be…manufactured."

"I'm going," Leanya announced. "They're starting the fashion pageant." She took Golde's elbow. "Come on, Rufus." Seeing the long face on Praxis she grabbed him on her other arm. "You," she said, turning back to Athens, "are going to 'buy' me a new dress."

He nodded with amusement and watched them go. Then turned to Persus with the private smile he reserved for her. "What do you think of it all?"

"The music is too loud…but this," she said, gazing around, "…*is* more exciting than Terres ever was." She regarded him carefully. "It'll change us, you know."

"For the better? Worse?"

"Don't know. I can see you getting lost in the whole currency thing."

He shook his head. "Not me."

"You think you'll be immune to the "twin brother of wealth?""

"What? Greed?"

"It always happened in the past. The ones who had the most were the greediest. And you're drowning in gold."

"But I don't *care* about it. I like it. I like seeing it around me. It's pretty. It makes women happy." He scanned the jammed hangar with a bemused gaze. "I just don't crave it for its own sake like they do."

Persus could hear the honesty in his voice. But Athens *was* greedy. He always needed more and more of everything. Adulation. Respect. Glory. *Ahhh,* she thought, remembering the stories of the Terresian kings and queens of old. Certainly they'd been wealthy beyond measure – in land, palaces, women, slaves, cities, fleets. But it was not the *things* they valued. She could see that Athens was thinking along the same lines as she. They did this so often that many times after a long silence they would speak the very same word at the same moment.

Greedy for power, she thought, but did not say. The expression on the governor's face revealed that the very same phrase was on the tip of his tongue. *There is nothing that Athens Ra desires more in the world,* echoed silently in her head.

"You keep that to yourself," he told her. "Our little secret."

TWENTY-NINE

A STAR-STUDDED NIGHT SKY *rips open a large vertical tear, its jagged edges brilliant white, the space behind it glowing deep purple. Glimpses of colored galaxies stretching into infinity. The white-lipped tear pulses with sensuous vibral throbs. A squadron of small amber plasma orbs – with nightmarish velocity – comes screaming out of the gash. Athens watches himself at his shuttle's controls, watching more and more orbs streak by its window. All missing the* Atlantos. *All missing the shuttle.*

Ahhh...a shiver runs through him.

One is inside. With him. There before his faceplate. One of the spheres. It stands perfectly still, unwavering.

The rupture again. Its purple and colored dimension throbbing behind the milkwhite lips...

Athens came awake with a slow surge of dread. He looked at the other side of the bed. Thankfully empty. He stood by the window, letting sunlight warm his back.

The dream again. How many times had he had it since their arrival here? And his brother's voice, speaking of Elgin Mars, his disappearance – *"The planet swallowed him up"*. The words haunted Athens more than he wanted to believe. *And the dream that kept repeating...*

He knew this was folly – *Leave well enough alone!* – he punched

256

in the code for a years-old report on his hub but hesitated. It was one he had considered reviewing many times over, but somehow feared. He knew he was being silly. *What was there to fear?* With a single tap at his wrist the projection blinked on before him in the sunny bedroom. There was still time to shut it off. *Shut it off!* But he had to know. "*The planet swallowed him up.*" Athens flashed forward through the replay – *Chyron: Aerosean OffWorld Mission. Day 3,147, -14 hours to lift-off. Site 62. The phaetronic drill beam morphing from red to orange to yellow... the drill rig exploding, leaving a phosphorescent white erection of pure Vibrus...a phaetronic beam entirely out of control...a long puff of red dust following the bluff above the Site 62 beach, running north and south...*

Athens paused the report. Curious, he magnified the line of red dust on the bluff. Rewound. Replayed. *The dust appearing moments after the blast.* Magnified further. *A split in the rocky ground.*

Poseidon at the Federation Energy conference table. He'd never said anything about a quake.

Athens punched in a report from later that day. Cyphus's report, a mission to find Commander Mars. *Mile 7 Beach, Day 3,147, -13 hours to lift-off. Cyphus stepping out of his shuttle onto the beach of a crescent bay, the ocean dark green chop...the pink sand beach ringed by a jumble of boulders strangely topped by a crescent-shaped rock like the profile of a jut-chinned man...a huge broad-boughed fern tree jungle behind it...the Scouting Team's shuttle nestled in the sand, its borehole spent and abandoned. The Mile 7 crew at the shoreline playing with solies. Drill Chief Tybo, in his blue worksuit torn in several places, faced streaked with red dirt, strides toward Cyphus.* Tybo, *unable to hide his distress, saying, "We've looked everywhere,"... then Cyphus, "We'll make one more sweep"... Tybo leading Cyphus towards the rocky escarpment between Mile 7 beach and the neighboring bay...a narrow walk-through in the boulders... Tybo leading Cyphus into the next cove, a "solie haven" with thousands of animals, a breeding ground, females sunbathing as their pups suckle. playful sand fights, races into the surf...The solies freeze with alarm, scatter in panic, diving into the waves...the ground undulating under Cyphus and Tybo's feet...boulders on the bluff tumbling down... "Damn planet," mutters Tybo.*

Athens closed out the projection, fingers trembling, heart pounding.

The quake at Site 62.

⚬

"Why no women?" Micah said.

"Stop whining. We don't always have to have women. There's plenty to drink." Athens filled his friend's cup. He liked the new shuttle's self-piloting feature as much as Micah's elegant design. The men were lazy spectators as the craft soared north up the continental coastline.

Micah yawned. "Too tired for bed with a woman in it anyway."

"You see? I know best," Athens said with a boyish grin. "I always know best."

"But so mysterious. 'A little jaunt up the coast, just the two of us.' Do you plan to seduce me?"

Athens pursed his lips in a pout. "I haven't longed for another man since..." He hesitated, his mind blank.

"Since our last month on Terres," Micah reminded him.

"That was *years* ago." Athens made a show of appraising Micah's face and body. "Anyway, you're not my type."

"We do *drink* well together," Micah countered.

"True," Athens said with a smile. "Did you ever bed Talya Horus?"

"Tried. Failed."

"*You?* Failed?"

"So did you. Also surprising. It must sting that your brother..."

258

"Don't remind me. I know why she wouldn't have you," Athens said. "She thinks you're a mutant, like I am."

"We *are* mutants," Micah said. "But that's a good thing. Mutants have more fun."

The shuttle tilted into a smooth and graceful approach to a pink sand beach.

"This is pretty," said Micah gazing down at the scene. "Look at that face in the rock."

They were hovering over Mile 7 Beach.

"It's odd, isn't it?" said Athens. "What does it look like to you?"

"*You*, with a big black mole at the end of your nose."

"Shut up."

"Why are we here?" Micah demanded as Athens opened the floor portal and activated the elevator beam.

"Because it's beautiful. A good place to relax and consume our jog."

They rode down together and stepped out onto the beach.

"What is that?" Micah said of pink sand piled into dunes.

"A borehole. A drill site they left in a hurry."

"Never seen one."

"I know. Thought you might like to."

"Think I'll be inspired?"

"I've known other holes that have inspired you."

Athens watched Micah stride in the direction of the dunes, and gazed up at the stone man facing southeast. He would have witnessed Mars's fate, Athens thought. His hands started trembling again, and he grabbed his fingers to stop them. It didn't take long to find the narrow rock passage between this cove and the next – the one he'd seen in Cyphus's report. He climbed up through the breach, then turned back to Mile 7 Beach. Micah was already peering down into the borehole with his artist's eyes framing a series of shots.

It came as no surprise when Athens topped the rock and

looked down at the next cove and found the "solie paradise" deserted, nothing like the scene he'd witnessed in Cyphus's report. Instead of going down he climbed further up to the bluff above the beach, not unlike the one above Site 62. Here he found a long quake-induced gash running parallel to the shore and on to what would be the next cove beyond, to the north. It was filled with black basaltic rock. Cooled lava. Perhaps this had driven the solies from their playground.

He began following the rift up on the bluff and…something caught his eye, in a pile of jagged boulders halfway down to the beach below. A color out of place.

Blue.

He slid down the sandy ridge and made for the boulders. He briefly lost sight of the blue and had to scramble carefully, as the sharp edges here could easily rip the skin.

There it was! He picked his way to what could now be clearly seen as a finger's length of synthex, a common fabric used for worksuits. The same blue as Tybo's crew had been wearing when Cyphus came to the site looking for Mars. *Had he met his end here? But how? With enough violence to rip his worksuit to shreds?* Tybo's worksuit had been torn in places. There were gusty breezes on these beaches. When he returned to the Complex he would have the piece of cloth analyzed for any of Elgin Mars's genomic markers. *Farfetched,* he thought, *but worth a look.* He stuffed the blue shred into a leg pouch and continued on.

As long as he was down in the cove Athens headed for the next rocky divider across the sand, pristine, with no sign of recent solie habitation, just the constant crash of green waves on the shore. At the stone pile separating this beach from the next, Athens began to climb again. He looked on the bluff for that continuation of the quake rift. But when he reached the apex the further cove came into view.

The sight awaiting him froze him in place. *Were his eyes playing tricks?* He could see very clearly that the cold black lava-filled gash extended not along the bluff to the north, but cut perpendicularly down across the beach leading like a roadway into the sea.

But piled on either side of the rift...*bones*. High piles of bones. Millions and millions of bones.

A moan escaped him. Heart slamming against his chest wall Athens climbed down carefully, trying to find a place to put his foot that would not crush the brittle skeletons. Parts of skeletons. There was no doubt. He could see by the shape of the skulls. The delicate little digits of their hands. They were solie remains. All that was left of the creatures' colony – the haven become a hideous boneyard.

He found himself paralyzed. What did this mean? What should he do? Who should he tell? *Nothing*, he heard himself say. *It means nothing*. A sad catastrophic extinction of a single colony of wild creatures, signifying nothing. *Leanya should really be notified*. Perhaps a disease had taken them. His breath seemed trapped in his lungs, and he began to tremble, his whole body shaking from the inside out.

No one. Tell no one! He heard in his head, *Not even Persus*. When he steadied himself, commanded himself to heed these words, he finally felt the trembling slow. He was able to suck in a breath.

He began to program his hub, but his fingers twitched, making it impossible. *Calm yourself,* he heard in his head. Where was this voice coming from? *Bloody stars, where is Persus when I need her?! Wait – she can never know. I must protect her. If she knows she'll be complicit. Complicit in what? What is this?! This is not my fault. Not...my...fault?* Why did he feel like it was? It was nobody's fault, but people...maybe people *should* know. Should he tell them? The colonists. It was their world. They had a right to understand its mysteries.

If people know, his inner voice was high and shrill with fear, *the sweet dream of Mars, of the Golden Planet will be ruined! Investigations! Worry! Blame!*

Had a human presence here led to the slaughter of our friends? Surely not!

Then Athens's eyes fell on the black lava road leading into the sea. The lava rift that – if followed backwards would lead up the bluff back behind the now deserted solie beach, and Mile 7 Beach. A rift leading south many miles down the coast, all the way back to Site 62. Poseidon's vibral drill going wildly out of control. Pounding into the Marsean mantle.

Causing the quake!

How could the quake cause the death of all these solies? *No. Impossible.*

He steeled himself. Used his enhancer to slow his heartbeat. Steady his hand.

Then as he stood facing the ocean a sudden vision filled his head – *the amber orb inside the rescue pod hovering before his eyes. The orb, the orb from the nearby dimension, losing its amber glow, reorganizing, transmogrifying into the face of... Ammon Ra. That imperious, contemptuous old man. Judging him. Discounting him. Willing him to fail...*

"No!" he shouted out loud. The source of his misery was far, far away from here. Soon to be sleeping away the millennia in a metal box on a dead planet flying back into the depthless dark of space. And here he was, beloved Governor Athens Ra of the Independent Colony of Mars.

With all the fortitude he owned he disappeared the abhorrent vision. He exhaled a ragged sigh. *I need never think of my father again. Ever. Ever!* He straightened his back, broadened his shoulders. *But there's work to attend to.* He scanned the beach below. *I have to decide. Choose my destiny. Do what great leaders do.*

He reprogrammed his hub. Held up his hand, palm out, high over the beach piled with bleached bones and watched as, soundlessly, the structure of their molecules was rearranged, disassembled. Crumbled into tiny particles. Into dust. But even this was too much substance, *evidence* to be left behind. With another flick of his fingers Athens disappeared the solies' dust, much as he had his father's face. All that was left now was the black stone rift bisecting the pink sand leading into the sea.

A final function…and a moment later not a trace of the quake's distal end was visible.

Nothing to see here! Nothing at all!

Athens turned back and began to climb to the boulders' apex and looked down at the deserted Solie Beach. *Good*, he thought. *Good. I'll put this behind me. No one will ever know. Mars, beautiful Mars.*

As he started down, his planet's name ringing pleasantly in his ears, he plucked the short length of blue synthex from his leg pouch. He held it up between two fingers for a moment… and let it go. A breeze took it skipping over the stones, the sand and into the sea. All that was left of the hero for whom the planet was named.

Athens raised his head to the stone man above him, the crescent profile overwatching the three beaches. He had seen everything that had happened here, whatever that had been. He knew all the secrets.

But, Athens thought with a long and grateful shiver, he would never ever utter a word.

He had invited Leanya to the City Residence for dinner. "I've had enough of beaches for one day," Athens told her as he picked at the meal his cook had prepared, sitting at one end of the long table next to her. It was generally filled with partying friends, but not this night. It was just the two of them. The place, situated near the Federation Center, was larger and many times more luxurious than the Halcyon beach house. Leanya had asked him several times as they ate why he was so quiet, but he only gave her his most endearing lopsided grin and said, "Because I'm contemplating all the different ways I'm going to ravish you later."

But now they were in his gilded bed and she was gazing at him across their pillows, bemused. "Well that's a surprise," she said, gently teasing, pushing a damp curl off his forehead.

"A once-in-a-lifetime event," he promised her. "It's what happens when you spend an entire day drinking with a rude buffoon like Micah. Shuts down all the…" he searched for the right words, "…vital juices."

"*Vital juices?!*" Leanya laughed, then rolled over, coming to straddle his hips. "Well let me see if I can get them flowing again."

❧

He was alone, dreaming, walking among a thousand solies on Solie Beach in brightest sunlight. It should have been a loud and raucous scene, but it was so silent Athens could hear the blood pumping in his ears. He was following beside a rushing river of bright orange lava bisecting the beach, a river that led from the bluff through the mass of animals into the waves, throwing up marvelous billows of steam. The steam should have hissed but was silent, too. It rose in a white wall heading straight out to sea. He followed it with his eyes across the beach to the daytime horizon, the green chop below, the blue cloudless sky above. Then all at once came a shrieking in his ears, a sound that grew to a heaven-ripping roar.

The Marsean sky opened in a great horizontal rupture, one that widened slowly, inexorably, revealing on the other side of it the bright purple universe.

❧

The shuttlecraft arrived at Halcyon Beach early for its pickup, as Athens had requested. The sun had not yet risen when he stepped aboard the disc and it soared off soundlessly into the orange sky. The governor needed time to think before the events of this momentous day began, and nothing calmed and straightened his mind as much as a slow fly-over of his beloved colony. The moment they were airborne he looked down, as his favorite sight was Halcyon Beach itself.

The pilot skirted the coastline, then headed inland over the grow-houses, and finally the mining complex came into view. It was eerie, thought Athens, this absence of activity in the places that were normally hives of activity. Even the dearth of traffic in the sky – a time when the space was normally thick with airbusses shuttling colonists to work – reminded him of the import of this special day.

"Once again to the coast," Athens instructed the pilot, "and out over the sea. I need more time."

"Yes Sir."

There was a vast continent inland, beyond the mining complex, but Athens was rarely drawn to explore, or even contemplate it. His interest lay solely in his little part of the planet – his world. The colony. He knew the mind of his people. He wanted more than anything for them to love him. Crave his leadership. Think the way they did. And guide them to the answers they wanted to hear.

He argued with himself as the shuttle soared over the ocean. There was no doubt in his mind that the people jealously guarded their possessions and had no wish to share this particular form of wealth with the home planet. Unlike titanum, gold was *unnecessary* for Terresian survival – so went the conventional wisdom. Terres would never miss having it. It might even complicate their tightly structured society. If it was all the same, the colonists would gladly keep it for themselves.

Lately there'd been grumblings, sentiments expressing a profound difference in values and thinking between the two worlds, and the idea of secession had actually been proposed. The "Marseans," as they now called themselves, had become entirely independent of Terres, and no one wished to return to the old life. "A fate worse than death," he'd heard many of them say. Yet

Athens was unqualified to come to any decision that affected every colonist on his own. Persus had suggested that a referendum be called on the issues, with each person allowed one vote.

It was to learn of the outcome of this election that Athens was now bound.

"Sir," said the pilot, interrupting the governor's reverie. "I think you should see this."

Athens looked down at Rufus Golde Plaza where the shuttlecraft was making its careful vertical descent not far from the newly constructed Governor's Residence, Athens's "city house." The square and the boulevards leading away from it were mobbed. Never had Athens seen so many Marsean citizens gathered in one place. As the craft descended he could see that they were cheering his arrival.

When the shuttle door opened Athens emerged into the warmest and most enthusiastic welcome he had ever known. People were shouting his name, some chanting, "Keep the gold!" Still others were calling for an independent Mars. A little girl stepped forward and presented Athens with a bouquet of flowers fashioned of pure gold. He found himself smiling, genuinely enraptured by the encircling affection, calling out to the people, taking up their chants, laughing delightedly, waving and embracing the babies thrust into his arms. He was met at the top of the steps by Persus, herself glowing with excitement. Feeling warm and expansive, Athens pulled her into a fond hug, sending the crowd into even louder cheers. Finally he turned and signaled the assembled with a double-fisted salute. Then to roars of thunderous approval, he turned and disappeared inside the Residence.

Even here were throngs of well-wishers, though most of them were Federation employees, mine officials and government representatives. Golde, wearing an outrageous jumpsuit of his namesake cloth, strutted around with his new bedmate, lovely and young, from whose throat, wrists and ears dripped exquisitely crafted gold ornaments.

Vice Governor Praxis took Athens's arm and steered him into

a first floor meeting room where the two of them were finally alone. The sudden silence and calm within was more disconcerting to Athens now than the chaos without had been. Praxis wasted no time with pleasantries.

"The votes have been counted and the results are in," he said, attempting to elicit an eager response from the governor. Athens turned away, deliberately peering out the window at the crowds to deny the vice governor any small pleasure from his reactions.

"On the first proposition…?" asked Athens.

"Overwhelmingly to restrict the exportation of gold to Terres."

"On the second?"

"The people have voted unanimously for a gold currency."

"And the secession issue?"

"Not so clear-cut a result. Fifty-nine percent voted to secede."

"That many?" said Athens.

"Yes Sir."

"How did *you* vote, Praxis?" asked Athens, turning suddenly to confront the vice governor.

"I…I…" he stuttered. "I believe, as the majority of Marseans do, that we have no responsibility to give our gold to Terres, provided we maintain our commitment to supply them with titanum."

"And do you wish independence from the home planet?" Athens persisted.

Praxis swallowed so hard Athens was sure he'd heard a *thunk* in the man's throat. He tried hard not to smile as the squirming vice governor carefully formulated his answer.

"Well, I… I've always considered myself a loyal Federation man and a Terresian patriot…"

"And you voted for secession," interjected Athens.

Praxis's face flushed so instantly and deeply red that Athens was forced to bite his lip to stifle his laugh. Humiliated, the vice governor blurted out, "Yes Sir, I did. And how did *you* vote?" he demanded, hoping to turn the tables.

"Me? Why, it was a closed ballot, Praxis. I never discuss my voting record with anyone. Now, is there anything else I should know before I address the people?"

Praxis began to fume so alarmingly that Athens wondered if the vice governor would explode. He knew such treatment was dangerous – that a person so close to the high command could turn on a moment's notice, and at the worst possible time. But it pleased him to irritate the too-deeply sun-tanned bombast who looked so ridiculous in his gold ear clips and ornately carved neckband.

And of course, Athens enjoyed the danger.

Praxis finally composed himself enough to rattle off a few more voting statistics, but Athens wasn't listening. He was gazing with warmest affection out his window at the plaza filled with colonists – the New Marseans – and looking towards their glorious and independent future.

ERTHE

Poseidon in Love

"In this mountain there dwelt one of the Earth born primeval men of that country, whose name was Evenor, and he had a wife named Leucippe, and they had an only daughter who was called Cleito. The maiden had already reached womanhood, when her father and mother died; Poseidon fell in love with her and had intercourse with her…"

– Plato's Critias, 4th Century BC

THIRTY

POSEIDON SAT CROSS-LEGGED on his bed. He'd closed the hut door-flap and spoke into his hub in the lowest possible tones. "It has been three moons and three days since the horses came to the Shore Village. Confused and frightened as the people were they adapted to the animals with grace and good humor. Several of the men – particularly Boah – have forged a rare partnership with them. I'm grateful the men forgave the weakness of their inexperienced teacher. In fact, delivery of the horses to the tribe has raised my stature to such a degree that I'm finally permitted all the privileges and respect of a…"

His voice trailed off. He replayed the last section of his report. "It has been three moons and three days…" A moment ago the phrase had come to mind naturally as he'd spoken. Not months, but *moons.*

When had that happened? When had his immersion into the culture reached its maximum? How had what was once alien become as natural as his heartbeat? Bloody stars, he was thinking in their language! A long sigh of astonishment escaped him and he laid himself down to digest the idea. *I will no longer record my reports. Only commit pertinent data to memory. Otherwise I will just…I will* live.

It had been some time since he'd contacted the *Atlantos*. He told himself daily that his presence on the ship was not crucial. Most of the crew were engaged in their own work in far flung corners of the planet. Zalen missed his leadership. He knew that. The captain was not fooled by the quasi-ScienTechnic rationalizations he was offered. But he would never beg. Zalen was a stern Terresian. Nor would he ever, in his wildest dreams, imagine that the man he'd known for so long been absorbed so seamlessly into a primitive Gaian tribe, or that the tribe completely inhabited Poseidon's head.

No, let me revise that. Cleatah *inhabits my head.*

Now as a respected tribesman he was free to seek her company, even bed her. With that image before him Poseidon felt a sudden hard knot between his legs.

Maybe it was anticipation. Yesterday she'd invited him to go with her the next time she traveled to the Great Plateau for medicine gathering. She would only know the proper day when it came, she told him. It was childish, he knew, but he worried that she would forget the invitation and go without him. He would have to be patient. One day soon she would come before dawn and call to him through his door flap. They would walk the path up to the plateau by moonlight. She would lead the way. He would watch her strong back and long tawny legs, the soft skins hanging at her waist, imagine the smooth muscled haunches beneath...

Another long sigh. "Cleatah," he whispered. *Was she Manya's "surprise?"* He must be patient. Time would tell.

⁓

The blow to the chest came as Poseidon turned and stood from the central fire. The surprise of it, as much as its power, caused him to stumble sideways and crash heavily to the ground. He looked up and saw, to his great astonishment, Boah towering above him – weaponless – but glowering with malevolent intent.

"Boah?" Poseidon said, scrambling to his feet.

"You will fight me now."

"I will not. I have no reason to fight you."

"You have taken my woman."

The others around the fire, all men who had come to talk about the coming hunt, formed a circle around the two of them. From the corner of his eye Poseidon could see women and elders streaming from their huts or moving from their home fires to the uproar in the village center.

Boah swung a fist at Poseidon who ducked to avoid it connecting with his head.

"Cleatah is not your woman," Poseidon said.

Both men and women around them began to vocalize their opinions. "She is not your woman, Boah." "Poseidon has stolen her from you." "Fight! Fight for Cleatah!"

It occurred to Poseidon then that this was an ancient custom of the Shore People: two males, one desired female. A fight would decide who mated with her.

As Boah lowered his head to ram his rival, Poseidon glimpsed Cleatah at the edge of the circle, firelight and shadow dappling her face. Poseidon crashed down onto his back with Boah straddling him, swinging with two fists at his head.

Poseidon's first wild blow missed Boah's chin but crushed his nose. Blood exploded from Boah's nostrils onto his rival, but his fists never slowed. Poseidon propelled himself upward with a head-butt that proved equally useless. Grabbing Boah round the shoulders he spun them both sideways. But they were rolling straight for the bonfire.

"Stop!" Cleatah's voice rang out clear and strong. "Stop now!"

All eyes swiveled to find her, bold but impassive, balled fists at her hips.

"Let them fight!" cried Brannan. "That is the way it is done. A man chooses a woman. If two men choose one woman, they fight. He who wins the fight wins the woman."

The brawlers were inches from the fire, but Boah's flying fists had not ceased for the elder's recitation of tribal ritual. One blow landed square on Poseidon's cheek and he felt the skin split over the bone.

Cleatah strode over and began kicking both men. "Stop!" She kicked harder, landing blows on their sides and backs. Boah finally ceased his attack and sat back on his knees, panting hard. Poseidon wiped blood out of his eyes. His head was ringing but he could hear Cleatah loud and clear.

"I am a woman, and two men wish to mate with me. But I will not mate with the winner of the fight."

Complete silence fell over the camp. This was unheard of.

"Then who will you mate with?" Elkon asked.

"The man I choose."

"A woman cannot choose!" Heydra insisted with a derisive shake of his head.

More cries of "A woman cannot choose!" rang out around the central fire.

"*This* woman chooses," Cleatah said.

Poseidon pushed a perplexed Boah off him and stood as tall as he could, unable to take his eyes from Cleatah, fierce as any hunter.

"I choose Poseidon," she said.

The moment he could never, in his wildest dreams, imagine was at hand. There was no time for hesitation or all would be lost. "She is mine," he declared, feeling the words as he spoke them to be the truest he had ever uttered in his life. He looked around and saw groups of women whispering among themselves, considering the import of such outrageous sentiments.

"She chooses Poseidon!" called one bold tribeswoman, "and he chooses her. Let Boah find another!"

He went to Cleatah then, bloodied but strong. They stood shoulder-to-shoulder, displaying less defiance than fortitude. Then joining hands they turned and sliced silently and unmolested through the crowd, a new tribal tradition burgeoning in their wake.

∾

The Spring plateau was teeming with life. Grasses were still green and un-trampled, trees bursting with new foliage, and the floor of the plain a carpet of varicolored wildflowers. They'd ridden out on Arrow just after dawn, Cleatah seated behind Poseidon, her arms linked around his waist. Sheeva, her protector, now quite accustomed to the man and the horse, trotted behind them. Sometimes Poseidon walked alongside, giving Cleatah clear sight of the world from the higher vantage point. Other times they both walked, allowing Arrow to run free, graze on the sweet grasses, or just amble companionably beside them.

More times than he could count he shouted aloud at the sight of some overwhelming magnificence, swooned at a gorgeous fragrance. He savored the lusciousness of a berry turgid with juice, delighted at the soft velvet of a flower's petal trailed along his cheek. It was not that he had never experienced such marvels, but that in this woman's company they were amplified, almost miraculous. They laughed easily together. In his whole life he had not laughed as much as the two of them had in this one morning.

They had never talked about their "choosing." It was more of a quiet confidence between them. Something that neither of them had spoken aloud before that moment in front of the tribe, but a knowing that they'd each felt as surely as a need to eat or drink or sleep.

Today was the day she'd promised for so long – accompanying her to the Great Plateau. Now as they walked Cleatah elucidated properties of the various medicine plants as she gathered them. She explained to him simply but beautifully the cycle of life, growth, death and rebirth of plants. Together they examined a flower inside and out, marveling at the tiny structures so perfectly formed for function as well as beauty.

She'd created a language all her own, though before today she'd had no one to share it with. She knew, instinctively, that he would comprehend, that her intellect would not frighten him. So the words – detailed descriptions of plants, their usage, anatomy and function, effects of the weather and the seasons on them, even the idea, sounding remarkably like molecular principle that everything, even a rock, was alive and moving – came tumbling forth like a great gushing river. There was no attempt to hide her joy in having found her equal, someone who could share all that had been unspoken and unrevealed until this day.

When the sun was at its zenith, the air shimmering with heat, Cleatah led him from the open plain to the shade of the forest. The cool on his skin felt lovely, and as he watched her stoop to carefully gather the tightly furled fronds of a fern he was struck by the odd combination of her strength and softness. There was a discernible definition to her muscles he did not see in Terresian women. Yet there was a rich female quality as well, one that made him long to touch her – any and all of her – skin, hair, face, breasts… something he had not yet dared to do. Their most physical contact had been the feel of her body pressing against his back as they rode, and that alone had set his heart racing.

Now all four of them were on foot – man, woman, horse and wolf. He glanced at Sheeva. There was hardly a moment when the wolf's eyes strayed from Cleatah. What trust the animal had accrued for Poseidon could easily be shaken by the lightest overstepping of an invisible boundary the animal had thrown up around her. By far the wolf's most astonishing olfasense was smell. Poseidon had learned his own bodily odors were changed more dramatically by emotion than by physical exertion and was keenly, if ironically, aware that it would be the beast who recognized his fears and his desires before the woman.

"You are quiet," Cleatah said. "What is in here?" She touched her temple but did not meet his eye. She'd learned that he would speak more freely if their gazes were not locked.

"I'm curious about Sheeva," he finally said. Poseidon could see Cleatah's lips curl upward into a bow, as though she relished the thought of telling this particular story. She hesitated, as good storytellers do, deciding how and when to begin the tale.

"When I found her she had been badly injured, a bone broken in her foreleg. Her pack was nowhere to be found, but a buron herd grazed nearby and I thought the wolves had gone for a kill, and this unlucky one had been trampled. It did not explain her family abandoning her, but I would never know the reason for that. She was weak and in terrible pain when I found her, barely able to growl at my approach. She was young, though not a pup. Perhaps it had been her first hunt. When a young man fails in his first hunt it is shameful. If he is injured it is a disgrace. Perhaps it was so of the wolf.

"I thought I would help her somehow," Cleatah went on, "but I admit I wished her injuries had been to the hindquarters, so my head would not be within snapping distance of her jaws." Her eyes smiled, remembering. "I believed she would not hurt me, but I moved slowly. You know, Poseidon. Like it was at the first with Arrow."

He nodded and she went on.

"She whined when I touched her foot, and looked up from under her heavy lids. Then she licked my hand. I set the bone and wrapped it with vines. I brought her water and a small kill to eat. She was very quiet, very still, but I slept next to her all that night and stayed by her side the next day and night. But we could stay no longer. Her nose twitched so violently I knew something to fear was nearby – perhaps a lion. I did not help her to her feet. I knew that if she could not rise of her own accord, if she could not walk beside me, my healing had been for nothing. But she did rise, not without a pained cry, but once on her feet she found her footing quickly, though careful on the broken leg. The splint I'd made held the bone tight and straight, and we arrived at the edge of the plateau before nightfall.

"The descent for the wolf was not possible, but I wished her to shelter in the safety of the village that night. I ran down and found Boah, knowing he would not be afraid. Once night fell we carried the wolf down and hid her in my hut. She knew, somehow, knew to be perfectly still, perfectly quiet. I brought her food every day. Her leg healed well. She came to love me and I her. I gave her the name Sheeva."

The wolf's ears pricked up at the sound of her name, and she looked to Cleatah, as if for orders. Receiving none she continued her easy trot.

"How did you show her to the tribe?" Poseidon asked. "Were they not frightened?"

"One night when we were all were gathered at the central fire Boah went to them and said, 'Cleatah is coming now, and she brings with her a friend. No need to fear.' I came slowly from the shadows into the light of the fire with the wolf at my side. I heard Boah saying, 'You, stay down.' 'No shouting.' 'If you move, move slowly.' They heeded him and Sheeva – may Great Mother bless her – stayed quiet and calm at my side. She didn't curl her lip or bare a fang. She sat at the edge of the fire pit. But when she grunted and lay down with her head resting on her paws there were gasps, and laughter all around. I allowed the people – one by one – to touch the wolf, telling them to gently speak her name as they did. The children wished most of all to lay their hands on this magical creature – once their enemy to be feared, now at rest, warming her fur at their fire.

"All trusted Sheeva and loved her, but it was to me that she stayed closest. She protected me as I had once protected her. She hunted small creatures and brought them home to share at our fire. So when one day she disappeared, as though she had never existed, the tribe mourned her. But no one more than me. Once again I was alone. But where before I had never known loneliness, now I did. How I had come to depend on my companion!

"Nearly a moon passed and one morning she returned, looking weary and bloated. With one look I knew her to be pregnant. In my hut that very night she birthed nine wolves so tiny they could fit in the palm of my hand. Every family wanted one, though the hunting men won out, for they argued rightly that wolves taught to hunt would bring food for the whole tribe.

"Each year Sheeva leaves us and returns with a brood in her belly. Her mate is nowhere to be seen, I think wary of the village and the tribe. After all, how can Sheeva tell him not to fear? So this is how she came to me, to the tribe, and how her children became the children of the Shore People."

Cleatah went silent, perhaps aware that she had never spoken so long or so clearly since Poseidon's coming. She stood and turned, carefully placing the ferns in her gathering bag. "Will you come with me to my bathing place?"

I would go with you anywhere, to the end of the Erthe, he thought but did not say.

Instead he stood, and trying to keep his composure followed her deeper into the forest.

෴

"It's time you bathed," she announced.

"Ha! I've bathed recently."

Cleatah could see that her remark had caused no insult but had been taken lightly, as she had meant it. "Not as you will today." She enjoyed provoking this man, for his responses were so unusual – not at all like the men of her tribe – the odd complexity of his feelings, so many of them transparent. The way he combined his words, the inflections in his voice.

She led him through paths soft with moss and hung with thick vines and brilliantly hued, cuplike flowers twining in profusion around gnarled tree trunks. Soon they could hear the rush and tumble of water, and in the next moment emerged at the base of a sun-dappled waterfall. From the expression on Poseidon's face she knew it was as lovely a sight as he had ever seen. She stooped at the stream's edge and began rooting around in her bag.

"Take off your clothes and start across," she called. "It is cold.

The water comes from the high mountains. Go on. I will meet you." From the corner of her eye she regarded Poseidon's naked body as he stepped into the stream. He was tall, but in the time since he had joined the tribe his muscles had thickened and firmed, especially his thighs and haunches as a result of riding the horses. Yes, he was a powerful looking man, and handsome to her eye.

She slipped off her skins and waded into the waist-deep water just as Poseidon emerged onto the far bank. He turned and watched her come across. He was staring at her naked body, her nipples hard from the icy cold. When they both stood on the opposite shore she led him downstream and away from the crashing falls to a tranquil, rock-lined pool near the river's edge. Steam rose in delicate tendrils from its dark green surface.

She wasted no time lowering herself into the water, unselfconsciously gasping and moaning in delight. Poseidon quickly clamored in after her, and she wondered if his haste was more to cover his nakedness than to experience the pleasure of the waters.

"Ah, ahhh…" Poseidon's eyes closed as he plunged in up to his neck. "Hot water," he said finally. "There is nothing in the world like it."

"You had springs like this near your village?" she asked.

"Yes, and I have missed them." He opened his eyes and looked at her. "Thank you. This is a joy."

After a while of soaking in silence she said, "Stand out of the water. There's a ledge here."

He obeyed her and found himself waist deep, steam rising off his arms and torso. When she turned to face him she had in her hands the soap root that she could knead into lather. She looked directly into Poseidon's eyes and held his gaze as she reached out and placed her soapy hands on his chest. She knew the expression she saw on his face was desire, and it did not displease her. She began to massage the lather into every part of his body above the water – arms, chest, back, neck. He stood obediently as she directed him to raise his arms so she could soap his armpits. She ignored the trembling she felt beneath her hands, and tried to ignore the thought of his male parts under the water.

"Rinse yourself," she commanded him finally, "and dunk your head." This he did wordlessly, but as he emerged from the pool, water streaming from his head and beard and powerful body, it was Cleatah who was suddenly trembling. She wanted this man. Wanted to feel him moving inside her... But that would have to wait.

"Now sit on the ledge. I am going to wash your hair."

"Wash my hair?" He looked at her and laughed aloud.

"Should I not?"

"No, no. I want you to. Then will I wash yours?" he asked with a playful smile.

"Just sit down."

He obeyed her, unable to suppress his smile. She lathered the thick mane, scrubbing his scalp with her strong fingers, enjoying the feel of his head in her hands. His head, she thought, was as intimate a body part as what lay between his thighs – the sinewy tendons at the back of his neck, the gristle of his ears, the bony temples.

"Dunk and rinse," she instructed now.

When he emerged this time she was holding an obsidian flake, one side a fine sharp edge. "Will you let me shave your face?"

"You bathed me at your will, and washed my hair. Why do you ask permission to shave me?"

She did not answer for a long moment, forming her words only as the thoughts came to her. "You may wish to continue hiding your face from me. That is your right." She did not add, *But I wish to see it as I did in my mushroom vision.*

"Shave me," he said, his voice cracking with emotion, his eyes fastened on hers. "I do wish you to know who I am."

Cleatah turned away then, pretending to make a lather with

her soap root, but in truth she was not prepared for Poseidon to see the tears of some unnamable emotion that were threatening to spill from her eyes.

∽

Following Cleatah into the meadow in mid-afternoon, Poseidon reached up and touched his face. It had been nearly an Erthan year since he'd been clean-shaven, and it felt wonderful. Even more gratifying was her expression when she'd finished shaving him and saw his hairless face. She had muttered "As I thought..." but had refused to explain herself. She'd simply washed her own hair and body, an act that Poseidon, watching her, found almost as erotic as her washing of his. But afterwards, in anointing them both with a fragrant oil – chest, forehead and temple – he sensed the entire episode was somehow a rite of purification.

In the height of the now scorching afternoon Cleatah led him through a field inhabited by a herd of grazing buron and a multitude of large black buzzing flies. She moved carefully but confidently, avoiding the several bulls that grazed with the females. Occasionally she stooped for a moment to extract a plant from what appeared to be piles of buron dung. He thought the actions strange after such vigorous bathing, but did not question Cleatah who seemed serious and intent in her gathering. When they'd left the field, however, and she was carefully stowing her recent finds in her gathering bag, he saw that she was smiling broadly, indeed looking extremely pleased with herself.

"What have you found?"

"The reason we have come out together today," she replied mysteriously.

"Show me."

"First let us go to a more comfortable place."

She took him to a shady grove of trees, a pleasant respite from the heat, and sat down facing him. The moss was very thick but dry and made for a luxuriant cushion. From her pouch Cleatah extracted her most recent find and laid it out on a bed of leaves in front of them. There were sixteen slender–stemmed mushrooms. She separated them into two piles, placing each pile on a large leaf, and handed one to him. The other she held up in front of her heart. She looked directly into his eyes.

"You and I, Poseidon, we both keep secrets. You hold yours in your head. Now you hold mine… in your hands."

He looked down at the mushrooms, unable to utter an intelligible thought.

"You do not know of these mushrooms?" she asked.

"I do not."

She was struggling for words. "They are filled with powerful spirits. The most sacred plants I have ever gathered. When I eat them I see…wonders."

"What sort of wonders?"

"Visions…" was all she said. "Visions."

Certain naturally occurring life-forms on Terres were said to produce hallucinatory episodes, he knew, but for many generations the ultra-practical Terresians had shunned such experiences. Cleatah seemed to be attempting to re-conjure and describe the indescribable.

"I travel…to other places, though I remain here. I….see things. Everything is beautiful. Everything is…" She made a chopping gesture with her hand and her face screwed up as she groped for the word. "…sharp. I cannot explain, Poseidon. We will eat them, together, here, now. I have eaten them many times before, but never with another person. I want you to share the wonders with me. To come with me to Ka."

With that she took up the first mushroom between her thumb and forefinger. "Great Mother, bless me, bless this man, bless our journey." She placed the mushroom in her mouth and began to chew.

Without hesitation Poseidon did the same. The taste was

bitter, even poisonous, he thought. But he trusted Cleatah, trusted her in a way he had trusted no other person in his life, and found that there was nothing he wished for more than to share with her a journey of wonder.

Together, one by one, they ate the rest.

&

Paralysis suffused his limbs as his mind reeled in color and light. Then in a shattering explosion of clarity Poseidon understood the sacred nature of this world. Everything was alive! *Not simply the myriad creatures and profundity of vegetation, but each and every element of the planet itself was imbued with vital, moving spirit. The mountains, rocks, sand, water, wind –* Erthe lived! *The edges of every object in his sight appeared sharp and almost painfully defined, but paradoxically, all were connected...intersected. There were no boundaries. Did the molecules of his skin not mingle with those of the oxygen surrounding them? What constituted ground, and where did the sky actually begin?*

For the first time he could feel *the spirit that animated the orange and black insect fluttering by, and questioned how it could fly. Surely muscles and aero-mechanics alone could not explain it. What mind of what creator could conceive of such a miracle? Or was it something other than mind? He stared hard at his own hand, perceived what he saw but was suddenly overwhelmed by its significance...or was it insignificance?*

Into his frame of vision another hand moved to grasp his own. Smooth and slender where his was thick and work-roughened. Fingers intertwined fingers and exquisite sensations moved up his arm in tiny, pulsating waves that threatened to overwhelm him. Cleatah. The woman of Erthe who was herself made of the planet's stuff – its water, minerals, air, spirit, knowledge. This woman who cared for him, had bathed him, shaved his face to see him more clearly, trusted him with her mushroom spirits. This lovely creature whose hand now entwined his own. Was she not the greatest mystery of all?

He had refrained from turning his eyes on her face. He knew it from memory already, knew each curve, the angle of the cheek-bones, the tilt of the eyes, the fall of dark hair that framed it. But he somehow feared looking into that face now. Feared its overwhelming beauty and its power to unhinge what was left of his precise Terresian sensibilities. Who was he now? What had he become? How could this have happened?

Her hand in his lay still and undemanding. She understood him, a man whose education and technos, whose very evolution surpassed hers by eons. A year ago he would have thought it impossible. What would happen to him if he coupled with this woman, joined his spirit with hers?

What would happen to him if he did not?

Then Cleatah slowly laid her head against his chest, gazing up into his eyes and all at once one of his myriad questions was answered. As he slowly gathered her to him and bent to kiss her mouth the movement itself seemed a destiny fulfilled. Her supple arms pulling him closer still, seemed to be welcoming him home. But the astonishing pleasure of the kiss itself took consciousness and hurled it from his mind to his senses in the space of a breath. Suddenly every nerve was inflamed — absorbing her perfect fragrance, the pleasing colors of her skin, hair, the luminescence of her eyes and unbearable softness of her skin, the ripe fruit of her mouth. He marveled at the animal way she moved in his arms, at the urgent sighs as she devoured him with her lips.

Their thin summer pelts fell away and they were naked, pressed tight along the length of their bodies. Limbs bent at angles to pull closer still. Kisses deepened. Cleatah's new-washed hair fell soft about his neck, his shoulders. His hands began searching the curves and soft mounds of her, long flanks, taut buds, moist clefts. She moaned and opened her thighs, warm and trembling, to receive him. Governed by impossible restraint he entered her slowly, gradually piercing her untouched center, liquid and sweet and tight around him. Her low moans he heard from a distance, but his own rough growls reverberated loud inside his head. Insistent fingers on his back and buttocks pulled him further inside. 'Deeper,' he heard her whisper, 'deeper, oh please…" and the once-languid thrusts found the rhythm of a slow gallop. Then time vanished. Bodies melted boundary-less one into the other, pulsing with fierce spikes of pleasure. Spikes quickened, deepened, urgent sweetness surging, massing like a great wave cresting, higher, higher, threatening to break.

And then it did.

They exploded with shocked cries of pure and joyous sensation. In a vision of perfect clarity he saw the lush bodies of the woman and the Erthe as one, and knew that spirit, that single infusing spirit would now and ever after be necessary to sustain his life. And as long as she lived he would never be lonely again.

Once night had fallen Arrow slept on her feet near the tree where, on a soft cushion of moss, Poseidon and Cleatah had laid down side by side. Sheeva rested beside them. Cleatah's hands explored his face, her gentle touch causing him tiny jolts of pleasure under her fingertips. He was aware that the world as he knew it before the mushroom was coming back to him: the colors beautiful, but no longer screaming their various hues. The definition and perspective of objects clear, but not abnormally sharp and ultra-dimensional. Sensations exquisite, but not overwhelming. Gently he took her hands in his and kissed them, then pulled himself up so he was resting on an elbow above her.

Somewhere in the long, miraculous stretch of the day he had come to realize that this woman would be his. But now he must reveal his secret – what he feared might turn her against him. How could she forgive him for so long and staggering a deception? Cleatah was gazing at him with wondering eyes.

"My secret…" he finally blurted, but then could not go on.

"You wish to share it with me now?"

He sat up and Cleatah, understanding the importance of the moment, sat up too. It took him a long while to speak again.

"Cleatah, I am not what I seem. I am not who you think I am, who I told you and your people I was... I do not come from an inland tribe. My people were not murdered in an attack on our village."

He could see that she was following his words, but those words were leading only to confusion. He was explaining who he was *not*. Now he must explain who, in fact, he was. She remained silent, choosing not to question him or urge him on but waited patiently, never taking her eyes from his face.

"You have never gone farther afield from your village than this?" he asked, and she nodded affirmatively. "But you know there is more beyond this?"

"Yes, I can see the mountains, and I have been told there is land beyond the mountains, and shores stretching very far north and south of our village. Also, the elders say the sea goes on for a long way beyond what we can see from even the highest plateau."

"They are correct. The sea is perhaps larger than any of you have imagined."

"Do you come from...beyond the sea?" she asked slowly, hardly understanding her own question.

"No, nor do I come from a village on the shore to the north or south of you."

"Then where?" Cleatah's confusion was growing into alarm, and he felt no closer to an explanation than he had when he'd started. He looked into the sky and saw that the moon had risen. It was huge and bright, and its features were clearly defined.

"How far do the elders say the moon is from the village?" he asked.

"They do not know, but think at least as far as the mountains, maybe more."

"And the sun?"

287

"Perhaps closer, for it gives off so much more heat and light than the moon."

"And how far are those?" He pointed to the stars, increasing by the minute in the blackness of the sky.

Cleatah smiled and shook her head helplessly. He knew she would be thinking that he was becoming harder and harder to understand. "The lights that move across the sky at night..." she said, "we do not know. They are just beautiful lights."

This woman who had but a short time ago possessed the knowledge of a great botanical scholar now seemed little more than a baffled child. This was far more difficult than he had ever imagined.

"Do you trust me, Cleatah?"

"Yes."

"If I tell you things, even if they are hard to imagine, will you try to take them as the truth?"

"I will. And I do trust you, my love." Impulsively she reached out and caressed his face with her hand, reminding them both of the extraordinary day they had shared, their intimate journey and – suddenly infusing him with the confidence to go on – the promise that she would hear him and somehow understand.

"Erthe," he began, "though you cannot see it, and therefore cannot know it, is enormous. And the land is not flat, but so large that it curves. In fact Erthe is shaped like this." With his ten fingers splayed and curved and joined at the tips, he formed a sphere.

"When I am at the highest point on the plateau," she interjected, "I can see a curve on the ocean."

"Yes, Erthe is round, like a davok seed. There are great areas of land, and even greater areas of water."

"How large is Erthe?" she asked.

"If you could walk all the way around it – if you could walk across the water – it would take you more than fifty moons."

Cleatah's mouth fell open slightly. Then she composed herself. "I am listening," she said.

"The moon is also round, the same shape as Erthe, and it is

also much farther away from the village than the mountains are. It is, perhaps, as many times away from the mountains as there are buron on the entire plateau." He could see Cleatah silently calculating so extraordinary a distance, but he knew if he did not continue he would lose his confidence. "The sun, also round, is…is even farther away than the moon."

"Are you certain?" she asked, perplexed. "How can it be farther but give off so much more light and heat than the moon?"

"Because," he went on, "it is so much larger than the moon."

"I understand this," said Cleatah slowly. "The mountains appear small from a far distance, but become large as you approach them. Still, Poseidon, I do not understand where you are from, and why you talk about the moon and sun and lights in the sky to explain it."

"I know this is difficult. I'm afraid…it is going to become even more difficult. Where I come from, we call the lights in the sky 'stars.'"

"Stars," she repeated, gazing heavenward.

"I know you can see many stars, but there are far more than can even be seen on the clearest night. These stars, small as they appear…"

"…are actually round and large, because they are so far away?" she finished for him.

"Yes, yes!" He was momentarily relieved at Cleatah's ability to comprehend such concepts, but descended immediately into desperation, knowing that his next statement would, despite her intelligence, prove completely unbelievable. Unable to go on in so teacherly a fashion, he gathered her into his arms and held her tightly.

"Poseidon," she said impatiently. She pushed him to arm's length and stared into his face. "You came into our village a clumsy stranger and…invented yourself a respected man. You are brave, you are kind, you are gentle. You have shared my deepest secret, accepted the visions fearlessly, joined your body and spirit with mine. I love you. From this day on you are my love. I want no other man, and expect that you will want no other woman. What distance your village is from mine, or how large it is, means nothing. You will still be mine."

"Do you promise me that, Cleatah?" he said. Promise that no matter what I say or do in the next moments, you will not run from me?"

"Run from you?"

"In fear. I may shock you, show you things to rival the mushroom's visions, but please, don't be afraid. I will never, ever harm you."

"Tell me. Show me. *Now.*"

Poseidon stood and presented his upturned palm to Cleatah. With his other hand he activated his wrist hub. He was relieved to see that she smiled at the tiny, blinking lights of many colors under his skin – like something out of her visions.

"What is this thing?" she asked. "This thing inside your body?"

"It is called a 'phaetron.'"

"Fay-tron," she repeated.

"I will tell you where I'm from. It is farther away than you can imagine, but in fact, in every important way I am a man like all the men of your tribe. The only thing that makes me different is that I possess the phaetron and its secrets."

"In the same way my possessing the mushroom and its secrets make me different from anyone in my tribe?"

"Yes!" He prayed that Cleatah's experience with the mushroom would somehow make this easier. "I'm going to show you what the phaetron – my mushroom – can do. May I put Sheeva to sleep for a little while, so she isn't frightened?"

When Cleatah nodded her assent, he leveled the narcotizing function on the wolf and she fell into a deep and instant slumber. Despite the warning, when Sheeva fell unconscious Cleatah gasped and reached for her. She laid her head on the wolf's chest to assure herself the animal was breathing. She looked up at Poseidon, astonished.

But he could hesitate no longer. He activated the light source and instantly the area under the tree burst into mid-day brightness. Now Cleatah flung herself back against the trunk. A clenched fist covered her mouth and her eyes were large, darting in every direction.

Placing a gentle arm around her he said, "Let me show you something."

"You have *already* shown me something, my love."

"Come here," he said insistently and drew her back down to the ground. He cleared away a large patch of moss to expose the soil beneath it, then picked up a handful of different sized stones. He laid the largest one – a smooth, light colored rock – in the center of the cleared patch. Around this he drew nine concentric circles, and on each of the circular lines he placed a pebble.

"I want you to imagine that this white stone is the sun. We call it Helios."

Cleatah was still trembling, but she nodded nevertheless.

"Nine worlds spin around it. This one, third from the sun, is Erthe." He took the third pebble and moved it in the dirt in a circle around the white rock. Cleatah looked confused.

"Does Erthe... do all the worlds move about in the dirt?" Are they not in the sky?"

"All right. Move back," he instructed her. "Don't be afraid." He activated another of the phaetron's functions and directed it at the stones on the ground. At once they began to levitate, and with another function punched in, the pebbles began to rotate in proper planetary orbits around the white rock.

He turned to find Cleatah goggle-eyed with wonder, all her fear having vanished with the miracle before her. Heartened, he picked up the tiniest pebble he could find and dropped it next to the stone representing Erthe. Instantly the little pebble fell into orbit around it.

"That is the moon," he said, "which flies around Erthe in this circle we call an 'orbit.' All of these worlds spin in an orbit."

"Orbit." Cleatah moved close as she could without disturbing the outermost stone's circuit. "What are the others called?" she demanded.

"Hermes," he said pointing to the closest stone to the sun. "Then there is Aphrodite, Erthe, Mars, Zeus, Kronos, Ouranos, Radon, Pluton."

Cleatah studied the moving configuration for a long moment, then looked up at Poseidon. "And which of these worlds are you from, my love?"

"Cleatah, you astonish me!" he cried, the worst of his fears assuaged. Suddenly he felt himself bursting with an emotion unknown to Terresians but must, he realized, be passionate love for this woman.

"I am from none of these worlds," he said, indicating the nine planets, and knelt to find one last stone. I am from *this* world. We call it 'Terres'." He dropped the final pebble into the space between Mars and Zeus. Immediately it began whirling around the 'sun' stone, and then hurled itself far out into its elliptical orbit on a slightly different plane. So far did it travel that it moved beyond the circle of light the phaetron had created under the tree, and did not immediately come back.

"Where did it go?" she exclaimed.

"Far away. It will take a long time to complete its orbit."

"Has it gone as far away as the stars?"

"Almost as far."

Her face creased into a mask of puzzlement. How...how did you get here... from there?"

Poseidon laughed aloud at the thought of so ungainly an explanation and pulled Cleatah into a warm embrace. "That, my love," he said, relief flooding him, "is a story for another day, many days. For a lifetime."

MARS COLONY

Disaster

THIRTY-ONE

S TAND IN THE light, Nonae," Athens instructed the red-headed woman. As she moved to the window of Micah's studio to allow the sun to shine down on the head-dress she was modeling, it occurred to the governor that the piece – hundreds of thin gold braids hanging down from a curved diadem like a long wig – would have looked better on Leanya's black, silken hair. Still, the headdress was wonderful on Nonae, the most mature of the women Athens was currently seeing. Her slender ivory limbs were an elegant compliment to the draped and slitted gown she was wearing, a style popular with colonial women these days. The simply designed garments showed off to the finest effect the golden body ornaments that they all wore in great profusion. The two of them had stopped at the artisan's studio before leaving for the theater to see the latest historical spectacle that everyone was talking about.

"Would you like the headdress?" Athens asked Nonae, giving Micah, who had created the treasure, a conspiratorial smile.

"You know I would," she replied, dandling her fingers sensually through the delicate gold braids. "Does it look good with my dress?"

"What do you say, Micah?" Athens asked his friend.

"I'd rather see it on you naked."

Nonae laughed, unperturbed. "I want to make you a gift

as well," she said to Athens, moving with fluid grace from the window to a display of the artisan's creations and appraising each one carefully.

"How much is it?" Athens asked Micah.

"Twelve hundred crells. But for you, *Governor*," Micah replied with friendly mockery, "I would only require a payment in raw gold to replace what was used in the headdress."

"You should pay *me*," Athens said. "Everyone at the theater will see it and come breaking down your doors."

"I think this is the one," said Nonae finally, holding a stylized golden mask over her face. "Do you like it? I think it would look lovely over your dining…"

Before she could finish, Persus, burst through the studio doors.

"Come quickly!" she said to Athens.

"What is it?"

"Horrible, horrible…"

"Tell me what's happened.

"The mine…both mines. They've collapsed!"

If the sights and sounds above ground were any indication of what lay below, Athens was sure he could not stand to see them. Lying amidst a landscape strewn with chunks of charred and steaming titanum ore, here and there scattered with pebbles of gold, the dead were – many of them – burned and mangled beyond recognition. Medics attended to the injured using pha-etrons to mend tissue and bone and stop hemorrhaging. But with no one having ever conceived of so enormous a disaster, the rescue and emergency team was hopelessly small and inadequate. The screams and moans of the victims, many of them clutch-ing at Athens's legs as he moved through their numbers, were unbearable to him.

"This way, Governor," said the shift manager, Glyss, guiding Athens and Persus toward a large jagged hole in the ground on which had once stood the mine's elevator terminal. A large beam emitter held in place with clamps now provided a makeshift blue elevator column upon which the grim-faced emergency workers were descending, and the injured continually borne up to the surface. The three of them stepped into the beam and began the descent. The smell of burnt ore, seared flesh and blood was nauseating, but Athens knew he must remain strong and appear confident, his leadership the only antidote to utter panic.

They rode the blue beam down through the skin of the planet, the once perfectly vertical tunnel in some places skewed, in others studded with titanum rock and boulders vomited up from the depths. Already claustrophobic in the shaft, Athens was forced to turn his eyes away from the constant stream of mutilated and suffering miners being transported topside.

The scene in the upper mine was nightmarish, as the devastation was nearly complete. The entire cavern was destroyed. Portions of the side walls had collapsed, and there were great gaping holes where neat rows of cells had been. The central column had fallen over, crashing into the forward mine wall. The men trapped and crushed in the cells beneath it were most certainly dead, and there was terrible resignation in the absence of rescue activity in that area.

Many of the six-legged phaetronic robots had been knocked from the mine walls and crashed to the cave floor. Others had simply gone awry, Athens could see. One of them – it's searing red beam meant to sunder rock from rock and still activated – had burnt a large gaping hole through the midsection of a dead victim hanging grotesquely from the cell opening.

When the heavy central column had fallen, all its many hundreds of yellow tractor beams had failed in an instant, releasing their endless streams of men and titanum ore in a rain of death to the cavern floor. In many places, however, Athens could see the floor itself had exploded upwards from below, leaving shards of jagged rock upon which some bodies lay impaled. In other places the upper mine's floor was gone entirely, with gaping holes that extended, he imagined, all the way down into the lower mine.

"What caused this?" Persus asked Glyss, gazing around in disbelief. "What could possibly have caused it?"

"They don't know, but perhaps an unexpected chemical reaction in the lower mine…"

"But…" Athens muttered helplessly.

"We have to make our way on foot from here, Governor," said the shift manager.

"We're right behind you," said Athens grimly. "Glyss…"

"Yes Sir."

"Does it get worse than this?"

"I'm afraid it does, though by now they may have cleared away most of the…body parts. Watch your heads here."

Athens saw Persus stoop to get by a ragged hole blown in the lower end of the central column, and followed her. Then Glyss led them down a ladder through what was left of the shaft, now nothing more than a pile of rubble. At the sensation of liquid dripping on his cheek Athens wiped it away to find his fingers slick with blood.

"Uugth." He shuddered involuntarily and looked up. Half a man's body hung impaled on shards of the central column's metal casing.

"I'm sorry, Sir," apologized Glyss. "Be careful not to slip on the rungs. We're almost down now."

Reaching the bottom of the ladder they found themselves in the lower mine. Here men were clearing mineral debris with their hubs, and others carting away bits of human remains. The lustrous glow of gold was absent, even in the bright illumination of emergency lights.

Athens spotted Golde with a group of men, mining foremen and engineers. Though they were speaking to him, questioning him and he was answering, he appeared to be somehow absent from the scene. His eyes were dull, his expression flat. His newly flamboyant personality had vanished. He was drowning in remorse.

As Athens approached the group all eyes fell on him, looking for answers, encouragement, guidance, hope. He found himself, for perhaps the first time in his life, entirely lost for words. In this terrible moment lay his greatest challenge. The colony needed him. The home world was depending upon him for its very survival. He could not leave this to Persus who, understanding the import of the moment, was standing silent. For a fleeting moment his thoughts flew to Poseidon, living somewhere on Gaia with a primitive tribe. His brother would naturally know the best course of action in such a situation. Suddenly Athens calmed. He placed an arm around the distraught Golde and looked squarely at the others.

"We cannot allow a panic," he said, surprised at how steady his voice sounded. "And we will stay focused, put our heads together – geologists, engineers, managers – and we'll find a solution, see this through."

He was gratified to feel Golde's tense body relax at his words. His heart swelled to see the admiring gleam in Persus' eye, and the faces of the others softening. This was his moment. He would prove once and for all that the Terresian grumblers had been wrong about him. That his father had been wrong. He was strong and level-headed and sure and no one – not even his brother – was better suited to lead.

THIRTY-TWO

"THERE WAS NO way of knowing that the organisms in the throes of metabolic process exuded a gas," said Golde, "and that mixed in certain proportions with the oxygen pumped into the mines, produced such a highly volatile condition." He was standing before Athens sitting behind his desk with Persus at his side.

"Unbelievable," Persus murmured. "that something that created such joy and beauty in our world could produce so much death and suffering."

"Not your fault," Athens told Golde.

"You believe that, Sir?" he said, his voice little more than a whine.

"I do. Don't you, Persus?"

"Yes, Golde. We're on your side."

"Because I've been hearing..." His slouch grew even deeper, "...that people are blaming me. Even though you...benefitted so greatly from the discovery..."

Athens's eyes flashed at the implication.

"All three of us share the blame," Persus said, evenly. "Praxis, too. And I don't see any way out of it except meeting it head-on. I say we call a congregation of the colonists. We'll stand shoulder to shoulder and explain it to them together. They'll understand.

We're only human." To Athens she said, "You can count on the people's love for you, Sir. Even…" she was finding it hard to go on, "even if you have to announce, for safety's sake, to cease all mining of gold ore."

Athens groaned at the words.

"I think if we explain that while the explosions might be rare," she went on, "they cannot be precisely calculated. Even a single death more is an unacceptable risk." She looked at the two men. "Don't you think they'll appreciate that?"

"They'll have to," Athens said. He sounded almost convincing.

Now, two days later, with several more dead of their injuries, Athens, sharing a platform with Golde, looked out over the mass of humanity assembling in the plaza outside the Governor's Residence. With a pang he remembered the last time they had gathered like this. It had been on the occasion of the Independence Vote, undoubtedly the happiest day in the colony's short life. Athens had been as bright and beloved as the gold ore he had gifted his people. The love they showered on him that afternoon had provided him the first genuine triumph over his brother's insidious presence in his life. In fact the hero, Poseidon, had been all but forgotten by the colonists. If he was recalled at all it was as a quaint memory of their Terresian past, of endless dark nights and sterile cities that paled in comparison with their shining present.

True to form, Vice Governor Praxis had distanced himself from the excruciating embarrassment on the platform, insisting that there was no need for his presence. *Coward!* He was probably hoping for Athens's destruction, leaving an opening for himself to fill. Athens could see concern growing on Golde's face now as the colonists were called to silence. He would speak first, give a scientific explanation of the incident, and prepare the people for the inevitable announcement that Athens would shortly make of the mine's closing, and his rationale for the decision.

"My friends," Golde began, clearing his throat three times

before he could go on. "I'm not much of a speaker, so I'll just make you this promise. There can be no more deaths or injuries under my watch. You can certainly understand my concern and appreciate my care for you, even if it means sacrifice…"

Athens recalled Persus reinforcing by constant repetition that Golde should be confident that he could convince the people that while the unlimited flow of ore would have to cease – and this would necessitate a radical shift in their economy – the existing gold would simply become a more rare and precious commodity. A change in attitude more than anything.

"…thus the explosion."

Athens was startled out of his thoughts, realizing that Golde was well into his presentation. He could detect in the audience a subtle but distinct shift in mood. They were very quiet, and Athens sensed they anticipated more disturbing news.

"I cannot begin to express my sorrow at the death of our friends who lost their lives in the mines," Golde went on, sincere grief creasing his features. And that is why we cannot allow such a disaster to occur again."

Athens realized the scientist had overstepped himself. This was an announcement they had agreed the Governor should make. Athens was about to step forward when a woman from the audience called out in a voice whose rancor startled him into keeping silent.

"You can't mean you would shut down the gold mining operation?"

"Only until a safe solution can be found," Golde replied.

"Are you sure there's a solution?" she demanded.

"No," said Golde sheepishly.

"This is unacceptable!" shouted a man in the audience.

"Unacceptable?!" cried a third colonist. "This is an outrage! Do you have any idea how many lives this will ruin!"

As more and more colonists began shouting out their opinions, most of them antagonistic, the rhetoric becoming more heated by the moment, Athens's mind began to race. He knew he should step forward – quickly – and work his personal magic to dispel the growing fury. But something held him back. Failure as the colony's leader was unconscionable. Loss of his people's love unacceptable. The germ of an idea had taken hold and was now enlarging and multiplying like the cells of a human blastula in the first moments of life. One of his genomists had recently delivered a groundbreaking report which, while rife with ethical problems, now seemed to offer Athens a feasible solution.

He watched Golde trying to deflect the ever more heated barrage directed at him. The scientist finally looked to Athens with a pleading look that said, 'Come rescue me!' Indeed, the moment had come that the governor should speak, and finally Athens moved to the podium. He walked slowly, gravely, and the crowd quieted as he approached center stage. No one could possibly know that in the crossing of that distance he had decided to sacrifice Golde at the altar of the colonists' outrage.

The scientist had stepped aside and gratefully relinquished his place to Athens. The silence of the vast multitude before him was astonishing, and he knew instinctively to use it, elongate it, enhance it for the most dramatic effect. He stared out over the sea of faces, turning slowly this way and that, as though he was caressing every one of them with his benevolent gaze. He allowed a small, pained smile to play at his lips. He opened his mouth to speak, then closed it again, as though overcome with emotion, and the effect was riveting. People strained forward towards Athens, breathless…

"Good people…" he finally began in the warmest of voices. "…we together have suffered a great tragedy in the mining accident. There's not one among you who did not lose a family member or a friend on that terrible day." He paused again, as though gathering strength for what he was about to say. "Like you," he finally continued, "I believed our operations – both titanum and gold – were safe. Never once was it explained to me that there was the remotest possibility of danger in either mine."

Athens kept his eyes straight ahead, and it appeared that he was restraining himself from turning to glare accusingly at Golde. *Do not think of him,* Athens commanded himself. *Someone must be surrendered to the mob.* It could not possibly be himself. He was the colony's leader. Adored. Trusted. He could never let them down. "The easy thing," he finally continued aloud, "would be to shut down the gold mining operation indefinitely, perhaps permanently. Simply restructure our society and economy to function without free flow of the ore. Certainly we would survive, because we are strong. But why, my friends, should we go without the thing that brings so much joy into our lives when there is a solution at hand?!" He knew that Persus would be wondering what he was about to say, but he refused to look down and meet her eye.

As the crowd stirred with interest and excitement Athens silenced himself again. He was formulating his thoughts in the moments just before the words flowed from his lips. He felt inspired, alive. "We will have our gold!" he cried, lifting his voice to be heard over the crowd. "We will have our gold and no human life or limb will be lost for it again!"

The colonists began shouting encouragement, though no one yet understood how such a thing was possible.

"Today is not the day for lengthy explanations about how this will be accomplished, but it is a day for promises to be made!"

The crowd roared it approval.

"Do you trust me?!" Athens shouted.

"Yes!" came the mass reply.

"And you know that I am a man of my word?!"

"Yes!!"

The sound of their voices was shaking the air.

"Then you have my promise that if you can survive for three Marsean years with the gold that exists, the mines will be reopened and not another human life will be forfeited!!"

As the cheering became wilder Athens leapt down from the

platform and moved out among the crowd. He wished to bathe in their adulation. It excited him, strengthened him…and it allowed him to forget, if only for the moment, the wreckage of a man who stood on the stage, arms hanging limply at his sides. Athens never wished to do Golde harm.

There had simply been no other way.

ERTHE

The Great Undertaking

...of the inhabitants of the mountains and of the rest
of the country there was also a vast multitude...

Plato's *Critias,* 4th Century BC

THIRTY-THREE

CLEATAH KNELT AT the altar feeling, for the first time in her life, shy under the gaze of Great Mother. She placed narrow strips of yew bark into the fire, watching to see if it flared, hoping to see some sign before the Goddess would begin whispering answers to the question her humble servant had already asked. But there were no signs. No colored sparks, no tiny poofs of moth dust or unexpected scents from the flames. And as Cleatah breathed in the close air of her hut she grew impatient. Great Mother was making her wait today. Today of all days! The most important question she had ever placed before the Goddess. She would ask again.

"Mother, tell me about this man who comes from the stars. You know him. He is your child as much as I am."

She thought she heard Great Mother singing then, very low but very sweetly. It was a song she sometimes sang about the Moon. Cleatah waited patiently for the song to finish, but then it became a hum and went on for a long maddening time.

"Great Mother," she began, hoping her impatience was not showing. "Poseidon is a good man. He teaches me many things and..." she thought for a moment, "...he lets me teach him many things." She smiled to herself. "Boah gets angry when I try to teach him anything. 'Those are *manly* things,' he tells me. He shows me his teeth – a joke…but not a joke." She closed her eyes and saw Poseidon behind her lids. "I like his hands. Strong. Long hard fingers. But those fingers…" She had to think about it. "Those fingers are sometimes gentle as a woman's. I see the way he pulls open the petals of a flower. And he really looks inside the flower. As though he had never seen one before. He asks questions. Many, many questions. And I like to answer them!"

By now Great Mother's humming had stopped and the only sound was Cleatah's own voice.

"I like the way he touches me, but you know that. You are there when we put ourselves together. You feel how he moves his hands over my body and how he moves inside me." Cleatah felt the blood rush up her neck to her cheeks. She sighed, blowing out through her lips, surprised. "See! Just the thought of him…" she still wondered why Mother was so silent. She was there. No doubt of it. But keeping still. Even the humming had stopped. And then she understood.

The Goddess was listening to her!

Cleatah placed a few more strips of yew bark into the dancing fire. This time the flames leapt up with a sharp crackle. This made her brave. She could speak her mind. The Goddess wanted her to speak.

"If I choose him," she began, observing her words as they fell from her lips, "my whole life – from now, I'm hardly more than a girl – till I'm old, a woman with sagging teats and stringy thighs, I will be with Poseidon. He will share my bed. He will father my children." These thoughts were clear as water from a spring, but as she continued the thoughts behind the words were new to her, hard to make sensible. "If I choose him he will show me things I have never dreamed before, even in my mushroom visions. He knows so much about the Erthe, the sky…all that's invisible."

"*Do you fear this?*" the Goddess said so suddenly and forcefully that Cleatah gasped with surprise.

But she said nothing. She had come to Great Mother to ask

her permission. To ask for her blessing. "No!" she cried. It was nearly a shout.

"*Do you fear the life he will give you?*" The Goddess demanded.

"I do not fear him. I want him to share my life. I want to grow old with him."

Then Cleatah heard something she had never heard before – it was Great Mother laughing. Cleatah listened. There were many kinds of laughs. One to share a joke. One to put you to shame. One to show your surprise. But this was different. The Goddess was laughing with pleasure…at her teachings understood. She had remained silent so that Cleatah was forced to answer her own questions.

When it came to Poseidon and their destiny, Cleatah suddenly realized, *she herself possessed the wisdom of Great Mother!*

She sat back on her heels, stunned at this thought. "I am my own best teacher," she said aloud, and with that the altar fire burst into a shower of crackling sparks, wrenching a laugh from her own throat. *What other sign could be so clear?*

"Thank you, Mother! Thank you. Thank you for bringing me Poseidon. With all the blessings of my heart, I thank you."

Poseidon found Boah on the Great Plateau where a few small huts and corrals had been built for the tribe's horses and the brotherhood who tended them. Rode them. Cherished them. The smallest of the enclosures held a few foals for their first taming. Boah was forehead-to-forehead with a young male, and he was speaking softly to him. The horse was perfectly still except for its ears which flicked occasionally, and Poseidon could, as he approached, hear Boah's voice. It lacked words – more the singing of "clicks" and "clucks" of encouragement. A strong hand caressed the long cheek, and the horse nickered contentedly. Boah laughed, then gave the animals a good scratching around the ears.

"Boah," Poseidon said, and saw the tribesman, recognizing the voice, stiffen. He turned quickly with the sense of an enemy at his back.

Poseidon held both arms at his sides and softened his features. "Is this the newest born?" he asked.

"Yes."

"She's got her father's markings."

"How would you know? Boah snapped. "You have no time for horses anymore."

"Cleatah was…"

"Do not speak to me of Cleatah." With that he strode across the corral and out into the larger pasture where several grown horses fed. He grabbed a bit and reins hanging on the fence and leapt up on the bare back of the nearest one, and without another word galloped away.

Poseidon followed, finding another bit. He took the back of a brown mare and rode after, savoring the feel of a horse beneath him. He kept his eyes on Boah, who was lengthening the distance between them. Poseidon doubted it was a challenge, just the mere desire to outrun him, but undeterred he leaned over his mount's neck and urged her on. Boah was right – he hadn't ridden much in months, but the animals felt good between his legs. If he knew anything, he knew how to make a horse run, and run fast. The distance between the riders shortened. With a backwards glance Boah realized the pursuit. With an explosion of dust beneath its hooves Boah's horse shot forward. Poseidon's pace quickened.

The race was on.

"Ha! Ha! Boah cried, lying low over his horse's neck. It seemed possible, Poseidon thought, to catch up. His own mount was itching for a run and suddenly the spirit of competition had overtaken the pair of them. Her strides were long and smooth and the closer she came to the horse ahead, the faster she ran.

"Good girl!" he cried, urging her on.

Ahead the dry ground had gone marshy. A series of narrow

waterways loomed. Boah jumped one, then another. Poseidon's horse cleared them but began to slow, lacking the confidence of Boah's mount.

Boah jumped a broader stream, landing hard on the other side. But when Poseidon's mount followed across the breach his footing faltered on the far side. They barely avoided a fall.

That was enough. It was not a race after all. Poseidon would not endanger a horse to chase an angry man who did not want to be caught. He pulled up on the reins and turned back the way they'd come, slowed to a trot and then a walk. He cherished the horse with some kind words and the flat of his hand on her neck, then set their sights to the corrals.

"She was mine," Poseidon heard behind him. He kept his eyes square ahead and stayed silent. "From childhood. I was her chosen one."

What was there to say? Poseidon wondered now. What words had he planned to use when he'd gone up to the plateau to see Boah today? *I'm sorry? She chose me? I will take care of her? You will always be her friend? I would like you as my friend?* None of these would heal the open wound of this tribesman losing his promised woman.

So he said nothing.

A moment later Boah raced alongside and in front of Poseidon's mare, pausing only long enough to urge his horse, with two back hooves, to kick clods of dirt up into Poseidon's face before racing across the meadow to the corrals.

※

They ran through the driving rain, a downpour that had turned the plateau into a vast bog. It was farther afield than Cleatah had ever traveled in her gathering forays, far enough from the village, Poseidon had calculated, so that the villagers would never be aware of the shuttlecraft's arrival.

He had prepared Cleatah as best he could in the past two moons, teaching her the Terresian language and customs. She had proven a superb linguistic student – learning vocabulary, syntax and grammar at an impressive rate. Customs and behavior had been more of a struggle. It was not so much a matter of comprehension as disbelief, and occasionally disapproval. She thought the Terresian ways cold and callous, especially with regard to the rearing of children. *How could a baby not grow inside a woman's body? Where was the affection, the physical bond when young ones were taken from their parents' homes to be "schooled" in large institutions? How could people live inside their houses so much of the time and not outdoors in the natural world? And why were the houses so large?*

Neither could Cleatah fathom the lack of love between men and women, something her people took for granted. *How could males and females simply bed each other throughout their lives, changing partners at will? That was behavior for youngsters.* Poseidon explained that for many thousands of years his people had, in fact, practiced such passions and customs as the Shore People now did, but that these had been discarded by their advanced society.

To live without the sun so much of the time, to sleep through their long winters, and to live without ties of love and affection seemed impossible to Cleatah, though because it was Poseidon insisting that these were the facts, she tried her hardest to accept them. As for the technos itself, Poseidon had withheld many details of Terresian mastery over the physical world. He had discouraged her curiosity about the phaetron, avoided demonstrating the cloaking function and the healing function, worried that too many 'wonders' might frighten and confuse even an intellect as impressive as hers. Lately, though, he himself had begun to think that such advanced technos was unnecessary, even slightly ridiculous. He would catch himself in such thoughts more and more frequently as the day of his re-uniting with the Atlantos's crew approached.

Now they were hurrying through the storm to meet the shuttle that would deliver them both into his world, and he believed he was far more apprehensive about this meeting than Cleatah was. He had prepared her for the idea of a flying machine that would take them high into the air and far past the mountains in no time at all. He had described the *Atlantos*, its crew, what they would wear, what they would eat. He explained their expectations of her.

But nothing, he mused, could prepare his associates for Poseidon himself – for what he planned to say to them, for what he had become. Now they were nearing the coordinates for landing.

"Poseidon!" he heard Cleatah exclaim over the howling wind. "There!"

He looked up and saw what was an extraordinary sight, even to his sophisticated eye. Cleatah must be thinking she'd stumbled into one of her mushroom visions. In front of them, five semi-circular rainbows sprouted equidistant around a thirty-foot diameter of ground, looking like a gargantuan spider with an invisible body and multicolored legs. Within the circle, it appeared that no rain at all was falling.

Before he could stop her Cleatah broke from him and ran for the fantastic cluster of prisms. When he reached her she was standing awestruck in the center of the circle, gazing up at the sky above her, which was mysteriously dry. The five half-circular prisms glowed with a soft, subtly pulsing brilliance. She twirled around and around in place like a wonderstruck child.

Suddenly the prisms vanished. The sky over Cleatah's and Poseidon's heads disappeared as the circular, silver shuttle disc, its five equidistant lights pulsing, uncloaked and materialized, hovering above them.

Cleatah gasped and Poseidon encircled her with protective arms, pulling her close. An instant later the blue elevator beam shot downward from the center of the disc. Poseidon slowly moved her toward the beam.

"I won't let you go, my love," he whispered. "I'll never let you go."

In the next moment the blue beam enveloped them and whisked them upward. They disappeared into the circular door and it silently shut behind them. The beam winked out of existence and a moment later the shuttlecraft disappeared entirely from the rain-swept plateau.

❦

The crew – scientists, technoists and flight specialists alike – sat dumbstruck at the circular table, eyes fixed on their commander…or what had become of the man who had once been their commander. The Terresian garments Poseidon had immediately donned upon his return could not disguise the bulky musculature beneath. His long unruly mane, the sun-bronzed complexion and work-rough hands were an affront to their sensibilities. And the wild glint in his eyes belied the normalcy of Poseidon's modulated voice. Only Talya lacked the bewildered expression of her crewmates. Poseidon had sought her out first, privately in her quarters, to apprise her of his "much-changed circumstances," in the broadest strokes possible. He could not have left Cleatah alone long enough to have a full confrontation with Talya, he'd told himself, and had only stayed a moment, silently admitting his cowardice, but knowing the showdown would come later.

Talya had kept to her rooms since then, but Poseidon insisted on her presence at this meeting. Now having admitted to his associates only the broadest truth – that the female subject Talya had discovered on her first field study – name of "Cleatah" – would not, in fact, be employed in either the genomic cross-fertilization or cultural stimulation protocol as planned and, more shockingly, that he would be remaining on Gaia after the crew's departure for Terres. Poseidon waited uneasily for the expected response.

"So you're suggesting an extended experimental program," said Cairns, finally breaking the silence.

"Actually, I prefer to think of it as my life," Poseidon said, feeling more relaxed than he expected to be. "I have no intention of returning to Terres with this or any future expeditions."

"He will be mating with the subject, 'Cleatah...'" Talya spoke the name pointedly, "...*himself*." She sat directly across from Poseidon, furious and dry-eyed.

"But why, Sir?" asks Phypps. "Forgive me, but I don't understand the decision. None of us do."

Poseidon looked around the table at the faces of his crew. Each was dear to him. Their intelligence, courage and dedication to their fields of study, as well as their unspoken commitment to progress and Terresian values had always provided common ground between them. Science had been all the fulfillment any of them had ever needed.

How... Poseidon thought...*can I ever explain love?*

"Friends," he began," I came to this world as you all did – to serve the humanity of both Terres and Gaia...and with every intention of returning home. But here I've discovered a simplicity that pleases me more than I could ever have dreamed. A mate I want to spend my life with. This existence *feeds* me."

"But these people are primitives," argued Ables. "What kind of stimulation, mental or otherwise, could you possibly be 'fed' for the rest of your life? And it will be a very, very long life at that. I don't have to tell you that one of our years is multiplied many times over on Gaia. The Terresian metabolism lived-out here will make you appear immortal. Your...woman," the geologist continued, unable to hide his disapproval, "will age normally. She'll become ancient while you remain..."

"Ables..."

"Sir?"

"I mean to stay, whatever the consequences," Poseidon said in the gentlest tone. He looked at his cohorts, stiff with shock and betrayal. "Your window for reconnection with Terres before she heads back into deep orbit is very brief, and will be upon us in less than six months. Preparations need to proceed in good time, but adjusted for my absence. I'm granting Captain Zalen my command. I'll be notifying Federation shortly. I wanted you all to know first." Poseidon stood. "I'll be in my quarters if anyone wants to speak to me privately. I welcome you all to come and meet Cleatah." He avoided Talya's eyes, but hard as he tried he was unable to keep his lips from twisting into a smile as he added, "She is a most extraordinary woman."

THIRTY-FOUR

ONCE SHE HAD assessed that 4251 was elsewhere occupied Talya went to Poseidon's quarters. She'd decided she
would see him in a place where they could be private and
she could quickly, gracefully exit if the need arose. And she would
need to escape, she was certain of that. She was about to face the
bedmate that had publicly rejected her for a primitive Gaian
tribeswoman. She must override her humiliation, remain calm
and altogether rational, she reminded herself for the dozenth
time since she'd left her own quarters. She knew the eyes of every
crewmember followed her as she passed – no doubt wondering
what she was thinking, what she would say to Poseidon. *They
were pitying her.* One thing she knew: she could not countenance
their pity!

Arriving at his rooms she knocked, and thankfully the door
opened at once. He stood there, as if he'd known she was coming
just then. Her spine rigid she pushed into the room without invitation, refusing to meet his eye. She moved directly to the dining
table under the window where only a short while ago they had sat
with Athens and Persus and Korber, the marvelous expeditions
to Gaia and Mars and her plans for an auspicious pairing with
Poseidon ahead of them. Talya laid both hands on the table to

steady herself. She hoped to scathe him, flay his calm exterior, cause him to feel as diminished as she herself now felt.

"I thought more of you than this," she finally said. Her voice sounded oddly hollow, echoing in her skull. "You are a well-bred Terresian man. How can you abandon your ancestry and succumb to these unhealthy… hungers?"

"There is no way I can explain it or apologize, Talya," he said, taking her hands.

She controlled her urge to rip them angrily from his grip. "You disgust me. I think you've taken on quite a bit more of the aboriginals' ways than you realize. You've lost all objectivity and grown ridiculously emotional." This last had been meant as an insult, but she could see no embarrassment in Poseidon's expression, instead the beginnings of a slow, almost shy smile. It was all she could bear. Talya pulled her hands from his.

"How can you do this?" she hissed.

"I did it…" Poseidon said, but paused for a long moment to put the words together carefully…" because I could not *not* do it."

"So I'm to understand that you are compelled to sacrifice everything – the knowledge, the resources and the beauty of our culture…for this crude *primitive*?"

She saw Poseidon gazing mildly about his quarters. "I used to think this beautiful," he said, annoyingly unperturbed by her comments. "But my perception of beauty has changed. My perception of knowledge hasn't diminished. It's expanded. The indigenous peoples do lack technos. Their culture is simple, but their lives are rich! They're… *connected* with this planet."

"Oh spare me your hyperbole! I can see the surroundings are lovely. I'm not blind. But you don't belong here." Talya's frustration was escalating, "You're our planet's most distinguished scientist. Are you simply going to desert us all for this… delusion?"

"I already have."

Talya turned away, her eyes stinging. She wondered briefly if she should go now, spare herself any further unpleasantness, but she had to know.

"So you 'love' this woman?" She could not keep the sarcasm from her voice. "Next I suppose you'll want to father her children."

"We do want a family."

Talya sniffed derisively.

"I've decided that I'll give the crew members a choice – they can go if they wish, but anyone who wants to remain here can stay, carry on in a personal capacity. Make a different sort of life for himself."

"Really? And what of the Terresian projects? With this one irresponsible act you'll dismantle hundreds of thousand years of evolutionary progress."

"Not at all," he replied in a maddeningly even tone. "Of course it will proceed on a smaller scale, but the mixing of my genome with Cleatah's, and our children's with other natives will, after a number of generations, have a significant effect on Erthe's human evolution."

Talya was suddenly silent. She was considering Poseidon's words, extrapolating from them an idea of her own making. Surely it was a mad scheme and not a little perverse, but the more she considered it the more feasible it became.

"I think perhaps I'll stay," she said finally.

Poseidon's expression of shock and confusion gave Talya some grim satisfaction, seeing on his face and in his posture the dismay she had wished for, but until this moment had been unable to elicit.

"If you don't want to carry on with the Terresian objectives, so be it," she continued. "But you wouldn't dare prevent me from proceeding with them if I chose to stay."

"I...I..." he stammered, but she could see his mind rushing, attempting to decipher the consequences of her staying on his personal fantasy.

"It sounds as if you've already begun animal domestication with the collection and training of horses," she continued, "and we'll introduce grain cultivation and agriculture as planned. There's no reason we shouldn't initiate the linguistics and written language protocols as well."

She smiled coldly, certain he realized her suggestions had nothing to do with civic duty. Poseidon was right. The interbreeding of a specimen such as himself with the extraordinarily evolved Gaian female would eventually produce a unique and magnificent race of human beings – indeed, the Terresian expedition's original objective. It was simply that she believed Poseidon's sexual preoccupation with the woman would be short-lived. No matter Cleatah's qualities, she must eventually bore a man of such complexity and intellect. And of the new emotions he was feeling, well, he would soon revert to the deeply ingrained instincts natural to a Terresian – coolheaded reason. His "love" for the woman was merely a fanciful whim, a temporary derangement of Poseidon's mind. Further, the female would grow old and ugly very quickly, while she and Poseidon would remain vital. When his insanity passed, Talya – her dignity, equanimity and beauty intact – would be there waiting for him. In their unnaturally extended lifetimes the two of them would have completed an extraordinary amount of genomic research and restructuring of the population. She and Poseidon made a brilliant team. They would be remembered on Terres together...heroes.

"So it's decided then," Talya said, managing a dispassionate tone. "We'll have to revise your plans, of course. I can't possibly carry on without equipment. And others may choose to stay. Of course I'll talk to Zalen and make sure, but I believe that during the return window the crew can outfit several of the shuttles with sleep pods so they can fly them back to Terres. We'll keep the *Atlantos* here as a base of operations. The library and laboratories will be essential to our operations, don't you agree?"

It was difficult to keep from smiling, and before Poseidon

could answer or object, Talya decided the moment had come to terminate the meeting. She never dreamed the outcome would be so gratifying, and suddenly she found herself brimming with confidence and genuine excitement. She did enjoy a challenge. She started for the door, then turned back to Poseidon with a pleasant expression. "When will you make the announcement?"

"Tonight, at the evening meal," he said, subdued.

She could see he was pulling himself together, but it no longer mattered. She had unnerved him, bested him. And it felt wonderful. She executed her coolest and most attractive smile from the doorway.

"Till this evening," she said.

THIRTY-FIVE

NOT SURPRISINGLY, NONE of the other crewmembers opted to stay.

Cleatah, however, charmed everyone before the first week was out. All who had labeled her a 'primitive' were astonished at her intellect and mastery of the Terresian language in so short a time. But it was her warmth and directness that beguiled them, much as it had Poseidon. He watched her interaction with Chronell, holding his hand in hers and examining his face as she correctly diagnosed an as-yet untreated condition, then prescribed a potion made of a native plant to cure it. After that Chronell privately approached Poseidon and shyly inquired if there were any other women in Cleatah's village who were anything like her. Poseidon was sorry to say that while the warmth was common to the tribe, this woman's level of intellect was not. In the end Chronell – as all the others – decided to return to Terres.

Word that Talya would remain on Gaia to carry out the genomic directives was met with almost as much disbelief as Poseidon's announcement. It was whispered that the planet had a strange effect on some Terresians, causing them to act in a most peculiar and dangerous fashion, and as plans progressed for the crew's reconnection with Terres it was with a sense of nervous anticipation that they longed to be gone, lest they fall prey to these untoward emotions themselves.

✌

Since Talya's private visit, Poseidon's mind had been churning almost out of control. At first her suggestion that she stay on had rocked him as violently as an erthequake. But as the days passed a notion sprang into his consciousness and took hold. He would lie awake at night, Cleatah long asleep, and ponder the plan. It grew complex and unruly, and when he finally slept, his well-developed Terresian dream-state allowed for still wilder and more grandiose machinations to flower.

Now as the shuttle disc left Erthe's atmosphere with Cleatah by his side at the controls, the daytime blue sky was becoming black-flecked with brilliantly glittering stars, and with the boggling sight of Erthe receding into a small, blue-green disc, Poseidon could think of nothing but the look of wonder on her face. They were alone – he'd insisted on piloting the vessel himself – and she stood very still at the shuttle's largest window, watching the moon grow larger and brighter by the moment. Certainly she had believed him when, under that tree on the Great Plateau, he'd explained the nature of the solar system to her, understood conceptually the moving pebbles representing the spherical sun and planets. But now here she stood, unmoving, yet flying through the air, with day turning to night – not slowly as the sun set, but in an instant. And here was Erthe's moon taking up more and more of the black sky, the details of its craters and mountains distinct, perhaps a little frightening.

Poseidon could read this all in his lover's expression, much as she could be awakened merely by his thoughts. They were becoming attuned in a way he had never remotely conceived feasible.

"You want to know how this is possible," he began. "How

325

we're flying through the air in a metal machine. How this shuttle and the *Atlantos* were built."

She nodded silently. Her eyes had softened, and it seemed to him that she was readying her mind, opening it for a large influx of intelligence.

"It all begins with 'vibration.'"

She waited patiently for him to explain.

"Vibration is invisible, but it's all around you. You employ it when you play the flute you invented. The breath from your lips makes the air inside the flute move very quickly, like a strong wind in the branches of a tree. Sometimes you can hear a sound in the leaves."

"That is 'vibration?'"

"One kind. There are many, many other things that vibrate. Actually, *everything* is vibrating, all matter, living or not. Everything in the world and in the sky – every stone, every grain of sand, every inch of skin on our bodies, every drop of blood – even if we cannot see it move. And each bit of matter vibrates at a different speed. A long time ago my people learned these things were true. That this principle defined our universe. And they discovered the power that dwelled in harnessing what they called 'the Vibrus.'"

"Like the music that comes from air vibrating inside the flute?"

"That's right. They found that the Vibrus, if controlled and directed in different ways, had many uses." He smiled to himself, realizing he had never been called on to explain the most basic principle in the cosmos to anyone before. "So many uses."

Then using the laser "blade" in his wrist hub he sliced the skin on the back of his hand, making it bleed.

"What are you doing!" Cleatah cried, stanching the flow with the palm of her hand.

"Let me show you," he said, pulling gently out of her grasp.

With a healing frequency he knitted the sliced tissue together. A moment later not even the faintest scar remained.

He could see that Cleatah was holding her thoughts tightly together. She was too proud to let her fear or agitation get the best of her. He reset his device.

"Look over here," he said, drawing her gaze to the shuttle's console.

A small diffracted image of Talya and Chronell standing together talking in the *Atlantos* Library materialized. With another adjustment their voices could be heard. He caused them to dematerialize a moment later. Then a small pebble – not an image this time, but solid matter – coalesced out of thin air. He placed it in her outstretched hand so she could feel the weight of it.

"Stay still," he told her, then oscillated it out of existence.

"This is how my people, on Terres, built their cities. Healed diseases. Learned to fly and travel between planets. The system that harnesses the Vibrus is called 'technos' and the machine that harnesses the technos is called a "phaetron." A single kind of stone must be used to power the phaetron. This is called 'titanum.'"

She was struggling to ingest the plethora of data, and Poseidon worried he had shown her too much, too soon. But he was driven to finish what he'd started.

"I have a brother whose name is Athens. As I came to Erthe, he traveled with 5,000 of our people to an Erthe-like planet called Mars." Poseidon turned and scanned the skies to find it in the sky. He pointed. "See the bright one there?"

"Your brother is there?"

"He is."

"Why?"

Poseidon sighed heavily. This would be harder to explain. "Our home world, Terres was once like Erthe and Mars. It flew around the sun like the others…till a terrible thing happened. A great rock from space – the size of the moon – collided with the planet and slowly, over a great length of time, Terres went flying farther and farther from the sun in a long, long orbit."

"You showed me this the day we told each other our secrets! This is 'the story for another day.'"

Poseidon laughed, relieved. "Yes, Love. This is that story. Now, when Terres is at the farthest end of its orbit, it suffers terribly. There's no light or heat from the sun. The land is covered in ice. There's no air to breathe."

"How do you live?"

"That is where 'technos' comes in. With the Vibrus and phaetron we were able to create protective domes. Think of great soap bubble, as large as the Central Range and infinitely strong. We live all together underneath it in cities."

"I remember the word," she said. "Cities are places where a great many tribes come together to live."

"Under the domes our cities have light and heat and air. Everything we need is under the domes. Everything outside it is dead."

She closed her eyes, trying to imagine such a thing. What he did not say was that even the years of Terres's "close orbit" to the sun did nothing to revive the land or seascapes. They were permanently and irrevocably bleak.

"Why did your brother go to...Mars?"

"You remember the word 'titanum."

"The stone that powers your..." She'd forgotten.

"Technos."

"Technos," she repeated.

"We are running out of titanum. Without it, our domes will fail and we'll all die. Titanum ore was found on Mars. Athens has gone there to mine it."

Cleatah had never heard these word either.

"You know how you go to a certain mountain on the Great Plateau to dig ochre out of the Erthe to use in your ceremonies?" She nodded. "Ochre is a kind of ore. The digging for it is 'mining.' But Athens and our people have to dig – we call it drilling – with great machines – deep into the ground on Mars to find titanum."

"You 'drill' with your machine...your phaetron? Into the planet's *body*?" She seemed unsettled by this thought.

"Then Athens sends it in great ships traveling through space, back to Terres."

"That is quite a story, my Love," she said with an incredulous frown.

There was so much more to tell, he thought. More that would only confuse Cleatah now – how technos was worshipped as passionately on Terres as the Great Mother Goddess was on Erthe. How all they knew was the daily life manufactured by the phaetron. That the people were content with technological representations of nature, like the sun and sky and weather. Comfort. Safety. Beauty. Refinement of culture. All under the domes. Any thought of moving the planet's population to Erthe or Mars was met with suspicion, derision, at least as long as titanum could be found in sufficient quantities to power the domes and SleepPhase chambers. Old habits died hard. He didn't know if he had the words to make this understandable.

"Once, soon after I met you," she said suddenly, interrupting his thoughts, "I had a vision, and I've never forgotten it. I was sitting alone on the shore near the village with water lapping at my feet. Colorful fishes nibbled at my toes. I was surrounded by children playing happily there. Girls and boys. There were hundreds of them. I remember thinking that they were, every one of them, my children, and they were all *your* children as well."

"How did you know they were mine?"

"Because they had your eyes. Your grey eyes...and I knew they were yours because I could never imagine – even then, in my dream – having anyone else's children."

Poseidon moved behind her and clasped her around the waist. "I've been thinking, Cleatah..."

"Your favorite occupation." she said with a smile.

"I've had a vision of my own…"

"Tell me."

"A great joining. A bringing together of our two peoples, our two cultures. We've already begun with you and me, but I've been imagining all the ways Terres and Erthe might be… woven together."

Finally Cleatah pulled her eyes from the moon and turned to face him. "Explain this. Tell me what you see. I don't understand."

"I see a city.

"Where is this city?"

"Close to where the Shore Village now stands."

She smiled, amused. "But where do these 'great many' people come from? Our village is small."

"We would gather them from every part of this continent. Many tribes inhabit it, and though each of them is small, together they would make a great many."

"But why? Are we not happy as we are?"

Now he looked away, staring at the Erthan moon looming brightly before them. This was the most difficult of all to explain.

"When I first decided I would stay I believed I'd be content with a life of simplicity, living with you, loved by you. And if you don't agree to this I'll be content – I promise you. But now I'm constantly visited by this imagining of something more. I'm asking for your consent, for your help. Without it I can't possibly carry out my plan."

"Just tell me."

"You know that I've fallen in love with this planet. And with you. But the people here…they possess a quality that we Terresians lost so long ago that we don't even miss it anymore. But we *should* miss the feeling, the passion, the love…"

"We're also a jealous people," she told him. "Sometimes hateful. Sometimes violent. And we are so…" she looked around her at the shuttle's gleaming control console, "…ignorant beside you."

"No! Not ignorant. What we lack, you possess. What you lack, we possess. Certain uses of Terresian technos focused on the natural resources of Erthe would produce an extraordinary marriage. I see…" In his excitement he became lost for words.

"Your city?" Cleatah finished for him.

"Yes! A city. A civilization. A culture of extraordinary magnificence! Erthan arts inspiring Terresian design. Terresian design forged into Erthan stone!"

"And the people?" she asked. "How would they know what is necessary to build this… 'civilization'?

"With your help," he said, taking her hands in his. "In the beginning you would teach them to never be afraid – of me, of what's different. Later, our children and their children's children will share our blood, our knowledge. It's in these offspring that I see the most beautiful aspect of our future. Terresian levelheadedness mingled with Erthan passion would create a splendid human being. An ideal society."

Cleatah looked away, overwhelmed.

"We'd begin slowly," he insisted. "I won't frighten the people with too much. I promise. But we would need a common language, and to learn how to grow food enough for a large population. We'd mine the stone and minerals necessary for building."

Worry and doubt creased her forehead.

"It can happen, Cleatah! It's no more impossible than your dream of our children by the seaside. But I can't do it without you. I don't want to do it alone."

He could see that his ideas were at once far too vast for her to grasp…and altogether clear. She was silent, unable to find words to express herself. When she began to tremble she turned away from him. But the sight that greeted her caused her to gasp aloud.

The pale, mottled surface of the moon – that sacred orb Cleatah had wondered at and worshipped her whole life – now entirely filled her vision. Poseidon's arms encircled her from behind, and tears began to gather in her eyes. This man, this stranger from another world, had given her the strength to stand toe-to-toe with Great Mother. To tell, not ask, the Goddess about her future life with him. This man had given her the very moon…and now he wanted her help.

She would, of course, deny him nothing.

THIRTY-SIX

"A GOOD DAY TO you!" Athens cried a moment after his diffracted image appeared in the *Atlantos's* library. He was in as cheerful a mood as Poseidon had ever seen him. This called greeting – "A good day to you!" – had become the Marsean's most common one, as the rising of the sun every day was cause for great celebration.

"Good day to *you*, brother. You sound as if the female company you're keeping is satisfying you well."

"To the greatest degree. And the mines are booming. What reason do I have to feel anything but glorious?"

Poseidon grew silent, and stayed silent till Athens said, finally, "What is it? Something wrong?"

"No. Nothing at all. However, I have decided… I've decided to stay on Erthe."

"Erthe. What is Erthe?"

Poseidon realized then how long it had been since he and Athens had seen one another. Spoken. Shared their thoughts. It might have been a hundred years that had passed, so much had changed. How to explain any of it?

"Erthe is Gaia."

Athens laughed. "*You*? You are *staying behind* on Gaia?"

"Yes."

"And the crew?"

"All are leaving during the window, except Talya."

"You devil!" Athens barked.

"It's not what you think."

"What I *think*?" I can't think at all. I'm phazed entirely...Tell me your plan."

"This is bound to be as much a shock to you as it's been to everyone I've told." Poseidon exhaled a contented sight. "I've come to love a woman of Erthe. Her name is Cleatah."

"From the Shore Village you've been living in for all this time." It was not a question. Athens seemed slowly to be making sense of it all. "But staying?" he said. "For what purpose? Are you becoming a tribesman?"

Poseidon could hear derision in the word. Yet he could not help smiling when he answered, "No. I have *been* a tribesman for all this time."

"And you're sending your crew home without you?" Athens was disbelieving, scornful. "At least when you left Aeros without Elgin Mars you came back with titanium. Now the Terresians' favorite hero is staying behind on a primordial world, keeping with him the greatest genomist of her time. And for what? A chance to rut with an aboriginal?"

Poseidon stifled his annoyance. But then none of his crew understood any better than this. He was certain nothing he could say would make Athens change his mind. Instead he said, "We are building something here."

"What, a race of monkey people?"

"That was uncalled for and rude."

"Forgive me for worrying if my brother appears to be losing his mind."

"When did you ever care what happened to me?"

"True." Athens reined in his flaring temper. "I imagine to do such a thing you'd have to have good cause."

Much better than you think."

"Well, I suppose it will be helpful to have my brother in close orbit."

"But not *too* close," Poseidon said.

Athens was warming to the idea. "Perhaps I'll like this brother better than the old one."

"May be. Especially if you ever need something from me."

"We've got everything we need on Mars. And more." Athens closed his eyes, imagining. "So there you are. You'll have a beautiful native at you side. I assume she's beautiful. But you will also – and for this I do not envy you, brother – have incurred the unbridled Wrath of Talya."

"True. But the prize is worth the challenge."

Athens shook his head, unconvinced. "Time will tell."

THIRTY-SEVEN

TIME GREW SHORT for the crew's departure. In less than a week the window would open and the crew would be departing for home. It was an orderly protocol, but in their faces Poseidon could see confusion and loss. When Federation had first learned of their commander's defection and finally believed it a certainty that the crews would be coming home in shuttles with the data gleaned from the Gaian expedition, but not their commander, they were aghast at Poseidon's decision, unable to counter his incomprehensible reasoning. Ammon Ra believed his son had simply lost his mind. His fellow scientists would face the indignity of returning home without him. At least Commander Mars had been lost to an heroic death. Perhaps worse was convincing Federation to allow he and Talya to keep the *Atlantos* with him on Erthe, when it was learned that Poseidon had abandoned his world and his family for the "love" of a primitive woman.

Talya Horus's motives were even harder to decipher.

Zalen had taken the news in stride, himself drawn to Gaia, but his occupation was entirely technos-based. Without it the man had no function. No purpose. Ables had attempted briefly to dissuade Poseidon from staying, but he could see in his commander's eyes the sheer, unconquerable determination of love, if not the concept. That was still a mystery to the Terresian psyche.

No one in the crew dared speak to Talya about her decision to stay. She was already known as a paragon of steadiness and restraint, but these days she doubled her reserve, lengthened her silences.

∽

He'd begun to take Cleatah into the *Atlantos* Library to begin her education into the larger world. Her revulsion for the dead air of the ship was overwhelmed by her fascination of the stories – great and small – projected by the phaetron into the space around them. Poseidon watched with delight as her mind, already a fertile landscape by virtue of the mushroom, absorbed masses of data as diverse as astronomy and genomic theory and the great geological wonders of her own planet.

This day he had seated them side-by-side in reclining viewing chairs, dimmed the lights and turned the pitch-black dome into an astrolarium with the universe spread out all around them. Even having experienced the 3-Dimensional Diffraction Projector in other lessons, Cleatah was rendered mute by the grandness and clarity of the galactic light show.

"I know you remember our solar system and the long elliptical orbit of Terres." He recalled her expression as she'd sat under a tree on the plateau and watched his demonstration with flying pebbles. "And you understand that our civilization, our technos, our history and our fate are all defined by that one single circumstance. How we've been forced to squeeze every aspect of our lives into the portion of the 'Terresian Year' that the planet is bathed in natural sunlight. I showed you how Terres's extreme orbit turned the planet into a wasteland. And how this created the desperate need for more and more extreme technos, and why mining for titanium is so critical."

She nodded her understanding, urging him to go on.

"There was a wonderful man who came on our expedition who died before we reached Erthe. His name was Samos Korbell." Poseidon paused to remember his sweet face. "He was a very great scientist. In fact it was he who taught me – and every other Terresian student at our Academy – about the creation of our two "sister planets" – Terres and Erthe. When he lectured to first year students, he would stand in front of them and in his most serious voice intone, 'Collision is Destiny!!' Then he'd go silent. He stayed silent for so long that everyone began to squirm."

Cleatah smiled at that.

"He insisted that we *must* understand the collisions that impacted the most ancient version of our Solar System....two billion years ago."

Now Poseidon momentarily projected that Solar System overhead in the night sky. Then he zeroed in and enlarged the four planets closest to the sun until they filled the Library dome.

"There, you see? Hermos and Aphrodise are in their expected orbits, closest to Helios. And there..." Poseidon paused for dramatic effect, "...there is the third planet from the sun."

"Why is it so large? Erthe is not that large."

"Because that is not Erthe. Two billion years ago the third planet from the sun was 'Tiamet.'"

Poseidon further enlarged and enhanced the planet till it virtually filled the upper reaches of the Library dome. They could now see details of Tiamet's vast oceans, its continents alive with forests, mountains and deserts, erupting volcanoes and shifting continents. "There was no life on land," Poseidon said, "but the oceans were full of it. Amazing creatures of every shape and size." Poseidon stood from his chair and struck a dramatic pose, gesturing wide with both arms. "Then Samos Korbell would call out to his students in a booming voice, 'And then the day of reckoning! The Great Fracture!'"

Cleatah laughed, delighted with Poseidon's performance.

Up above them, Tiamat had shrunk slightly so the whole dazzling array of the solar system's planets, moons and rings was again visible. And suddenly as they watched, a massive comet the size of a small planet, streaming white and gaseous, raced into the solar system past the outer planets, clipped one of the Marsean moons, and slammed into Tiamat with unconscionable force and velocity.

Cleatah gasped, and watched spellbound as the mighty world ripped apart, separating at the seams, its molten core, rocky mantle and atmosphere chaotically roiling and re-coalescing into something new. She grabbed Poseidon's hand as one giant fragment shattered into billions of burnt shards of stone that, in a slow-motion dance, re-assembled themselves into a ring of asteroid-sized rocks flying within the original path of Tiamat.

"That is what we call "The Rocky Belt," Poseidon said.

A second part – sucking into itself both oceans and land-masses – reformed, then propelled itself into a new stable orbit between Aphrodise and Mars." Poseidon added, "This became the *new* third planet from the Sun – what we know as 'Erthe.'"

Cleatah was silent, riveted to the scene above.

"The final fragment," Poseidon went on, "also coalesced land and sea into a solid planet. This became Terres. Her orbit, some-what less stable than Erthe's, found its place between Mars and Zeus. But the story isn't finished." He paused, allowing the profu-sion of information to penetrate before going on. In fact, Cleatah closed her eyes and breathed slowly, chewing on her lower lip.

Finally he continued. "Remember the moon of Mars that was dealt a glancing blow by the incoming comet?" She nodded yes. "That moon's wobble," he went on, "in time, gave way to an orbital shift, and *that* to a complete expulsion from Marsean gravity."

Then above them Mars's vagrant moon careened through space on a collision course with the new planet Terres. It struck and flew off into the night. The blow was far less destructive than the comet had been to Tiamat, but it was large enough to destabilize its orbit and set it on an altogether different 'plane.' *That* was when Terres began its journey over many millions of years, farther and farther into the black reaches of space...and its unnaturally long elliptical path. Ten thousand Erthan orbits to every one of Terres's," Poseidon finished.

He turned to Cleatah, expecting her to be moved, even overwhelmed by what she'd just seen, but she was quite sanguine. 'I understand," she said, then smiled. "Great Mother is far greater than I ever knew."

He exhaled heavily.

"You don't believe. I know that. You will one day."

He held out his hand to her. "Enough for now?" he asked, certain it had been.

But Cleatah was not moving from the viewing chair. "Your brother Athens..." she said, pointing to Mars above them "...is there digging in the ground for titanum ore. "Show him to me."

Poseidon felt himself caught off guard. "Athens now, or as a boy?"

"You and Athens as children. Your mother. Your father."

Poseidon hesitated. He was shaking his head helplessly.

"If you can show me the planets in collision, surely you can show me your tribe."

The footing here was dangerous. Like quicksand. Athens, from his earliest years, had proven intractable. He'd brought out the worst in their father. Had shown Poseidon to be no great hero for his brother, hardly any help at all against the barrage of cruelty inflicted daily. Only their mother softened the blows. Poseidon had never dwelled on his shame of failing Athens. Now he was being forced to come face-to-face with it.

"Show me something," Cleatah demanded. "Anything."

He reluctantly skimmed the family MemoryFiles and settled on one that at least dazzled the eye and showed their mother in a fantastical light. All four of them were in it. As the solar system faded from the Library dome a new scene was projected before them – a crowded amphitheater, gorgeously lit and costumed during a theatrical spectacle. Poseidon looked over and saw Cleatah's eyes widen, and her mouth falling softly open. "This is a Terresian 'theater.'" He swept his hand before him. "People called 'actors' are pretending to be great tribal leaders, 'kings' and 'queens' of days gone by – 'history.' Theater is a kind of ritual. Different people act out the parts of the ritual to help them remember something important to them. It makes them remember why they are a tribe."

"Cleatah sat forward, her eyes fixed on the stage, her senses on fire. "This is a beautiful ritual."

"You see the woman in the center of the stage? The one with the glittering headdress? We call it a 'crown.'"

"I see her. Is she a queen?"

"Yes." Poseidon smiled. "She's also my mother. Athens's mother. Her name is Manya."

Cleatah looked at Poseidon with stars in her eyes. "*That* is your mother?"

"Yes. She was the greatest actress of her day."

The memory clip reversed angle suddenly, revealing in the first row of the amphitheater Ammon Ra flanked on either side by a boy. Poseidon at fourteen was already recognizable as the man he would become, but Athens at five was a sweet-faced child whose eyes were fixed on the extravagently attired figure of his mother. It was clear by his enraptured expression that there was no distinguishing fiction from reality, the queen from his mother.

"There you are!" Cleatah said excitedly. "Not yet a man. And that is your father?"

"Yes."

Her eyes narrowed. Poseidon could see that Ammon's rigid posture and steely expression disturbed her, but she said nothing.

With the sound of commotion onstage they saw Athens's eyes widen with alarm. In fact, on stage, another of the characters – an assassin – had seemingly plunged a sword into the queen's back. It's point erupted from her chest. She fell to her knees, clutching the bloody sword with her hands. While the audience quietly gasped at the illusion of the expected death in this classic play, Athens, with a heart-rending shriek for his murdered mother, exploded from his seat and made a leap for the stage. Far too high for a successful landing, he was knocked back and fell on the floor. He picked himself up and tried scrambling up once again. The effect on the sanguine audience was embarrassed amusement and quiet laughter.

Poseidon could see his own fourteen-year-old expression of horror as Ammon Ra slowly rose from his seat and scooped the distraught little boy up and carried him, kicking and crying from the theater. Onstage, the action continued. Poseidon locked eyes with his mother, "dead" on the stage floor.

He was close enough to see she was silently weeping.

Poseidon dematerialized the MemoryFile. Cleatah sat immobile, staring straight ahead.

"Your father...?"

"You saw there. A bad man. He poisoned my brother's heart."

"But Athens lives. He is the chief of his tribe on Mars."

Poseidon recalled their last comm. What good would it do to burden Cleatah's mind with the bitterness that had hardened Athens into a hateful man, one who had no use for a "monkey woman" like her?

"Will I meet him one day?"

"I think he's happy on Mars," Poseidon said. "Let's leave him there."

❧

There was one transmission to Terres that Poseidon on one hand dreaded, and on the other joyfully anticipated. When Manya materialized before him, her long silver hair falling around her shoulders like a cape, she quietly regarded her son's startling

342

transformation – his tanned and muscular physique, the long wild mane.

"I understand you've found something on your voyage that 'surprised' you," she finally said with tender indulgence.

"I have."

"And what is she called?"

"Cleatah."

"Is she as beautiful as her name?"

"I'll let you see for yourself." He beckoned, and Cleatah came to his side. Manya took in the sight of her for a long moment, and exhaled a contented sigh. "Hello, Cleatah."

Cleatah didn't speak for a long moment, simply gazed at Manya's face. "Poseidon showed you to me as a queen, in a spectacle. You were very..." she searched for the word,

"...grand." Her hands outlined the intricate headdress and costume she'd been wearing. But now that I see you here, like this, you are so much the way I imagine Great Mother!" She turned and smiled at Poseidon, then looked back at Manya. "I feel like I know you already."

"And you apparently know my son very well. I think he's in very good hands."

"Thank you," Cleatah said gravely, crossing her hands over her heart. "Thank you for Poseidon. He is my life now. My family."

Manya nodded, her eyes brimming, lost for words. Cleatah stepped away leaving mother and son their last moments alone.

"I've named a mountain after you," Poseidon said, deciding a touch of levity was called for. "She's very majestic, 'Manya.' Fiery. She nearly killed me."

His mother laughed a throaty laugh. Poseidon could see in her a more profound serenity than he had ever remembered. "Since your father told me your news, I'd been thinking, 'Well, he won't be coming home.' But now I see you *are* home. Good. My life will end knowing both my boys are content. What more could I ask for?"

Poseidon thought on this for a long moment. "A splendid final dream," he finally said.

"Perhaps I'll dream of my namesake – Manya – blowing her top in a violent eruption."

He laughed at that. "I love you, Mother. More than you know."

"I do know."

"Thank you…" his voice was ragged, "…for a heart that can feel."

Tears were coursing down Manya's cheeks now, and he reached out across the miles, in vain, to wipe them away.

"Sweet dreams, Poseidon," she whispered, "and a long and joyful life."

THIRTY-EIGHT

WO DAUNTING TASKS still lay ahead. The *Atlantos* needed a hiding place, as did the two shuttle discs that would be left behind. Zalen and the technos crew were consulted. Talya rightly insisted that a location central to the planned city, provisionally called "Atlantos," was crucial. Of course the Shore Village must be preserved intact, and Cleatah requested its close proximity to the city. Zalen suggested entombment of the ship under the crust of the Great Plateau. Poseidon rejected this. He wished for closer proximity to the ocean.

They settled on burial of the larger craft at sea-level, south of the Shore Village, where the plateau curved naturally into a massive amphitheater, the ground at its base layered with black sand that covered lavic rock hundreds of feet deep. The shuttles left behind – so they would be more readily available for flight – would be hidden in two horizontal caves high up on the plateau's palisades.

Till now the Shore People knew nothing of Poseidon's true home, or that he possessed tools or weapons beyond a spear, blade or arrow. He had been accepted as the mate of Cleatah, and he'd proven himself courageous and worthy as a tribesman. But the greatest obstacle required Cleatah's counsel. "Should the tribe," he asked her, "be allowed to see the *Atlantos* fly? To hover and vaporize rock and sand? To watch as it lowers itself down beneath the ground, and the discs slotted into the cliff face?"

"It is too soon," she replied. "There's no way to prepare them for such a sight. They'll die of fear." It was just as Poseidon had suspected.

"Before I came to the village, when I found the horses, I put them to sleep so I could safely separate Arrow from the herd. You remember I did the same to Sheeva while we ate the mushroom."

"You want to do this with the tribe?"

"It may be best."

And afterwards?"

"We'll cover the vessels completely so no one will suspect it had happened. My worry," Poseidon said slowly, measuring his words, "is what they will think when they lay eyes on the great ertheworks necessary to build the city."

She thought silently for a long moment, as though gazing into the months and years ahead. "By such a time they'll know you to be far more than a Shore Tribesman." She caressed his cheek with her hand. "You must not worry. Put the people to sleep. Bury your ships. We still have to gather the tribes and bring them across the continent, teach them to speak one language. Surely that's enough for now."

So it was done.

With the Shore People narcotized, Zalen flew the ship to the seaside, found the center of the miles-wide amphitheater, and directed the phaetron's beam downward. Black sand was blown away into a low circular mound below the craft's perimeter. The highest frequency boring function then vaporized the lavic rock, carving out a tremendous space to a depth capable of hiding the vessel completely. Zalen skillfully maneuvered the *Atlantos* into the manmade cavern, and the sand was re-deposited atop it. The discs were slotted into their horizontal caves, stone doors set in place to camouflage them.

When the Shore People awoke from their sleep, no one, save Cleatah, was the wiser. And the heart of Atlantos was once and forever set in stone.

THIRTY-NINE

"I AM MOTHER TO not a single child," Cleatah said, teasing him, "and now you want me to birth a civilization."

Poseidon watched as she rose from their bed and plucked up a shirt to cover her morning nakedness.

"Why would anyone from the gathered tribes listen to me? Elder men, wise women? I'm young. They'll have their own ways."

"I believe they'll follow you. They'll love and revere you."

His eyes lingered on her sleepwarm body, and he wished she would be slow covering it. He never tired of the sight – the tall, supple form and graceful movements, the full breasts and prettily muscled limbs. That dark mane never failed to thrill him. Cleatah was, to his greedy eyes, as much a wild animal as a woman, eliciting sensations and primal instincts that he'd never known he possessed. At night when he reached for her, even in half-sleep, she came willingly. She curled and wove tendril-like around him, nestling her face with short, fragrant breaths into the curve of his neck. If Poseidon kissed her – anywhere – she came slowly awake in his arms, always glad to have been roused, then commencing to rouse *him* to extents he could never have imagined possible. Only an hour before, Cleatah had been straddling Poseidon, riding him, moving in voluptuous rhythm to pleasure herself, having learned there was no better way than this to pleasure him.

347

But today he needed to bring his Terresian sensibilities to the fore and, with Cleatah, to direct their thoughts and efforts to the "Great Undertaking." The months ahead promised to kindle all manner of creation, from the grandest to the minutest scales. What was yet unspoken – and uneasy – was Talya's part in all of it. In the ship's kitchen a few days before he'd observed the two women standing side-by-side. They were equal in height and both slender, yet they couldn't have differed more. Cleatah's posture was unselfconsciously lithe, agile, her breasts fuller, limbs more muscular. Talya stood ramrod straight and seemed to wear her skin and clothing as an armor. She ever-so-slightly recoiled at Cleatah's nearness.

Talya had blanched when he and Cleatah announced their intentions to gather the tribes from the farthest reaches of the continent in order to found their new society. She spluttered at the idea of a new civilization, her normally frosty skin flushing pink with one of the rogue emotions to which she'd lately fallen victim.

"Can you hear yourself, Poseidon? You've gone completely mad." She'd turned away from them to retrieve her meal from the diner-window, but he knew she was only hiding the embarrassment of her emotion. "I won't have anything to do with it."

"It was your choice to stay," he said. Like it or not, this is the future of Erthe. You can do what's necessary to help us, or you can stand by as an observer. You need to decide quickly, though. We're moving ahead at once."

Poseidon had seen the subtle trembling, and the tapping in on her hub a program to calm herself. Then she'd swiveled to face them again. "I suppose you expect me to start an exponential breeding protocol with this 'gathered tribe' while you build your city."

"No breeding program," Cleatah had unhesitatingly corrected Talya. "Once the tribes have come here, they'll mate among themselves as we in the Shore Village have always done."

Talya had turned to Poseidon then, her eyes flashing dangerously, infuriated by Cleatah's quiet assurance. He knew that Talya believed he'd take her side against this unreasonable argument. She'd been mistaken.

"In every way possible," he told her, "we'll proceed according to natural laws. Erthe's laws."

"There will be no more 'terminations' of tribes whose brains are too small," Cleatah added.

Talya gaped at them disbelievingly. "You want me to put aside the genomic protocols laid out by Federation? Had I known that…" she spluttered but could not finish.

Had you known, would you not have stayed? Poseidon thought, but did not say.

"I'd like to speak to you alone." Talya hissed at him.

"There's nothing you can say to me that Cleatah shouldn't hear."

Talya's closed-lipped mouth worked in silence as she'd chosen her words carefully. "This is anarchy," she finally said, calm and steady. "You've commandeered a world, Poseidon. A Terresian world."

"Erthe is its own world. Our interventions have brought evolution far enough. We have to stop playing God."

Talya laughed bitterly. "And what are you doing, if not playing God?"

"Call it what you will. The decision's been made. The city's infrastructure will be laid down with the phaetron – erthe-moving, primarily, to spare the people back-breaking work. I imagine this will 'elevate' me in the people's eyes."

"I would say so." Her tone was caustic.

"You know very well there's a difference between using technos to move stone, and using it to manipulate the species at a cellular level," he said.

"We've always done it. Do you presume to be the single man who unilaterally derails so crucial a Terresian program?"

"I do." He'd spoken in an unmistakable directive. "Human

genomic interventions stop now. The population will reproduce as it always has, at a rate and with mutations determined by natural circumstances alone. There will be no more tampering."

"You call my *work* tampering!" Her skin glowed red with rage.

"It is tampering," he replied, with a calm that could only incite further fury. "And it stops now."

That had ended the conversation, and Talya had avoided them for several days. Today had been set aside for their meeting in order to begin the physical plan for Atlantos City and its environs. As Poseidon and Cleatah walked side-by-side through the deserted ship from their quarters to the hub, turning down the hall of laboratories, he wondered if working long hours in Talya's space, amidst the highest levels of technos, Terresian thought forms, and the silent but omnipresent phaetronic Vibrus that permeated the body of the craft, would rattle his mate.

She always longed to have her feet planted in the soil and sand, rock and vegetation, to hear only natural sounds and feel only Erthely energies pulsing beneath and around her. She'd reluctantly agreed to sleep in Poseidon's quarters while their creation took form. But it had become her habit before every day broke to slip from bed, and fearlessly riding the blue beam to the surface, emerge into her own world. Poseidon imagined that first inhaled breath, the joy and relief of sipping the smells of her beloved planet. There too, waiting patiently for her mistress, was Sheeva. All attempts to bring the wolf into the *Atlantos* had failed, and even her fearlessness and devotion to Cleatah could not surmount the animal's revulsion and dread of the unnatural and claustrophobic interior. On most days the pair of them would descend the cliff face and walk the beach north to the Shore Village. Cleatah visited with her people, speaking to them of the world-shaking changes that were coming. She spoke to them of *the future*.

It was hard for me to understand 'future,'" she'd told Poseidon. "How will I explain it to them? Every day is the same as the day before, and the same as the day after. Only the shaking of the ground or the most terrible storms with winds that blow down our huts make us think of past times. 'That was the day before the great shaking that killed Boah's father,' someone might say. But they will never consider a storm or a quake in the *future*."

When they entered Talya's laboratory they found her standing in front of a diffracted rendering of the Great Plateau, its fertile plains laid out in a neat grid of farms and lushly planted fields, irrigated by a massive system of canals. Far in the distance was the volcanic range, Manya still and peaceful, towering above the other peaks. It was clear that Talya had no intention of revisiting their last conversation about human genomic manipulation, and had decided to move forward. Contribute in some other way.

"What are we seeing here?" Poseidon asked.

I've devised a system to maximize food productivity."

"What is this?" Cleatah demanded, pointing to the center of the Great Plateau, slashing her two middle fingers first horizontally, then vertically, indicating the unnaturally organized cross-hatched pattern of farmland and canals.

"It makes best use of the land," Talya answered, unable to keep the condescension from her voice. "More food can be grown this way. Rivers that twist and turn back on themselves may be pretty, but they're wasteful. The canals distribute water to farms with the greatest efficiency."

"You would change the course of a river?" Cleatah glanced back to Poseidon. "You would not permit that." It was a statement more than a question.

I might." He knew his answer would evoke Cleatah's displeasure, but Talya's ideas were sound. "We have to think first about feeding a great many people. We can't bring the tribes here only to let them starve."

Cleatah returned her gaze to the projected likeness of the Great Plateau. "I don't understand. How did it come to look this way?"

"Let me show you," Talya replied, wiping the "finished image" of the farmlands away with a swipe of her fingers over the trans-screen. What was left was the plateau as it existed before the *Atlantos* had arrived, its two graceful blue rivers descending from the mountains and flanking each side of the broad plain. The first superimposition Talya now produced showed the crisscrossed grid of canals dug into the plateau which was devoid of its grass-lands. The next superimposed image showed the re-directing of the rivers into the canals, leaving the natural waterways arid and lifeless. Another image overlaid the patchwork of fields, their circles and squares inscribed with planting rows in the brown soil. Finally the dry grid was superimposed with green plantings, looking very much like a vast fertile garden, one that would have been envied by Terresians, its proportions and fecundity almost too extravagant to believe.

Cleatah stepped back. While she now understood the pro-cess of terraforming her world, she clearly disapproved. Yet she remained silent. She'd won the argument over the unnatural breeding program that Talya had wanted to adopt. Cleatah was supremely sensible, even-tempered, Poseidon thought. While she had quickly learned the idea of standing firm on her most cherished principles, she had also mastered the equally critical concept of compromise.

Poseidon came to Cleatah's side now. "This is a good plan. What you can tell us is the kind of food that will best nourish and please the gathered tribes. You cannot know what those of the farthest villages eat, but perhaps you can speak to us of the foods favored by the Shore People – aside from what comes from the sea. Then we'll show you what we've brought from Terres and from other continents on Erthe. Let you taste it. Together, the three of us will decide what to plant in the fields."

"And the men will no longer hunt?" Cleatah asked then, remembering an earlier conversation with Poseidon, one that had disturbed her profoundly.

"Not in the way they've been doing," Talya answered, enlarging the image of an area of grassland enclosed by sturdy wooden fences. With a flick of her fingers thousands of buron appeared, grazing contentedly inside the vast pens. "The herds will no longer roam freely. They'll be contained so that they can quickly and easily be slaughtered for food."

"Some buron of both sexes will always have free range," Poseidon told Cleatah.

"So we will continue the Ceremony of the Bull?" she asked him.

He nodded, glad to be pleasing her. He knew she worried that without the natural grazing of large hooved animals the sacred mushroom would be more difficult to find, though she would never have said so within Talya's hearing. Poseidon could see by the glint in Cleatah's eye and the thin line of her lips that even the assurances of some free-ranging buron had not placated her entirely.

"Come with me to the plateau," Cleatah said suddenly, her tone commanding. "Both of you. We'll stand there, look out over the plain, not here in front of this…this…"

"Diffracted imaged," Talya finished for her.

Cleatah closed her eyes and Poseidon saw she was willing herself to calm. He guessed the word she'd sought to describe the plateau but did not yet have in her vocabulary was "abomination." Poseidon could see that his mate dearly wished to give Talya a sharp swat, as one might chastise an irritating child. But more than anything she wanted to be free from the confines of the ship, striding along with the wolf at her heels.

It was clear he needed to level the field.

"Cleatah…" he said. She turned and looked at him. "Explain the principle of phaetron technos."

She spoke slowly and precisely, reaching into the depths of her memory. "It is the principle that all matter and energy, at their most basic levels, are nothing more than vibrational frequencies.

It is the unifying principle of the... micro and macro-verse. Everything that exists is given form and energy by vibration."

"That we sometimes call...? Poseidon asked.

"Vibrus," Cleatah said." She smiled, pleased with herself.

Poseidon could see Talya holding both hands behind her back. He imagined she was tapping out a calming program on her hub.

"So," Poseidon said to her, "Why don't we walk the plateau and you can show us the places of greatest fertility. You know what grows there now. That will help us know what to plant in the future. You can show us where the herds normally roam."

"They'll need to drink. All the animals as well," Cleatah said, and glanced at Talya. "You will leave one of the rivers running freely."

"Ridiculous," Talya said. "That destroys the entire agri-grid."

Cleatah faced Talya squarely. "You will do as I say."

Without another word Cleatah strode from the laboratory. Poseidon and Talya locked eyes but said nothing. He could see color rising from her neck to her cheeks to the top of her ears.

Then he turned and followed his mate out the door.

FORTY

COUNTLESS DAYS AND endless nights were devoured by dreams and imaginings of the first civilization on Erthe – "The Great Undertaking." Cleatah and Poseidon talked of nothing else, and he never failed to be astonished at how open and flexible her mind was to new ideas. He realized, though, that so alien a sight as a city would be impossible for Cleatah to conjure unless she had experienced it herself. She stood next to him in the center of the Library and slid the cylinder into the diffractor. As Atlas City materialized around them she was silent. She turned in a full circle to view the wide boulevards, the massive public edifices and many-storied residences towering on both sides of her. In the cloud-dappled blue sky of the contour dome a family hovercar buzzed overhead, causing her to duck. Then she laughed, remembering it was all an illusion, and she took up his hand as she sometimes did when they were walking through a mushroom vision. Sleekly dressed Terresians passed them as they "strolled" down the street together.

"It's all too close," she finally said. "And too big."

We can build the homes smaller, and place them farther apart."

"But where are the trees and the grasses?" she lamented. "And water. Where is the water? I won't live in a city – even with you – if I cannot sit in the shade of a tree or put my feet in moving water."

"What we have on Terres are 'gardens,'" he'd explained, and led her to the Central Plaza, walking her through the carefully manicured beds of flowers, shrubs, and trees in perfectly ordered rows.

She stopped, and he could see wheels turning in her head. "Could we not put a garden on the roof of a house?"

"I suppose so."

"With trees and flowers, medicine plants and hanging vines? So that birds and insects would visit there."

Poseidon closed his eyes and conjured a street with a row of such dwellings. "They'll need water to nourish their 'hanging gardens.'" Then his imagination took flight – a system of pipes to every home and building in the city, expanding outward to an aqueduct – perhaps two – that would be fed by the rivers roaring down over the Great Plateau from the far mountains.

That was how it continued – the creation of their city, their society. A germ of a notion conceived of by one, fueled by the ideas of the other, spun out, built upon and extrapolated to proportions previously inconceivable and fantastic. Why, asked Cleatah, should not hot as well as cold water be piped down from the plateau, a place where many people could enjoy bathing in a warm pool? And how wonderful would it be, Poseidon asked, to build a permanent track for racing horses, a "stadium" where the whole population of the city could gather for celebrations?

The actual shape of their new city came to them one warm afternoon as they sat in the sand of the Shore Village beach, gazing south to the site of their anticipated metropolis, under which the *Atlantos* was now buried.

Cleatah began tentatively. "Remember when you showed me – with pebbles flying in the air – our sun and the planets twirling around them?" With her finger she etched a small circle in the sand. "Helios," she named it, then drew orbit after orbit around that, each larger than the last. "Can our city have this shape?"

Poseidon stared for a long while at the ring of concentric circles, then slowly traced a finger between two of the rings. "Let this be a waterway." He pulled his finger around within the next two orbits. "Let this one be land. Here...water again. And see, buried under 'Helios' – the central island – lies the *Atlantos*." With a short straight slash of his finger from the central isle across all the ring islands and waterways to the sea, he said, "This broad canal will connect all the island to the ocean, a 'harbor' where our vessels can shelter from storms. What do you think of it?"

"It is very beautiful..." Cleatah concluded with a playful grin, "...for a city."

᪥

A serious void remained in their planning. The most formidable mission of their endeavor was the gathering of all the aboriginal peoples of the continent. Only Cleatah, a single native female, and Poseidon would be shouldering the entire burden. Despite his integration into the society of the Shore People he knew himself to be an inauthentic man of Erthe.

"Boah will help us," Cleatah said.

"But he knows nothing of who I really am, where I'm from... What my technos is capable of doing. He's strong. Fearless. But I think it will frighten him."

"You don't know Boah," she said simply.

Cleatah went to the village alone and came riding back to Poseidon on the Great Plateau with Boah on his mount, Kato. His posture was taut, defensive. The stranger had stolen his promised woman. There was no forgiveness for that.

"I've told Boah that the world will be different now, by your hand and mine," she said. "That many changes are coming, and that if he wishes, he will help us. I told him that you are a man from a village far, very far away, and that you and your kind can do many things that men of our tribe, or nearby tribes, could never dream of doing. He doesn't believe me. He says you are a good enough hunter, and you did bring the horse to our people, but that is all. I said you would show him that there is much more that he should know about you."

Boah glared at Poseidon, much as he had the night of the challenge for Cleatah –distrustful, and supremely confident as a hunter of his skill should be. "Show me," Boah said simply. "Show me now."

"Look at Kato," Poseidon said. "I'm going to make your horse sleep. I will not touch him. I will not hurt him. You know I would never harm a horse. Watch."

Poseidon directed his wrist hub at Boah's mount, his head high, strong jaws working the sweet grass he had just grazed upon. Instantly the horse stopped chewing. His head drooped and a moment later the powerful legs folded under him. He fell into a deep stupor. Boah ran to Kato and examined him, saw that he was breathing normally and in no distress. He stared wordlessly at Poseidon, unable to form a question to ask.

"You tell me when you want me to wake him," Poseidon told Boah. "You decide."

Boah glanced at Cleatah. He thought hard and decided to wait. He paced about, displaying admirable self-control for a man whose horse had just collapsed into an unaccountable sleep. Several minutes passed before Boah strode back to Poseidon and, eye-to-eye, demanded. "Now. Wake him now!"

Poseidon deactivated the narcotizing function and instantly the horse began to stir. Kato lifted his head and shook it, then scrambling to his feet snorted and pawed the ground, as if impatient to be on his way. Boah was breathing hard. The muscles in his arms, shoulders and neck tightened. His hands balled into fists. But he was silent.

"There is more that I can do, more that I can show you," Poseidon offered.

"This is all you need to do," Boah replied. "I know now that you are more than a man. You are a god."

"No, Boah. We're the same in our bodies in every way. But I possess what I call 'technos.' It's hard to explain. Perhaps Cleatah can make you understand it."

"Poseidon is just a man with a tool," she said without hesitation. "He carries it under the skin of his arm."

Boah shook his head slowly from side to side.

Cleatah went on. "Think of a spear. It is *your* tool. With it you can change something – change a living buron to a dead one. With a rock-grinding stone tool you can change loto root into food. Poseidon's tool is a powerful one. It can heal. It can put living things to sleep. It can move heavy things without touching them. It can make you learn things, see things. None of the people of the shore or the plateau have this tool. It is one that comes from Poseidon's people…" She gazed at Poseidon for permission to say, "…and they are not the people he told us were his tribe when he came to us. We can explain that to you later, but now you must believe us when we tell you that Poseidon is simply a man with a very great tool."

While Cleatah spoke, the tension in Boah's muscles began to dissipate. His breathing became slow and easy. He thought for a long time, his forehead creasing into a spider web of lines. Then he said, "Is a horse a tool?"

"Yes!" Poseidon cried, his face erupting into a smile. "A horse is a very powerful tool." He beamed at Cleatah.

"Do you trust me, Boah?" she said to him.

"I do. Ever since we were children I have trusted you."

"Then trust me when I tell you that Poseidon is your friend. That you can trust him with your life." She took his hand. Took Poseidon's hand. Joined them. "We have work to do. Traveling far from home. Gathering many tribes together. Building a great new village near the sea. We are asking for your help."

Boah held Poseidon's gaze. His eyes veered to Kato,

remembering the benign effect of the newcomer's tool on his horse. He turned back and studied Cleatah's face.

"You are not a god," he said to Poseidon.

"No, my friend. I am not."

"I will help," Boah said.

※

Not finding Talya in her laboratory, Poseidon had gone to her quarters where he found her eating a solitary meal at the table, an eye-level trans-screen scrolling data, lighting up her face. She looked over and saw him.

"Where's 'your woman?'"

"It's just me."

"What do you want?"

"Maybe a private goodbye. Maybe…to say I'm sorry."

"Goodbye." She turned back to the screen.

He found himself tongue-tied. He'd come here to make amends, but he refused to grovel.

"You realize, don't you, that this is an *insane* idea," she said. "How exactly do you plan to entice the tribes to leave homes they've inhabited for thousands of years and follow you back here to populate your 'shining metropolis?'"

"Natural human persuasion."

Seething with exasperation, she wiped her screen, but sat staring straight ahead, refusing to look at him. "So you'll forego demonstrations of technos entirely?"

"I have my reasons."

"So you won't be viewed as a god."

"When you did your original field work with the tribes," he said, "you cloaked yourself for the same reason. You were right about that."

"How kind of you to say," she snapped.

"Ah, let's not fight, Talya."

"No, no, let's not fight." She skewered him with her icy blue eyes. "Because for your grand scheme to work, you need me."

"You're right. We do."

"'We... do,'" she repeated pointedly, and shook her head with an expression of sincere incredulity. "Who would have ever guessed at your astonishing capacity for callousness?"

"You know..." He was struggling. "You know I never meant to hurt you."

"I think you believe that. And you believe you would never do anything to hurt your darling 'Erthans.' But has it ever occurred to you that this plan of yours might come to a bad end for any of them?" Her tone had become contemptuous. "No, no, it's simply the fulfillment of your daring dream – a glorious adventure fueled by the *purest* of intentions."

He felt heat rising in his cheeks. "Twist it any way you like. Be a part of it...or not. But if you undermine it in any way..."

"I'd never harm you!" she said, genuinely abashed. "You know that."

"Of course I do. If anything happens to me, you're stranded alone on this 'godforsaken planet.'"

He started for the door and she stood, as if to follow him, caught up short by the truth.

But he was angry now. "You know, if you tried just a little, you might actually find something to enjoy in our marvelous new city."

Her eyes hardened. "Oh, just *go*. I'll scream if you say another word."

Suddenly grieved for his unintentional, his undeniable betrayal, he walked across the room, gathered her in his arms and held her. She was stiff with resentment, but in the briefest moment before he released her he felt her soften, lean into him and sigh softly, and in that moment he remembered why he'd once had feelings for Doctor Talya Horus. Then she stiffened again and disengaged from his arms. He turned to go.

Pleasant journey," she called after him.

FORTY-ONE

*F*LYING ABOVE THE *Great Plateau, over vast plains, mountains and rivers, down to the far shores of the continent was a shiny metallic object in the shape of a long-hafted, triple-headed spear. Manya's voice portentously announced this weapon was a "trident." Its handle and each of its three sharp-tipped prongs named Poseidon, the trio of tines Cleatah, Boah and Talya. The trident flew amidst the puffery of white clouds and pierced whirling black cyclones, but never strayed from its true course till finally it focalized its target and descended with increasing speed towards Erthe. Slamming into the soil it threw up a monstrous cloud of dust that coalesced into a fabulous city of concentric circles.*

✍

The four of them had gathered around a fire the night before their departure to ride out into the villages. Cleatah poked at the embers with a stick, watching Talya and Boah across the fire, talking together.

Cleatah leaned over and whispered in Poseidon's ear. "She wants him in her bed."

He laughed quietly and shook his head. It was impossible, he thought. Talya's revulsion for intimate contact between Terresians

362

and "the primitives" was too deeply ingrained to allow such a thing. Boah was no stranger to Talya. She had observed him, while cloaked, during her early field work in the Shore Village, though on their first official meeting Boah had been struck speechless by the sight of her. Never had he laid eyes on such a creature – the fine yellow-white hair, delicate features and long, pale limbs. He'd been paralyzed and could hardly utter a greeting.

Since that time Talya had emerged from the *Atlantos* several times to meet with the others to discuss their formidable endeavor. Clearly ill-equipped for interaction with the tribes, it was agreed that her tasks were best accomplished at the ship's home base. This night it seemed that Talya's initial condescending amusement at Boah's inclusion in the team had transmuted into respect for his native intelligence and – maybe Cleatah was right after all – a touch of lust.

"We should all get some sleep," Poseidon suggested. "We'll leave before dawn. Will you make your prayers to the Great Mother tonight?" he asked Cleatah and Boah.

"We will," Cleatah said, smiling at Poseidon. Then she turned her gaze on Talya. "And what prayers will you be offering tonight for our great undertaking?"

Talya was taken off guard. "I…I wish for every…success, and that you all return safely from the journey."

Poseidon struggled to remain straight-faced as Talya stood and abruptly left the campfire, Boah's eyes watching as she went. And he was reminded once again that the two women in his life were far more evenly matched than he could have ever thought possible.

FORTY-TWO

THEY WARILY APPROACHED the village of the Foothill
People – miners of flint, quartz and obsydion – as they
were known to be a fierce and stubborn lot. Their settlement was laid out along a river, and their houses were built into
stone cliffs. Their men were known as masters at fashioning the
best and sharpest tools, ones they traded with nearby tribes.

The men and elders who came out to meet the approaching strangers could see they were well-armed, but their posture
seemed in no way belligerent. Cleatah and Boah on horseback
stayed at the edge of the village, with Sheeva sitting attentively
at their feet. Poseidon went forward alone, on foot. In their language he told them their offer in the simplest terms possible.
They laughed at him. Why, they wanted to know, should they
leave their home for 'a very large village on the eastern shore
where the sun rises?' They had lived here always. Food was plentiful, and few dared attack them by virtue of their weapons. But
they listened intently as he spoke. He showed them a large blade
made of honed steel – a material that fascinated them, having
never seen it before. But even as Poseidon demonstrated cutting
rock with his blade he could see that some of them had their eyes
fastened on Boah and Cleatah, more specifically their horses.

At first Poseidon ignored their blatant stares, tempting them

364

with the secret of his steel implement and a promise to show them the mines where the ores that made them could be found. Some of the headmen were fascinated, but their attention was finally drawn away by several younger men who were moving cautiously towards the horses and Boah, and to Cleatah who had slipped to the ground. With spoken words she was giving the wolf instructions to remain motionless.

Boah began to speak in an open way to the young tribesmen, showing them that the horses were harmless, even friendly. He was offering rides, causing nervous laughter. With that, the elders left Poseidon to watch this curiosity. A demonstration of Cleatah mounting her horse with the help of a foot in Boah's clasped hands was all it took. The bravest of them was hefted into the saddle behind her. A walk, a trot, and a few moments of galloping, and the man was whooping with joy and terror.

The three of them were asked to share a meal in the headman's magnificent stone dwelling with its soaring natural arched ceiling – sweet white-fleshed fish from the Wild River and meat of the oryx cut into thin slices with their razor sharp blades. Poseidon asked them again if they'd leave their village and come with them. He promised them steel tools and horses. He also promised peace and safety, though he added that they would have to live among many more people than they did now – a great many more, and far away from their settlement and houses in the cliffs. Some of the elders sat back, talking among themselves and glaring at the strangers suspiciously.

Then Boah spoke quietly to Poseidon. "I think just a few want to come," he said. "They want the horses. The elders do not want to leave their stone village, their mines and their forests, as I would not. So let them who wish to stay, stay, and those who wish to go, go. Later those who leave with us might come back here and tell others to join them."

It was decided that Boah, with this wise strategy, should be the one to speak further to the elders. In the end more than half of the men, women and children agreed to leave their village to follow the trio.

The gathering of the tribes had begun.

In another mid-continent settlement far from lush vegetation, the women suffered terribly in childbirth without the medicines of the plateau and forest, and many infants were dying. During the Trident's time there a woman gave birth, and with the medicines Cleatah had brought with her she saved the life of her child and also eased the mother's suffering. With the urgings of the women this tribe, too, deserted their village down to the last elder.

While moved by Poseidon's surreptitious healing of a pustulant leg wound, Arak – headman of a western tribe that was steeped in dark superstitions – became angry at the "miracle." Unwilling to relinquish leadership, he stood eye-to-eye with Poseidon and growled menacingly, "A man cannot be a god. If we go with you we will be punished!" Every one of his followers refused to leave their village to go with the demonic horse beasts and a wolf that obeyed the commands of a woman.

FORTY-THREE

"TALYA, I'M SPEECHLESS!"

"I doubt that very much."

Standing in the circular library of the *Atlantos* she could see Athens's image before her. He appeared to be sitting oceanside under the spreading canopy of a giant fern, a golden goblet – she supposed filled with jog – held lightly in a be-ringed hand. On an ornate table at his side was a plate of some unrecognizable food, slippery and glistening and raw, probably from the sea. *He must have diffractors everywhere*, she thought, then said, "Working hard, I see."

"To what do I owe the pleasure of this visit?" he replied, ignoring her sarcasm.

"We haven't seen each other since we parted ways on Gaia. I simply thought it would be neighborly."

Athens drank deeply from the goblet. "You are many things, Talya, but neighborly is not one of them. You need someone civilized to talk to, and the best you can do is me."

"Do you mind?"

"No, no! I'm delighted to share your company, whatever the circumstances. You're looking very…"

The pause was so protracted that Talya found herself annoyed, in the way she was always annoyed by Athens's insolence. But he was right. She was desperate for someone to commiserate with.

"So you think I look old and haggard?"

He laughed aloud. "No. You're still the most beautiful woman I've ever known. What you do look is *furious*. Rage is radiating from every pore. It's rising from you like…"

"That's enough. You're enjoying this far too much. I think I've made a mistake calling on you. Why don't we just…"

"No. You need me to say these things for you. You're incapable of saying them yourself. But you're feeling them, and that alone – feeling emotion at all – must make you think you're losing your mind."

With the stinging truth of his words she felt hot tears welling. But she was still not disposed to lay herself entirely bare. "Poseidon's made a catastrophic blunder," she said.

"I couldn't agree more."

"Everything he's worked for – his science, his reputation…"

"You. Throwing you away was his biggest mistake."

She swallowed hard but refused to let a single pathetic tear escape from her eye.

"What of this great undertaking of his? This civilization of brutes?" Athens pinched one of the gelatinous morsels between thumb and forefinger and popped it in his mouth. He smacked his lips and licked both fingers, slowly and with purposeful sensuality.

Talya stifled her revulsion. "He's very determined. As far as he's concerned, it's progressing according to plan. I will admit…" she began, but hesitated before continuing.

"What will you admit?" Athens wheedled, sitting forward in his chair.

"They're an interesting species. Genomically they're nearly identical to Terresians. I've discovered several small anomalies – quite inexplicable. But for all intents and purposes, they are *us*, though woefully lacking culture."

"And culture is what my brother intends to offer them?"

"Not precisely."

"What then?"

"He plans to take bits of their 'culture' – from all the scattered tribes – and introduce only certain motes of Terresian knowledge, then meld them into something altogether new, but 'natural' to the planet."

"'Certain motes'? What does that mean? What about our technos?"

Now Talya laughed. She knew how bitter it must sound. "He expects to use it very sparingly, if at all. Your brother is so inflamed, so inspired by the 'native accomplishments' that he raves on and on in his transmissions from the field. I *try* to show enthusiasm, offer suggestions. 'Could the night sky gazers be taught navigation by the stars in the vessels built by the future ship builders? Might the textile weavers bring with them not only their looms and designs, but seeds of the plants from which they've harvested their fibers, ones that I can propagate genomically and grow in great profusion?'" Talya sighed despairingly.

"So even once his brilliant new society is a reality, you will still be living among savages."

"I don't know, Athens!" she shouted, then groaned with defeat, "I don't know."

His voice grew uncharacteristically gentle. "Why did you stay? What possessed you?"

"I know he's going to change his mind eventually."

"That's true enough, but still…this 'Cleatah' – what does he see in her that he could do such a thing? All I can imagine is pure animal lust," he went on, "which surprises me, really. I didn't think he had it in him."

"Unlike you."

"Quite right." Athens was unperturbed by the jab.

"Well, I suppose I should ask you about yourself," she said.

"To be neighborly?" he teased.

"Just tell me your news. Not women."

"Why not women? Isn't that news? Or does it make you jealous?"

"Athens!" she snapped threateningly.

"All right, all right. Well, you know we've had our own catastrophe here."

"The collapse of the mines. I heard."

"I'm happy to say we're on the way to full recovery – a massive improvement in efficiency and safety. And I have one of your own to thank for it."

"One of my own?"

"A genomist. Gifted man..."

And then Athens, all arrogance dissipated, all mockery dispelled, began to speak in the most glowing terms of his own beloved Mars and its radiant, limitless future. His talk of a society in which Talya could live most comfortably was quite soothing. She found herself fully engaged in the conversation, plying this once-irritating buffoon with questions and opinions of technos and alternative scientific approaches. All of them were cordially welcomed or intelligently rebutted. He was enjoying their conversation, too.

Only once, very briefly, did this fleeting thought cross her mind: the grandiose dreams of the brothers Ra were not so very different at all.

෮

"Let me see you," Talya demanded.

"Not now," Poseidon said quietly. "I'm in the middle of the encampment. It's dark – just a sliver of a moon – and I haven't got long. There's a birth we're attending."

She was momentarily annoyed, but then thought it better this way. She would hate to have him see her overly avid as she described her newest protocol.

370

"I'm going to begin the horse breeding program immediately," she said.

There was silence on his end, though she could hear the clamor around him. His precious "Gathered Tribe" had become a seething mass of humanity, and Talya wondered what was keeping it from becoming a rabble.

"I realize I wasn't to start until you returned, but you've promised your hoard 'many horses,' and I think it's wise to begin multiplying the herd now. When I go into the Shore Village to collect materials I'll remain cloaked."

"Talya, it's dangerous to work with animals that large. You've had no experience around them."

She found herself enjoying the alarm in his voice, so she calmed and flattened her own even more. "I'm perfectly capable of learning their anatomy and behavior. If necessary I'll use the narcotizing function when I work." She waited a moment more while he tried and failed to invent rationale to dissuade her, then added, "You have no need to be concerned. I'll be perfectly fine."

"Of course you will," he finally agreed.

Am I hearing relief in his tone? she wondered with a sudden flare of irritation. *The more busy and contented I am, the less Poseidon will have to think about me.*

"Please transmit your expedition times, and let me hear from you once you're back on the ship."

"I told you not to worry."

"And I'm ordering you to report as specified."

"Yes, sir."

She heard him sigh.

"I hope the birth is successful. Good night."

She clicked him off before he could say any more. She smiled, pleased at having unsettled him. And pleased, too, at her fascinating new endeavor.

FORTY-FOUR

THE FOREST OF the North was already known to Poseidon, he'd told Cleatah. With the diffractor he had explored it many times. But what he knew of it concerned him. It was hot and dense and wet and crawling with life, both miraculous and dangerous. Talya's anthros summary revealed a large tribe – the Arran – spread like tentacles throughout it. He had described the place to Cleatah, and now as they left behind those already gathered who were camped on the open plain with Boah overseeing them and neared the forest, she could feel her desire to walk its verdant, slippery paths, seek its medicines, grow into a fever. Poseidon set his wrist devise to locate the fastest, safest route to the main village.

"I haven't journeyed alone with you since our voyage to the moon," she said as they regarded the dark tangle of trees looming before them.

"I can think of nowhere more different from that as this place we're going. But remember, we're here for the tribe. Much as you want to investigate every medicine plant you see, we simply cannot take the time."

"If we find the people, we will find the medicine," she told him, ending the conversation.

It took only hours tramping through the crush of greenery

to make contact with the first small encampment of the Arran people, a dark-skinned race despite the dearth of sunlight through the thick canopy of leaves. It took three further days of hard trekking to locate the central village, a sprawling compound of stick and thatch houses carved from the forest, surrounded by a wall made of thick branches.

They were greeted with curious stares. No Arran had ever seen such pale skin as Poseidon's before. They were made welcome nevertheless and shortly discovered who led and who was most trusted among the tribe. A headman named Kull made decisions of daily life, but when the invitation to leave the forest was made to him it became clear that "Ta'at" the spirit doctor would need to be convinced.

Cleatah followed behind Poseidon, and he behind Kull, as they made their way through the crowded village, hundreds of pairs of eyes watching them pass. Ta'at stood at the large-leaf door of his hut, stooped nearly in half, fingers clutching a staff as gnarled as his fingers, but his skin was as unlined as a child's. Next to him, straight and tall as the ancient one was hunched was a young man of Cleatah's age, his forehead high and broad, the thick black hair straight and falling to his shoulders.

They were led inside and invited to sit. The young man, Thoth, did the talking, though prompted frequently by his grandfather. When the offer had been laid before them Ta'at had conferred with his grandson.

Thoth said, "My grandfather would like the people of the village to go with you to the new land by the water. But there is something to stop us going. Plants that cannot be left behind."

"Are they food, Ta'at?" Cleatah replied. "We promise there will be food enough for everyone."

"It is not food to eat," the old man said, surprising them.

Cleatah and Poseidon fixed their eyes straight ahead, though she wished desperately to confer with her mate. Finally she spoke. "Are these spirit foods?"

The old man had to peer up from his stooped head, but his gaze was steady. His silence endured for what seemed an eternity. Then he nodded.

"There are two vines that twist around the sagron tree," said Thoth "and they must always be moist."

Now Cleatah spoke to Poseidon in Terresian. "Can you not promise him that their vines will grow on the Great Plateau? They may survive in our small wood, where the hot and cold springs flow. You must promise them. The phaetron – I've seen it do wonders."

"You wish me to use technos?" he asked incredulously.

"For this, yes. Ta'at is a Green Teacher. We must have him."

"All right. Promise him."

She turned back to the men and said, "If you bring the vines, they will grow."

Ta'at inclined his head towards his grandson again and whispered to him.

"Something else," said Thoth. "We cannot leave our ancestors behind." He turned his body to reveal two mottled human skulls in the center of a small altar. "Many others, all the bones of our tribe, lie in a cave nearby. Many, many bones."

Cleatah saw Poseidon silently calculating, imagining a compromise. Ta'at and Thoth never took their eyes from his face.

Finally Poseidon touched his forehead with two fingers. "Let them know they may take as many bones as they can carry."

Once the answer was given Cleatah and Poseidon were shown out and allowed to sleep in an empty hut, creeping insects that lived in the thatch falling on them all through the night. In the morning they were called back to Ta'at's hut where the old man, his son and Kull were waiting. No one spoke but Ta'at.

"Erthe and the Great Mother choose the Gods," he said regarding Cleatah with a warm gaze. "I see they have chosen you. The Arran will follow you, every one of us, from the forest. We will bring only the skulls of our ancestors." She felt Ta'at boring into her mind, like the tree beetle who tunneled far into the bark of the yew. "And we will bring our vines. You have promised me they will grow."

"I will keep that promise."

"You have been to Ur." Ta'at said. His words were uttered as a statement...and a truth. "I see it in your eyes."

Cleatah hesitated before she spoke. She believed she knew what he was saying, and it excited her. "I have been to...another world, but your 'Ur' and mine may not be the same place."

She saw confusion on Ta'at's face, and it was much the same as hers. Surely his vines took him to another world, but how could she think that it was the same as Ka? Did different plant medicines not provide different healings? Why would the juice of two deep forest vines deposit its drinkers into the same world as eaters of mushrooms? Was there one Ka, or were there two?

"You have met the Uth-Cray?" Ta'at said. This time it was a question, proffered cautiously, suspiciously.

Now Cleatah was tongue-tied. That was a word Poseidon had taught her, one she liked. She had to think how to untie it. In Ka there were only creatures of the daily world that were brighter or bolder or spoke to her in clear voices. "Who are the Uth-Cray?" she finally said.

Ta'at laughed. Really laughed. From the belly. He laughed long and hard. "I cannot explain," Ta'at said, wiping tears from his dusky cheeks. "But one day I will take you to meet them."

Cleatah took Ta'at's hands in hers and smiled broadly. Then she and Poseidon stood. What was left for Kull and Thoth was the plan for an orderly retreat from the forest. Thoth held open the leaf door, stopping Cleatah with a hand on her arm.

"My grandfather is old, very old. I fear the journey will kill him."

Cleatah nodded.

"I have been taught the making of spirit vines into juice."

"Good," she said, "then you will carry on for him when he dies."

But Thoth's forehead was knotted with worry. "There is much I do not yet know about Ur and the Uth-Cray. I cannot learn it all before he dies."

"I see much life left in your grandfather. He may live for a very long time."

Thoth grinned and Cleatah saw that he was a beautiful man.

"He would be very pleased *never* to die. He says he dreamed of your gathering, the many people for us to live among – 'the more to share the spirit vine with,' he told me."

She smiled inwardly at that. Lately she had dreamed of giving the mushroom to the people as well.

"If my grandfather dies…"

"There is no need for worry, Thoth. I will not leave you alone in this or any other world. It is my promise."

Tears glittered in his eyes.

"We will be waiting with the others on the southern edge of the forest," she said.

FORTY-FIVE

TALYA HAD LANDED the shuttle on a broad beach north of the Shore Village and walked south, activating the cloaking function only when their boats and nets spread out on the sand came into sight. The beach was deserted, everyone having climbed the stairs to the village in time for the evening meal. There was plenty of daylight left for this – her sixth foray of the horse breeding protocol. She was no longer surprised at her pounding heart and the sense that her neural network was firing at maximum levels. Annoying and enflaming Poseidon with the announcement of her mission had been immensely satisfying, but execution of the program was, surprisingly, proving to be its own reward. She'd always found her research in human genomic revisioning enjoyable, and never expected that applying the Molecular Sequence Reorganization principles to the Gaian horse population to be so challenging. She saw the role that the horse played in even the simplest human society. Those Shore People who had mastery over horses were thought to be elevated, potent individuals. Already Boah had become as respected a man as the oldest elder. Therefore, in Poseidon's experimental civilization, whomever controlled horses at their elemental level would possess limitless influence.

As Talya climbed the empty steps the smells of charred meat

and fish assailed and mildly nauseated her. She'd never gotten used to the idea of eating flesh and thought it amusing that Poseidon now relished the taste of it. Invisible to everyone, she sidestepped the families sitting around their cookfires. A small child running in a wild circle came careening into her legs and was knocked back by a solid but unseen barrier. She moved past quickly, heading for the corral at the base of the plateau.

Talya remembered the growing intoxication during her initial cloaked missions – recording the horses as they grazed, hunted, raced and mated – and recalled the unexpected disappointment she felt once the collected images had been phaetronically assembled, integrated, and recreated in her laboratory. While her detailed study of the three-dimensional bio-facsimiles – the muscular, skeletal, vascular, digestive, nervous and reproduction systems – was fascinating, she found herself longing for the physical presence of the living animals.

The next series of data collections were, as Poseidon had warned, more potentially hazardous, and had indeed required separating out and narcotizing each animal in the herd. Testicular sperm aspiration and egg harvesting with phaetronic devices she had designed and fabricated had proven daunting at first, but in the process Talya reaffirmed her admiration of these magnificent beasts, and she found herself strangely gratified and humbled to be probing them in so intimate a manner.

Then once again she had found herself back in the laboratory, in the tedious process of preserving and storing the samples. Colors, markings, temperament, relative strength and speed of each individual had been recorded. But it was the subsequent genomic re-sequencing, necessitating long weeks in front of her trans-screen, that grated on her the most intensely after the stimulation of field work.

In multiple transmissions with Poseidon, Cleatah and Boah she'd discussed the role of horses in the culture. Some would be needed for simple transportation, and for this a smooth amble was preferable. Large, heavy horses would be required for plow-ing and pulling ore wagons; lighter, faster and nimble mounts for hunting and racing. She had then chosen pairings of mares and sires, and at the genome level reshaped complexes of preferred characteristics. Finally she injected a single chosen sperm directly into the chosen oocyte, fertilizing it.

Today – finally – she would be depositing the first of the embryos into the mares. She approached the corral with its heavy scents of grassy dung, sweat and musk, with what was perhaps unjustified confidence. There was no way of telling if the intrafal-lopian implantations would take hold and generate a live birth.

She entered the enclosure. The horses had grown used to her presence, and she walked among them, stroking a flank or a muzzle. She located the first mare and spoke calmly to her. Within moments the animal was following Talya to an empty corner of the corral. Slowly she lifted her wrist hub to the female's head and activated the narcotizing function.

It was, she realized, as the animal dropped to her knees and came to rest on her side, the first completely satisfying moment Talya had experienced since arriving on the planet.

FORTY-SIX

YAZMAN, BIRTH DOCTOR of the Ladoon, stood at Poseidon's and Cleatah's fire in the center of the encampment. Shadows danced on her wizened face.

"Ta'at is dying," she said.

As they followed her through the field of slumbering humanity and fires burning down to embers, Cleatah watched Yazman's skinny, rod-straight back as she made her way to a camp on the edge of the gathering. There they found Kull and dozens of Arrans, and many Green Teaches clustered silently around two campfires side-by-side where they watched as Thoth squatted, stirring two bowls of dark liquid. Nearby a roofless enclosure of skins and weavings had been erected, and Cleatah suspected that inside it Ta'at lay dying.

She squatted down beside Thoth. At once she could feel the fear in him.

"Some think your coming here brought death to him."

"Is that what you think, Thoth?" she asked gently.

He nodded, but there was no anger in him. "It is as it should be. He said to me that we are in safe hands with you." He looked up at her. "What if my mixture is wrong?" he whispered.

"It is not wrong," she soothed. "You have done it correctly many times before."

"But never to give to Ta'at before he dies." Thoth look down at the bowls again, perhaps to avoid her eyes. "He wants only you and me with him. Kull is angry."

"Why?"

"In all his years Kull has never drunk the spirit juice or met the Uth-Cray. He is a fierce a hunter, but he does not like the sound of the Uth-Cray."

Cleatah knew that when The Gathered were settled on the Great Plateau she would journey to Ur. She had looked forward to it with all her heart, but now she would be forced to go unaccompanied by Ta'at. Thoth would have to suffice as her guide. Thoth, who lacked surety in himself in almost all things.

Leaving Poseidon to sit vigil with the Arran men, she and Thoth entered the enclosure. She was glad they had not roofed it over. The luminous stars filled her with confidence that this death would be overseen, as all were, by Great Mother, but also by the special gods Ta'at worshipped. And by the Uth-Cray. Before long the nearly-full moon would be overhead, a further comfort.

Ta'at was sitting up, propped on both sides and around his shoulders with soft bedclothes, and he looked to Cleatah not at all like a man about to leave this world. He waved a happy greeting at her, and she sat herself on one side of him. Thoth kneeled on the other. Now displaying none of the hesitation or doubt she knew he was feeling he handed the single bowl of spirit juice to his father.

In their conversations Ta'at had attempted to describe Ur. Sometimes it sounded like her mushroom visions – a world of brilliant lights with stars throbbing and colors dancing together. But there were differences. In Ur giant snakes would speak to him, there were bird-headed men, and a great wind took him sailing through the sky and under the water. It was, Ta'at said, "a place where death is known." Of the creatures he called the Uth-Cray the old man reported, "They are slim-limbed, their skin the color of ashes, and their eyes – very large – are as black as the space between stars." He found them gentle beings and smiled when he spoke of them.

But Thoth had no such comfort in their company. Silently they threatened him with their small slit mouths closed, as if speaking from their minds directly to his.

"What do they say to you?" Cleatah had asked.

"They warn me."

"Of what do they warn you?"

He shook his head in confusion, unable to answer. When Ta'at would suggest that he, too, had initially feared and distrusted the Uth-Cray, Thoth grew agitated, arguing, "No-no, you just say that to calm me."

But now Thoth showed great restraint, unwilling to delay or hinder his father's passage to Ur in any way. Ta'at closed his eyes and whispered something unintelligible before he put the bowl to his lips and drank.

Cleatah and Thoth sat with him as the time passed and the nearly-full moon took its place in the sky above them. Ta'at spoke of the stars as though they were old friends and told his grandson that he would miss seeing his beautiful face. He would be waiting in Ur – he swore this – for the time Thoth would join him there.

But when Ta'at stopped in mid-sentence to raise his hand in greeting to someone unseen, and his mouth curled into a beaming smile, they knew he had found his way to the other world and that the Uth-Cray had been there to welcome him.

FORTY-SEVEN

"BOAH!" HE HEARD a woman calling from far across the sprawling encampment.

He turned to find her waving him toward her, calling in a language he did not understand, and urged Kato through the crowded field. As they carefully picked their way through, he surveyed the swelling masses that numbered nine thousand, gathered around hundreds of campfires, men returning with game, shelters being erected, food being prepared, children playing. Even as numbers of what was now "The Gathered Tribes" grew, with fierce hunters and warriors among them, Boah never felt his strength or assurance fail him. Men, women and children looked up to him, even as they did Cleatah. It was clear to the gathered that these two were tribal people, like they were. Not so Poseidon. While never arrogant or overbearing, wearing the same skin pelts that Cleatah and he wore, and refusing to use his powers, instinct somehow fueled the people's suspicions of him. He was somehow different from any of them. Boah knew he himself was thought trustworthy, and nothing to be afraid of. Sometimes he wondered if his newfound potency came from Kato. Everyone envied his horseworthiness. And most men relished the day they would reach the promised land where horses were waiting for them to ride, like Boah did.

At the campfire of the woman who'd called for his help Boah jumped down from Kato's back where a crowd had gathered. It was no longer a fight, as one man was down and bloodied, hardly moving, and the other kicking at him viciously. The woman was shrieking in a language Boah did not understand. Surely the one on the ground was someone dear to her.

He wasted no time, moving behind the man kicking the helpless one. He dug in his heels and choked the man's neck with a crooked elbow, locking his wrist with the other hand. The fighter grunted and struggled against him, but the hold grew only tighter. "Will you stop?" Boah said, not knowing if the man understood the words. But his tone was calm. The woman and some of the crowd pulled the wounded man away.

Suddenly all the fight went out of the brawler. Boah released his grip. The man turned and glared at him. There was still fire in his eyes. Boah remained calm. The crowd grew closer.

Why were you fighting? He gestured with upturned hands.

The man's nose was dripping blood. Every time he breathed, some spattered on Boah. "He laid a hand on my woman," he said in a dialect Boah understood.

Boah looked at the crowd and gestured, *Go back to your fires. Everything is all right.*

"Did he hurt her?" Boah said.

The man shook his head.

"Did she want to be with him?" Boah was remembering...

"No. She wants only me."

Boah smiled and slung an arm around the man's shoulder. "This happened to me once. I fought for the woman. But she wanted the other man. So I would say today is a good day for you."

The man nodded with tight-lipped gratitude.

"Where is your fire?" Boah asked, mounting Kato. The man pointed far across the encampment. Putting down his hand, Boah swung the man up behind him.

As they rode through the camp, heads dipped in the deepest respect.

✌

They'd been particularly commissioned by Talya to recruit the Harrar, a tribe of the Southern Mountains who, according to her data, were a people of robust constitution, extraordinary longevity and potential for high intellect. Even she had been impressed with their circle of elders who studied the heavens. "Some of your 'star-gazers,'" she'd told him with a less condescending tone than usual. "They've managed some astute observations about the precession of the equinoxes, which is rather extraordinary, considering how near they are to the equator. You'll like the Harrar. Not quite remarkable...but noteworthy."

On Arrow and Tide, Poseidon and Cleatah climbed into the highlands to make contact and, with any luck, they would bring the Harrars out with them. They were close now, the village just one rocky ridge beyond, when a barrage of arrows and razor-pointed spears came flying out of nowhere, whistling perilously close to their heads.

"Ride!" Poseidon shouted. As he activated a shield around their horses he saw thirty or more naked, ochre-painted figures darting from boulder to boulder, some reloading their bows – a lithe band of warriors bent on murder. More arrows flew, but the shield deflected them, and within moments their mounts had carried them out of range.

"Are you hurt?" he said.

"Not hurt, but Tide..." She indicated an arrow embedded in her stallion's flank.

Poseidon pointed to a precipice above, then glanced behind them. The ochre-painted men were quickly falling behind, picking up their arrows that had mysteriously broken in mid-air.

385

He pulled Cleatah down from her horse and examined her and Arrow for injury, all the time watching for an ambush.

She gentled the stallion while Poseidon closed the wound on its flank and phaetronically scanned the area. The attackers were on the run, still fleeing in the opposite direction. Once it was safe they remounted and rode on. As the village, surrounded by a high stockade of narrow tree trunks with their tops sharpened into points came into view, a sturdy, clear-eyed young man – a Harrar lookout hiding behind a boulder near the gate – stepped out and showed himself, but then shrank back at their approach.

"He must have seen the attackers' arrows falling short and breaking before they hit the ground," Cleatah said. "He's afraid of us. Let me..." She walked slowly but directly towards the man with her friendliest smile and her hands outstretched before her. Poseidon could see the tension melting from the tribesman's muscles. A smile in return. Convinced of their peaceful nature, the man hurried them into the village and locked the log gate behind them. There were neat rows of huts set around a central courtyard. And a high railed platform along the fencing appeared to be the star-gazers observatory. Nearly two hundred armed tribesmen, women and children had gathered there.

"They are the Maurrad," the Harrar headman, Palak, confirmed after they'd found shelter inside. "They came from nowhere, between this moon and the last. They killed many of us before the wall could be built. But they keep coming and coming. Each time there are more." There was real terror in the headman's eyes. "They are eaters of flesh. They are coming soon!"

Cleatah's hand covered her heart. She said quietly to Poseidon, "There are tribes that are known to roam, with no village for a home. They worship nothing and slaughter everything in their path. Flesh-eaters are feared above all. If a body is eaten, the spirit can never join the ancestors."

"How large is the Maurrad Tribe?" Poseidon asked Palak.

The headman looked around at his people who'd assembled

in the village center. They numbered more than two hundred. "This many," Palak said, indicating them, "and again this many… and again."

Poseidon flinched. *Six hundred attackers!* He moved behind a hut and quietly raised Talya on a voice comm. "The Murrad. Why weren't we warned?"

"Because they're nothing but a myth." She sounded annoyed. "I heard legends in villages all across the continent about these nomadic monsters that steal in at night and eat babies. It's nonsense."

"They're real, Talya," he said. "We're with the Harrar people, and an attack on their village is imminent. Perhaps six hundred of them…"

"Let me check your coordinates." She was momentarily silent. "If they come…"

Poseidon could hear shouts and wailing within the stockade. "They *are* coming. Now!"

"Then kill them. You have the means."

His mind was racing. "I'll narcotize them."

"Don't be ridiculous."

"They'll be incapacitated. Then you'll come here and recalibrate them."

"Genomically recalibrate six hundred murderous savages?"

"You'll do it. It's an order." He closed the comm and quickly joined Cleatah. Palak and every able-bodied man were assembled and watching through gaps in the tree-trunk blockade, knowing their defenses were inadequate against so many maniacal demons. They would fight, but they were reconciled to meet their grisly deaths. Poseidon climbed to the star-gazer's platform and looked out at the rocky ground in front of the village. Now swarming over the hills like an army of giant red ants were many hundreds of the grotesquely painted Murrad, shrieking with a blood-curdling song of murder. He quickly set his hub in a wide narcotizing arc, but in the moment before he could activate, the hoard was suddenly, violently, and uniformly felled in their tracks. They lay sprawled and broken, piled atop each other.

Death, not sleep, had rained down on them. *Not by his hand, but by Talya's.*

The Harrars who were watching, baffled, began shouting joyfully at the miracle, but in the next moment – and to Poseidon's horror – every one of the enemy bodies… dematerialized. They were gone, as though they had never existed. The shouts of joy turned to moans of terror at the dark magic, and the men shrank back from the wooden fence. Their eyes found Poseidon standing above them.

This stranger had single-handedly vanquished the Murrad. Then he'd disappeared them!

Palak pointed up at Poseidon silently, and all the villagers fell to their knees. Women began weeping. Cleatah shook her head in bewilderment.

"Talya…" Poseidon whispered despondently. "Oh, Talya."

FORTY-EIGHT

I N THE DAYS it had taken the Harrar to pack up the lives of countless generations, talk of the "God Poseidon" had only escalated. He and Cleatah sheltered outside the village with their horses, now that there was no danger threatening. But any time they stepped foot inside the compound, silence would fall. People would drop to their knees. Women would come with bowed heads and offerings of food and little handmade treasures. If he tried to speak to them, or even smile their way, they would cower. Neither were the sharp-minded star-gazers immune from the fear of being in such close proximity to a powerful deity. Cleatah had no remedy for it. Her suggestion to Palak that Poseidon was simply a "carrier" of Great Mother's powers fell on deaf ears.

"Let me cut myself," he said to Cleatah, "to let the people see I bleed the same as they do."...

"It will only confuse them further. Make them more afraid."

But this weighed heavily on his mind, the whole way down the rocky hillsides to the plain where The Gathered Tribes were waiting. The journey was therefore excruciatingly silent and awkward. Poseidon knew what was ahead. The moment the Harrar began mingling with the people, stories of the terrifying god who could slay six hundred men in a moment without a single spear or arrow or blade, then make them all *disappear,* would multiply exponentially among even those who had come to trust him, and accept him as one of them.

The moment the Harrar and the Gathered were united, Cleatah found Boah, and the three of them rode off together to find privacy in a nearby forest. Poseidon raised a diffracted Talya, and the Trident was once again united.

Talya gazed at them defiantly. In fact she appeared quite pleased with herself. But no one spoke for a long while. The circumstance was too entangled for a simple shouted argument.

"If I had done what you asked, there would still have been repercussions," Talya finally began. "The entire Murrad hoard falling senseless in front of the village?" The question was left hanging.

"You took six hundred human lives!" Cleatah cried.

"And saved you, Poseidon, and all the people of the Harrar Village. You're just angry because I disappeared the bodies. Less easy to explain away. Great Mother might somehow have put them to sleep..."

"I was convinced of Poseidon's Godhood when he put one horse to sleep, and woke him up," Boah added.

"That's right. And think of this," Talya added. "If I'd come to recalibrate the lot of those appalling creatures, we'd have had to narcotize the Harrar during the procedure, and *then* what? Do you think when they woke they'd have let the newly sweet-hearted baby eaters walk away unharmed? You're really not thinking clearly. Any of you."

"There was always meant to be a time, Poseidon," Cleatah began haltingly, "when you would need to reveal your powers to the people. You remember. We spoke of it several times."

"I remember," he said. "But that moment is *years* away, after The Gathered Tribes has learned to trust me. To accept me as they do you and Boah."

"What's done is done," Cleatah said, sounding more assured. "We should move forward from the place we stand now."

"Well at least *someone* is thinking logically," Talya said, folding her arms across her chest.

If he could have, Poseidon would have taken her by the shoulders and shaken her hard. Her revenge came in many different forms and packages. Instead he gave Cleatah his full attention. "What are you suggesting?"

"Now or later, you will have to face the peoples' fears, their questions, their worship. You'll need to decide what to reveal." Cleatah took his hand in hers. "Decide what lies to tell."

"So...show them now?" he asked.

Cleatah smiled. "Show them now."

⁓

Poseidon looked out over the assembled. They stood in a great mass facing east. Cleatah and Boah flanked him, wearing expressions of the greatest solemnity. Realizing that the one whom some, despite the denials, believed was a god – was about to speak, everyone grew very quiet. They never realized their silence was unnecessary, as Poseidon was even now programming the voice projection and language function of his hub so that he would be heard clearly and understood by all.

"Good people," he began, "I know you believe that I am a god. That I possess powers that only Great Mother possesses. Perhaps ones that even she has never shown you before. Today I would like to prove to you that you are mistaken. That I am not a god at all. That I am made of flesh and blood and bone like you are. But I have something I have to show you. Something that will only convince you further that I *am* a god." He paused in order to compose himself. "When Boah and Cleatah and I came to you, we lured you away from your homes asking you to join with many tribes unknown to you, traveling into strange lands, having little shelter from the elements. You gave your trust to three strangers with wild stories of a great village far away

391

by the sea. One with many large and beautiful huts made not of pounded mud and grass, but of stone. With food and medicine gardens, easy hunting and fishing...and horses for all who desired them. We made you a promise, and today we will show you the great village. It is called a *city*.

"I wish I could explain how this vision can be shown to you if I am not a god." He spread his hands in front of him with a helpless gesture. "It may be frightening, but I swear to you that what you see and hear now will not harm you in any way, and that this is Great Mother's gift as much as it is ours. Anyone who does not wish to witness this vision should turn away now, but if you do watch, you must promise not to move from where you stand, and you must remain calm. When you see the place, know that it is *your* place. You will – with my help, the help of Cleatah and Boah, and the leaders of The Gathered Tribes, build this city. Then it will be yours to live in. You and your children, and your children's children. Let anyone leave now who does not wish to witness a vision of their new home."

Among the many thousands of tribesmen, women and children, it seemed not a single muscle twitched. Not a person turned away. The silence was absolute. Even the birds ceased their calls. The wind, as if Poseidon had sent a request, suddenly died. He could hear blood pounding behind his ears. He clutched Cleatah's and Boah's hands.

Poseidon turned back to the people and said, "Behold a new world. Your world, your home. 'Atlantos!'"

Then with the merest touch to his wrist he engaged the diffractor. At once the air began to crackle and spark. A moment later, there on the plain stood a fantastical metropolis of three concentric rings – both land and water – a circular city. It was nearly encircled by the cliffs of the Great Plateau, though a towering seawall high enough to hold back the greatest waves completed the span. Water-filled canals glittered in the sun. Upon them hundreds of vessels, their white sails and bright flags snapping in a crisp breeze, moved in and out through a massive sluice gate to the ocean beyond. On the outermost "ring island" could be seen the tiny figures of men loading and unloading cargoes onto docks and into warehouses. A marketplace filled with stalls teemed with women in colorful shifts. Another canal separated the outermost ring island from a middle ring isle. On this were built grand public buildings, pretty white, red and black stone residences amidst lush trees and flowering gardens where children were playing. Plazas, roadways and bridges spanning the canals like spokes of a wheel were crowded with carts and horses.

Poseidon chanced a look at the peoples' faces and saw their transfixed gazes and slack-jawed astonishment. Women held their children tightly to them, and the fiercest of hunters froze where they stood. He sagged with relief. They had not run screaming in fear. Shown a glimpse of their inconceivable future The Gathered Tribe had, in a moment of remarkable trust, accepted a wondrous vision born of the most impossible of dreams.

His gratitude knew no bounds.

FORTY-NINE

I
T HAD FALLEN to Talya to ready the Great Plateau for the many thousands arriving any day now. At first in her solitary endeavors after the Trident's departure she had been lonely, and angry at herself for missing Poseidon's company so keenly. But after occupying herself in the world of horses it had slowly insinuated itself into every sinew, every corner of her brain. It was work, still, but now it was passionately explored and rendered.

The subject was suddenly beautiful to her eyes and made her heart pound. Genomes were no longer hard numbers, but living things. The very *essences* of living things. The sparks of life. Inspirations came floating from behind her shoulder as elemental wisps and whispers – elegant solutions to formulae, inventions of technique, the urge to preserve the biological forms as art. Talya's wait for Poseidon to tire of Cleatah might be long, but she'd found a way to make the best use of her time on this planet.

The plain above the village had proven more fertile than even she had expected it to be. Its volcanic soil crisscrossed with her network of canals was already a paradise of fruited trees and vegetal crops. Tools, like buron-driven plows, had been fashioned by Poseidon's direction and design and were waiting to be used by the first generation of farmers. Corrals were in place for the tremendous herd of buron that had been driven across the plain with the Gathered Tribes. This infrastructure remained cloaked from the Shore People's sight, and a vibral perimeter subtly steered them away from developed areas to their hunting grounds and bull ring.

The many cloaked visits she made to the Shore Village horse corral had proven exhilarating. She delighted in both the plethora of healthy mares and foals she'd produced and the tribe's astonishment and joy. Of course they credited their Great Mother for these gifts, and made generous offering to her. Everywhere Talya walked in the village she saw flower-covered altars. It amused her to think that the offerings had, in fact, been made to herself.

Finally on this Spring afternoon gazing out at the Great Plateau a thin veil of dust began billowing on the horizon, and suddenly she had her first sight of Poseidon's 'Gathered Tribes.' As they came she could only marvel at their numbers, far exceeding his original expectations. The act of delivering them, even to Talya's critical eye, was a triumph of organization, sheer will and faultless vision. No one would ever know it, but the roiling mass of humanity excited her.

There were, she decided with a self-contented smile, countless opportunities afoot.

∽

On one horse, with Sheeva running along behind, Cleatah and Boah had ridden ahead to the Shore Village with news of the coming. Everyone had been told of this venture before their departure three years ago. But even then the trio knew they had failed in their attempts to explain the magnitude of the event when Brannan asked if the gathering was like Poseidon's much-celebrated horse round-up.

Now as they slid from their mounts shouts of joy and embraces warmed Cleatah heart. She'd lived for so long among masses of strangers. Home to her had never seemed so sweet.

A gathering in the village center quickly became a noisy throng with children darting like insects between the people. It took some time before tribesmen and women settled themselves to hear a report of their unfathomable future.

Cleatah beheld the assembled, and she looked at Boah one last time before she spoke. "Honored elders, friends. Boah, Poseidon and I have brought home with us what you may see as a great herd of tribes."

There was talking and shouting. Nervous laughter. An infant began to cry.

"We hope that when you climb to the plateau," Boah told them, "what you see you will understand is not an invasion of enemies, but a blessing of new friends and tomorrow's families bestowed by Great Mother herself."

Everyone quieted and Cleatah thought – hoped – that his words had managed to soothe them. But suddenly erupting from the stone path leading to the plateau came shouts, fevered and fearful. She turned to see a hunting party – some on foot, some on horses – descending not as ordered and self-satisfied men normally returned from the hunt, but terrified. Agitated. Their eyes wide and showing their whites. Children fled to their parents' arms, and a cry went up among the villagers.

"What have you done, Cleatah, Boah! Where is Poseidon?"

"We've done as we said we would," Cleatah answered calmly. "Poseidon is at the head of a great many tribesmen and women and children."

"Where will they live?!" Hydra called out. "How will they be fed?"

"We have brought with us a herd of buron larger than you have ever seen," Boah said. "These can be eaten. There are many fine hunters among the men. These people will build a village on the Great Plateau. And they will sustain themselves with no harm to the Shore Village."

There was more shouting.

"You will like these people!" Boah cried above the uproar. "I have made many friends among them." He smiled his winning smile. "Some of the women are very pretty."

There was male laughter at that, and the heat of the moment began to cool.

Cleatah said, "All of them have left their homes to come here."

"Why have they done such a thing?" Elkon demanded.

She swallowed hard, the answer sure to sound like the ravings of someone bitten by a rabid animal. "In great numbers there is great strength." She was silent as she gazed around her at the familiar faces. "If you choose you can join with them, live among them, mate with them. There are many ways you can help them, and they will be very, very grateful. Or you may want to stay here in the Shore Village instead. See them little. It is only as you wish it to be."

"Now if you like you should come and meet your new neighbors," Boah said, swinging up on his horse's back and pulling Cleatah up behind him. "They are the Gathered Tribes," he added with some pride, "and they are eager to meet you."

∽

The Gathered Tribes' coming together so easily into one people had taken Cleatah by surprise. In all her plans and dreams with Poseidon, nothing had prepared her for the teeming mass of humanity now inhabiting the Great Plateau above the old Shore Village that was called Itopia. The numbers that had agreed to leave their own villages to follow three strangers riding on the backs of tamed horses never failed to amaze her.

Now they were living in the close quarters of the sprawling mud and thatch settlement in remarkable peace and good-natured cooperation. The people seemed, in fact, to revel in their new-found neighbors. Why – when fear of the unknown was the prime mover of this species – did this population thrive and grow in open-mindedness and hunger for new experience? she often wondered.

Cleatah's sandals slapped the dusty path snaking between the modest huts, greeting the women tending cookfires or weaving at looms outside their doors. Men gathered in circles for tool-making as they had in the Shore Village. But here the slight differences were apparent – eyes rounder or narrower, tall reed-like stature or shorter with broad chests, skin a honeyed tan or bark brown, raised scars on the back in the shape of a star, or tattoos covering a face.

Most had yet to learn their neighbors' languages, but here there was sharing by demonstration. "See how I carve this spear point?" "Let me look at the strong shaft you've made." "Teach me." "Let me help you."

It sometimes brought Cleatah to tears.

And now, making her way to the gathering she had called at High Helios with the sun at its zenith in the sky, she felt her chest bursting with anticipation and, if she was honest, not a little fear. She had scoured the whole settlement, inquiring after each tribe's medicine man and midwife, and made an invitation to them. It was a gathering of "The Green Teachers," she'd told them simply, and was gratified that each of them understood perfectly. *No need to be afraid,* she said to herself for the hundredth time. *They all want to be here. They are open-hearted and will make it easy on me.*

She came into the small plaza where the common, open-sided hut had been erected for just this occasion. To Cleatah's surprise they were already gathered, seated in a circle like a flower with several rows of petals, chattering and gesturing broadly, some with heads touching as they whispered secrets.

Joy leapt in Cleatah's chest at the sight. It stopped her dead in her tracks, but this sudden cessation of movement brought all eyes under the thatched roof to her figure – the tall woman in pelts like they wore, the woman who had come with two men and unknown magic to their tribes and who'd brought them here to this village of unimaginable size.

A way was made for her to walk through to the center. As she moved, ever so carefully, ever so slowly in order to *feel* the men and women she had brought here – the healers and teachers, the repositories of their peoples' knowledge – she felt a buzzing in her ears and a palpable wave of warmth flowing from all sides, converging on her skin and hair and in her throat.

She stood in the center, and as she began to speak the many languages she had taught herself, she slowly turned in place so her back would be turned on no one for long.

"Welcome, all of you. You know who you are and what you are. You know why I've asked you here. Every one of you is the keeper of some wisdom of healing, of birth and death. Today we come for the first, but not the last time, to share the Goddess's teachings. There are some plants that are common to us all – like *annubis*." Cleatah took from her pouch the five-leafed weed that grew across the whole continent and showed it to everyone who nodded and murmured familiarly. "Good for pain and worry," she added. "You..." Cleatah smiled down at a deeply wrinkled man, "...may know a secret potion to clean an infected wound. You," she singled out a young, bright-eyed woman no older than herself, "may have discovered a special medicine plant that eases the agonies of childbirth. We are one people now. If we, here today, freely gift each other with our knowledge, then all of us will have all of it to use for our benefit."

"What is *your* secret medicine?" said the black-skinned young Arran man – Thoth – whose grandfather, Ta'at, had died on the way to Itopia. He had a friendly smile – a beautiful smile – plastered across his handsome face. The sight made Cleatah unaccountably happy.

"My secret medicine" – now it was her turn to smile – "will from this moment on, no longer be secret. In fact it is not a green plant, but a mushroom. And it less heals the body than it does the mind." She took a handful of her mushrooms from her pouch and twirled slowly so all could see them laid in the palm of her hand. "But healing the mind is the least of the mushroom's properties. When eaten in proper amounts…" She hesitated, carefully choosing her words, "sitting quietly in place, it will take you on a journey to…another world."

The gathering erupted loudly, but Cleatah spoke over the voices.

"It is as though you step through the doorway of your hut to the outside, but it is not the outside you know."

"I know this world. It is called Ur!" Thoth cried out over the commotion, and all eyes turned to him. "I do not eat the mushroom. I drink the bitter juice of The Two Vines."

"Is it the same world as hers?" said an old man bent nearly in half, pointing at Cleatah.

"I don't know," Thoth said, "if my 'Ur' is her 'Ka.'" Then he grinned with impish delight, "but I think we will soon be finding out."

FIFTY

POSEIDON WAS ALWAYS awed that Itopia – a Terresian word that meant "good place" – had materialized in little more than three years since the Gathered Tribes' arrival on the Great Plateau. The village had been built, mines dug and fields cultivated with startling cooperation and ease. Even the concept of foods stored for use in leaner seasons had been quickly accepted.

Of course none of it would have been possible without a common language. The phaetron had synthesized a basic tongue from Terresian and all the languages on the continent – a language called "Terrerthe" – and it fell to Cleatah to teach it. People were unwilling at first to abandon their tribes' languages, even angry at her attempts to force on them something as primal as the way they made themselves understood. But little by little the many diverse languages fell into disuse, only clung to by the oldest and most stubborn.

From their pounded mud hut in the center of the village Poseidon and Cleatah oversaw the miraculous creation of a people. He used technos sparingly, though his wish to be perceived as a human like any other had been sacrificed in his spectacular visioning of the city back on the Central Plain. Learning would evolve naturally with tidbits of inspiration or innovation to excite the peoples' natural gifts. Perhaps their greatest joy was watching a class of artisans emerge. The weavers, potters, basket-makers, painters and sculptors of stone were pleasantly shocked to know they would not be forced to hunt, cook or garden in order to survive.

Poseidon knew that for any civilization to grow or evolve, hard metals were necessary. With his geologist's knowledge, he dug side-by-side with the mining tribes for iron and carbon ore, and with them built the first smelting furnaces on Erthe. They began producing steel. Steelworkers designed sturdy cutting tools. Too, the phaetron had located shallow veins of a reddish metal the miners named "orich," and this was dug from the ground and fashioned into artifacts of great beauty. Granite cut from the cliffs with steel tools were worked into immense rect-angular blocks by a small army of stone masons and at Poseidon's direction, rolled on tree-trunks to be piled on the headlands of the Great Plateau.

Other tools and mechanisms were invented. Introducing a flat "sledge" to the top of the wooden rollers led to a wheel, and then to a cart using wheels-on-axles. Instruction in the principles of mathematics, the laws of gravity and simple physics were given to the cleverest of the inventors leading to the development of winches, levers and pulleys.

Those with a passion for horses became, with Boah's leader-ship, herders of the buron. It was hard, dirty and sometimes dangerous work, but the magnificent beasts allowed them to ride on their backs for work, as well as the thrilling pastime of racing. The men of this "Brotherhood of the Horse" believed themselves the luckiest men alive.

Hunters continued their traditional ways, hunting on foot the wild buron, antelere, lyox and wild turkeys, and even the tusked elephants that were discovered in a large herd on the far northern coast.

Those with a love for the sea began building sturdy vessels

that used rudders for steering and were safe in the sea beyond the waves. Islands off the shore that had never been visited by the Shore People became a frequent destination. The invention of the first sails to catch the wind was intoxicating. Everyone had crowded onto the beach one night to gaze out at the black ocean. They could hear the roar of waves and saw only glimpses of moonlight on the wavering foam. Then all at once the sea was illuminated before them, as though the stars had fallen onto the surface of the water. It was a parade of newly built vessels, each carrying a firepot that lit up its sails and sailors, a spectacle of movement and light from north to south and far out into the waves.

A fellowship of enthusiastic "star-gazers" was born. They needed no help in calculating the best seasons for planting, harvesting and fishing, and celebration days to worship the seasons. Once they'd begun discovering the planets Poseidon had taken them all out to the Shore Village beach. With everyone gathered round he'd focused a phaetronic beam into the sand. The gazers watched astonished as the minerals turned the silicon into glass. Next were lessons in cutting and polishing, and before long they'd begun – with their first lenses – a rapturous exploration of the night sky. Distant planets. Moons. Galaxies. Stars. And a teacher who was their eager student.

The first of the major constructions to be completed were the North and South Ramps, wide curving expanses of paved roadway that led from the plateau down to the seaside, necessary for ingress and egress to the site that would one day become the city. A minimum of technos had been required for the ramps, just an elegant design provided by Poseidon, and strenuous but not backbreaking labor by thousands of men of The One Tribe. They'd worked tirelessly for the better part of that first year, many of them learning new skills and cooperation with their fellow Itopians. When it was completed Poseidon directed the workers to transport the granite blocks down to the seaside. No one questioned the order. It seemed impossible, but it had taken little more than three years for The Gathered Tribes to become "The One Tribe."

⁂

It was celebration day in Itopia.

Poseidon gazed out at the sprawling settlement. Night had fallen and fires were lit. Musicians were making fantastic sounds. Drumming rhythms moved women in their cloth garments to dance and sway in the firelight, their long hair flying, their ornaments clicking. Earlier this day, after a bountiful harvest had been gathered from the land, sky and ocean, they had celebrated their new society. In the morning, with the greatest solemnity, the men of the Shore Tribe had performed their ancient Ritual of the Bull. The sacrificed animal's sacred blood was divided and dispersed to the fields, the orchards, the corrals and the sea in hopes of continued abundance. For the feast, the one hundred buron that had been slaughtered were prepared in one hundred different ways. Mountains of grain were ground into flour and thousands of loaves of bread were baked. Everywhere were piles of ripe, succulent fruit that people could eat at their pleasure. People wearing woven garments and ornaments of quartz and orich, and beads made of seashells, wandered through Itopia visiting with neighbors and friends, showing off their healthy infants and prettiest handicrafts.

At midday there were games – running, wrestling and jumping. They threw thin iron discs to great distances. But nothing caused greater excitement than the horse races. With ceremonial pomp, Heydra had come forward to announce the significance of the horse to their tribe. He recounted the now-mythic legend of Poseidon's roundup, and Cleatah's part in saving the first herd from a terrible death. In the races, Poseidon competed alongside Boah, the Shore People and the new horse brothers as an equal.

Race after race was called for, *insisted* upon, and run with unflagging courage and endurance. The shouts and laughter left the people hoarse and happily exhausted and the winners – suddenly heroes – were hoisted upon the shoulders of the crowd.

Cleatah came quietly to Poseidon's side and placed her hand in his. He could feel her trembling.

"I know," he said.

"I can hardly believe the time has come."

"Do you think they're ready?" he asked. "It's one thing to see the vision of a city projected onto the plain. It's another to make a display of such raw power.

"They finally trust you, god or no god. You're simply their Poseidon."

She stood before him and kissed him on the mouth, lingering there sweetly, unrushed, as though the moments to come were no more significant than their daily intimacies.

"I'll be with you," she said, then smiled. "The worst that can happen is that they all run away screaming."

He laughed at that, held her close for a moment more, then together they went to gather The One Tribe at the headlands of the Great Plateau.

&

The people assembled on the lip of the plateau grew very quiet, as they had on the day Poseidon showed them the spectacular diffracted image of their future home. He'd decided that the time for speech-making was over, so he simply turned his back on the crowd to face the ocean and steadied himself. He'd learned over the years how to regulate his emotions and bodily variations without his enhancer, though he was tempted now to employ it. Instead he inhaled deeply and took a final glance at Cleatah.

He'd begun with the seawall, a structure necessary to complete a tremendous circle – a three-quarters-round natural amphitheater in the cliff-face of the Great Plateau. Having previously calibrated his hub with the large phaetron on the *Atlantos* control deck for maximum force, he directed its levator beam at the pile of granite blocks assembled nearby. There was a communal gasp as the first of them was lifted and tractored into position along the seaside. Despite the displays of Terresian technos that Cleatah had previously witnessed, Poseidon could feel her trembling at the sheer power of the Vibrus. To be honest, he'd never before employed the device in a project of this magnitude, and even he was awed by the display.

One after another the blocks were stacked precisely into a crescent shape with a gaping hole in its center. Row after row of blocks were set, several deep, till the two matching walls were a hundred feet high, and twenty feet thick. Ore miners, smelters and metal smiths had been working night and day for months to fashion a solid orich sluice gate for the center of the seawall. Engineers invented a mechanism of vertical rails, winches and chains to raise and lower it, and the whole device had been positioned within a solid rock "frame." Now, praying for a perfect maneuver, Poseidon lifted and settled the colossal gate into place between the two equal sections of wall like the final piece of a puzzle.

From the previously silent crowd behind him a great cheer went up, and when he turned to the people, he could see that every one of them had been suffering a cold sweat along with him.

"Wait," he said. "There is more."

He turned back to the now-enclosed construction site. Like a master artist at a vast blank slate Poseidon projected onto the black sand the city's enormous round template, illuminating it in sharp concentric circles of light. Then with its "vaporize" frequency at maximum, a phaetronic beam began churning up the volcanic rock. Three 100-foot-deep and 100-foot-wide circular channels, each smaller than the one before, were dug. These completed, a

300-foot wide, dead-straight "Great Harbor" that bisected the channels from the central island out to the sluice gate, was carved away. This left two wide ring-shaped islands. Though no one but Poseidon and Cleatah realized it, the small round island at the center perfectly overlaid the body of the *Atlantos*.

ATLANTOS CITY

"And beginning from the sea they bored a canal of three hundred feet in width and one hundred feet in depth and fifty stadia in length, which they carried through to the outermost zone, making a passage from the sea up to this, which became a harbor, and leaving an opening sufficient to enable the largest vessels to find ingress. Moreover, they divided at the bridges the zones of land which parted the zones of sea, leaving room for a single trireme to pass out of one zone into another…

— Plato's *Critias,* 4th Century BC

FIFTY-ONE

THE NORTH RAMP was a wonder, Poseidon thought as he and Cleatah walked, among the early morning crews, down its wide expanse of paved roadway to the emerging metropolis. The two of them still lived in their hut in Itopia, and each morning they would walk, or ride on Arrow's back, down the North Ramp amidst the workers, exchanging pleasantries, Cleatah besieged for advice on issues ranging from child-birthing to the correct poultice for a burn. Those men who styled themselves the Horse Brothers who had taken it upon themselves to tend the growing herd, build fences for pasturing, and oversee breeding, could not forget that it had been Poseidon who'd brought them the horse. And Boah, first among the Horse Brotherhood, showed nothing but respect, even reverence, for the man he now called his friend.

From this height there was a good view of the emerging city. Poseidon had marveled at the stonemasons' quick study of cement mortar, and their designs for sturdy aqueducts and elegant bridges that connected the ring islands. These had been put forward and executed by men who less than ten years before could build nothing but simple mud huts. Along the circular canals hundreds of docks were built, ready for the day that water would fill them. The stonemasons had scratched their heads at

Poseidon's instructions to build large empty structures along the far edge of the outer ring island – warehouses – with long piers jutting out into the canals. They could not yet conceive of a "future" in which these buildings would be filled with goods traded from across the sea in three-masted ships on continents yet undiscovered by sailors.

Poseidon felt Cleatah's hand snake through the crook of his arm. He saw her eyes fixed on a small family – a man and woman and two small children who were toddling down the ramp near them. He couldn't see Cleatah's face but he was sure there would be longing in her eyes.

"Soon," he said to her.

"Not true. It'll be years before we can have children of our own. But I do ache for them."

"I know. I'm sorry…"

"Not your fault, Love. I knew what we were getting into."

He laughed ruefully. "I'm not sure I did."

They'd reached the bottom of the ramp which let out onto a modest marketplace where farmers had begun bringing their crops, bakers their bread, herders their soft goat cheese balls and grape growers their mildly intoxicating kav. Few people lived in the city yet – most returning instead to Itopia every night, but the workers preferred to choose from the growing array of foods in the colorful market stalls than carry it down from the village above. The market was a genial place to gather. To share some figs and cheese, enjoy the juiciest gossip from the Itopia alleyways, grumble about how over-proud the Horse Brothers were becoming, stealing all the most beautiful women for themselves.

"Mother Cleatah!" a young woman tending a baker's stall called out. "I have something for you."

They went to the tented table where the fruit hand-pies were steaming in the still cool air. "One for you," she said, handing a pie to Cleatah, and so shy as to barely meet his eyes, another to Poseidon, '…and one for you, Father."

His heart leapt at the title. Slowly the people were coming to trust him, in no small part because he was Mother Cleatah's life-mate.

"Thank you, Elfa," he said, and basked in her surprised smile for having remembered her name.

Cleatah reached into her waist pouch and brought out a few leaves of teff and placed them in the girl's hand. "These are good for your cramps," she said.

"You remembered," Elfa said.

"You remembered how much we love your pies," Cleatah said.

Ahead was the front façade of the newly completed Arboretum – a tall graceful mud and raw timber structure, its door inlaid with green foliage in cut glass.

"I won't be home tonight," Poseidon said, and kissed her.

"Star-gazers?"

He nodded.

"Lots of surprises for them?"

"The last time I thought I'd be teaching them how to calculate the solstices, they told me they'd been doing it since time began."

Cleatah pushed through the door into the unfinished arboretum antechamber, now piled with bags of soil, sacks of seeds and boxes of saplings. Out in the middle of the vast covered garden – each section growing with a different tribe's most prized and sacred plants – sat the circle of Green Teachers. So intent were they on the teaching – Thoth adding pieces of gnarled vines to a boiling cauldron of black, foul-smelling liquid – that no one looked up to greet Cleatah.

"When the brew is drunk with intention, great healings can occur," he told the teachers, "and if fear can be vanquished, you may be welcome into the world of the Uth-Cray."

"Uth-Cray?" Myman repeated, his forehead creased with confusion.

"Powerful spirits," Cleatah said, surprising them all with her presence. "As powerful as they come. Put away your fear. Listen to young Thoth. And drink his potion."

❧

With sounds of pounding and metallic clanking and with granite dust aloft in the morning air Poseidon crossed the newly completed arched bridge spanning the Outer Canal to the Outer Ring Isle. Here the first three levels of stone blocks had been raised for what would become a gymnasium and horse racing "stadium" and a small army of shirtless, sweating masons lifting with winches and pulleys the beginning of the third level. The adjacent stables building was farther along in construction, with walls completed and the roof trusses in place. Passing before its huge double doors Poseidon could see that all forty stalls on either side of a wide central aisle were completed, as well as a loft spanning half of the building to store feed. Off to one side was a smaller structure that had become the butt of jokes among the masons – a "bath house" for the horses. The idea had originated with Boah and the Horse Brothers, and though outrageous, found a champion in Poseidon.

For this the Brotherhood began whispering among themselves the title for him – "God of the Horse." Embarrassing as it was to be considered the god of anything, Poseidon found himself more and more convinced by Boah that there was no harm in it. That the deification could only elevate the role of horses in their burgeoning society. He teased, in fact, that if Poseidon did not want the title, he'd be glad to take it.

"There you are!" he heard echoing from inside the stables. Boah, in the flesh, was striding towards him leading a quartet of horses pulling an empty wagon. He was more impressively virile than he had ever been, Poseidon thought, and smiling broadly. There was a confidence about Boah now, born of the place he had forged for himself in the Brotherhood and the wider society of The One Tribe. He had proved himself a natural leader of men, and there was no shortage of women who wanted to share his bed.

"What's making you so happy?" Poseidon demanded.

Boah climbed up into the driver's seat and Poseidon joined him. With the merest snap of the reins the horses took off trotting down the wide dirt avenue and headed back over the bridge.

"I'm no happier than usual," Boah said.

"Lilia again?" Poseidon inquired, trying not to smile.

"No, I slept here at the stables last night, on a bed of sawdust. It was very comfortable. More than my bed in the village. I was making plans."

"What sort of plans?"

"The stadium will have a racetrack within its walls."

"Yes, we decided that. And risers that can seat the whole population of the city."

Boah's face shone with impetuousness. "What if…" he began, seeming to be seeing something more that the roadway ahead, "…there was an archway at each end of the stadium, and a racetrack – a much longer one – was cut following the circle of the whole Outer Isle?"

"All the way around the Outer Isle?" Poseidon tried to imagine it. "So a horse could exit the south portal, run this long track along the whole ring isle, and enter the stadium again through the north portal?"

"Exactly! We could leave room for a single row of race-watchers on either side, behind a railing. No seats necessary. The track would be dirt – hardly any trouble to build…"

"Or maintain," Poseidon added.

"A race could start with several laps around the stadium, but then the horses and riders would race out of sight. Only those along the longer track would see the progress. Imagine the excitement in the stadium, waiting for the riders to return!"

"And then," Poseidon continued, already seeing such a race in his mind's eye, "they could end with several more laps around the stadium track before the finish."

"Yes!"

"Well you *were* busy last night, even without a woman."

Who said there was no woman? I only said it wasn't Lilia."

Poseidon laughed. "Your horse brothers will like the idea, and everyone else will think you're mad."

"Only until they've seen the first race."

"They're going to take my god-hood and give it to you."

"I'll take it," Boah joked. "Or we can share it. Whoever wins the race that year, *he* is 'God of the Horse.'"

"Very sensible, my friend."

"So you'll draw up the plans?"

"I will draw up the plans."

The cacophony of construction on the Middle Isle was so deafening that there was no thought of further conversation. Hundreds of residences in every stage of completion lined the main thoroughfare in the center of the ring island, with many perpendicular streets leading off to the canal on either shore, where more homes were going up.

Every few blocks was a small neighborhood temple or bathhouse, the latter some of the prettiest buildings anywhere, with a graceful row of pillars without, and tiled hot and cold pools within. Artisans could be seen painting frescoes on the walls in bold patinas.

Poseidon smiled to see two men planting a roof garden on a pretty little wood and plaster cottage – from Cleatah's dreams to this reality. He imagined the joy these homes would bring to the people of The One Tribe but wondered how he could muster the patience needed for the city to be completed, the populace to inhabit it, enjoy its comforts and entertainments.

He was especially proud of the Academy, a clutch of several large public buildings – classrooms – being built around a grassy quadrangle, not surprisingly resembling Atlas City's ScienTechos learning center.

The cart rumbled over the bridge to the Central Isle. This, above all, was torn apart, the residence for he and Cleatah and the family they would one day create, was nothing but cleared land, a pile of boulders and crates full of trees that had been carted down from the Great Plateau that needed planting. The only element of form and substance was a round hedge in the dead center of the island. It was already tall and filled-out. Poseidon had used his hub to enhance the greenery's growth to hide what was within it. There was a single cloaked opening in the hedge and, if breached, its path led through a spiral of hedge whose center was the portal to the mothership *Atlantos* buried beneath it.

Just now, emerging from the opening, was Talya, dressed in simple, skin-tight overalls. She was serious, as though only work was on her mind. There was barely a smile for Poseidon, or for Boah who had come to fetch her. As Poseidon climbed down from the wagon, Talya climbed up, taking his place. Their eyes did meet momentarily, but there was something less than friendliness in her expression.

"Meeting with the farmers?" he asked.

"The arborists. Their stone fruit is not thriving. I'll see what the problem is."

"She's coming with me to the high country stables as well," Boah said. "She says she can breed a stronger, faster horse."

"I have no doubt she can," Poseidon agreed.

"How is the lovely Cleatah?" Talya said with a chilly smile.

Poseidon felt his fingers clench into fists, but he steadied his expression.

"Not pregnant yet?" Talya added.

It was a rude enough remark that even the mild-tempered Boah scowled.

"Tell Joss I'll be sending a work crew to finish the stables up there," Poseidon said, altogether ignoring Talya's question.

Boah snapped the reins so sharply that the cart lurched forward suddenly, throwing Talya off balance, forcing her to catch herself gracelessly. She gave Boah a withering glare. He smiled back at Poseidon who saluted him with two fingers to his forehead.

Then he disappeared in through the green cloaked hedge curtain.

ᕗ

Though he and Cleatah were so often inside each other's minds these days, Poseidon was certain that she knew nothing about what he was planning to do this day. As he rode down the ship's central elevator beam and stepped off on the laboratory level he realized how unaccountably happy he was feeling. Terresians never thought in terms of "blessings." They took for granted all the good things in life and were sanguine about any bad fortune that did befall them. Except for the fate of their planet – which was tragedy on the greatest scale imaginable – they saw its killingly long orbit, the darkening and desiccation of the atmosphere as wholly out of their hands. But under the contour domes everyday living was astonishingly pleasant and for the most part controllable.

Nothing could be further from this reality on Erthe. Natural life was paradisiacal, and yet each and every moment of every day was fraught with the gravest of dangers. A small scratch, if left untended, could fester and might kill you. A rogue wave could sweep your child from the beach and out to sea where a shark might devour it whole. And yet the Erthan species – the one that Poseidon and Talya had come here to "improve," in fact needed no improvement at all.

They were marvelous in every respect.

Their diversity was mind-boggling. Their innate intelligence, ingenuity and ability to learn, their artistry, their capacity for compassion, love of family, devotion to tribe, impulse towards peace, their enjoyment of every sensual pleasure, their passion for living...

The human species, thought Poseidon as he entered MedBay, *is a study in evolutionary perfection.* And he, despite the place of his birth on a distant planet, had become one of them. Perhaps he was not fully trusted by every member of The One Tribe. Not yet. But that trust was growing daily. Today Elfa had called him "Father." And of course, the one who knew him best, the one who loved him, *the only one who truly mattered,* accepted him as her mate. Knew that under the skin, in his sinew, his heart, his mind, his intention, Poseidon was an Erthan.

He went to the equipment shelf and pulled out one of the smallest robotic surgeons, then attached it to the right side of a treatment chair. Searching the controls for the correct protocol, he punched it into the device. He sat himself down and waited while the softly whirring chair tilted him back into a comfortable alignment.

If Cleatah knew what I was about to do, would she approve? He wondered. Certainly she had never suggested such a thing. *Would she be angry? Would she be pleased?* But here, lying outstretched in the surgical chair, Poseidon realized that for all the adoration and reverence he bore for the miracle that Cleatah was, he was taking this action neither for her approval nor in fear of her disapproval. This action was his alone. The ritual that would, once and for all, make him human.

He steadied himself and slipped his arm into the surgical bot and activated the protocol. He barely felt the analgesia puncture his wrist or the scalpel slicing the skin and the connective tissue below it. But there was, indeed, pressure when the robotic surgeon excised and lifted the phaetronic wrist hub out of his body.

For the delicate and protracted repair and regeneration of the arm tissue, Poseidon decided he would be best asleep. He programmed a narcotizing function on himself, and he had barely a moment for celebration of his newfound humanity…before sleep swept him off into a sweet dream.

FIFTY-TWO

HOW COULD IT be, Poseidon wondered, that they had arrived at this singular morning less than fifteen years since his team returned to Terres from Mars? It was nothing less than miraculous. He and Cleatah stood atop the massive Seawall. In moments they would give the signal to open the Harbor Gate and begin filling the city's system of canals. He found he couldn't take his eyes off her, wind whipping the long dark hair against a tawny cheek. She was radiant, regal in the white tunic that grazed her ankles, though the strong sinewy feet appeared misplaced in her worked-leather sandals.

From this vantage Poseidon could see thousands of pretty residences and stately public buildings on the Middle Ring Isle with its tree-lined roads and neighborhood plazas. Along both sides of the still-empty Great Harbor and circular canals, and on the arched bridges that gracefully spanned them were all the people of The One Tribe, now the citizens of Atlantos. Poseidon knew he was not imagining a thrumming human Vibrus in the crowd, the air of high expectation for this moment of communal triumph.

Though the Stadium on the Outer Isle was still incomplete, its promise burned in the hearts of everyone. Using human labor only, it was taking far longer than expected. Even with an army of masonry workers, every spare hand mining and cutting stone blocks, using winches, chains and ramps, finishing the grand edifice had proven difficult. He had wanted the "new engineers and architects" of the city to think through its design and construction. He wanted desperately for the Stadium to be a product of Atlan ingenuity. The pride of the city.

Out of sight but critical to this new society was the terraformed Great Plateau, now connected to the city below by its two massive North and South Ramps. There the buron herds grazed within a vast fenced pastureland, and the horses used to manage them were kept and bred in the High Atlantos Stables. Fields and orchards, watered by Talya's efficient irrigation system were thriving and abundant. Itopia was still a bustling settlement, occupied by farmers and herders who wished to be near their work, but also maintained houses for their families in the city below.

Farther across the plains were the mines – orich, quartz, granite, iron, carbon, shale and salt. The miners were an independent breed. Most chose to live where they worked, wishing only to visit the city on occasion. They and their families had taken up the architecture of fabulous cliff dwellings, living in the very mountains they mined.

Finally, from the northern end of the Seawall were steps leading down to the beach and Shore Village. Only the elders still called it their home, though family and friends regularly made the short journey into the past to visit with them or remind themselves of their old lives and place of origin.

"Well…"

Cleatah's voice snapped Poseidon from his reverie. There was an edge to it. Something new. The merest hit of reticence. Resistance. Or was it defiance? But there was no time to question it now. He inhaled a long deep breath of sea air and steadied himself.

"My friends," he began, the phaetron amplifying his voice throughout the entire city basin, "you were once many tribes with many languages. You joined together to become the Gathered Tribes, then arriving on the Great Plateau you adopted a single language and transformed yourselves, again, into The One Tribe. Here today, surrounding you are the fruits of your labor. Know that each and every one of you holds a place in Cleatah's heart, and in mine, for you brought our dream into being. So it is to you, the people of Atlantos, that on this glorious morning we dedicate this city."

With a nod of his head the signal was given. Two hundred men heaving chains through a massive winch set into the Seawall slowly lifted the gargantuan sluice gate. Millions of tons of seawater began cascading through the portal, slowly filling the harbor and spreading sideways into the curving canals. A great roaring cheer could be heard rising from all parts of the city.

It was then, in the moment of their greatest triumph, that Poseidon felt a tightening in his gut. Brief, but sharp enough to be noticed. It was a clutch of some distant, nameless foreboding. *But how could it be so?* This was a marvelous day. Sunlit and over-brimming with hope and promise. He dared to glance sideways at Cleatah who was gazing out over the city and the people – now "Atlans" – citizens of their new civilization. He moved to reach for her hand, something to assuage his fear. But he could read her thoughts and the language of her body, and this is what she was thinking:

What have we done? There is no turning back now. Then he saw her shoulders settling ever-so-slightly and heard a long sigh shudder past her lips.

No reassurances here, Poseidon thought and pulled back his hand.

Let's go down and walk along the canals," she finally said. "I want to visit Boah's house."

She turned and started down, but Poseidon hesitated so he could take one last look at the city from the wall. Cleatah stopped and turned back to gaze at it with him. The harbor and all the canals, while only inches deep in water, were neverthe-less rippling and glittering in the sunshine. Already one could appreciate the full magnificent symmetry of the alternating rings of water and land.

"It's beautiful," she said and smiled, but she didn't linger. *What have we done? There is no turning back now.*

❦

They chose to traverse the Middle Ring Isle – the one that boasted the majority of private dwellings – on foot. It was a day of cel-ebration, for once the harbor and canals had but a few feet of water in them, everyone who had built a water craft – and there were almost as many varieties of design as there were designers – was eager to set the boats into the water. Nearly every home on both shores of the Middle Ring Isle had its own wooden dock. The canals quickly filled with vessels and happy families sailing or rowing about, enjoying the sights of their city from this new vantage point. Those from the inland tribes who had never been on boats allowed themselves, terrified and giddy, to be taken on their first water journeys. Others stayed on the banks of the canals and watched the astonishing flotilla drifting past. Laughter could be heard echoing down the waterways, and there came over the city a slow easy grace born as much of the popula-tion's contentment with their lives as with the unique design of their new city.

As they walked, Cleatah and Poseidon were greeted with affection by everyone. They enjoyed the sight of the many new homes, some of quarried black, white and red stone, others of brown rammed-erthe. Atlans were gathered with their families and neighbors admiring a black-and-white patterned wall here, a roof of layered slate there, a hanging garden blooming with lush vegetation. They sat at tables large enough for a family of ten to recline among soft cushions of colorful textiles. Something as simple as a wooden table instilled pride, as the idea of furniture was a wholly new one for a people who'd previously known the simplest of beds in rough huts, and nothing more.

They found Boah's home on the inner rim of the Middle Ring Isle, close to one of the two bridges that connected the Middle Ring to the Central Isle. A crowd was mingling there. Boah was a popular man for the help he had given to so many since the gathering of the tribes. He had friends from every sector of Atlan society.

On the dockside of the lovely but modest erthan house, in the shade of a long vine-covered portico he had proudly set his table of polished cedar wood – a gift from one of the city's finest woodworkers. A simple rowing vessel that paid homage to the boatcraft of the Shore People was tied to Boah's dock. While there was fruit and bread and fish aplenty the table groaned particularly with succulent cuts of meat, tribute from the faithful Horse Brotherhood, men whose lives as hunters and herders had been blessed by Boah's generously shared knowledge of the beloved beast.

Tanned and muscular, his limbs fairly bursting from the short, sleeveless shift of nubby cream cotton, Boah beamed a broad white-toothed smile at the sight of his two best friends.

"Poseidon, look," Cleatah said quietly in his ear. She was staring at the back of a tall slender woman speaking to several Atlans near the table.

The woman wore a long, finely woven azure shift nearly to her sandaled feet, and a matching shawl that gracefully wove round her head and shoulders. When she turned slightly her face was revealed in profile.

It was Talya.

"Look at that," Poseidon whispered, as pleased as he was astonished. Since her brief, anonymous appearance at the visioning of the city to The One Tribe, Talya had remained as sequestered from the people as she had during the great gathering and the years at Itopia. The one exception, it suddenly occurred to Poseidon, was Boah, whom she had seen sporadically as she carried on with her work.

Now as Boah came to Talya's side he placed an arm around her shoulder, and she smiled up at him with a radiance Poseidon had never seen in her. They were clearly more than friends and work mates.

"Friends, neighbors, Brothers of the Horse," Boah began, speaking to the assembled with confidence and authority. "This woman is called Talya. You do not yet know her, but you *do* know her brother...our beloved Poseidon."

A gasp caught in Poseidon's throat, and he felt Cleatah clutching at his hand. From the corner of his eye he could see she was barely controlling her expression, one that outwardly exuded placidity and happiness. Then he caught Talya's eye. Her look – unrecognizable to anyone but himself – begged him to support her lie. *What harm will it do,* he thought suddenly, *if it makes her life more pleasant to be known as my sister?*

Now everyone followed Talya's gaze, and they were smiling at Poseidon with the warmth and affection he had come to depend on for his own contentedness. There was so much happiness around them. So much good...

He smiled back at Talya and intoned simply, with a respectful nod, "Sister."

Boah puffed further with pride as he went on. "You have not known her, but she knows you. With the magical tools of her family's tribe she has made our fields and orchards fertile and abundant, and grown buron with the tenderest and sweetest flesh. And Brothers," he continued, gazing at the horsemen, "if you wonder why, year after year, our horses run faster and longer, wonder no more. Give thanks to Talya."

With that, Boah lifted from a basket on the table a fabulous necklace of cut quartz stones and shimmering mother-of-pearl shell beads. Talya's mouth fell open with shock and delight.

"With Erthe's offerings," Boah said, slipping the strand over her head and around her milk-white neck, "I honor our sister... Talya."

The horsemen began first, with their signal of brotherhood, a closed-fist slapping into a cupped palm. Then one by one the Atlan women came and embraced her. Small children tugged playfully at her azure shift and suddenly Talya laughed, loudly and uninhibitedly – a sound, thought Poseidon, that he had never ever heard her make before.

It pleased him, he realized with a swelling heart, beyond measure.

FIFTY-THREE

"THERE WAS A fire between Boah and Talya today," Poseidon said as they reached the bridge to the Central Isle. "You saw it, too."

"Everyone who was not blind could see it," Cleatah replied with a smile. "And those without eyes could smell it."

Poseidon laughed.

"I was just thinking of Talya as well," she said.

"Of introducing her to the Green Teachers?"

He knew her so well, Cleatah realized. He did not read her thoughts so much as *share* them. The Green Teachers' influence had become the greatest of all in Atlantos. Plants for food, medicine, oils, soaps, plants for weaving and dying were of supreme importance to the people. And then there were the plants for visioning – her mushrooms, Thoth's bitter potions, and smoke from the leaves of a bush that grew in great profusion along the foothills of Manya and her sister mountains.

She and Talya had worked together in her laboratory to find constant and plentiful sources of food. Too much time spent in the ship's confines sickened Cleatah, made her weak. She even struggled with her studies in the *Atlantos* library, always feeling when she emerged onto Erthe's surface that she had somehow escaped with her life. And the two of them argued, rubbed each

427

other raw. *Talya and her unnatural growth programs!* It seemed wrong to tamper with the Great Mother's plants and animals. You might grow and eat them, hunt, corral and slaughter them for food. But to *change* them from within? Talya could transform the essence of living things, reshape the way they grew. More seeds on a stalk of grain. A flower petal's deeper shade of red. A horse with the size of its father but the markings of its mother. This frightened Cleatah. Made her angry. How many times had Poseidon defended Talya, reminding Cleatah that this was Talya's work? Her greatest delight.

Then one year a swarm of locusts the size of a storm cloud had destroyed an entire planting of grain just before harvest. The people protested loudly. When they'd lived in their own villages there was always enough to eat. But here, with so many mouths to feed, a failed harvest of the grain they'd come to depend on was frightening. But their greatest fear was that they had angered Great Mother by leaving their homes and putting their lives in the hands of Poseidon, a creature who was neither a man nor a god. Loss of the entire crop was a sure sign that she was mightily displeased.

There seemed to be no calming them. It was then that Talya – ever-calm as she was – revealed Protocol 9. A fast-growing variety of grain was sown, and increased watering by way of her irrigation canals avoided a dreaded famine. No one ever knew that a woman working with phaetron technos in her laboratory deep underground had saved them. In the peoples' minds the Great Mother had taken the Atlans back into her favor.

But that single act had earned Talya Cleatah's undying gratitude and respect.

She had invited Talya to meet the Green Teachers then, but she had refused, still preferring her lonely laboratory. Today, having seen her at Boah's house out among the people, Cleatah had decided she would invite Talya again, though she hadn't mentioned it to Poseidon.

They'd arrived at the bridge to the Central Isle and paused to gaze out over the canal. They'd crossed this bridge hundreds of times during the city's construction, but water had never coursed in the curved channel before.

"Did you know that Talya and Boah were working with the horses together?" she asked.

"I did not. I've been…preoccupied."

It was Cleatah's turn to laugh.

Poseidon had recently taught her that word – "preoccupied." He liked to tease her, accusing her of being preoccupied almost every day. And indeed she was. Sometimes she would even forget to answer him when he spoke. She would gaze far into the distance and see things. Things that were not yet there. Things that would be there in the future. Her work at the Academy teaching Atlans to speak, read and write the common language. A temple for the Green Teachers.

Crossing over onto the Central Isle they passed its "navel" where behind a towering circle of hedge hid the portal to the *Atlantos* – a place that had come to be known as "Poseidon's Grove." She'd learned to activate the blue elevator beam that would suddenly wink on and whisk her into the vessel below. These days Cleatah was able to effortlessly navigate Poseidon's technos. It never failed to surprise her.

But beyond the Grove on the Central Isle was a green landscape, lush with ancient trees, grasses and flowering shrubs. She remembered the first time Poseidon had brought her here. Back then, she'd stood staring around wonderingly at what he'd already constructed, though far from complete – a meandering rock-and-boulder-lined stream that cut through the center of the green, utterly wild meadow. And then suddenly her wolves Araba and Sky – daughter and son of Sheeva – had come bounding towards them. They halted, panting and whining at their feet, pushing themselves under Poseidon's and her hands for caresses.

Cleatah had stood staring around her, wonderstruck.

"What *is* this place?" she'd whispered. "And how are the wolves not afraid to be here?" Many times she'd attempted to bring them from Itopia to wait for her in Poseidon's Grove while she worked in the *Atlantos* with Talya. They'd refused to even cross the bridge to the island, ears flattened against their heads, eyes downcast in embarrassment of their fear. She'd long ago ceased trying to bring them.

He'd told her it was their home. "If the wolves can be happy here, so can you."

But she was already moving in long strides behind a thick row of ancient-looking trees.

"Those will be residences and stables," he'd called after her. "Some of your favorite Green Teachers and their families will live there. Some horsemen." She saw houses there, made in the new fashion out of stone. They were still unfinished. Roofed shells with large window holes that she could see would let in light from every direction.

"I want my horses near me," Poseidon had said. "And you know how preoccupied you are, busy at the Academy. Someone will need to tend the medicine garden."

She'd turned to him wide-eyed. "What have you done?"

He gestured to a small red footbridge that crossed the stream. Cleatah went on ahead to a low thicket of flowering shrubs. On the other side she'd found an expansive garden. She walked its narrow footpaths, ecstatically counting dozens of varieties of medicine plants, inhaling the familiar sweet and pungent fragrances. Some of the plants had been laid out in neat rows, others spread in natural patches. Clusters of leafy vines hung from trees that shaded the whole perimeter of the garden.

"You've brought everything I could ever need from the Great Plateau!"

"And from other villages as well. More are arriving every day. This way you'll have medicine from all corners of the continent."

She'd thrown her arms around his neck and kissed him then.

But he'd begun pulling her from the garden with a teasing smile. She knew he was bringing her to their future home, a residence Poseidon had himself designed and built for her. He was very proud, almost shy about it. The place was a long and graceful structure, not overlarge but lovely in its combining of rock, erthe, whole timber and slate. The length of it undulated with the soft contours of nature. Not a single straight line could be seen, as though to the builder they would have been an affront. At the structure's center there was no door. Instead was a tall, wide entryway framed in gnarled tree trunks, finished to a burnished glow.

"You don't like closed places," Poseidon had told her as they passed through the arch, "so I made the outside and inside one space."

They had entered a spacious, high-ceilinged chamber nearly as bright as the day itself. She'd angled her face upward and saw the sky above her through a thin transparency of glass. It was the gathering room. On the walls were textiles of every color and design. Arranged on the floor below them sat intricately woven baskets and shapely pots, some as large as a person. Gifts from every tribe. An enormous stone hearth had been built into an entire wall. She'd marveled at the immensely long polished stone table overlooking a wide window archway. Beyond this was the Great Harbor canal lined with granite blocks that stretched in a perfectly straight line from their new home, past the Middle and Outer Isles, all the way to the Seawall. Even from this distance she'd been able to see the still-lowered sluice gate.

Cleatah had given Poseidon a helpless smile. "How can we live here? It's so big."

"Think of all the things you've learned. Will learning to live here be so hard?" He'd taken her hand. "Come, let me show you." He pulled her through a smaller doorway to be greeted first by the sound of crashing water, then by a warm mist that, when passed through, revealed a tall irregular chamber, its walls made

431

all of white granite boulders. He turned her to see the corner behind them.

There, painstakingly recreated, was their secret waterfall from the Great Plateau. Two streams of water gushed down in a continuous flow – one cold, one hot. The waterfall was decorated with clusters of glittering quartz stones and long flowering vines. There was even a supply of the root Cleatah used for lathering soap.

It was then she'd felt a tightening in her throat. She was unsure how this "bathing room" made her feel. As Talya changed nature, Poseidon – with his technos – had *re-created* nature.

"You don't like it?" Poseidon asked, astonished.

"I do. Of course I do. I just…"

"Shhh. Come on." He'd led her through a final doorway.

This room's light was dim and soft, and here the torches were ablaze. There were no walls to be seen – only rich red patterned textile panels hanging from the high ceiling to the floor. Cleatah's nostrils were touched by familiar sweetness. She'd followed the scent and to her delight found her altar to the Great Mother. Her old oil lamp burned before the carving of the goddess she had worshipped since childhood.

"You brought my altar from Itopia?"

"It wouldn't be your home without it."

Then she saw the bed. Between the broad expanse of gorgeously carved posts were arranged a profusion of furred pelts, woven coverlets and cushions. And laying across it was a white shift. At its waist had been laid a red belt of an intricate weave – one of the western tribes, she guessed.

"Will you put it on?" he asked her.

Cleatah fell silent. She had not yet relinquished her skins. She raised her hands in front of her.

"I'm not going to force you, love," he said with a crooked smile.

"I don't know…"

He'd held the garment up to her cheek. It was soft – a very

fine weave, she thought. And it was fragrant – as though it had been imbued with mattock and elsin. She imagined how the shift would feel against the skin of her breasts and belly, her thighs and haunches.

She'd pulled off her vest and the pelt that covered her from waist to knee. She stood naked before Poseidon.

"Lift your arms," he'd commanded her. She did as she was told and he slipped the dress over her head, pulling it down along her torso. It tickled her side and she'd laughed nervously, feeling like a silly young girl.

But when Poseidon carefully tied the belt around her waist and stood back his face was lit with delight and not a little surprise.

"What?" she said. "What do I look like?"

He could see she was at a loss. "I don't have a mirror. You have to trust me, Cleatah. You look amazing. Like the Great Mother…in human form."

"You shouldn't say such a thing!" She'd started pulling the shift over her hips.

"No, please. Leave it on." He'd pulled her to him. Held her long body against his own. Buried his face in her hair.

"You like it better than my skins," she said.

"Maybe."

"Because I look Terresian?"

"No! You could never look Terresian. You're just…beautiful."

It *had* felt wonderful against her skin, so light, with its flowery fragrance. She took a step, expecting her limbs to be imprisoned by the narrow lines of the dress, but the seams ended at the top of her thighs. She could stride in this garment as well as she could in her outfit of pelts.

"I'll wear it again on the First Day," she'd promised him. The day they would open the sluice gate and fill the canals.

"Then shall we take it off now?" he said with a sly grin. "Mustn't get it dirty."

She'd raised her arms and closed her eyes as he'd dragged it slowly up her torso and over her up-stretched arms. She felt his warm lips on her breasts, and her knees faltered. With a low laugh in his throat he'd caught her up and pushed her back on the bed. Its thickly furred coverlet had felt soft and cushioned behind her back. *If this is civilization,* she'd thought, *if the gifts of the ship's library were hers for the taking and the wonders of Talya's technos could feed the people, then she did like it. She liked it very much.*

But here, now, on the night of the First Day Celebration, as they approached the residence – fully completed, lights glowing warmly from within – Cleatah recalled the foreboding she'd felt just hours before, watching the avalanche of water as the sluice gate opened and the canals began to fill. It had clawed at her belly. There'd been a brief tightening of her throat. It was not just the thought of herself giving up her skins for the pretty white shift Poseidon had given her to wear, but that the whole populace of Atlantos was now at the mercy of Terresians and their technos.

What have we done? she thought. *There is no going back. There is no going back...*

Poseidon led the way through the arch to their new home's "gathering room" where a fire roaring in the stone hearth was the only sound to be heard. He sat her down on the pale wooly rug and took her into his gaze. "Do you know what you've done, Cleatah? You've birthed a civilization. You've become the mother of a people." He ran his fingers down the curve of her cheek, and his voice grew husky. "Do you think it might be time you became the mother of our children?"

She was startled by the question. For so long she'd put it out of her mind – the painful longing that tore at her every time she saw a baby at its mother's breast. Now she remembered her dream of Poseidon at the water's edge and the many grey-eyed little boys and girls who played at her feet. All of them hers. All of them his.

"Yes, my love," she said as she untied the red belt and lifted the dress above her head. Worry scattered like wisps of clouds on a windy day. "It's time we made a child."

FIFTY-FOUR

EVERYONE HAD GONE, leaving just the two of them alone together. Talya and Boah lay stretched out face-to-face amidst a long nest of cushions in his fire-lit garden. Kav had loosened their limbs and voices. She remembered the evening, how she'd laughed more frequently the more intoxicated she'd become. Now she found herself staring at this man, this primitive she had come to know, her eyes fixed immodestly on all parts of his body.

His thick forearms with a feathering of sun-bleached hair.

His obsydion eyes with firelight dancing in them.

His mouth, lips and teeth. *What will be the effect,* she wondered languidly, *when these are applied to parts of* my *body*?

Not a word had been spoken of it, not a touch of skin on skin, yet she'd been certain that she and Boah would couple this night. Perhaps soon. She hoped soon.

She discovered to her surprise that she had been leaning in closer and closer to him. His scent – Erthan, clearly not Terresian – was mildly salty, mildly sweet. Not as pungent as he was after a hard ride. In this moment his smell was altogether pleasing. Arousing. This surprised her. Olfaction had never before played a part in coupling. She wondered when he would first touch her. How? Where? But he did not reach out across the small space

435

between them. *Is he going to touch me at all?* she thought with the merest hint of panic. *Have I only imagined his intentions?*

Such speculation was forgotten with the next laugh.

It was then she realized he had been waiting for her to move first. Not so long ago she'd disparagingly thought Boah nothing more than a primal man. Now it was apparent that he was cerebral as well...and very much in command. *All right, I will be the first to move.* She leaned in and laid her fingers on the back of his hand. With a slow smile he grasped her fingers and turned the hand over exposing her palm, then sank his lips into it as though it was a luscious half-fruit.

In that instant her soft gynae flesh pulsed sharply, twice, then a third time. She felt warmth spreading to her belly, her pubis and thighs. As Boah moved his slightly opened mouth across her palm and fingers, sucking on their tips, Talya closed her eyes and felt her heart racing. The insistent thump startled her, but no more than the warmth between her legs turning to wet. With her other hand she buried her fingers in his long, thick black hair. She heard him sigh with deep satisfaction.

Suddenly he was lying full-length right beside her, pushing away cushions and lifting his tunic over his head. She startled again at the nearness of him, the expanse of naked skin, tawny and taut. His hands, perfectly strong and perfectly tender, touched her everywhere, moved her this way and that, lifted a forearm overhead so his lips could explore the cup of her underarm. He pulled her blue shift up to her hips, and more slowly still, spread her thighs wide apart.

Her hands were busy, too. The pleasure at the simple touch of them on his flesh surprised her. She sought and found his soft double sack. She felt his muscular rod grow slippery under her fingers. But far from relaxing into her hand he took her body and lifted it with ridiculous ease, placing her astride him, pulling her down on him. With that she lost all sense of time and reason. All the places on her body she'd imagined him taking in his mouth, he did. She heard herself crying out, whimpering, begging for more of this, more that, *There, there! Please, oh please!*

Then with another turn she was on her back. He was inside her, stroking with a slow intentional rhythm, pulling her legs higher, then pushing them apart. She was groaning loudly. Never in her life had such a sound escaped her lips. The sound brought her a moment of sanity. *I should engage the enhancer, pace the crescendo, intensify the climax.* But the moment ended with a sudden flurry of arms and legs and a swift sweeping spin of her body that set her onto bent knees. The enhancer controls were out of reach, both wrists pinioned above her head in Boah's large sinuous hands.

His face burrowed in wet silky hair at her neck.

He was thrusting deep, galloping joyously.

She was his ride.

The rhythm began to coax from the deepest place in her a sweet sensation that with every stroke redoubled, strove, magnified, redoubled again. *Slower,* she told him, *slower. Barely move.* Then, like the points of a thousand-petaled flower opening at once Talya blossomed with a fury so sharp and so sweet that a braying cry burst from her throat. The sound was not pleasure. Not really. It was pleading, praying, beseeching.

Let it never stop. Please, please, please...

Talya came lazily awake in a warm tangle of limbs and strong sexual scents. There was moonlight enough to see Boah's beautiful face next to hers, and cushions strewn about them round the fire that had long ago burned itself out. She was naked, her shift lying in a careless heap just out of reach. Some of her muscles had begun to ache and she was deliciously sore between her legs. At this thought memories and sensations flooded through her, threatening to once again swamp her, rock her like a small vessel in a rough sea, just as they had done before.

Before, when she'd lost every last shred of inhibition or control. Before, when she'd been laid bare, rutting for hours like a wild animal with Boah.

It had seemed perfectly natural as it was happening. Then she remembered: she had never engaged the enhancer. Yet the coupling had been…*what had it been? Prolonged. Frighteningly raw. Primal. Insanely satisfying.*

Nevertheless, the desire to separate from the man was growing into an urgent need. She knew any attempt at disentangling their bodies would wake him, so with a few taps at her wrist he was narcotized. As she wrestled out of his sleep-heavy arms and legs she felt the spell of the evening lifting. She paused once to smooth back a dark thatch of hair from Boah's brow, and a pang of some unspeakable emotion – *yes, it was emotion* – fluttered briefly in her chest.

Talya stood and slipped the rumpled blue shift over her head. The shawl was nowhere to be found, but the necklace he had presented her was at her feet, the quartz stones glowing dully in the moonlight. She picked it up but hesitated, resisting the urge to put it around her neck, keenly aware that she was drowning in sentiment.

I really must get hold of myself. I must.

Tying the leather sandal straps around her ankles she stood erect, took in the remains of the celebratory feast on the cedar table and moon-dappled water in the canal, and wondered at her own appearance. Was she ravaged, like the carcass of roasted buron, or as serene as the tiny waves lapping against Boah's dock? She gazed down one last time at his sleeping form, so peaceful and sated, then turned and started back to the *Atlantos*.

It was the first time the ship had felt deserted and the hum of the vibrus so unnaturally loud to her ears. The monotone grey metal surfaces contrasted sharply with the colors and textures still impressed in her mind's eye from the evening before. She felt a surge of familiarity and relief as she reached her laboratory, but as the door slid open a sharp and unexpected stab of longing assailed her.

Poseidon.

How had it happened that the source of her fulfillment was someone other than her chosen mate? A sudden startling epiphany stopped Talya in the doorway. She stood, overtaken by the understanding of Poseidon's unquenchable passion for Cleatah. He had lost himself in the sensual realms and had no intention of finding his way out. Now she comprehended that for a Terresian such sensations, once allowed a foothold, could be permanently desired. Addictive.

She would not allow them to control her. No. It was unthinkable. Irrational. Embarrassing. She moved from the doorway into her laboratory, as though the intentional step was a reclaiming of her sanity. She went directly to the cabinet where an array of hubs were stored, and with a clatter she set the necklace on a counter and reached for the small gynae phaetron. Without hesitation Talya set it to the "abort" function. She was nowhere near the fertility phase of her cycle. Nevertheless she lifted her shift and slipped it inside herself. *No sense in taking any chances.* Perhaps it was a symbolic act. No matter. She would not, under any circumstance, become a slave to her desires or emotions.

But later in her quarters, steam rising from the shower stall, Talya hesitated before stepping naked into the water. She wiped an open hand across her shoulder and chest and brought it to her nostrils. Faint but definite – what was left of Boah on her skin. She let the hand drop to her side, then angled it up to caress her belly and slowly snake lower to her pale silky triangle. She let a single finger discover the moist cleft and closed her eyes at the shock of pleasure it produced. A moment later she was setting her wrist hub to "Orgasm – Strong."

Then she stepped into the pounding shower and let the phaetron do its work.

MARS COLONY

Amber and Grey

FIFTY-FIVE

"I'M PREGNANT."

Joya rolled off Athens, allowing her long fragrant hair to sweep across his face and neck. She lay next to him so that her face was close to his.

"Mine?" he asked, mildly surprised.

"Yes."

Athens pulled back so that he could see the whole of her lovely face. "Will you carry it to term?"

"I haven't decided. Probably not."

The fetus, he knew, would gestate quite as well – and more safely – in the breeding laboratory, and it would save Joya the discomfort and bodily distortion of pregnancy. Still, the idea of offspring was curiously appealing.

"Is it a boy?" he asked, stroking Joya's belly. It was flat and perfectly toned.

"A girl. She'll have my hair and eye color."

This cheered Athens. Joya's silky black hair and eyes were her nicest features.

"But the gene-scan gives facial bone structure predominantly to you." She ran her fingers over his angular jaw, rough with stubble. "She'd be better off looking like me," Joya teased.

"I agree. We'll modify any parts you don't like."

She lowered her head and twirled her tongue around his nipple, bringing him almost instantly to arousal.

A child, he thought, and was reminded suddenly, warmly, of his own mother. He remembered snuggling in her arms, having the top of his head kissed. "What if I told you I wanted you to carry it to term?"

"What if I told *you* you were being ridiculously sentimental?" She bit down playfully on his tender flesh.

Athens grimaced in pained pleasure. "I'd say you were acting impertinently to your governor and needed to be punished." In the next moment he decided his tumescence was far too delicious to waste on such pointless babble and slid his fingers into the warm, wet folds of her. He paused for a moment to decide exactly how he wanted to take Joya this time, but found himself instead to be thinking, *A daughter, a beautiful daughter…*

⤚

Athens knew he was dreaming. Not the regimented working dreams of SleepPhase, but one of the sweet, lazy dreams of Mars. *He was in his bed at the beach house gazing through the large glass doors of the upper deck, to the sea. But there were no blue crashing waves, no cloud-dappled skies, no birds soaring and diving. It was night, and all he could discern out the glass was deep blackness and glittering stars. He might have been looking out the window of the transport that had brought them to Mars, the stars were so bright, so close.*

He felt a warm hand grasp his hard sex and turning his head slowly saw Joya smiling that pouty-lipped smile he loved so much. He looked down to see her fingers, long and soft and white moving slowly, rhythmically over its shaft, caressing the head. He heard his breathing quicken and felt the pleasure rising, beginning to intensify. I should tell her to slow her stroking, *he thought.* I don't want this to be over so quickly. *But now he noticed something odd – the acrid smell of burning rock.*

The smell of deep space.

Fear gripped him, unreasonable and chilling, though the pleasure in his loins continued to build and build quickly, paralyzing him. It is all right, I'm dreaming, *he thought,* things are always odd in dreams. *Slowly he lifted his eyes to the glass doors. Just beyond them, hovering above the deck, were three plasma spheres, glowing orange and pulsing to the rhythm of Joya's strokes.*

What are they doing on my deck? *he thought, panic rising.* What are they doing on my deck!

He felt he should look down again, though he knew it was not what he wanted to do. He did not want to look down to where the raw pleasure was growing, growing... Not with the amber spheres suspended ominously outside the glass. He should really not take his gaze from the orbs. But his eyes defeated him. He felt the slow creak of the lids as they lowered, his gaze lingering on his chest, then to his belly and past it, where the hand was working him.

But the hand was not Joya's. The fingers were long, far, far too long, with bony knuckles, lacking fingernails. The hand's color was grey. Grey! And it moved in terrible rhythm at the end of a spindly grey arm. Above, a face he recognized...

Athens shrieked in terror and insane pleasure as he came and came and came.

ERTHE

FIFTY-FIVE

RISING NAKED FROM bed in the thin dawn light Talya found a heel of bread and a fat crumble of white cheese on Boah's table and downed them ravenously. Their nightly exercises always left her hungry – for food and more copulation. He was always obliging though more and more – to her great irritation – he spoke of children. She would share his bed gladly but children were out of the question. She'd recently had to say it aloud, and watched him flinch at the words. Nevertheless he continued to bed her, pleasure her…and himself…most nights of the month. People spoke of Boah and Talya as though they fit naturally together. *We do fit together 'naturally,'* she thought with a twitch deep inside her, and smiled. In that way she could not get enough of him.

She pulled on her shift, unsurprised by his absence in the house. There was some horse business to be seen to at the city stables. He would meet her later in High Atlantos. She stepped out into the sea-crisp morning and saw that he'd tethered the horse to the cart so that it would be ready for her. Her tool cases were laid out neatly side by side with Boah's things – horse blankets and bridles, several shifts and a pair of sandals – all he would need for his extended stays in Itopia. The Brotherhood had lately been objecting to his life in the city, so far from the buron grazing pastures and the grasslands where the horses ranged and bred. Boah had told her it would please them if he stayed in the settlement more. She had not objected. They would still have their trysts at his home on the canal, but now when she went to High Atlantos for work she would stay a night or two in the old village with him.

From Boah's house on the Middle Ring Isle Talya crossed the bridge to the Outer Ring. She sat on the seat at the front of the wagon, the horse pulling it. She'd never enjoyed riding. Though the rhythmic gait stimulated her pleasantly, she felt vulnerable with her legs spread wide over the beast's back. Clopping along past the South Market she could see it coming to life even before the rising sun peeked over the Seawall. Vendors called out friendly greetings to her, and she called back to them. Talya still marveled at the ease with which she had been accepted into Atlan society once she'd emerged from her solitude.

She turned the cart onto the South Ramp that rose in a sweeping curve to the headlands of the plateau. The cobbled surface of the long ramp caused the cart to clatter noisily, rattling Talya's bones and setting her teeth on edge. Like so many aspects of the city, its construction – though an amazing feat of engineering – was rough. It was even beautiful in its way, though lacking refinement.

Not unlike Boah, she thought. There was always a whiff of the savage about him – though now he was famous as the "First Man" of the Great Plateau.

Above the city stretched High Atlantos. It was home to many who saw the fields and orchards, mines and herds and the Itopia settlement as more their domain than the circular isles, canals, bridges and houses enclosed behind the Seawall. Where would the city be without the food the plateau provided? The water? The horses?

The horse still held a power over men like no other. The beasts made them stronger, more fearless. Better hunters. If you were a Horse Brother a woman would smile at you before she would another man. There was strength in the Brotherhood. Strength that came from loyalty and a shared love of the animal. The men rode together, ate together, bantered comfortably, laughed rowdily, competed good-naturedly. Without effort, men from many distant tribes had forged themselves into a single sub-tribe with unbreakable bonds.

They toiled happily to keep the pastures green with sweet grasses, assisted at the birth of foals, improved their herding, and raced for the simple joy of it. Their women wove them blankets and short tunics of a pattern and color all their own. They were keenly aware that they'd been blessed by Great Mother, and gifted the horse by Poseidon.

They were the proud men of High Atlantos.

Boah led them by virtue of his knowledge, something so strong and inborn that no one questioned it. He was generous, humble and soft-spoken. He'd told her that when he was young he'd been loud and sometimes bullying. Now he found that the quieter he spoke to men and horses the harder they listened. Only when a buron herd ran amok, or a brother was endangered did Boah's shouts shatter the peaceful plateau. They were commanding. Surprising. Frightening. Some claimed he could turn a stampeding herd back on itself just with the sound of his voice.

Talya thought of him and smiled.

Close to the lip of the plateau ledge the view of the city was complete. She always stopped her cart here to gaze down at it, never failing to marvel at its perfect symmetry, a virtue she much admired. It had been a stroke of genius – the concentric circles – making such excellent use of the water and the land. Whenever she took in the sight she mused ironically that Poseidon was a geologist, not an architect. The talent must have been latent in him.

Seeing she was alone on this part of the ramp Talya quickly activated the bio-locate function on her wrist hub. The triangulation complete, a small diffracted image materialized in front of her showing Poseidon on the Outer Ring Isle at the still unfinished Horse Race Stadium. This was another of his wild schemes, all of which were meant solely for the pleasure of "his people," as he so quaintly referred to them now. She could see him gesturing broadly over a vast sprawling complex – the stadium, stables and stalls that lodged all the animals employed in the metropolis, and the extravagant indulgence that never failed to amaze Talya – a bath house for the horses.

The greatest proportion of male Atlan horses lived in the city, with only the breeding stallions living in High Atlantos, stabled with the females and their offspring. The city's horses were seen by many as the society's greatest resource, available to all as needed. No one "owned" a horse and, though common property, each of them was equally cherished and pampered.

Talya was content to view the image without sound. When she secretly observed Poseidon like this – an activity she knew he would despise – she preferred him to be silent, as so many of his actions and sentiments irritated her. Some, like his surgically removing the phaetron from his wrist, she found preposterous.

Then into the picture walked Boah, his eyes following Poseidon's gesticulations, the two men certainly imagining what would become the city's most magnificent structure. Now Boah pointed "there" and "there." Poseidon nodded and smiled, seemingly pleased with his friend's ideas.

The sudden clattering of cart wheels on the ramp above Talya took her by surprise. She deactivated the diffracted image and it winked out instantly. It was time she moved on. This was too important a day to be late. She tapped the horse's rump with a long slender stick and it trotted on.

As all who traveled to the top of the South Ramp Talya was greeted by the immediate sight, sound and smell of the great buron herd that grazed unhurriedly and uncrowded, enclosed by fences and gates. The shaggy pelts on their backs suffused the pastures with a rich musk that floated wherever the wind took it. As she traversed the long well-constructed road beside the pasture there was time to consider the Brotherhood and horses – the reason for this day's visit to the plateau.

Her stature among the Brotherhood had been increasing with each of her genomic progressions – a larger horse to carry a heavier load, a faster mount to win races, a thicker foreleg for endurance, a gentler breed for women to manage them more easily. Each success raised her higher in the Brotherhood's eyes and increased the men's solicitousness. Though she dealt with horsemen very naturally – speaking without pretention, eating and laughing with them at their campfires – it was whispered that this milk-skinned, sun-haired woman, and sister to their beloved Poseidon, possessed strong magic. That she was herself a goddess.

The grasslands were a place of bucolic loveliness – rolling green pastures and ponds dotted with tall, luxuriant trees and the graceful mares grazing there with their young. The stables were ahead, and the horse pulling her cart picked up speed, eager for the company of other horses and the men with steady hands. The ones who knew the words to whisper in their twitching ears to calm them.

When Talya arrived at the birthing barn it appeared by the size of the crowd that the entire Brotherhood was in attendance, all of them milling excitedly near the barn's wide-open door. Two of them helped her down from the cart. Her equipment was taken down and the horse and trap were led away. She could feel men's eyes burning into her, admiring and undressing her. Of course she was aware – and Boah lost no opportunity to remind her – that while their respect was sincere, every one of them wished to bed her. They all envied Boah his possession of her affections. She strode to the far stall where a gathering of horsemen as large as the one at the door announced the day's grand event.

"Boah has not come?" It was the man called Joss who'd spoken, his gravelly voice tinged with disapproval. He was kneeling at the side of a brown and white mare that lay in the straw in the final moments of her labor. Talya could see the deeply tanned, muscled back and long sinewy arms of Boah's second-in-command, and found she could not tear her eyes from the naked haunches showing out the sides of his leather loincloth.

"He will be here, perhaps not before the birth," she said.

"A most important birth," Joss said pointedly.

Talya went to his side and knelt beside him.

"Will the foal be pure white?" he asked. There was a rough challenge in his words.

"White, as I promised. And a female."

Joss turned and fixed her in his gaze. There was something feral about him. Dangerous. The glittering black eyes, the tightly pulled skin over lean cheekbones. A single crooked incisor might as well have been a fang.

"This is one promise that should not be broken," he said.

"Have I ever disappointed the Brotherhood?"

The mare was laboring hard now. Her side, lathered in sweat, heaved with every contraction. Joss moved quickly, reaching up inside her and ruptured the grey amniotic sac. A foot dislodged, then a second. The foal's muzzle appeared. Joss spoke gently to the mare, rubbing her flank with an open palm. Now a head and neck appeared, wrapped in the sac. Joss peeled it away as it came.

Talya hardly breathed as the shoulder, abdomen and hips emerged. Finally the hind legs. With all of the sac peeled away it was clear that the horse was pure white.

But it was limp. Lifeless.

Talya could hear agitated murmuring around her. What good would her promise of the first pure white horse born of two brown-and-white parents be if the thing was born dead?

Joss worked quickly, clearing the infant's nasal passages. He leaned down, placing his mouth over the foal's nose and began to breath. Another man knelt beside the small body and rubbed it briskly with a rough cloth.

With a sudden jerking spasm the foal kicked all four hooves. Everyone fell back, giving it space. *Giving* her *space.* Talya noticed with a small thrill – it was a female. A moment later the horse scrambled to an awkward stance on gangly legs.

Joss helped Talya to her feet and they turned to face the assembled Brotherhood, now crowded outside the stall door.

"A healthy white female, as Talya promised!" Joss cried, his voice trembling with pride.

The Horsemen came crowding around them chanting, "Talya! Talya! Talya!" She liked the feel of all that male flesh so close, the salty scent of them, the husky voices celebrating her name. Then in the crush she felt it – unmistakable. It was Joss's arm snaking around her waist, his wiry fingers caressing the small of her back. Talya's heart lurched for a single perilous moment.

Then she leaned back into his fingers…and smiled.

There was no warning of the first jolt or the colossal roar of the erthe grinding against itself. When the barn's vaulted ceiling began moving and groaning, sending dust down on the horsemen's heads they fled towards the door shouting in terror.

With inconceivable strength Joss lifted the white foal in his arms while two horsemen covered Talya's body with their own and made their way over the convulsing floor towards the light of day.

What greeted them was a scene beyond imagining. The grazing meadow was a bright green sea of angry rolling waves. Mares and their foals had stumbled instinctively towards each other, and now in a large disorganized herd were running in panicked circles.

Then in a moment that would be seared forever into their memory Talya and the Brotherhood watched as a wide gash ripped open the ground beneath the herd's feet. She would remember the moment as altogether silent – though of course there would have been crashing and rumbling as the quake continued to batter the erthe as the horses screamed and died.

She did not hear the horsemen's openmouthed wails, but saw them falling to their knees, covering their faces with their hands.

Neither did she hear the sound of her own bleating, help-less cries.

FIFTY-SIX

BOAH HAD BEEN thrown to the convulsing ground outside the City Stables. As he staggered to his feet he could hear from inside the panicked crashing of hooves on wooden stable doors. His horse brothers were leading wild-eyed animals outside. Padras, his head bloodied, called out, "The feed loft collapsed! Go find help to get the horses out!"

Boah took off running. Poseidon and many of the Brotherhood had gathered this morning at the Stadium to make plans for the first Atlantos "Race Day." But as he came round the corner of the Stables he was stayed in his tracks, paralyzed.

A large section of the arena wall, newly completed with fabulous marble statues of horses and riders, was now a pile of rubble.

Some brothers wandered dazed in the dusty debris. Others had begun digging in the ruin, with desperate calls for help. When he saw Poseidon among those finding it impossible to lift the giant blocks and pieces of statuary from their brothers Boah went to him and, shoulder to shoulder, began to move the stones.

Boah glanced at Poseidon's wrist. "Use your device," he whispered urgently.

Poseidon shook his head, frustrated. "I have to go. Get to the Seawall. Something worse is coming!"

Boah watched him run for the Stables for only a moment, then put his back into the rescue.

&

The Brothers had collected the surviving horses in the corral. All were agitated, frothing at the mouth, with fights breaking out among them. Poseidon scanned the pen. In the melee it was hard to make out one horse from another. *Please be here, please...* He whistled shrilly – twice, once, twice, their signal – and suddenly Arrow was there at the fence, snorting and nodding her pleasure to see him. His heart quieted at the sight of her. He went in, took her out and swung up on her back.

They galloped off, making for the nearest Outer Canal Bridge, passing the line of docks and warehouses where workers struggled with fallen walls and gravely injured workers...none of which he could help.

He could not be sure without his hub, but from the strength and considerable duration of the tremors, and the direction of the ground movement, he believed the rupture was offshore. He knew what this portended.

Fool. Fool! Fool!! echoed in his head.

&

In her Academy Terrerthe language classroom, Cleatah struggled to her feet the moment the ground ceased to shake. All about her were people bleeding and crying, bones broken, half-buried beneath fallen masonry. Some were dead.

She found among the students two Green Teachers who had survived, as she had, unscathed. "Elona, Brant," she called to them. They turned, stunned and confused but heartened to see Cleatah standing unharmed. "Go to the Arboretum. See who is there. If they're unhurt, send them out to their wards. Let them do what they can."

They turned to go.

"Elona, bring me back my satchel, and we can work together here."

The woman nodded dully. When she turned she stumbled on a dead man, his head crushed, one of his eyeballs popped from its socket.

"Keep your eyes ahead," Cleatah told her. "Hurry!"

Cleatah surveyed the classroom. Her unhurt students were stirring, looking around them, reaching out to help each other. A young man called to her, "Here, Mother! This woman is bleeding badly."

Another voice from across the room, "Please help me! Please!"

"You, Zonar. Take off your shift. Rip it into long strips." The one-time Arran tribesman was at her side in a flash, and together – grunting with effort – they lifted a stone block off the leg of a young pregnant woman. "Malla," she shouted at a wizened crone across the room, staring helplessly around her. "Find me some wood for splints." Cleatah knelt by the pregnant woman's side.

"I'm Luna," she said weakly."

"I know," Cleatah told her with a gentle smile. "I remembered because that was my mother's name."

"Aaaiggh!" Luna cried. Her breath was ragged. "It hurts so much!"

"I'm going to make it better." She turned and called out, "Zonar!"

He picked his way over, wearing just a loincloth, his tunic in narrow strips hanging over one arm. Cleatah took them gratefully. "Will you find old Malla? Help her collect splints. Bring them to me here." She turned back to the young woman lying stretched out at her knees. "This will hurt…badly…but just for a moment." She placed a hand above the break, and one below.

"Scream as loud as you can. Understand? Let Great Mother hear your pain. "I'm going to scream with you."

Luna managed a smile.

"Now…"

❧

As Arrow crossed the Outer Canal Bridge Poseidon saw to his relief that the Seawall had been largely unscathed by the shaking – all but a small section to the north of the sluice gate. A phalanx of men of the Wall Watch, though unnerved, stood faithfully at their posts. They were gazing nervously inland towards the city, concerned for the quake's damage and injuries of loved ones. Their heads swiveled to see Poseidon riding hellbent towards them.

He leapt from his mount. "There is a wave coming!" he called up to them. "A great wave! Look for it! When the water recedes, when there's no more water in the sea, then it will come. A white line of foam from north to south. It will rear up to a terrible size! When you see the line of foam you must come down from the wall and run inland! Gather anyone you find and take them with you!"

Four ground-level Watchmen were standing tall, waiting for his orders. "We have to close the sluice gate," he told them. "Quickly now! We should be all right. This is why we built the wall. It will hold." He wanted to believe his own words, though he found time to curse his excised wrist hub. If it were still in his arm he would know the size of the wave, if it was taller than the one hundred foot high Seawall, and how long before it arrived.

The gate's massive mechanism, but a year before, had required two hundred men and heavy chains to winch the gate open. Its design for emergency closure was different, needing just three men and the force of gravity to close it. Once the lever was released the metal behemoth would slice down through its vertical grooves on either side of the Seawall and in moments seal both the tall portal and the deep channel below it.

"Heave!" Poseidon cried, and they threw their weight behind the giant release lever.

It did not budge.

"Heave!" they all cried with him.

The second attempt was as futile as the first.

He looked above him and saw the fractured section of wall, and fragments of stone all around his feet. Some of them must be lodged in the winch and chain!

Bloody stars, the sluice gate was wide open, and a long, unstoppable wave was coming!

He saw in his mind's eye the catastrophe unfolding. The swell of water surging through the open gate, the canals refilling quickly with the force of the seismic surge and with its extraordinary wave length, coming and coming until it flooded the city carefully enclosed behind the Seawall and by the cliffs of the plateau.

And here he stood, helpless. The hub could have made quick work of the blockage in the winch. With it, he might have projected a warning to every part of the city for the people to stay away from the harbor and canals. To climb to the highest rooftops.

The Wall Guards were still waiting loyally at the winch but now Poseidon shouted for them to run. Abandoning the lever he dashed to Arrow and mounted in a single bound, setting his mind to meld with hers. He only had to think "Home!" and Arrow received it. She danced in place only long enough to set her target, then shot for the Outer Canal Bridge.

⁂

The horse pounded beneath them, Talya's arms clasped tight around Joss's waist. The newest portion of the South Ramp had collapsed, and they'd had to ride up again, across the plateau's lip and down the North Ramp. It was jammed with bloodied Atlans streaming out of the city, fleeing to something simple, familiar, not heavy stone walls crashing down around them.

It was slow going in the panicked crowd. Her heart pounding, she wanted to shout "Faster!" in Joss's ear. From above she could see some damage. A portion of the Stadium wall collapsed. Several of the inter-island bridges down. The Seawall, thankfully, appeared intact.

At a full stop now, her nerves frayed. Fingernails bit into her fisted hands. *Can't wait like this!* She programmed her hub and directed it towards the mob climbing the ramp. Invisibly, painlessly and, to Joss – impossibly – a path through the crowd was miraculously cleared before their horse, all the way to the ramp's bottom.

"Great Mother," he whispered in awe.

"Go!" Talya cried.

⚓

Idiot! The word raked across Poseidon's mind. *Fooled twice by this planet. Anything but benign.* This mistake, this bloody mistake, compounded by his premature, credulous removal of his hub, would cost not one friend his life, but all the people of Atlantos. Drowned, when water poured in through the sluice gate… like rats in a bowl. He banished recriminations for now – plenty of time later – and was vaguely aware of the normally placid waters of the Outer Canal broken into chop, slamming skifes and triremes hard against the stone piers.

Gain entrance into the Atlantos. *Secure a hub. Triangulate quake coordinates*, he enumerated. *Release the sluice gate. Find Cleatah…*

Luckily the layout of the city byways – its bridges and streets – went from the Seawall to Central Ring Isle in a dead-straight line. They rode past warehouses and ship yard…then a narrow overpass that spanned the Racetrack… the rest of the Outer Ring Isle, then clattered over the Middle Canal Bridge.

He traversed the Middle Ring Isle, with its many homes and neighborhood temples, its dead lying at odd angles, and maimed – many wandering dazed, bloodied. There were quiet signs of shock rather than screaming panic in the streets. He saw ahead that the largest city bath house had collapsed, masonry and water filling the street. Geysers of steam rose from what remained of the hot pool. "Please, please," cried a man, his skin red, blistered and peeling from his body, a small limp child in his arms with ghastly burns. *Eyes straight ahead,* Poseidon commanded himself, keeping up the pace. *You cannot help them.* A tall marble pillar had fallen and blocked the whole width of the road ahead. Arrow saw this, picked up the pace, and just as her muscles tensed beneath him and he flattened against her neck, they were suddenly airborne, flying over the column, landing with a sure-footed thud. Not missing a beat they headed for the Central Canal Bridge. They were halfway across it when, with no warning, came a second jolt. Brief, yes, but violent.

The bridge collapsed out from under them before they could halt their tracks. They fell, together with the bridge rubble, into the chop of the Central Canal, Poseidon flung off of Arrow's back, his skull narrowly missing the sharp keel of an overturned skife. Arrow, her eyes wild and uncaring of the detritus buffeted about, paddled towards him. He closed the distance, desperate to be back astride her. They would calm one another. Think as one. They would make it to the shore of the Central Isle. They would…

In the roiling water the knifelike keel of the overturned skife, came crashing towards him, slicing through his thigh. A moment later it slammed broadside into Arrow. Poseidon heard her scream. She began to flail, blood bubbling up around her. He tried to catch her eye but he thought, *She does not see me. She sees nothing but darkness.* For a moment the water spun her, exposing the cruel gash that had rent her ribcage in two.

And then she was gone. Taken down by the terrible frenzy.

He came to his senses. *No time. No time.* He forced his arms to move. He swam for the Central Isle shore. For the fringe of yew trees that backed a narrow sand beach. He clawed his way onto land, bearing the grisly pain in his leg, helplessly replaying the panic in Arrow's eye in the moment before her life was extinguished. *No time, no time. Stand up!* He took only one breath, then pulled himself erect…and began a hobbling run.

Emerging from the yews to the north of the Residence that stood blessedly intact, he made for Poseidon's Grove. Even from here he could see that the ground's movement had skewed the circular hedge, all in one piece, to a small but unnatural angle. The sight stunned him, then set his mind in forward motion.

The hedge is skewed. The elevator beam must be damaged. The beam damaged, the only entrance to the ship is compromised. How will I get inside! His legs barely carried him the distance across the Central Isle and red bridge to the Grove's entrance. Inside the green spiral – off kilter – disorientation threatened. *Steady!* he commanded himself. *Focus!* On in the center, the beam activator poked from the ground at the same angle as the hedge. Foot pressure elicited no response. His heart sank. The portal to the *Atlantos* mocked him, resolutely closed. He sank to his knees, and ripped away the grassy cover. There was the hidden door that, once activated, would normally have slid open. But the mechanisms were bent. All his human strength was useless against Terresian technos. *Useless.*

"Move away," he heard above him. "Poseidon, step aside!" It was Talya. She was tapping at her wrist. Falling to her knees she burned a slot through the metal, inserted her fingers and with the enhanced strength of ten men, pulled back the door. Instantly the blue elevator beam blinked on, streaming straight down within the angled metal tunnel.

"What's wrong with your hub?" she demanded.

A sudden blaring alarm coming from below saved him from speaking the awful truth. Its sound grew deafening as they descended the beam and emerged at Laboratory Level. Warning lights along the corridor were pulsing red.

"No...no...no..." he muttered.

"What? Poseidon. Tell me."

"A Core melt!" he shouted, then thought, *The sluice gate is open...* "Talya, you need to go to the Residence!"

"What?!"

"Dining room. Balcony over the Harbor. Use your hub. Black beam."

"I don't understand!"

"The sluice gate is jammed open. Debris in the gears. A *wave* is coming! If the sluice is open the city floods!"

"How long before...?"

Bile rose in his throat. "I don't know."

"How big is it?"

"I don't *know*."

"*Why* don't you know?" She looked at his inner arm.

"No time to explain!"

"I'll generate a dome over the city," she asserted, glancing at her own hub.

"With something that large we'd need the ship's phaetron, and with a damaged Core... I don't know...Please, just get to the Residence. Black beam, straight down the Harbor, slight north angle. You'll find debris in the winch and chains. Deconstruct carefully. Don't damage the mechanism." He knew his eyes must be wild. "I'll take the Core."

"Poseidon, your leg..."

Blood was pooling at his feet.

"Just go. Now!"

He pounded the first control he saw and silenced the screaming alarm and pulsing lights. He turned and staggered to the equipment bay. Inside, he slid out the broad drawers housing phaetrons carefully arranged by size and function. Surgical devices, repair hubs, wrist implants – his excised hub among them. *Hand held? No. Would need both hands to work. There, an older model. Antiquated. One that strapped onto the wrist. It would do.* He fastened it as he chose his suit. *Not pressure. Not propulsion. Temperature control!* He paused long enough to pull up his tunic, exposing the grievous wound, then knit the thigh muscle, fascia and skin before pulling on the climate suit. Grabbed a helmet and ran back along the corridor to the central elevator beam.

As he rode down he punched in Seismic Triangulation on the hub. Instantly coordinates projected before him, along with a diffracted view of the seafloor. He was familiar with the two thousand mile long, six-mile-deep Marius Trench, two hundred miles east of their coast. He could see clearly that a thirty-five-foot upthrust in the fault had caused the rupture, and the vast displacement of water was even now sending a seismic sea wave in their direction. He comm'd Talya.

"We have thirteen, maybe fourteen minutes."

He could hear she was breathless, clearly running. "How large is it?"

He did a further calculation – the varying angle of the seafloor off the continental coastline. "Deep water…then shallows two miles out," he said as much to himself as to her. "A hundred feet or more."

"Higher than the Seawall?"

"Slightly." He'd reached Level One Operations. The titanum Core Anteroom. "Get to the Residence," he told Talya, then closed comm. He found the door was jammed. *Perhaps the ship's entire Central Corpus had been damaged.* He wasted no time blowing the anteroom door open. The hub was old but functional. His suit sensors blinked on. *Temperature elevated. Titanum toxicity elevated. Would the door to the CoreShaft need blowing in as well?* No. It opened easily. He stepped in.

The Core made of thick piled titanum discs rose a hundred feet through the center of the shaft towering above him to the top of the ship.

Its color is wrong, he thought. It glowed with a dull brownish red. He scanned it but found no damage to the Core itself. He surveyed the Core Wall next. *And there it was.* Not five feet above him was the breach – a vertical crack glowing with white heat. It rose above him thirty feet.

"Protocol. Core Wall breach," he said aloud.

The hub complied promptly with data. Heat was building exponentially in the Core. The wall needed sealing quickly. Codes and procedures needed to close the rupture flashed before him. He went to work, scaling the ledged wall, beginning at the lower end of the crack. *The protocols and device were working well.* He made his way slowly up the vertical breach.

The first heat on his back was mild, yet alarming. *Just work. Close the gap. Don't think about it.* But the thought came – his failure. *Impulsively, sentimentally removing his wrist hub. The* Atlantos *obliterated. The city vaporized. A chunk broken off the continent. And wave far greater than the one bearing down on them now from the Marius Trench. It would drown all the islands to the east of Atlantos. It was large enough to travel the whole breadth of the Eastern Sea to crash down upon the shore of South Platos. Titanum toxicity spewed into the atmosphere circling the globe. A hole blown in the sky.*

Poseidon took hold of his flailing emotions. *Concentrate. Work. Climb. Repair. Ignore the heat on your back. Work. Climb...*

Talya stood on the dining room balcony, the Great Harbor stretched out in a straight line before her. It was crowded with vessels, few of them moving with any purpose...all the boatmen confused. One of the triremes was listing dangerously in the water. She could see the crew milling about on the tilting deck.

She focused her hub on the damaged Seawall and sluice gate straight ahead and bought up a closer image. A penetrating ray revealed the inner works and there, as Poseidon had described, were several rock shards from the collapsed wall lodged in the gears. Unused to working from such a distance she coolly calculated her obstacles. The sinking trireme and crew were in a direct line to the winch mechanism. The black deconstructing beam would pierce the ship's hull, sinking it faster, and perhaps perforate some crewmen's bodies. If she narcotized them, laid them flat on the ship's deck out of harm's way, they could drown with the sinking ship.

She calculated and targeted the largest stone shard, set the protocol in place. *The trireme's hull would be sacrificed. If a man or two died there, it was the price to be paid for saving the city.* An unexpected wave of fury rocked her as she calibrated the beam. *Poseidon's fault! Without his hub he'd been helpless.* He could have closed the sluice. *Fool!* She reigned herself in. *Stop. Concentrate!*

The black beam activated, it shot straight down the Great Harbor to the Sluice Gate winch.

∾

On the language building's broad outdoor steps, crews had naturally formed to rescue the still living, but when it was learned that Cleatah was just inside, they called her out to minister to the injured. A whole row of granite lintels had toppled and crushed several people beneath it.

Many of the rescuers were naked now, their clothing torn into bandages to stanch bloody wounds and hold splints on broken bones. Elona had returned with Cleatah's medicine satchel, and her herbs had quelled some suffering and quieted much of the moaning and crying. She had lived through quakes before, she thought as she steadied her hand to pull a long spike of granite from a man's shoulder. These were terrifying reminders of Great Mother's displeasure, but rarely were there more than a few collapsed mud huts, and even more rarely was anyone injured or killed. There were tales told by the elders of great waves that swept away villagers, and floods that raged along the Wild River, but this was different.

With no altar to kneel at, no hot water spring as her anchor, she found herself summoning the Goddess nevertheless. *Are you there?* she called silently. *Is this your doing? Have we so displeased you, building this city?* No answer came. *Not surprising,* Cleatah thought. *Too much noise and tumult, Far too many people around me. Too much pain and suffering. Too much death to expect Great Mother's voice to be heard inside her head. Was she trying once again to answer her own questions?* But *Ah, another voice came whispering* as she packed a brown velt poultice into the long deep wound where the spike had impaled the injured man. *Another voice… Poseidon's voice. And her own. The two of them speaking as one, as they did so often.* The thought that they had shared as they stood on the Seawall on the First Day Celebration, looking out at the city they had built together. It had never been spoken aloud, yet was as clear as if shouted into a box canyon.

What have we done? There is no turning back now.

"Cleatah." It was Elona. There was urgency in her voice. "Come quickly. Luna's child is coming. Now."

"Bandage this man," she told the girl, coming to her feet. "I'll see to Luna."

"I'll pray Great Mother is watching over her," Elona said.

Cleatah said nothing. The Goddess was silent.

Even through Poseidon's climate suit the skin on his back was beginning to sear. He took a moment with the hub to deaden the pain. He needed to concentrate. Just a few more feet of repair and the vertical breach would be closed. He looked down. The metallic suturing below him was holding, but – with a quick phaetronic scan – he saw that the Core's heat behind him was only rising. He re-traced protocol. The crack needed complete closure to resume normal function and stem the titanum's meltdown.

Cleatah's face materialized before him. *No! Focus!* The strap-on hub flickered, faltered briefly. *Don't fail me now! Please, please!* Only inches to go. The hub reset. A dull ache crossed his back. *Don't think about it. Kidneys replaceable. But annihilation... His fault. The Goddess is angry. Sending the quake. Ridiculous. No Goddess. Tectonic plates shifting as they have for millions of ye...*

Finished! Closure!

Poseidon clung to the wall, staring at the knitted breach. He turned behind him expecting to see the Core's red glow fading. It wasn't dimming! It was pulsing now. The pain in his back surged with a vengeance.

Too late. He had taken too long. He had stupidly buried the ship in a seismic zone. His fault. Everyone dead. City destroyed. Poisoned planet. Cleatah, oh Cleatah...

And then it stopped – the pulsing Core. The searing heat.

The shock of success loosened his grip. He faltered backwards momentarily, then clutched for dear life. His heart crashed against his ribs.

It was over, the Core stabilized. Then his mind cleared. *Not over. The sluice gate. Talya at the Residence. The black beam.*

The wave.

⋙

From the residence balcony on the Central Isle she could see the water had receded in the Great Harbor and circular canals, flowing out of the Sluice Gate, leaving vessels teetering on the stonework floor. She diffracted an image and saw the spectacle of an ocean receded for miles out from the shore. And then she saw it.

The wave, just now finding the continental shallows and rearing up into a terrible wall tens of feet higher than the Seawall, stretching from north to south as far as the eye could see. Finally she could hear the roar of the water coming. The second of the large rock shards was gone from the winch but the third was wedged between the massive chain links and the winch lever. She targeted it with the black beam.

There! Dissolved. All of it.

The roar was louder. *The gate was not dropping! No time!*

She targeted the steel chain links themselves, slicing through them.

Still nothing!

Then all at once the Sluice Gate began to move, a slow screeching descent down between its channels, the winch beginning to turn and finally – overburdened by weight and gravity – it fell heavily, and with a resounding thud crashed onto the channel floor.

An instant later the wave struck. Water overtopped the length of the parapets in a violent waterfall, sending all those who had not run fast enough tumbling and drowning. Two guards, clutching each other with terror, disappeared in the turbulent water. It was rising fast.

Clutching her throat Talya watched the tide begin to flood the city. The Outer Canal began to fill again. Piers were washed away by the crashing onslaught. *This is not happening*, she thought. *This is not happening...*

But the Seawall was holding.

The Sluice Gate was holding.

And slowly, slowly the surge overtopping the wall lessened... receded...ebbed to a trickle.

She stared, disbelieving. Yes, the waters were flowing into the Harbor and canals, raising their levels, but they barely touched the land of the ring islands.

And then she remembered...*the Core...Poseidon...bloody stars...any moment the end of it all...*but no, the Core would have blown by now. He must have prevailed. She exhaled, then again. Felt her body again. Her heart crashing in her chest. She used the hub to calm herself. Even so, she felt hapless, mildly unhinged. She closed her eyes. A blur of images, sensations – *the High Atlantos horses falling to their deaths in a dark, grinding abyss… the feel of her breasts pressed against Joss's back…the sailors in the Great Harbor that she'd sacrificed to the black beam…*

She found herself wandering the deserted Residence, barely damaged in the quake. Built by Poseidon as a fortress of his love… for her. Every gracefully undulating wall, the polished tree trunks arched around the entryway. A cozy pile of skins set before the hearth. She imagined them there at the fire sitting back-to-back, laughing quietly. Making plans. They were always making plans. Their creation – all of it – The One Tribe, the fabulous city even Talya had to admire. She felt her belly tighten, her jaw clench.

She wandered into their sleeping chamber, saw the beautiful baskets and masks, the woven hangings. Gifts from "their people." The altar. Cleatah's altar, the embers still aglow. *Bloody Great Mother,* she thought, then turned to go, avoiding any sight of the conjugal bed. She would not look at it. It would destroy her. She pounded a fist on the doorjamb and swallowed her bitter pride.

Uncaring that he might be seen, Poseidon projected a narrow phaetronic bridge across the Central Canal, calm now and filled as much with debris as water, and raced across to the Middle Ring Isle, stopping for no one, sights fixed on the Academy campus. *Would he find her? Was she hurt? Dead? Not dead, please not dead!* As its damaged buildings came into view he could see the grassy quadrangle laid out with the injured and those who were tending them. *So many, so many…*

He grabbed the first man he saw. "Cleatah. Have you seen her?" The man shook his head numbly and wandered away. *Her classroom. Of course. She would be there.* His heart lurched as he saw the building's collapsed façade. *Where are you, Love? Where are you!*

And then he saw her. She was kneeling at the side of a man, smiling down at him, his hand clasped in hers.

Posedion stopped, barely breathing, and stood staring at the miracle that she was. This woman that the Erthan Fates had bestowed upon him. She looked up and saw him. Her head fell back and her lips moved in silent thanks.

"Poseidon!" He turned to see Boah slide down from his horse. They met and embraced, clinging together fiercely. "Cleatah?" he dared whisper.

Poseidon pushed him to arm's length. "Over there," he said with a small laugh. "She's... indestructible."

Boah's face softened and he expelled a hard sigh. Then he gazed over the quadrangle, awash in misery, moans and cries for help wafting on the morning air. "We should get to work," he said.

Poseidon grasped the hub strapped to his wrist, trembling with gratitude. Today, with Terresian technos, he had saved the city, materialized a bridge over raging waters. Now he would heal the wounded.

He had never been more confused.

FIFTY-SEVEN

WITH DOOM DARKENING their sights Cleatah and Boah led the searchers down the north Seawall steps to what had, before the wave, been the beach of the old Shore Village. The killer tide had scoured away much of the fine black sand, leaving a hard crust of lavic rock – points of the shallow reef now sadly shorn of its colorful living skin – poking up above the water's surface, and dead sea creatures rotting in the sun.

All in the party knew what lay before them, for in the two days since the catastrophic quake naked bodies, and parts of bodies of the Shore Village elders, had come crashing pitifully up against the seawall. Then as the tide receded it took its gruesome cargo with it.

On that terrible day, after the Sluice Gate had slammed shut the Shore People who lived in the city had rushed to the top of the seawall to watch in dread the seething black ocean that had overflowed its ramparts.

And blessedly stopped.

Though the Shore Village itself was raised on its own tiny plateau above the black sand beach it could not have been spared the water's fury. Poseidon had tried to prepare the villagers for the inevitable findings – the men and women whose fathers and mothers, aunts and uncles had chosen to stay in the only home they had ever known. The elders had showed little interest in leaving the ocean's edge for the city that had sprung up behind a strange man-made mountain of stone – ironically, a mountain that would have saved them from the sea rising up in a towering wall of death.

What must they have thought as the thing approached? Had they known what they were seeing? Or would they have gazed in curiosity at the receding water and the frothy white line stretching north to south? And if, in the final moments, had they apprehended the impending disaster would they have sought to flee up the footpath to the safety of the Great Plateau?

The people of the city, except for the Wall Watch, had been spared the nightmarish vision, but those guards – now set apart forever – would become famous with the telling and re-telling of what they had seen. The ocean disappearing, laying bare the sea floor for miles. The reefs on the shallow continental shelf and the previously hidden precipice where the sea bottom could not even be seen. It was here, the watchmen would say, that the wave – little more than an onrushing raised white line – had suddenly reared up like a thousand horses on their hind legs and become the hideous towering breaker that had sent them fleeing down the wall like terrified children.

As the search party approached the village plateau it tore at Poseidon's heart to see that the ancient stone steps he had climbed the day of his first coming had washed entirely away. They were forced to scramble on hands and knees up the unforgiving cliff face and were met with the sight of what had been the Shore Village…now scoured entirely clean. Not a hut, not a tree, not even the low rock wall that delineated the settlement's boundaries had been spared the water's onslaught. It was bare ground all the way inland to the steep footpath that led to the headlands of the Great Plateau.

It might have appeared as if nothing at all had happened on

this sandy shelf above a black sand beach near a blue sea and its dainty waves. Only the battered carcass of a giant grey shark with flies buzzing round its sunken eyes and feasting on the wide expanse of gum above several rows of razor teeth told a tale of the wave that had, in a terrible roaring instant, obliterated the noble elders and the age-old village of the Shore People.

The searchers wept quietly where they stood, trying in vain to conjure the village, to fathom the loss of what they had once been and everything they had known. They did not say so but Poseidon guessed they were giving bitter thanks for the city they had chosen for their home. The city that had saved them.

"There is nothing here," Cleatah murmured, slowly shaking her head. "Even their spirits have been swept away. All we have left of them is in our hearts."

She turned and walked back the way she'd come. One by one those who had been the Shore People followed her down the cliff and back to Atlantos.

FIFTY-EIGHT

ALL THE PEOPLE of the city and those of the Great
Plateau were gathered in the morning shadow of the High
Atlantos Stables. The streets and houses and markets of
the metropolis below were abandoned, and Itopia was once again
overflowing with members of the One Tribe who had assembled
for a celebration of life and memorial for the dead.

There was much to mourn. The elders of the Shore Village
were gone and hundreds had been killed by falling stone in
Atlantos City. In the mountain settlements workers had died
when mines collapsed on them. More than half the mares and
their young had been swallowed up in a single horrible instant
by Erthe herself.

Yet the city and its people had been saved from the wave's
wrath by Poseidon's Seawall. And of profoundest importance on
that otherwise tragic day, a pure white foal had been born and
survived the devastation. In the weeks following, this horse had
become a symbol of the Brotherhood's hopes and all Atlans' future
dreams. The Great Mother, it was often repeated, would never
have spared the foal had she wished to curse their new society.
The little creature was her blessing and her promise, and it was
not lost on the Horse Brothers that Talya was the Great Mother's
helper in bringing it into the world. Once viewed merely with

lust and jealous fever, the beautiful woman who held the secrets of life in her smooth white hands was these days venerated and adored like no other female, save Cleatah.

This morning at the Grave of the Horses – the ominous abyss that now rent the grazing meadow in two – everyone was gathered. They were listening to Boah who stood high on a rock platform to be better seen and heard by the congregation.

"…so while the loss is great and we honor our dead and will never forget them," he called out in Terrerthe, "…we have no more time for mourning. The Brotherhood has promised horses to the mountain settlements whose mines must produce ever more ore to build our city. To the docks for our ships, and the warehouses for the cargoes they will bring from across the sea. The 'Stadium' will soon be repaired, and the first 'Race Day' is coming."

At this there was happy murmuring in every part of the crowd.

"The time for spilled tears is past. There is no time to waste. We look to Poseidon's beloved sister Talya, who brought forth the white foal with her life-giving tools, and who promises in the coming years to increase our herd tenfold!"

The morning rang with shouts and Talya's chanted name, and clenched fists punched the air. Now Poseidon climbed up to join Boah on the platform, placing an arm around his friend's shoulder.

"So begin the games," he called cheerfully. "Light the cook-fires. Set the tables with the bounty of our fields and pastures. We – the people of the far mountains and the city, horsemen, orchardmen and farmers of the Great Plateau – we are all Atlans, and we are here to banish thoughts of death and destruction. To celebrate life – all that the Great Mother has provided us – and the promise of a shining future!"

Talya heard the cheers going up around her, composed in equal measure of true elation and faith in the peoples' beloved leaders. When the crowd began to disperse Poseidon and Boah stepped down from the platform where she and Cleatah met and embraced them. When the family of Brannan came and pulled Boah and Cleatah away to show them a stone tribute for their grandfather she found herself standing side-by-side with Poseidon. They gazed out at the milling assembly – men and women talking with animation, laughing at each other's jokes, children chasing each other and shouting happily, and wolves mingling comfortably among them all. She was loathe to spoil so fine a moment, but there were things that needed to be said.

"Do you ever think how close you came to losing this?" she began. "All of this?"

"Every day. Many times a day."

After this admission Poseidon's protracted silence began to gall her. *Was this all he would admit to?* "Then do you plan to re-implant your hub?" She was aware her voice was sharp as a metal probe.

"I've thought about it."

"*Thought* about it? Why haven't you done it? What more has to happen to prove you cannot simply abandon our technos on a whim?"

"It was not a whim. I'd thought long and hard before I removed it."

"I suppose Cleatah applauded it when you did."

"She was pleased. Of course she was."

"And was she pleased when its absence nearly drowned Atlantos and killed every living thing in the city?"

Talya was sure the silence that followed was Poseidon's refusal to dignify her harsh question with an answer.

Finally he spoke. "When she was consoling me…"

Talya cringed inwardly at the thought of this tender intimacy between them.

"…she reminded me, as she often does, that I am not a god."

"But you *are*, Poseidon. And so am I. What powers do gods have that we do not? The difference between you and me is that I choose to use everything at my disposal to help these people. You've let sentimentality overtake reason. No matter how much you wish to be an Erthan, you will never be one. You are a Terresian born and bred, and you will *die* one."

He turned and faced her. "What makes you so bitter? You have everything you could possibly want here – much, much more than you could have had at home. You are respected. No, let me correct that. You are revered. Famous. You have two lovers…"

Talya found herself reddening at the thought that her sexual habits were so commonly known and so easily accepted.

"…and every horse brother who doesn't share your bed wishes he did. But I would argue that, all this considered, you are no goddess. You're simply a woman with advanced technos. A woman who refuses to be satisfied with an embarrassment of riches."

Talya felt her cheeks stinging with the rebuke.

"All that said," he went on before she could speak, "I concur with your logic about my device. I'd planned to ask for your help re-inserting it."

Desired as they were, his words shocked Talya to the core. How could she feel so humbled by Poseidon's concession? This was one emotion she would never reveal to him. To anyone.

"I'm glad you've come to your senses," she said in the gentlest tone she could manage. "When we return to the city…"

"Much appreciated," he said, cutting her off.

Clearly finished with her judgment and criticism, Poseidon turned and disappeared into the crowd.

෯

Thousands of fires blazed in the dark of the winding footpaths of Itopia Village. After a long day of games and feasting, celebration was still in the air. The rude mud dwellings of the Gathered Tribes' first settlement were largely unfamiliar to Talya as she walked among them, as her visits to Boah's new quarters here were few and far between. Even her recent encounters with Joss took place at odd moments in dangerous settings outside the encampment.

Thoughts of Joss never failed to arouse her, particularly the latest experiments with her enhancer to augment the already-explosive climaxes she'd been enjoying. Still, at this moment Talya was craving the attentions of Boah. She noticed a kind of desperation in her search for him tonight, and while this irritated her mildly it made the hunt for him more exciting. She'd only caught glimpses of Boah during the day's celebration. She'd cheered for him in the races and refused to intrude at a somber gathering of the Shore People to privately memorialize their elders. Boah's preeminence in Atlantos, second only to Poseidon's, had become unequivocal today, and the urge for his company was proving irresistible.

His cool reserve in the face of the rivalry with Joss had proven almost Terresian. While her bedding with the two of them had caused an uproar within the ranks of the horsemen, Boah himself had remained utterly composed – affectionate and desiring her company, but lacking the smallest hint of possessiveness or jealousy. He had been heard saying, "Talya is my woman. She is not my mate." And to her great relief in recent weeks he had finally stopped suggesting she bear his child.

Everywhere Talya stopped to ask at Boah's whereabouts people had been welcoming and kind. Many offered her food and drink, and spoke of the honor they felt with her presence at their table.

He was close now. She could feel it. Several horsemen who knew him well had recently seen him on foot, traveling in the direction of a group of dwellings on the outskirts of the settlement. She would enjoy sex with him tonight – less savage, less excessive than what she had with Joss. More refined. Well, perhaps that was an exaggeration. Boah had proven a good student, but he had retained enough of the animal quality that set Erthan men apart from Terresians.

Then she heard his unmistakable laugh – warm and deep and booming. It surprised her to feel, at the sound of it, a sudden twitch between her thighs. Perhaps tonight she would let him know how much she missed him in her bed. Talya rounded a corner and stayed just beyond the light of a fire between a cluster of huts, now crowded with people. She recognized the textiles of a shore people from across the continent, with vary-colored shells woven into their designs. There was more laughter. She sensed they were members of a large family – and there again was Boah's laugh.

She stepped into the firelight as the crowd parted and there he was, his black eyes flashing, smiling his brilliant smile...at a pretty, small-boned woman whose belly was swollen with pregnancy. She gazed up at him adoringly, and he kissed her cheek with the gentlest touch of his lips.

Talya's heart began crashing against her ribcage. She fought paralysis and stepped back into the shadows before she could be seen. She stumbled away on the dark footpath and steadied herself against a mud wall. Her discipline proved stronger than her pain. She rebuked herself for such maudlin emotions and pulled her thoughts together. *Of course Boah would expect offspring. It was a wonder he hadn't any children already. And the woman he'd chosen was timid and subservient – exactly what he would desire in a mate.*

A "mate." The word stung her unexpectedly. *"Talya is my woman. She is not my mate.* She sniffed sharply and straightening her spine pulled herself tall. She composed her features into a semblance of tranquility and began retracing her steps back to the center of Itopia. She would waste not a single moment more on such preposterous Erthan self-indulgences. She was better than this. A proud Terresian.

Her heart rate slowed. With every step Talya felt the forced smile she had plastered on softening. She willed her equilibrium to return. *I will be fine*, she told herself.

I will be fine.

FIFTY-NINE

CLEATAH WAS SITTING among the ones she loved the best, her nearest and dearest in all the world – Poseidon and the Green Teachers. Nothing could make her happier. They had gathered for a quiet counsel around her dear friend Thoth's gently burning fire, and talk had been of fertility.

Yazman spoke of the moon's cycle and the fecundity of crops. There was no arguing with Yazman. She was old and had watched the growth of countless plantings long before Talya and her tools had increased the size of the Atlan harvest.

Zane asked why certain female wolves filled their dens with pups season after season, and others were barren.

"Those females who are fertile have a scent that only male wolves can smell that draws them like a bee to a sweet flower," was Tolmak's answer. He was a master of healing potions. Cleatah had learned much from him since their meeting. She trusted all the Green Teachers, but none so deeply as Tolmak. He absently folded a large leaf between his long bony fingers.

Cleatah asked him – all the time holding Poseidon's eyes with her own, "Why do I not conceive?"

Tolmak stared down at the once-large leaf, now a small pile of squares, then tossed them into the fire where they slowly browned and crinkled into nothing. "You ate silphan for many years. How many years?"

Cleatah counted in her head. "Nine," she answered, suddenly alarmed at the implication. *Have I eaten the preventative seed for too long?*

"No, you haven't erred," Tolmak said, reading her thoughts, or perhaps her expression. "It will take the tarax and ackil you are eating now a little time to overcome the silphan, which is very strong."

Cleatah saw Yazman slip something into Poseidon's hand. She was very fond of him and enjoyed giving him advice, even when it had not been requested. He always indulged her.

"What have you given him, Yazman?" Cleatah said with a grin.

"She's given me a smooth red quartz stone," he told Cleatah. "You must hold it in your right hand when we make love."

Yazman leaned in to whisper to Poseidon again.

"When we make love in the moon's *crescent* phase," he said, then turned to Yazman with a teasing smile. "What if I wish to make love to her in the full moon, or in the new moon or in the half-moon?"

"Make love to her enough," Zane remarked, "and you will need neither the tarax, the stone *or* the moon to get her pregnant!"

Everyone laughed at that, all but Poseidon who gazed at Cleatah with such naked desire that she blushed. But as she held his eyes she saw, over his shoulder, Talya standing behind him, still as a stone.

"Join us, Talya," Cleatah said.

"Poseidon turned. "Yes, come sit with us."

Zane and Yazman moved to make room for her.

"No. Thank you. I'm...I'm meeting Joss," she replied, unmistakably flustered. "I'm meeting Joss," she mumbled again and turned, disappearing into the shadows.

SIXTY

S HE DID MEET Joss. To a chorus of lewd shouts she pulled him from a bonfire circle of raucously celebrating horsemen. They found a darkened path and he took her roughly – the way she demanded it – her hands and face pressed up against a hard mud wall. When he finished, leaving her unsatisfied – as she had wished – Talya dropped her shift and straightened. Refusing to meet his eye she left him behind her and walked away, feeling the scrapes on her hot red cheek with trembling fingers.

With a few touches to her wrist hub she cloaked herself, and blessedly invisible to the still celebrating Atlans she found her way through the dark, fire-dappled settlement to the deserted city below.

✌

Alone in the echoing silence of the ship Talya drank herself into a frenzy. The jog, never meant to be imbibed so extravagantly, sent her brain spiraling to unheralded heights of imagination, only to crash through the floor of consciousness into a raw abyss of confusion and pain.

A day passed. Two. She drank. She seethed. Tore off her clothes and tossed in bed for hours, pulse racing, nerves firing, heat seeming to flare from her pores. She was sure sleep had permanently evaded her. She leapt up and pulled off her shift, despising its primitive weave, and donned a fine Terresian garment instead. Then light-headed and weak-kneed she reeled down the deserted corridors of the *Atlantos* reviling her weakness and praying to rid herself of such violent sensations. But the mind reeled, too:

How have I come to this? How? I'm Terresian, calm and rational. And now I've succumbed to the same fever that possesses Poseidon. No, not the same. *His is a passion of 'love.' Mine…mine is of* fury.

What a fool I've been!

Why did I not leave with the others? How could I have so badly miscalculated the passage of time? The Terresian constitution should have caused the months and years here to speed forward, easing the wait for Poseidon to regain reason. But no. My execrable bio-rhythms slowed! *Time drags. I might as well be an Erthan! Boah and Joss… drowning in sensual pleasures…even the horsemen's worship…nothing fills the void of this life – cold and silent and black as space. And now there'll be children to bind Poseidon and that smug, devious thief closer still. Imagine how he'll react to* offspring! *Fatherhood will catapult him into paroxysms of emotion.*

Wait. She stopped and stood, holding the wall to stop her swaying. *A thought came to her – random – the germ of an idea, a seed.* The warm, quiet hallway was a perfect medium for growth. *Close your eyes and see it.… There it is, the seed, the seed, warm and throbbing with the imperative to grow, bursting its shell. Sprouting. Breaking ground. Snaking and curling upward. Flowering. Oh!… it is a dark and twisted thing. An appalling scheme. Not like me! Treacherous and rotten and glutted with passions I despise.*

No going back. Not now – not to Terres nor the safety of moral ground. If…I…must…exist endlessly in this place, I will mold it, redefine it, suit it to my *desires. I will behave immoderately – as the primitives do. Twice humiliated is entirely enough.*

I will never suffer like that again.

᠅

Still drunk and giddy Talya stepped from the pillar of blue light and emerged from the newly repaired spiral of Poseidon's Grove, at once activating her cloaking device. Invisible to members of the household who had now returned from High Atlantos she crossed the stream on the red bridge and passed the darkened homes of the Green Teachers that lived within the environs of the Central Isle. She approached the residence.

Moving through the open entryway she was struck, as she always was, by the palpable peace and quiet of Poseidon's home. *Irritatingly peaceful,* she thought. It was as though a tranquil existence had become the single focus of his life. *How pathetic.* Talya reached the couple's bedchamber, but before entering she scanned through the wall to be sure they were there and sleeping. When she saw that they were she moved cautiously to the doorway. Pointing the phaetron at the pair of them she activated its narcotizing function.

She moved to the bed. There were the two bodies curled comfortably together, already in the deepest sleep state possible. The sight of them was wrenching but she steeled herself and went to Cleatah's side. Quickly she pulled down the light coverlet. They were both naked. Talya could not help but stare at Cleatah. She was lovely – perfectly formed and softly rounded in the womanly places. Her face in repose was undeniably exquisite. Talya glanced at Poseidon's nakedness, once so familiar to her, and her anger flared again.

Then a cold efficiency overtook her. There was no more hiding behind intoxication, no reasonable excuse for this. She knew precisely what she was about to do. Talya rolled Cleatah on her back. Fully narcotized the woman's head and limbs fell into unnaturally limp positions. She was utterly helpless, and for perhaps the first time in her life Talya assumed complete control.

She opened the small metal case that held her gynae phaetron and extraction tools.

And then, casting all doubt and all honor aside, she set to work.

SIXTY-ONE

"YOU'RE LOOKING BEAUTIFUL as ever," said Athens to Cleatah's diffracted image. "And keeping my brother very happy, I see." He was in his Marsean bedroom overlooking the sea.

Poseidon thought that aside from a dark weariness around his eyes Athens looked well, if ostentatiously outfitted in a short tunic of spun gold. The handsomely defined muscles of his arms were encircled with fine-worked bracelets of the sun yellow ore. He held at his hip his little girl Athena – not yet two – her short black ringlets matching her huge sparkling black eyes.

"We thank you for the gold," Poseidon said. "A generous gift, considering how short a time it's been since your mines have been operable."

Talya, Poseidon, and a hugely pregnant Cleatah had gathered in the *Atlantos's* library for the interplanetary comm. Via the phaetron Athens had been sending to Erthe a great quantity of artifacts and magnificent jewelry. At their feet was the day's offering – three raw bars of his precious metal.

"I'm happy to say both the mines are within weeks of opening again."

Athena whispered something in her father's ear and he set her down on the floor where she fixed immediately on the gold clasps on Athens's shoes. The child seemed unaware of the Erthe family in front of her, perhaps disinterested.

"And much improved as well," Athens continued. "We expect the titanum output to triple, at the least."

"Triple?" Poseidon was incredulous. "You won't be sacrificing safety for increased productivity, I hope."

"Not at all." Athens' smile was confident, self-satisfied. "Talya, come here. Let me look at you."

She stepped forward and raised her hand, palm facing him. He raised his palm to hers, and though millions of miles separated them their hands appeared to touch.

"Is it possible," he said, "that you're more luscious than when we last spoke?"

"Anything is possible," she replied with a teasing smile.

"I wish this blasted device could transport you to Mars." Athens held her eyes for a long moment, then turned to his brother. "And how is the great city of Atlantos progressing?" he inquired, pacing about the bedroom.

"Slowly but steadily," Poseidon replied. "The artisans are still learning their crafts. And some of the stone work is laborious and time consuming."

"You're mad to deny them the phaetron."

"You know where I stand on that. If we're to thrive as a great society the people must learn industriousness. But as long as it's work they enjoy and they reap the rewards of their labor they have no complaints about working hard."

"I've found myself another solution to the problem of hard work," announced Athens matter-of-factly.

"And that is?" Poseidon asked.

"Drones."

"What do you mean?"

"You know what a drone is, Talya. Tell my brother."

"In the laboratory we can genomically produce large numbers of organisms that are identical to each other," she explained.

"What form do these drones take?" Poseidon asked.

"Human. Well, *almost* human. Actually, sub-human and super-human."

Poseidon was growing alarmed. Cleatah was altogether confused. Only Talya remained sanguine. It was clear this was no surprise to her.

"You remember I said we'd be tripling production in the gold and titanum mines?" Athens continued, not waiting for a reply, "Well, we will accomplish our goal using these creatures. They're extraordinarily strong and incredibly stupid. We've bred males only, and they entirely lack aggressive or sexual tendencies." Athens grinned with self-satisfaction. "They're perfect working machines." My colonists will never have to put themselves in danger again."

"You can't be serious." Poseidon was slack-jawed. "What you're describing are humanoid slaves."

"Why was I so sure this would be your reaction?" Athens's look turned suddenly sour. "Talya, tell him why this is a brilliant idea."

"It does have its merits," she said evenly, "provided the drones are well-treated."

"Of course they will be. They'll be fed the best food, receive the best medical care... and they'll do a little hard work underground." He fixed Poseidon with a wicked smile. "Even *you* believe in hard work, brother. Of course the colonists are ecstatic. I've created an ideal world for them. A life, more or less, of pure pleasure." He regarded Poseidon petulantly. "You don't approve. Well, it can't be helped. Anyway, it's done."

"Done?" Poseidon was confused.

"We've been incubating them for three years. There are growth-accelerating chemicals... "he smiled at Talya, "We so appreciated your help." He held Poseidon's eye. "The drones are fully developed in every way necessary. They've been learning their skills. They're ready to go into the mines."

"This defies every humane principle we've ever learned!"

"I will *not* lose another colonist in the pursuit of gold," Athens said.

"Then lose the pursuit of gold!"

"I don't have that option."

"Of course you do. You have a choice. How can you even consider so contemptible a decision?"

An ugly expression twisted Athens's features. "Because if I don't give the people what they want they'll find someone else who will." He looked away. "Everything comes so easily to you. I've worked hard for what I have. No one, nothing, *nothing* will take it from me." He faced Poseidon again with a sour expression. "I wish you could have been happy for me. But I suppose that would have been too much to ask." He turned to Cleatah. "Good health to you in your delivery." He nodded straight-faced at Talya.

In the next moment the image of Athens and his tiny daughter dematerialized. All that was left of their presence were three golden bars glittering on the library floor.

SIXTY-TWO

WITHIN THE RED stone birthing house a warm herbal mist hung above the women who'd gathered for this unrivaled occasion. Cleatah's hands rested lightly on the mountain of her belly that rose above the warm saltwater tub. She was grateful to see kneeling around her the most adept of the Green Teachers murmuring with quiet concern about the twins they all knew were about to be born. Many of the tribes believed a double birth to be a dangerous omen, but now one of their own – their much-revered teacher – was giving birth to twins. She was certain they would find their fears groundless after all. To Cleatah's surprise Talya was among the women, listening and watching closely to learn what she might do to help.

When the next violent contraction seized her Cleatah shrieked and clutched the sides of the tub. She was vaguely aware of a warm hand atop her own, and a fragrant cloth wiping her brow. When the spasm passed her eyes fluttered open and she found that Talya was her comforter. She had changed somehow, emanating a new warmth and kindness. She had even taken Boah's fathering of Zeta's child with good grace, and had mourned with them when the boy was born dead.

Another contraction gripped Cleatah and all thoughts dissolved into fierce sensation. Zane began whispering encouragement and instructions as the first infant thrust itself into the world, its skin warm brown, like Poseidon's. Cleatah's head rolled from side to side, but as another pain ripped through her, her gaze fell on Talya. Her eyes were gleaming, her lips curling upward. It seemed a smile of pleasure, but there was something more.

Something strange about it.

Cleatah suddenly recognized the expression…but then with a final, resolute push her second son – a light-skinned boy – came wailing into his life. All else was forgotten.

All was forgotten but joy.

⁓

Later Cleatah lay on a wide couch in an adjoining room of the birthing house, one son suckling as the other was rocked by Yazman. The doors swung open and Poseidon stood at the threshold. He didn't move to enter, simply stared at the scene, enthralled.

"Poseidon, come see your sons," Cleatah said.

Only then did he move to her side and kneel so that his face was close to hers and he could see the milksweet features of the infant. "He was the firstborn," she told him, "and so, as we decided, he is named Atlas."

Poseidon first caressed her face, then with a touch as delicate as the fluttering of a butterfly's wing he laid his fingers on the infant's cheek. His expression was utterly wonderstruck.

She gestured for Yazman to bring Atlas's twin to the couch. "This is Geo," Cleatah told him.

Poseidon looked up and saw the younger boy being held out to him. He hesitated – this man who was as fearless as any she had ever known – trembling apprehensively.

"Take him, Poseidon. He's yours."

He stood and took the child into his arms, gathering him to his heart. He seemed unable to take his eyes from the infant's features. A small cry escaped Poseidon's throat and suddenly tears began spilling from his eyes.

Cleatah clutched his hand and held it to her lips. "Do I take it you like your sons?"

"Almost as much as I like their mother. Thank you for this gift, my love. Thank you..."

A noisy crowd of Shore People burst into the room. As was the custom, some bore flowers, others food and jugs of kav. The new parents were instantly surrounded with everyone crowding around to see the infants. The celebration had begun that would go on for many days and many nights. The sound of flute and drum burst forth, a song of thanksgiving raised in the newborns' names.

✃

Night fell and the music and celebration spread to all parts of the city. Joyful sounds echoed down the waterways and the spar-kling, twirling "fireshow" in the sky that Poseidon had launched left everyone shouting and awestruck.

Cleatah and the twins had been moved in a spirited pro-cession from the birthing house on the Middle Ring Isle across the arched bridge to the Central Isle, and now the three were resting within the Residence. People were feasting and dancing outside around a roaring bonfire in the courtyard. Their songs were ancient chants in praise of Great Mother and the gods of Erthe, but they sang new ones as well – songs of their city, of the horse and brave horsemen, and the deeds of their beloved Poseidon and Cleatah.

Poseidon watched as men and women moved in sensual rhythm to the drums, their faces glowing in the firelight.

"You must be very pleased." Talya's voice came from behind.

He turned to find her standing so close he could feel her breath on his face. There was a genuine pleasantness to her smile, and her eyes appeared unnaturally bright, he thought. Perhaps it was the reflection of the fire.

"You know that I am," he said, unable to withhold a grin.

A tribesman and a young woman came to dance before them, gyrating and thrusting suggestively. Her eyes were closed, his face ecstatic.

"I'm pregnant, Poseidon," Talya said.

"That's wonderful news!" Impulsively he embraced her, then pushed her to arm's length. "Who is the father?"

Before she could answer Boah emerged from the dancers and swept Talya into his embrace. As Poseidon watched they began to move together rhythmically, sensually, never taking their eyes from one another's faces. It was extraordinary. He'd never seen Talya move like that. Never seen such passion in her. Boah's hands encircled Talya's waist, and his hips and muscular thighs pushed closer to hers. *Thank the stars*, Poseidon thought, *she has allowed the true gifts of this planet – these people – to soften her, heal her wounds.* And now she was pregnant with a Erthan man's child. It was the final gift of this blessed day.

All at once Poseidon was seized by a rogue emotion so fierce it rocked him on his feet. Though he was surrounded by friends and well-wishers he was overwhelmed with emptiness. But he knew the remedy. In the next moment he turned from the fire, the music and revelers, and walked through the archway into to the Residence. There awaited all that would fulfill him.

There awaited his family.

SIXTY-THREE

"TALYA IS HAVING my baby!" Boah had waited to shout out his announcement till the horsemen had settled down in the shade to eat their morning meal. He happily accepted the backslapping and even some crude jokes about riding the Queen Mare.

"About time," muttered Tork.

"Is that why your eyes are red?" Patak said.

"We did drink a fair amount of kav," Boah admitted.

There was raucous laughter at that.

Talya had, in fact, waited until he was very drunk to tell him she was carrying his child. Thankfully he'd been sober enough to make love to her.

"So you'll lifemate with her?" Elkon asked. He was a fellow Shoreman, and this was the way of their tribe.

"Of course. She's having my baby."

"Joss fixed him with a playful grin. "The first of many?" His old rival for Talya's affections looked genuinely pleased.

"If the Great Mother allows it."

"Remember the time in the village when you fought with Poseidon to mate with Cleatah?" Elkon teased.

Boah felt himself flushing with mortification at the memory.

"Back then we thought him a puny stranger who could barely hunt."

"And now," Tork said, "he will be uncle to your children. His children and yours will be cousins."

Boah grew serious. "Our two families will be joined by blood." He gazed around at his friends. "I'm very proud."

"Look at him," Joss teased, "he's puffed as wide as the feathers on a wild turkey's breast."

Everyone laughed at that.

"Enough!" Boah cried with mock severity. "Let's eat. We've got horses to attend."

Joss nodded a sincere affirmation to his friend before he bit into his bread. Here he was surrounded by his horse brothers, knowing that the luminescent being they all so admired, even desired, was finally and truly his own. A child was on the way, and kinship with Poseidon's family was secured.

His happiness was boundless. There was nothing more that he wanted. Not a single thing on Erthe.

MARS COLONY

Abomination

SIXTY-FOUR

THEY SAT IN rows at tables the length of the enormous hall – two thousand of them outfitted in simple blue coveralls. They could barely be considered men, so young and tender were their hairless faces, but their bodies under the thin fabric were hard, muscular and mature. Brown-haired and blue-eyed, each and every one of them was identical in every way, even the same vaguely triangular birthmark in the center of their left cheek. They might have been considered handsome had their jaws, in repose, not sagged so prominently as they did, or had the light in their eyes not been so dim.

They ate their meals – large plates of hearty grain and vegetable stew – in a silence punctuated only by grunts, chewing, and the clink of utensils against bowls. The drones had been carefully seated so that no one sat directly across from another, for although the creatures had shown little interest in communication or even eye contact, these were the experiment's early days, and it was best to be cautious. No one knew what mutations of intellect or aggression lay dormant in them.

A series of three loud metallic beeps signaled the drones that there was a minute remaining to finish what was in their bowls. At the sound of another long beep they stood, pushing their chairs back. Then they turned, all of them to the right, and in a calm and orderly fashion filed out.

One drone remained seated at the far end of each table. When the hall had cleared completely they rose in unison, and without a sound or a word of direction from the overseers began moving down the line stacking the dishes. In the course of the morning meal not a word had been spoken nor a rule broken. It was Athens Ra's great Marsean workforce.

And it was, indeed, perfect.

The newly reconstructed titanium mine once again hummed with activity. The central column's descending and ascending blue elevator beams delivered workers down to the cavernous chamber, and chunks of ore to the surface. A new and improved generation of six-legged ore-cutting robots climbed the vertical walls tearing chunks of titanium from the cells, and yellow tractor beams drew the bounty into the central column. And while miners rode the yellow beams across the chasm to and from the cells as they once had, now there was no cheerful camaraderie, waves or work songs to make the time pass more pleasantly. There was only silent, mindless labor, the hum of phaetronic beams, the crunch and crack of rock shorn from the two hundred-foot high seam of titanium.

A small crew of overseers – Marsean colonists paid handsomely for electing to spend their working hours in the mine – had little to do as the drones, while subnormal intellectually, were more than capable of learning the rote tasks necessary for their jobs.

Far below in the baking heat of the gold mines the overseers moved about in air-cooled protective garments. Scientists had never discovered a way to improve working conditions without jeopardizing the gold extraction but it had been unnecessary. The new workforce was able to survive the stifling heat unperturbed.

Inside a cell at the titanum mine's 15th level four of the brawny drones stood in silence as the robot's red beam gouged huge chunks from the leading wall. When the twenty-second burst of intense energy ceased they began to lift the rocks out of the cell opening and heave them into the yellow tractor beam. Productivity had increased due to the size of the ore chunks freed. The colonists had been able to lift boulders only a third of the size and move them at a fraction of the speed than the drones now could. With another burst from the robot's red beam the ore-releasing process began again.

Suddenly the worker closest to the cell opening turned sharply and ducked reflexively as a large jagged slice of the wall collapsed above him. His swift reaction saved him from receiving injury to his head and torso. The other three waiting patiently for the twenty-second burst to cease made no comment, hardly acknowledging that the accident had occurred. A moment later the quartet began lifting the released ore from the newly-made pile and throwing it into the yellow beam.

It was only when the drone closest to the cell opening reached to retrieve a boulder that he noticed his left arm below the elbow was missing. He and the others stared at it in silence. It was a clean, bloodless severance, the wound cauterized by the slicing red beam in the instant the arm passed through it. The hand and half the forearm lay at the drone's feet. He picked it up with his remaining hand and looked to the others with a quizzical expression.

He was impervious to pain, as his creators had consciously excised from his and the other drones' genomic structuring all pain and temperature sensory sites. It was the same bio-mechanism that allowed his identical brothers toiling in the gold mines below to move about unprotected and unperturbed in near-scalding temperatures.

The armless man, as though suddenly recalling a learned instruction, turned from his work-mates and climbed out the cell opening. Still clutching his severed arm he straddled the ever-moving tractor beam and rode it across the abyss to the central column. Once inside he sought an overseer, the nearest one having his back to the drone. He tapped the colonist's shoulder and when the man turned to see him holding the arm the overseer's eyes widened in momentary surprise. Then he called for assistance. A supervisor and a medic were there in moments. They examined both the severed forearm and the stump which had finally begun to breach the cauterization and was now oozing blood.

It was quickly decided which of the two overseers would escort the drone topside, and before they stepped into the blue elevator beam the colonist discarded the severed arm, tossing it into the ore elevator where it was quickly pulverized.

✍

The drone's bleeding had become profuse by the time they reached the medical facility. While he still showed no signs of pain or panic he was pale from the loss of blood and shock, and needed support to walk the final steps to the treatment room.

A young, pretty female tech sat scanning a report. She looked up and saw the overseer and the injured drone. "Another one?" she asked unperturbed.

"We're still working things out down there. One wrong step and 'thwap!' Good thing they don't know the difference."

"Let's get him on the table." She looked up and smiled, "Myles, isn't it?"

"You remembered," the overseer said, pleased. It occurred to him that the attractive gold earbobs he'd seen the other day at his artisan friend's studio would look lovely on the young woman, but she was all business.

Together they lowered the worker down and strapped him to the table. He didn't struggle and seemed to be getting weaker by the moment. The tech, unperturbed by the patient's blood that pooled at her feet, chose an instrument from the shiny counter, one with a transparent cup at one end. She centered the device on the bloody stump and activated it. Instantly a film began forming over the open wound, stanching the crimson flow. The film thickened. It was first grey, and one could see tiny lines beginning to form. A moment later the lines could be recognized as blood vessels which quickly filled, and suddenly the layer of new skin was pink and healthy. Its edges knit so perfectly with the severed forearm that no seam was apparent. Color returned to the worker's face. His breathing evened and normalized.

The tech relinquished the first tool and moved to a shelf on which stood a row of instruments. They were all similar in that one end consisted of a small phaetronic device. Each was adapted on the other end with a soft, transparent receptacle of a different size and shape. The tech chose the one she deemed suitable and began to fit its see-through sock-end over the drone's newly healed stump, leaving the long sheath empty.

"Accelerator," she said offhandedly, naming the device for the overseer. "This is the part I like the best." She smiled as she switched the device on. "It just takes a minute," she said. She used the time to clean the bloody floor with a quick sweep of her wrist hub, then turned back in anticipation. "There!" she said, pointing at the drone's stump.

The change was noticeable. Two small bumps had appeared in the center of the new skin and were growing larger at an astonishing rate.

"Those are the arm bones. They're two of them, but they grow so close together at first they kind of look like..." she smiled, this time rather coyly. Indeed, what had been two bumps now merged into one, and this protruded outward, straining against the stump's derma looking ever more phallic.

"Will it bust through the skin?" Myles asked.

"No, no. See there." The tech pointed. "New skin is being

produced to keep up. Tiny muscles have already started developing inside. And nerves... Well, that's it." She was dismissing the
overseer, but the flirtation was obvious. "See you next time?"
she said.

Myles was suddenly shy. "Next time."

As the door whooshed closed the tech was already helping
the drone to his feet. She led him through another door that
opened into a medical ward of sorts. It was a spare dormitory
where nearly a dozen drones reclined quietly on tables. To each
was attached one of the devices, the transparent film covering a
different body part. The distal end of a thigh bulged out where a
knee joint was slowly rebuilding itself. The right side of a drone's
face under the accelerator was regenerating a cheek and ear.

The tech found an empty table at the end of the room and
carefully laid the drone down on it, speaking to him absently –
more out of habit – knowing that he barely understood her words.
The colonists who worked the mines had all been instructed to
treat the drones gently, though overt kindness was unnecessary.

"We'll just put you here next to your friend. He lost an arm,
too." She strapped him on the table, placing a small cushion
under his neck. "You'll be out of here in no time."

The tech moved away, not even glancing at the other patients,
and exited the otherwise unattended ward. The drone turned
his head to look at his identical brother lying next to him, just
staring mindlessly at the ceiling. If he had looked more closely
he would have seen beneath the transparent sheath a forearm, in
miniature, lengthening and developing at a slow but perceptible
rate.

On its end was the bud of a perfect embryonic hand.

ERTHE

Abomination

SIXTY-FIVE

"IT'S A GIRL, a *girl*!" Cleatah cried, unable to conceal her pleasure. Today it was Talya reclining in the warm saltwater birthing tub and Cleatah kneeling between her friend's knees. Cleatah held the partially submerged infant in one hand and cleaned the tiny body with the other as the women in attendance bathed Talya's face, neck and breasts with damp herb-fragrant cloths. Someone murmured that the new mother looked serene, nothing like a woman who had labored for eighteen hours and delivered her first child moments before. Cleatah guessed, but did not say, that Talya had employed the pain-suppressing function of her wrist hub.

Yazman tied the umbilical cord in two places several inches apart. Then with a brief, silent blessing Cleatah took up a small sharp knife and severed it. She gently floated the infant – as pale-skinned as her mother – to Talya's side and slid the baby under her arm, helping it find a breast. She began to suckle immediately.

With a pang, Cleatah thought how much she hoped for a daughter next time.

There was low whispering and relieved laughter as Yazman and the other women began tidying up the birthing chamber. They could hear the men who'd gathered outside to wait for the moment when they would be allowed to enter.

"This is Boah's first living child," Cleatah told Talya, "so his celebrations may go on for weeks." She smiled down at Talya who remained silent and contented, completely consumed with the little creature cradled in her arms.

∽

Later, when Talya was resting in the adjoining chamber Boah was shown in. He was wide-eyed, his face soft with emotion. Cleatah watched as he fell unselfconsciously to his knees at their side and kissed the tender, sleeping bundle, then kissed Talya.

"I've been waiting at home with my brothers," he said. "I put in a good supply of kav, but we all stayed sober till we heard that you, that...*she* was all right." He swallowed hard, unable to take his eyes off the child.

"Here, hold her," Talya said, and he lifted the delicate girl from her arms. "Get your fill. I'm going to take her back to the *Atlantos* for a little while."

He started to object, alarm creasing his handsome face.

"I need some time alone with her."

"The two of you must come live at my house."

"I'll send word to you."

"You'll call for me soon?"

"I will. I promise."

Boah stood and reluctantly moved to the door where Cleatah stood. He embraced her and departed.

"Why don't you give her the other breast?" Cleatah said, coming back to Talya's side.

She moved the infant carefully, first laying the girl on her back between Talya's breasts. It was Cleatah's first sight of the child's face. She could see its head was perfectly formed, the cheeks already pink and glowing, the lips a pretty bud-shape whose corners turned up as if in a smile. Then she opened her eyes to the world for the first time. Cleatah's breath caught in her throat as a gasp. She stared disbelieving.

The child's eyes were grey.

✦

Despite the aching exhaustion, Talya had clearly seen Cleatah's recognition of Poseidon's own daughter in her child, and for a moment regretted the searing bolt of agony and confusion in her rival's eye. But the emotion was short-lived, nothing more than Talya's own vulnerability in that moment. She was barely aware of Cleatah rising to her feet and fleeing the birthing chamber. The regret had quickly evaporated and was supplanted by an equally foreign and unexpected sentiment. It was directed at the tiny, squirming infant at her breast who, with uncanny instinct, had begun suckling hungrily.

Is this what is meant by human 'love' – this jumbled upwelling of warmth and joy and fierce possessiveness? Talya experienced a moment of disquiet, even panic. She attempted to reconcile who she'd been just minutes before with the person she had suddenly become. All rational thought seemed to recede along with her calculated reasons for creating this child – the lust for an inviolable bond with Poseidon. The pleasure of reprisal for Cleatah's theft of Talya's chosen mate.

Now suddenly there was only this grey-eyed, velvet soft creature lying in her arms, feeding on her body. Someone of her own that no one could steal from her. Ever. One that nobody else could possess or control. If this was what it meant to be Erthan, she thought, a slow smile creasing her features, she would have no trouble living with it.

None at all.

SIXTY-SIX

POSEIDON STORMED INTO Talya's quarters to find her leaning over Isis who lay sleeping on the bed.

"How did you do it!"

"Isn't it obvious?" she answered, aware that the familiar Terresian chill had returned to her voice. "I harvested your sperm."

"When?"

She'd never seen him so angry. In fact it looked as if he might strike her. *There was so little Terresian left in him*, she mused. *A pity*... "Does it matter when?"

"Just tell me."

"Soon after I learned Cleatah was trying to conceive, but before she actually had."

Poseidon looked as though he had stopped breathing.

"She'll never have the daughters she wants so badly," Talya added. "They'll all be boys... and they'll all be twins." This had been an extra small cruelty she'd devised that night she'd performed her genomic modifications. The superstitious regarded multiple births as abominations.

Poseidon turned away suddenly, as though he couldn't bear to look at her.

"I went to your rooms with only the thought to direct the outcome of your children. I extracted Cleatah's ovum and made

514

the changes in them to produce the 'twin effect' before reintroducing them into her body. Of course men are responsible for the sex of their children. I made certain the necessary genome for females would never again be produced in your sperm."

"*Why* Talya! Why did you do such a thing? If I thought for a thousand years I could never imagine a more obscene violation, such a senseless act."

"It made perfect sense to me." Talya came deliberately around Poseidon to confront him. Her eyes were blazing. "I didn't want her to have any female children – girls who would grow up to look like their mother whom you so adore. When Cleatah begins to age – as she soon will – you would have had her daughters to remind you of her, when she was still young and beautiful…"

"You're *insane*."

His words had no effect on her. Now she moved to the bed and picked up the child who had awakened and was crying hungrily. Talya looked back at Poseidon and smiled, pleased with herself.

"Funny, I didn't conceive of the idea of impregnating myself until I was already working on you. It was a sudden revelation, and I thought it rather brilliant. Cleatah would never have a girl, but *I* could… Oh, don't look at me that way."

"I'm not sure I can look at you ever again."

"Perhaps," said Talya, a wicked glint in her eyes, "but you *will* have to look at our daughter." She held Isis out for him to hold.

He stared at the helpless creature, the pale gold hair and delicate features that already resembled her mother's.

And the grey eyes.

"Look how beautiful she is. They're your eyes, but my coloring. Just think. The first and only fully Terresian offspring on the planet. Her lifespan will be enormously long and…"

"Quiet!"

"Outraged, are you?" she said, looking up at Poseidon who was – she noticed with surprise – staring down at the baby with something akin to wonder. "That's right. She's yours. She's mine. Nothing can change that."

"Bloody stars, Talya, "have you no sense at all of what you've done!?"

Her face hardened defiantly.

"You will change her eyes. Now. Make them brown, like Boah's. We'll go to your laboratory and I will watch you do it."

"I'll do no such thing."

He fixed her with a killing glare. She was unmoved.

"I want you out of here," he finally said. In a week you'll pack your things and move to Boah's house. For now you're confined to the ship. Don't show your face on the surface. And access to your laboratory…" He shook his head.

"We are not going to live with Boah. "My work is here."

"You're not listening to me. Your work here is done. When you leave the *Atlantos* it will be for the last time."

"You wouldn't dare…"

"From this day on you will have no use of technos on this ship, and I swear to you that if I learn you have – for any purpose – used your wrist hub I will cut it out of your body!" He inhaled a ragged breath, trying to calm himself.

She watched him take the placid infant into his arms. He looked down at his daughter, his features roiling, then moved to the door.

"What are you doing? Where are you taking her!" she said, moving towards him.

"You stay here," he growled, pushing her aside.

"Don't hurt her!"

§

Poseidon shut out the ridiculous plea. *Hurt a newborn?* And yet, as he rode the central beam upwards emerging into the Grove, he found himself clutching the girl so tightly she had begun to whimper. With a touch of his hub she was narcotized and fell limp in the crook of his arm. He hurried round the spiral hedge making desperate plans with one step, abandoning them with the next.

Once in plain sight of anyone who might be about in the Central Isle meadow he quickly cloaked the baby, trying to position the arm cradling her into a semblance of normalcy. But few people were about. The Residence courtyard was quiet. Cleatah, he saw with his scanner, was nowhere within her medicine garden walls.

At the Central Isle dock he unmoored a small skiff and placing the sleeping girl in the floor, un-cloaked her. Then he unfurled the small sail and caught the breeze that always blew down the straight, 300-foot wide Great Harbor. The sluice gate was there in front of him. He wondered where he was headed. *Into the circular canals, slouching low to stay unobtrusive, speaking to no one passing by giving himself time to think? He needed to think.* But he'd passed the waters of the Central Canal before he knew it. He'd gone by the Middle Ring Isle and its canal, and the Outer Ring Isle, too, when he found himself approaching the towering Seawall flaring out on either side of the sluice. The Gate Guards, recognizing Poseidon, waved down at him. He hid the tiny form at his feet with his body and managed to wave back. He found he needed to brush wetness from his cheeks – wishing it was sea spray – and sailed gratefully under the sluice into the ocean's chop.

He bore north up the coast, and what was once the Shore Village came quickly into sight. Abandoned altogether these days, children refused to play here, fearing a ghost wave, or a real wave like the one that had swept the elders out to sea. The whole beach was Poseidon's own. He scraped ashore at the far north edge, the place where all those years before he had descended from the Great Plateau to present his disguised self – the wildman – to the Shore Tribe. To *Cleatah's* people...before he had even realized he had come to claim her for himself.

Furling the sail he dragged the skife across the beach and sat heavily in the sand. He could see nearby where the woman used to wait for fishermen to come and drop their catch to be cleaned. Their krall to be pierced and pulled from their spiral shells. He was wandering in his mind, letting it take him away to more pleasant memories when a soft mewling from the skife reminded him what lay within it. The very reason he had pulled up on this shore.

He stood and looked down at the child, still sleeping, perhaps dreaming what dreams a newborn could have. *Did she miss floating in the salt sea of her mother's womb? Did she miss the warmth and wetness? Dislike the harsh cool air on her skin?* He picked her up and brought her out of narcosis.

At once she began to wail, but he refused to speak to her, even a single soothing word or sound. He knew how to do such a thing. His boys, Atlas and Geo, quieted instantly when he took them in his arms, tiny fussy bundles of outrage, causing Cleatah to cluck with indignation at his success when hers had failed.

But this *thing* in his arms. This milk-white, beautiful monster, did not deserve his soothing ministrations. *His blood?* Yes, every bit as the twins were. *But his child? His beloved offspring?* No! She was made of theft and deceit, hatred and jealousy. Even the name Talya had chosen stung like a thousand tiny cuts. The ancient Terresian deity named Isis was the Goddess of War. She had presided over some of the most infamous scenes of mayhem in battle, her sword-wielding arms covered in blood, unyielding and looking for the next fight.

How dare Talya name his child Isis?

A wave of rage swept over him, and like a mindless thing he strode into the surf. As the water reached his waist he held Isis higher and higher until, with small waves slapping his chest, he had thrust her high over his head.

What am I doing? he thought with dull panic. *This is for Cleatah. She must be spared the pain of this child's existence. The bitterness. The shame. The detestable presence of the woman whom they had drawn into their family. Whom Cleatah had come to call Sister.* No. Isis would not be allowed to live. *End it all now. Give her back to the salt sea. She would hardly have known what it was to be alive.*

He began lowering her, his elbows bending with terrible hesitation, pulling his child down to her death. Strangely, her crying had ceased. There was just the sound of lapping water and his own harsh breathing. She was lowered now to the level of his gaze. He tried to look away...*but she was staring at him!* Calm. Perplexed. Comforted in his strong broad hands.

He tried to tear his gaze from hers but she held him there. *Like old Ta'at,* Poseidon thought then. *Seeing the other side, seeing the peaceful Uth-Cray waiting there for him.* Poseidon lowered her further till her back was submerged. *It must feel cold to her,* he thought, yet she did not cry. She did open her eyes wide, though, and he saw what he never wished to see in a child that was not Cleatah's.

There *he* was staring out staring out from within the grey irises. There he was.

"Bloody stars," he whispered, tears mixing with spray, "you are mine." He clasped the wet bundle to his chest and began to heave with silent sobs.

"You are mine."

SIXTY-SEVEN

HE'D BROUGHT ISIS back to the ship and down to Talya's genomics laboratory. There he had taught himself the protocol and changed his daughter's eyes to a warm brown. Locking the door codes so Talya could not enter, he'd returned the girl to her mother without a word. He rode the beam up and walked haltingly to the Residence, trying desperately to find the words with which to face Cleatah. But she was gone. The twins were with Yazman at her house.

One of the horses was missing from the stable.

He took one of the other mounts, a young gelding called Pacer. Had it been Arrow he would not have had to give her direction. She would have known to head west, to making her way across both ring islands and their bridges and up the South Ramp to the Great Plateau. Instead he had to guide the horse past the High Atlantos Stables where he had been born.

Many of the old paths had been obliterated by the patchwork of cropland and grazing fields, and those that led into the forest were mostly overgrown. They left the dirt path to follow a rocky stream for a short time, only to return to one that resumed on the stream's far side.

In a green glade he found Cleatah's horse. Poseidon dismounted. Even after so many years' absence he quickly located the path in the thicket that the two of them had taken to the waterfall so many times.

Though he was certain he would find her there the first sight of her – naked and waist-deep in the river, bathed in the fall's violent spray – jellied his knees. For some time he did not make his presence known, as just the act of watching her in the old place steadied him. What he would soon be forced to reveal would open new wounds and try her spirit, even as she attempted in the purifying waters to heal the ones she'd already suffered.

Poseidon removed his clothes and waded into the river. When he was halfway to Cleatah she turned and saw him. His heart sank. The crashing waters had done little to calm the raging animal inside. Even the sight of him did not move her. She turned her face away. He closed the distance between them and with the thundering cascade a chaos around them he pulled her to him. Her body was stiff, unyielding. Steeling himself, he took her hand and led her to the shore to a place where the falls would not drown out their words.

She was silent as he spoke, knowing every word would punish her further. That he had changed the child's eyes, that no one would ever know she was his, even Isis, could never soften the blow of Talya's cruelest of all acts.

Worse, that he did not know how to undo any part of what she had done.

"It wasn't enough that she stole his seed to make their child together," Cleatah said to the downward rushing water.

Poseidon had gone. She had said to him, 'Get out of my sight.' She'd seen him shrink before her words and withering gaze. Now she was alone facing the falls, calling out to the Goddess. "Was it not enough to allow us nothing but twins? Did she have to steal any hope of my having daughters as well?! There will be no women of our line, Mother. *No women!*"

Behind the roar of the water where the Goddess's voice had so many times been heard, there was nothing. No answer. No explanation. No apology.

"And Poseidon?" She spat the name, trembling with outrage. "He says he cannot undo what she has done. He does not know how. They changed the color of the girl's eyes..." She laughed mirthlessly. "Locked the woman out of her laboratory...as though that would be enough."

She felt a single sharp stone amidst the smooth ones under her feet. She ground her soft arch into the point till she felt pain. "I told him to punish her. He looked helpless. *Helpless.* He asked me, as though there was no good answer for it, 'What is the punishment for such a hideous thing?'"

"'You tell me,' I said. 'What is the punishment for *murder?*' He went pale. Shook his head, ashamed."

Now she plunged both hands into the steaming cascade, searching there for the familiar voice of truth and reason. But there was silence amidst the roar.

"Talya murdered our daughters!" She was shrieking now. "Now and forever! Why, Mother? Why did you send me this man, this great and joyful life, if it was only to punish me this way? To steal all the girls of my body?!" She turned her back on the waterfall and stood in that place, motionless. Hardly breathing. Trying to fathom Great Mother's silent repudiation.

She doesn't care," Cleatah finally thought. *I am abandoned.* The idea buckled her knees. "I trusted you. I have kept your altar burning day and night the whole of my life. I did all the work you put before me. And this is how I am repaid?" She felt like a petulant child saying such a thing, but she thought, wildly, that this accusation – finally – would cause the Goddess to answer. To defend herself. Make her excuses. Because Cleatah *had* been a good and faithful servant. A tool in Great Mother's hands. Always. And here was her reward. The worst punishment a woman could be dealt. But no guidance came. There was nothing. No words. No singing. No laughter.

And nothing to suggest that Cleatah herself possessed the answer.

She was through. She strode to the rocky edge and vaulted from the pool. She pulled on her shift and tied the belt around her waist so tightly she winced. But the pain was welcome. In the absence of Great Mother's voice, it was at least a sensation, even if it was of her own making. She laced her sandals and straightened her back. Shook out her hair. As she strode from the pool she could feel the Goddess's hold on her weakening. That tie to the source of all wisdom. For a moment she felt strong. Sure of herself.

Then a sob escaped her. She stopped in her tracks. She pounded her chest with her fist, defiant. Once. Twice. Three times. She could live without Great Mother. She would speak to the wind and the water. She would always hear the teachings of the plants. The mushroom visions. She would give all her love to her sons, however many Poseidon would give her. But this betrayal, Mother's betrayal, could not be forgiven.

Nothing would ever be the same again.

ERTHE

SIXTY-EIGHT

CLEATAH WAS SUDDENLY gone.

It had not taken Poseidon long to realize that she had not simply left the Residence for an early walk to the Academy. There was an eeriness, an emptiness about the Central Isle. Something somber to the point of doom. With terrible trepidation he went below into the ship.

Neither Talya nor the child was there.

Fear seized him. What had Talya done? He knew her to be capable of the most despicable acts, but violent abduction? Cleatah was strong, but she was no match for the phaetron. She'd been so troubled in the last week. He'd tried and failed to make amends for Talya's betrayal, but she had been distant and largely silent. When she did speak aloud to him and the twins it was tenderly, but in increments the telepathic conversations that they frequently shared had become harder to hear. They finally ceased altogether. This unnatural silence between them explained how he'd had no warning at all, no call for help.

A terrible thought gripped him. *Could he not hear her because she was dead? How had he allowed any of this to happen? Talya's crime. His beloved woman gone without a trace. His fault. His fault...*

SIXTY-NINE

IT WAS UNCLEAR what had woken her from a sleep like death. Before she opened her eyes all was utter blackness, but she could feel a bone-rattling shake beneath her supine body, and her arms – *how peculiar* – were pinned tightly to her sides. There was a dull ache in her right arm, and the dampness at her chest could be nothing other than her breasts leaking milk. Then she heard Isis crying in a place behind her head. Talya tried without success to open her eyes. The sound of her child's cries clawed at her insides, and warm liquid came rushing forth in two small floods.

"Isis," Talya cried weakly, aware that her voice was cracked and feeble. "Isis!" With all her strength she lifted her eyelids. Her head swam in the daylight, though she was shaded from the sun by a plain-woven cloth. Her back, flattened along the bottom of a cart, was jounced violently by what must certainly be uneven ground beneath the wooden wheels. *This could not be an Atlan road.* Now she understood she was bound tightly, pinioned within the confines of a length of cloth, immobile.

Talya could see nothing to her right or left, as the arched shade cloth touched the high sides of the cart. But the rear of the cart was open. Lifting her head from the cocoon and looking straight ahead she could see out the back. What stretched before her was as terrible a sight as she had ever seen.

Wilderness. Vast grassy expanses of the Great Plateau with snowcapped Manya and her sister-mountains nothing but tiny mounds in the distance from where this wagon had traveled. Atlantos, she calculated with a sinking in her gut, was far, far behind her.

Isis had stopped her wailing. Instead were wet sucking noises and the soft, satisfied grunts Talya knew so well. Someone was feeding her child!

"Where am I?" she cried, finally finding a voice loud enough to be heard. Yes, she had been heard. Isis was crying again. *Crying for her!* "Who is there? Where are you taking me?" She felt the cart rumble to a stop and heard the driver climbing down from the seat behind her head. Talya's heart pounded in her throat. The vision that appeared at the cart's opening could not have been more stunning.

It was the strident figure of a long-forgotten Cleatah, a wild-haired female attired in ragged-edged, rough-sewn animals pelts. Her posture was that of a hunter, though where a spear would have been held diagonally across her chest was instead strung a soft cloth sling. Inside it hung Talya's tiny child, red-faced and bawling.

"Give her to me," Talya demanded, her voice hoarse with longing.

Cleatah stood silent and still, unmoved by the baby's cries or its mother's commands.

"What are you *doing*, Cleatah? Where are you taking us? Tell me now."

Without a word Cleatah climbed into the wagon bed and laid Isis down at Talya's bound feet. Again the infant stopped crying, perhaps at the sight of her mother's face or a whiff of her familiar scent. Cleatah came on her knees to the front of the wagon and with one hand lifted Talya's head. With the other she held a water flask to her prisoner's parched lips. Talya wished to resist the gesture without receiving some answers but her thirst was unbearable and she greedily drank till she was sated. Before she could resume her questioning Cleatah backed away, climbed from the wagon and lifted Isis out, again placing her in the sling.

"No, don't take her!"

To Talya's dismay her daughter quieted and began suckling at Cleatah's milk-heavy breast.

"Please, give her to me. And tell me what's happening!"

Cleatah stared impassively at Talya as though she was trying to make sense of the scene before her – a scene that Cleatah had herself created.

"At least let me feed her," Talya begged.

"If you did she would sleep and never wake up," Cleatah said, breaking the silence. "For now, Poseidon's daughter will drink my milk."

"What did you give me? How…?" A stinging pain shot suddenly up from Talya's right wrist, shocking her into silence. When she attempted to move it inside the binding the whole arm ached. Her blood froze with the realization of the pain's origin. "What have you done? My hub…" she said with growing horror, knowing that Cleatah had sliced it out of her.

"Nothing you haven't done to me. To Poseidon. You can never hurt us again."

Talya's rage crashed violently inside her skull and chest. "You will let me out of here! Instantly!" she shouted. "Give me my child!"

Cleatah's expression might have been pity, or revulsion. "That's enough. We have a long way to go." Gently rearranging Isis' little limbs in the sling so the feeding was easier, Talya's captor turned to go.

"Cleatah, wait! Wait! Does Poseidon know what you've done?"

Talya heard the Gaian primitive who had bested her in every conceivable way climb back into the seat and take up the horse's reins. She heard Cleatah click her cheek twice, and with a sharp lurch the cart began to move.

MARS COLONY

SEVENTY

FROM THE DECK of his majestic new home Athens gazed down the length of Halcyon Beach and found himself very pleased. The broad ribbon of fine pink sand – flanked on one side by the sparkling blue-green sea and on the other by palatial residences built since the re-institution of the gold currency – had become the colony's favorite playground. And today, on the yearly anniversary of their arrival on Mars, a holiday colonists had named "Landfall," it seemed as if every last soul had come out to celebrate.

His latest companion, Patrice, a truly marvelous specimen of female beauty, moved to his side and took his hand, little Athena taking the other. He had never understood, nor spent much time contemplating, why he had abandoned his affair with Joya, his daughter's biological mother. They had been so compatible. Perhaps it was the dreams – the nightmares – he'd begun having when he was with her – the amber plasma spheres, glimpses of odd triangle-faced creatures with bulbous black eyes. They had decreased in number since he'd begun seeing Patrice. *Or had they?* Maybe he'd just gotten better at forgetting.

Together the three of them started down the long steps to the beach. Patrice wore a spare costume designed to expose much of her flesh to the solar rays. Like so many of the colonists she had become devoted to bathing in the sun's health-giving emissions, a pastime that had had the effect of somehow softening the naturally rigid Terresian demeanor. They'd hardly stepped foot on the sand when Athena broke away to romp with some neighbor children and their pet solies at the water's edge. Knowing she was perfectly safe he and Patrice moved along the beach crowded with carefree families lounging on the sand and playing in the gentle surf with their whiskered companions.

Watching the scene Athens contemplated the importance of the drone workforce to the general contentedness of their society. They really could not be underestimated. Those few colonists who still worked in the mines were supervisors. This was on a strictly volunteer basis, and the colonial mine workers were among the best-paid individuals on Mars. Farming and manufacturing were technologically and robotically performed, and each person was only required to work one or two days out of every ten. It was a perfect arrangement. Those few genomists who opposed Athens's labor force on moral grounds had long ago been transferred to other projects. While he still privately chafed at the memory of Poseidon's disapproval, he had come to believe the drone project was the best decision he'd made since their arrival on Mars.

Vice Governor Praxis had been, and was still the project's most vocal opponent. Athens believed the opposition was simply a measure of Praxis's personal hatred for the much-loved Governor. He continually threatened to alert the home world of Athens's "slave labor force" which, Praxis said, was contrary to every ethical Terresian principle. But the threat was laughable. There could be no meaningful communication with Terres for thousands of Marsean years, as it had finally flung itself into its deep space orbit and Long Orbit SleepPhase had begun. For most of the colony, the home planet had become a dim and rather unpleasant memory. Athens therefore allowed Praxis to keep his post. It wouldn't do for the colonists to perceive their governor as a tyrant who brooked no dissenting opinions. The

Vice Governor had become nothing more than a pesky insect that Athens would occasionally swat away. He took great pleasure in humiliating him, the more publicly the better.

The colonists were therefore free to pursue the process of real civilization on Mars. Perhaps it was not the lush paradise that Gaia was, but his people had created a fabulous land of leisure, decorated by artistic wonders created in abundant gold. While the filthy and dangerous work of mining went on out of sight and mind, they enjoyed lives of contentment with time enough to pursue any and all interests… and of course, plenty of time for recreation. Adults devised toys, sports and games – from simple physical competitions to intricate mind challenges. Children who, on the home planet had spent most of their waking moments in serious education, now discovered the world of play. They were delirious with it, abandoning themselves to all manner of natural pleasure. It was a perfect arrangement.

That was why, thought Athens as he surveyed the happy scene at Halcyon Beach on Landfall Day, he had chosen not to alarm his people with the disturbing reports of solies found dead on some of the more remote beaches to the north. Actually the solies themselves had not been found. Rather it was bits of them strewn among the rocks, or a horrible mash of bone, muscle and fur that appeared to have been chewed up, digested and spat out again. Too, there was a growing number of the creatures gone missing from colonists' households. Athens had authoritatively announced that these disappearances were simply the natural habit of the animals. As much as the people loved their solies they were wild creatures whose impulse was to periodically return to the deep. A vague memory of some unpleasantness surrounding solies on Mile 7 Beach would occasionally assert itself, but like his nightmares, they seemed to fade in importance as the years passed.

He had quietly decided he would commission an investigation into the deaths and get to the bottom of it. He would do it soon. But it was too magnificent a day to be worrying about such things. All of it could wait.

Colonists saw the honored couple walking up the beach and cleared a choice spot for Athens and Patrice in the shade of an overhanging tree fern. Many approached to pay their respects to the Governor and brought offerings from their family's picnics. Athens warmed with pleasure, knowing that the beachgoers felt a sense of completeness and contentment that their leader was among them in their celebration.

He was thinking that he should call Athena to sit and eat with them when the first scream shattered the idyll as surely as a hammer blow to delicate crystal. A woman stood – rigid in the sand – her arm outstretched, finger pointing to a monstrous head so recently emerged from the waves that seawater still cascaded down its hideous, scaly snout. A solie struggled frantically in the beast's fanged jaws.

Worse than the sight itself was the creature's inexorable movement – unperturbed by the hordes of people before it, it advanced from the sea through the shallows toward the beach. Colonists scattered, shrieking in panic. Some had enough presence of mind to grab their children. Others desperately splashed into the surf to snatch their youngsters from the horror that had appeared in the suddenly treacherous ocean.

Like an unfolding nightmare three more heads appeared and began following the first monster that had emerged from the water onto the sand. Even on their short front legs they stood twelve feet high with long sleek bodies and a single posterior flipper. Their dark green, scaly torsos were dotted with dozens of large raised patches of an undulating, jellylike substance. Here the skin was a transparent membrane, and beneath it a colorful network of red and blue blood vessels could be seen. From the beasts' shoulders protruded six heavily muscled tentacles, several of which were independently searching out and snatching up solies, now making a desperate dash for the waves. The first unlucky solie had already been devoured, and a second in a tentacle's crushing embrace was being delivered to the creature's razor-toothed maw.

The other three amphibious monsters had in the next moment come ashore, hungrily eyeing and picking off their chosen meals. By accident – or perhaps curiosity – one of the beast's huge tentacles wrapped itself around a man trying to rescue his little girl. His scream of agony caused every colonist to look back at the scene they were fleeing. And now disbelief mingled with horror and repulsion as they watched the creature take its first taste of human flesh. By some small grace the man had lost consciousness, or perhaps died, before his limp body was devoured.

For an instant Athens's senses failed him, panicked and paralyzed by the magnitude of the atrocity before him. Then a terrible high-pitched trill from the man-eater alerted the other three amphibians that this new warm-blooded prey was good eating and they, too, began scanning the beach for humans.

The sound also thrust Athens into action. He looked back frantically for Athena but saw she had been swept up by a neighbor and was being carried under his arm off the sand. Then Athens took off running down the beach toward the living nightmare.

Unbelievably, the events had not yet completed their horrible unfolding. More than twenty colonists had set their phaetrons to the rarely employed "kill" frequency and were attempting to clear the beach of humans previous to initiating their counterattack. But before this was accomplished the four amphibians began a strange metamorphosis. It appeared as if large chunks of skin were being sloughed from their bodies. In fact it was the veined, jelly-like bulges that were disengaging themselves from their hosts – dozens of independent, parasitic creatures who now skittered across the pink sand with such speed and agility that many had found solie and human victims before anyone had had time to aim their weapons or flee.

The result was instantaneous and sickening. Attaching

themselves leech-like to any area of open skin, the jelly creatures began extracting bodily fluids at so accelerated a rate that the person was incapacitated before defense was possible. As the lucky scattered to safety, victims fell writhing to the ground, seeming to shrivel before everyone's eyes, with the parasites ballooning into large blood-filled sacs so overloaded they were barely able to make their way back to their host creatures.

Now on the front line of men with phaetrons Athens picked off several dozen of the parasitic jelly creatures. He and a few others had a straight shot at the amphibians. They took aim and fired. Two of them were felled instantly, crashing to the ground and dying with shrill, ear-splitting screams. The other two, reacting with a speed not imagined in such large cumbersome creatures, disappeared into the waves before another phaetron round could be fired off.

Weary and sick with revulsion Athens and his shooters now moved among the remaining parasites, vaporizing their turgid, struggling bodies to spare witnesses the grisly sight of exploded bloody membranes.

Finally it was done.

Dazed colonists straggled back onto Halcyon Beach to retrieve the bodies of their loved ones. Wondering briefly if his refusal to alert the Terresians of the earlier killed solies would come back to haunt him, he suddenly and painfully realized the Martian idyll was over and that a terrible kind of night had settled over Paradise.

ATLANTOS CITY

SEVENTY-ONE

BOAH HAD BEEN waiting – though no one would have said patiently – for Talya's summons. No woman treated a man like she did, yet no man would dare to command her. His brothers refrained from comment, though at the city stables where he worked these days to be close to her and the child he could see them watching him differently. They wondered why he'd been kept from seeing his daughter until Talya called for him, yet they'd stayed blessedly silent about it. But this day as he and Joss tended a bloody injury to a mare's flank, Boah knew he had waited long enough.

"Clean her?" he said to Joss.

A moment later he was out the stable door and trotting down the stone roadway without having met a single horseman's eye. All he could think of was his daughter, the flower-petal skin, the delicately arched features that he knew upon first sight resembled her mother's. When he reached the Outer Ring Baths he couldn't remember how he'd gotten there.

He stripped off his sticky tunic and at the warm fountain washed the blood from his arms and face. Then he stepped into the pool where thankfully few were bathing. He soaked only long enough to achieve the cleanliness needed to visit his family. He smiled to himself as he toweled off, silently repeating the words in his head.

His family.

He needed desperately to see them. Talya and the child. His daughter. As he took a fresh tunic and started for his house he allowed himself to venture future thoughts. *What name would they give her?* – pretty little filly with a sun-yellow mane. He would teach her to ride. No matter that Talya never got on the back of a horse. The girl would very naturally ride. All the Brotherhood would love her like their own child.

At home he paused only long enough to tie his long hair back into a tail and to grab the fine blue and yellow blanket woven respectfully by the horsemen's women, and dash out again. He reminded himself to walk and not run so he wouldn't be sweat-covered and disheveled to see his women.

When Boah finally crossed the Central Canal Bridge and neared the circular hedge that now hid the ship's entrance he saw Poseidon standing there. His tall frame seemed strangely stooped. Boah could see his features were torn with anguish.

"What is it? Is it Talya? The child?" He tried to move around Poseidon, but he blocked the way with his body.

"Tell me what's happened!"

Boah could see Poseidon trying to rearrange his features. He opened his mouth, then closed it again. Then he leveled his gaze on Boah and with much difficulty held steady. "You're a man who speaks only the truth, Boah, and you speak it from the heart," Poseidon began. "Now I have to tell you a truth…that will break your heart." He waited before he went on, composing himself as best he could. "They're both healthy." He fell silent again, this time for so long that Boah thought he would not speak again.

Boah shook his arm. "Tell me!"

"At the High Atlantos Stables…" Poseidon finally continued, though haltingly, as though each word was poisoning his mouth, "…you've seen Talya choose a particular sire for a particular mare." As Boah nodded his understanding Poseidon exhaled several times, pushing his fingers through the thick thatch of hair above his forehead. "In that same way...she chose a sire for her own child."

Boah nodded, certain that Poseidon was speaking of him. But his friend's expression had grown even more desperate.

"She led us all to believe it was you. It was not." Poseidon could only whisper the words. "I am the sire."

The muscles in Boah's body clenched reflexively. Poseidon raised and opened his hands before him in an attitude of surrender.

"She stole my seed while I slept. I *promise* you this. She stole it with technos, and impregnated herself with it."

Boah suddenly understood how it must have been for the mares and foals when the abyss had opened in the High Atlantos pasture during the great quake...tumbling and falling, limbs flailing helplessly

"Cleatah has taken her and the child away from the city," Poseidon went on.

"Cleatah...?" Boah's head spun, envisioning the consequences of Talya's deed upon his oldest friend. He replayed the words "taken her and the child" several times over in his head. It meant they were gone already. Vanished from his life, like one of Poseidon's Terresian cloaking tricks.

"We'll tell everyone that Talya has been called away on urgent family matters," Poseidon said, eyes glassy. Boah could clearly see that the man was as stunned at Cleatah's actions – her abduction of Talya – as he himself was. "No one will question a mother taking so young an infant with her. No one has reason to question the story."

"The child..." Boah said aloud – the only spoken words of his lament. The muddled confusion inside his head gave way to sudden clarity. He was crashing headlong into one of Talya's merciless betrayals after another. Theft. Cunning. Lies. Physical violation. And the stinging truths: Talya was no sister to

Poseidon, but a jealous lover. The daughter he believed his was another man's child. His own seed had been spurned, regarded as unworthy.

An invisible hand squeezed Boah's guts, forcing him to turn from Poseidon. He blindly retraced his steps home. His family was no more. It had, in fact, never been a family at all.

Once in his door he collapsed as though physically beaten and lay on the bed, motionless. His future visions began to fade. His bright-haired daughter riding low on the back of a fast pony. Gone. Talya, beautiful and wild, feeding wood into the blazing hearth of their home. The light banter he and the horsemen shared dwindling to whispered pity. Misery supplanted misery. Cleatah, his dearest friend on Erthe, suffering horribly at Talya's hand. Now Cleatah, in reprisal, had exacted a terrible punishment on all of them.

And the child, like a length of delicate cloth, would forever be torn between so many angry hands. *The girl.* He captured a small sob in his throat.

He had never even learned her name.

SEVENTY-TWO

THEY HAD TRAVELED nine days, stopping only to sleep and eat. Each night Cleatah would free Talya's legs and right arm, allowing her to feed herself, walk about so her muscles would not shrivel from disuse, and void her bladder and bowels. She would make a bed for herself and Isis next to Talya in the cart.

Many times Cleatah saw Talya stare disbelievingly at the cut-and-sewn flesh at her wrist. She wondered if Talya thought that Boah or Poseidon might still be coming to rescue her, bring her and her child back to the city. Cleatah knew that Talya was "seething." Poseidon had taught her that word. *A quiet agitation.* She had known it described the sea or the clouds, but now Cleatah knew seething could describe a person as well.

After a few days Cleatah's rage had softened enough so that she could give Isis to her mother for feeding. She found she missed the baby's suckling. She missed her sons. Her breasts ached for them. They were only eight months old, and she hadn't wished to leave them. There was nothing in the world she had wished to do more than be with them.

But she had to be rid of this woman.

It was still unfathomable, the act that Talya had committed. It was hard to know what inflamed Cleatah more – that

Isis was Poseidon's child, or that she would never give birth to a daughter. The latter was worse, she finally concluded – the fate of bearing no female children in all of her life. It was a punishment she could hardly comprehend. Poseidon had taken blame for his ignorance of Talya's monstrous assault. But now Cleatah wondered if she herself had grown so soft in her new "civilized" existence that she no longer sensed danger as it approached.

Saying nothing to Poseidon she had carried out her plan, asking no help from anyone. At the last, once Talya's bound and inert body rested in the cart with the horses stamping and snorting impatiently to be off in the crisp night air, she had gone to Yazman – who with her family shared the Central Isle – and told her their destination. The only one Yazman might tell was Poseidon, when he came looking for her. She did regret the moments of fear he would certainly experience when he found them missing. Yazman might also relay the message to him that she did not wish to be followed. The decision would of course be his.

Cleatah prayed day and night to Great Mother that he would not follow. As they crossed the continent she spoke to him silently, hoping that the distance between them would not prevent his hearing her. She was used to this unspoken conversation that flowed endlessly between them. For all these years it had been soothing to know he was with her inside her head, even if he was out of her sight. It had made her feel safe, always. Now she worried that in the last days she had silenced the conversation to accomplish her plan without him knowing. Perhaps she had silenced it forever. *Please, Great Mother,* she prayed, *let him hear me again. Let him hear me with all these miles between us.*

As each day passed she worried less that Poseidon would pursue them, but she was unsure of Boah. He would know nothing of why Talya and his daughter had gone, under what circumstances, or where. Would Poseidon tell him what he knew? What, if anything, would he reveal?

It was not her concern, she'd finally decided. Her task was

to remove the woman from their lives. Poseidon might object to his daughter's absence. In fact, this was Cleatah's only regret. The child was blameless. Isis was a dear and beautiful baby. Suckling the girl had afforded Cleatah a different sort of pleasure than she experienced with her boys. And Cleatah would without question protect the child with her life. She was, after all, Poseidon's blood.

Her mother – if Cleatah was entirely honest with herself – she wished dead.

∽

They reached the Taug Village at dusk on the twelfth day out. Behind it a wide river meandered by its lightly wooded shores. Isis was crying as they approached, and Cleatah hoped this would gentle the spirits of the Taug people who now watched a wagon pulled by two horses cross the settlement's boundary.

This was one of the tribes that had scorned the strangers and their four-legged beasts ten years before during the gathering of the tribes. The Taug whispered suspiciously among themselves for days after Boah's demonstrations with the large devil animals and Poseidon's impossible feats. Today Cleatah had a young baby hanging at her breast, and called out a peaceful greeting as she approached.

They allowed the cart to roll up next to the just-lit central fire where the women were handing out the nightly meal – a boiled knot of meat and a whitish mush in a small gourd bowl. The men, as she had remembered them, looked strong, bright-eyed and healthy. The women were well-fed and contented, the children lively and playful.

The headmen approached her, and several elder women crowded in behind them. Cleatah began to speak imperfect Taug. It was understandable enough. She had practiced her speech and worked to make a complicated request sound simple and understandable.

She wished for the village to take in this woman and her child. Cleatah had brought gifts to exchange for the favor, but if the woman and baby could be given a hut of their own she would work as the other women did and become a member of the tribe.

She told how, when her own tribe – the Shore People – had allowed a stranger into their midst, it had proved a blessing. Under no circumstance should the woman be allowed to leave the Taug village. Cleatah remembered that this inland tribe fished from the river's edge with nets, and had only the simplest of boats. If Talya had visions of escaping it would be on foot with an infant across the vastness of the continent.

The headman consulted with the elder women and turned back to Cleatah. *Was this woman very ugly or deformed?* they wanted to know. *Was she sick or crazy?* Cleatah assured them Talya was none of these. In fact she was a much-revered woman, but now she was being punished for an ill deed, and the tribe did not wish to have her in their presence. *Would this woman treat the Taug ill?* They asked.

Cleatah had thought long and hard about this and had concluded that the tribe was in no danger from Talya. Without her wrist hub she would be entirely helpless. Of necessity, her days would be spent learning how to survive in this place and how to keep her daughter safe.

Talya would at first be unhappy, she told the headmen and elder women, but she would harm no one.

It was finally agreed that the Taug would take her.

Cleatah returned to the covered cart and lay Isis down. She freed Talya from all her bindings. "Make yourself presentable," she said.

Talya ran her fingers through the pale hair, now stringy with sweat and grime, and tucked the fabric that had imprisoned her arms into a semblance of a garment.

"You will be careful what you tell the child," Cleatah told her, her voice laced with threat. Talya was silent, trembling. "Her father is Boah. Poseidon and Athens are your brothers, her uncles. They, like you, come from 'a place very far away.' Poseidon and his family, and Boah, live across the plateau in Atlantos. Athens lives 'across a very great ocean.'" Cleatah climbed out of the cart. "Now come out. Bring the child."

Desperation shook Talya. "Are you coming back for me?"

She watched Talya gather Isis into her arms.

"Will you come back?" It was a pleading whisper.

Cleatah said nothing. Then she turned away.

⤚

The first indignity of her banishment had been a bath in the icy river. As soon as Cleatah, the cart and two horses had disappeared out of sight the women had surrounded Talya, one of them taking Isis from her arms. The rest laughed and poked curiously at her unnaturally pale skin, bruised in places from the hard wooden cart under her back and buttocks, and her filthy yellow hair. She could tell from their expressions that they thought her unpleasantly thin, and next to their plump curves and ruddy cheeks she must have appeared freakish. But she stank, so even the icy water that made her prickle all over was a relief of sorts. She allowed the women to scrub her, though never taking her eyes off the girl who dandled Isis on her lap. Surely relieved to be done with constant jouncing travel, the child was giggling and patting the girl's face with her fat little fingers.

How could this have happened? How could she have so underestimated Cleatah, her passion and her fury? In her wildest dreams Talya could never have foreseen so brilliant a revenge brought down on her head. Not only were the Taug hundreds of miles from Atlantos, they were one of very few tribes who had shown no interest in joining the others in a new society. They were unimpressed by horses. They shunned the very idea of cultural evolvement. They were as backward a tribe as existed on the

549

continent. Without her phaetron Talya was paralyzed, at these people's mercy for every necessity.

There was irony in her gratitude towards Cleatah who, in her unceremonious farewell, had announced coldly that she hoped never to set eyes on Isis or Talya again. Talya had worried on that terrible journey that her punishment would be losing her child as well as her place in Atlan society. But thankfully Isis had been returned to her.

She would keep to herself until she could make a plan. At least these women were kind. She'd make herself unattractive to the men who – watching her bathing ordeal from a distance – seemed more curious than aroused. Perhaps Boah was already on the way to save them. Certainly he would want her back, want his child – no one would tell him the truth of her parentage. What of Joss and the Brotherhood? Would they not demand to know her whereabouts? And Poseidon – he could never have agreed to such rough justice. She was confident that this horrible village was in no way her destiny, or that her daughter must be raised among savages.

Talya gazed downriver and saw the morning light blinking like a thousand tiny suns on the rippled surface. She heard a shriek of laughter from the shore and thought of how far from her home on Terres she had come... and how much farther she would have to travel before she was through.

MARS COLONY

SEVENTY-THREE

THIS WAS TERRESIAN science at its best. The sharpest minds contemplating the inexplicable and making a civilization-altering discovery. The solution was so simple and elegant that there was only celebration within the small cadre of scientechnoists who laid claim to it.

Then why do I feel so desperate? Persus wondered. *Why am I terrified to bring the findings of the Physics Men to Athens?* Governor Athens. She found it harder all the time to keep her distance. To keep perspective. He was like luscious food to her, always a finger-length out of reach.

The Governor.

There had been a blackness hanging over him since the phibions' attack on Halcyon Beach. The hastily made plan to move the entire colony inland was a dismal alternative to their idyllic existence. People told themselves that the solies were lovely creatures but there'd be plenty to enjoy without them. Without the beach.

Gold. Games. Technos. Bed.

She knew Athens would not take well to the report. He already looked ill. Haunted. These days he muttered about bad dreams, huge black eyes... *Black eyes?* When she'd asked if he meant Athena's eyes he'd nearly snapped her head off. But she was sure today, for Governor Athens, would mark the boundary to a darker place still.

Of course she had no choice. She herself had commissioned the study, though the Physics Men had been arguing the problem since the accident in space – a mystery too delicious to ignore. And with titanum and gold production reaching an all-time high there was much leisure time for contemplation. Long nights together in someone's laboratory. Every trans-screen lit. Fingers flying over the equations. Fat, juicy formulas. Many shouted suggestions but only one perfect solution. These men played at science like a game.

Their joy will be Athens's destruction, she thought many times a day. She needed to steel herself. *No, it will be all right. He is stronger than he appears. Of course he is.* She stepped through his office door. Arranged a pleasant look on her face.

"We need to go," she said to the back of his chair that was turned to the window. He was silent, still, as though screwing up the nerve to speak. "Sir?"

"Yes, I'm coming."

She waited, but he did not move.

"How can we relocate inland? The people will blame me."

"You know that's not true. Everyone saw those creatures. What they were capable of."

"We'd be leaving the solies behind to be butchered by them."

"We'll think of something. Relocate the solies to inland lakes."

Finally he turned and looked at her. "I like that. Your idea?"

"Yes, Sir."

A moment later they were on the move, side by side. He towered over her, and for the hundredth time she bemoaned her pathetic stature and short, heavy legs. Then she admonished herself – this was no time for such selfish and petty considerations.

Very soon Athens would be needing her help.

❧

"But we've *always* suspected alternate dimensions," Athens said, annoyed and quite relieved. He'd been vaguely dreading this physics report, but here nothing was new. "During Gaia Approach...you proved it. Correct?"

"Correct," Clax said, trying hard to hold Athens's eye.

"The proof of an alternate dimension is also our problem," Enoc said, putting an irritating emphasis on "problem."

Athens had enough problems already, he thought.

"You understand there's a thin fabric, a membrane that separates our known dimension from the other. By our physical assaults on Mars..."

"'Physical assaults?'" Athens probed.

"Drilling, Sir," said Clax. "We're quite certain that drilling has had more than a superficial effect on the planet's mantle. We've also been tearing holes in the...fabric."

Dark dread began to settle over him. "What do you mean, 'The evidence is also our problem?'"

Monas finished for the others. "The tears can *grow* from the point of origination. Or possibly multiply. Some of them are in and above the ocean."

Athens froze. *The vision of a hole torn in the sky, a purple universe behind it...*

Monas continued. "We believe the phibions are coming through the tears, Sir. When we first postulated it we had sensors installed along the coast. Every time the sensors detected a new tear occurring, the incidence of incursions escalated dramatically."

"The solies?" Athens whispered.

"They're a new food source for the phibions, not an ancient one as we all believed. That's why the poor little things have no defenses."

The implication was ghastly. He, the colony's governor, was directly responsible for the solies' demise. "What does this..." he could barely form the words "...have to do...with the accident in space?"

"What the data shows," said Enoc, trembling with triumph, oblivious to the effect of his words, "is that, like the small rending in the dimensional membrane from drilling, a larger tear was made by our transport and the *Atlantos* at the approximate location of the accident."

"How much larger?"

"We don't know. But this is where the plasma spheres…"

Athens groaned.

"You *do* remember the amber plasma…?"

"Of course I remember them!" he snapped at Clax. *They are in my dreams, you idiot!* he thought but did not say. "Which is it then?" His voice was shaking. "Holes where we drilled? Holes in the ocean? Holes in *space*! And how are you so sure it was made during this mission? What about the previous Mars mission – my brother's expedition? They were drilling in the crust…There were quakes…"

"It could have been, yes…"

"Then why are you blaming *me?*"

"We're not laying blame on anyone, Sir."

Athens knew he sounded frenzied. Even he could hear the whine in his voice. He felt himself shrinking. *Oh why hadn't Persus minded her own business?* He stared at the Physics Men. He'd made them uneasy. There they all stood, larynxes bobbing up and down in their skinny throats.

Clax swallowed hard. He looked at the others who were waiting for him to finish the rendition of their findings. What all of them in the room now knew was that the answer would be a blow to the governor.

"We have reason to believe a tear now extends at least from the planetary orbits to Mars."

"*At least*?!" Athens shouted.

"It may encompass the entire solar system…and farther out into deep space. We just don't know yet. We're continuing to study it."

"Yes, you do that," Athens said, turning to go. *Poseidon had known all along what had happened to Elgin Mars. This was his reason for insisting on the Gaian expedition for himself and leaving this murderous planet to his fool of a brother. Something frightening on Solie Beach. The next beach over. A pile of bones…a crack in the sky. He'd been betrayed. Betrayed!* "And in the future you, Persus…" Athens spat her name, "You will ask for my personal commission of any scientechnic studies of this magnitude. Is that clear?"

"Of course, Sir."

As he made his exit he knew his composure was as thin as the bloody interdimensional fabric. He hoped it would hold steady until he was safely behind his office door.

ERTHE

SEVENTY-FOUR

"YOUR FAULT!" ACROSS a hundred million miles Poseidon could see the hatred burning in his brother's eyes. "This is your fault."

Poseidon had no answer, no excuse to refute Athens's claim. He stood in the *Atlantos* Library dumb, still trying to absorb the accusation, accept that his actions, his Site 62 excavations – the massive implosion of his phaetronic drill beam – had set in motion the spectacular demise of the Marsean paradise.

His brother's single triumph in life.

"You…" Athens began.

"I didn't *know*. No one could have known. Oh, Athens…" He wished desperately to lay blame elsewhere. Terres's extremity, their need for ore. The salvation of civilization itself. But it was by Poseidon's hand alone that the drilling had triggered the quake. And the quake had opened a galaxy-long gash between two dimensions. *What angry God had set his sights on the brothers Ra?*

Athens hadn't spoken again. He just stood there, silent tears rolling down his cheeks.

"Can your Physics Men…?" Poseidon began.

"Don't you blame them!"

"But their probe…?"

"The membrane had already been weakened on Mars, long before our technos breached it again. My men can do nothing. It is so far beyond their understanding... They are children, Poseidon, trying to influence creation itself."

"What can be done about the phibions? In their own dimension they can't hurt you."

"You're not listening! They have come through the tear. They have found our world very hospitable indeed. They have taken up residence in our waters. I'm told they're *breeding*." Athens shuddered visibly at the word.

"What weapons can kill them?"

"Black beams modified for organic tissue. It's so...archaic. We can kill them one at a time as they come onshore." He laughed ruefully. "Like our ancestors' hand-to-hand combat."

Poseidon knew how alien violence of any kind must feel to the gentle Terresian psyche. This killing of giant monsters and muculent parasites that lived on their scaly bodies, therefore, must be crushing to their very essence.

"I want to speak to Talya," Athens said, almost a whine. "She may have ideas..." His voice trailed off.

"She's not here, Athens."

"Well find her. I *need* to speak to her."

"She and her child are living elsewhere."

Athens's silence, and his glare, demanded explanation.

"She violated Cleatah. She violated me. We sent her away."

"You *banished* Talya from Atlantos?"

"It needed to be done."

Athens fixed Poseidon in his gaze. "*She* did it, didn't she? Your monkey woman? She took revenge on Talya. Sent her away. To where? There's nothing outside of Atlantos City."

"She's safe, Athens. I promise she's safe."

"When does she return?"

"I don't know."

With that, Athens's hands shot out and curled around

Poseidon's throat. Had a hundred million miles not separated them the force would have snapped his neck. As his fingers balled helplessly into fists Athens slumped, utterly defeated.

"Good bye," he said.

"Athens, wait!"

But a moment later he was gone from the Library, leaving behind nothing but the qualities of rage and unimaginable horror.

All Poseidon wanted was Cleatah, here. Now. For comfort. For assurance of his goodness. His innocence. *No*, he thought then, *she is too forthright than that. Too much a guardian of the natural world to side with him.* She would clearly see his transgression and the damage it had done. She would mourn the debasement of their sister planet. And she would judge him. She would not forgive him his technos and its shameful part in destroying the Goddess's masterpiece.

"Come home," he whispered miserably. "Come home."

SEVENTY-FIVE

THE GREAT PLATEAU was all but behind her. Cleatah had already passed the mining villages never making the slightest detour, so eager to be back that even the necessary stops were an annoyance. Her body craved her babies. Atlas and Geo would be little boys soon, rough and tumbling and seeking the company of older boys and men who would harden them, teach them the manly arts. But for now they were hers, seeking the softest parts of her, nestling in the curves of her body as they fed, making sounds like the sweetest birds, fragrant from hair and feet, tiny fingers tangling in her hair as their budlike mouths pulled and sucked at her breasts.

She summoned thoughts of Poseidon. He was her love, the pleasure between her thighs, her teacher of all things marvelous, the deep well of her trust in the goodness of this life. Every day of this miserable journey she had fixed him in her mind's eye – at the Academy Tower with the star-gazers sweeping his hand across the glittering fires in the night sky. With the stone masons at the site of the Horse Stadium urging them on to feats of artistry in their burgeoning craft. With the boat builders igniting their dreams of voyages across the distant sea.

But her happiest visions – the ones that had eased the loneliness of empty plains and endless mountain chains – were those of Poseidon at the Residence. In the gardens. Always Poseidon with the boys. His capacity for the emotions of love and caring had swelled with the birth of their sons. He was prone to fits of helpless laughter and even tears. Despite his never-ending labors in the city he spent every possible moment with his children, riding them on his back, composing chirping little songs for the simple pleasure of making them laugh.

He would be waiting for her return. He might be angry at her outrageous actions, but he had honored her judgment and her punishment for Talya. He'd chosen not to follow them nor allowed Boah to follow either. He would forgive her. She was certain of it.

The horses were straining against their traces, drawn by the scent of a familiar sea. Cleatah clicked twice in her cheek, but they needed no urging. They were taking her home. To her love and her family.

They were taking her home to Atlantos.

SEVENTY-SIX

THE BROTHERHOOD WAS well-aware of the two women's absence from their lives. Talya's was perhaps more keenly felt, as Cleatah – having retired to the Residence with the birth of her twins – was less a public figure than before. She was missed, but her strong silent presence – much as the black rock upon which the Central Isle had been built – was unquestioned and as soothing as mother's milk. But the horsemen's questions to Boah about their patron and mother of his newborn daughter were met with genuine bafflement. Even if he'd wished to, there was simply no way to explain the web of Talya's treachery and lies, or Cleatah's unexpected revenge. Only Joss dug at him with questions, suspicions, but these, too, went unanswered.

Boah had fallen into an unnatural silence among his friends and suffered alone in an impenetrable gloom. The days grew into weeks and the torment seemed endless. This day at the High Atlantos Stables he was tending to a boil on a mare's hoof when shouts began echoing through the rafters: "She comes!"

Boah dropped the horse's foot. He ran for the door. In the distance, approaching from the south was a solitary cart and solitary driver. Heart in his throat he leapt on the nearest mount and galloped off, riding west for a distance to avoid the Grave of the

Horses. The cart was in his sight but with a sinking heart he discovered it was occupied by Cleatah alone. *What had he expected?* he thought miserably. *That Cleatah would have had a change of mind and brought them home?*

When his horse met the team she continued driving them, her face and posture rigid. He rode alongside, but found himself bereft of words. The obvious question – the only question – hung in the silence between them.

Finally she said, "They are well, Boah. Far from here, but safe and cared-for."

They approached the chasm outside the grazing pasture.

"Cleatah. Stop. Talk to me!"

She drew the team to a halt and climbed down as Boah dismounted. He went to her but refused to embrace her until questions were answered.

She peered down into the darkness of the abyss. "I took them twelve days ride to the south. To the Taug." She spoke in hushed tones, never meeting his gaze. "They're fishermen and weavers. A prosperous village on a river. They're traders. We visited them during the great gathering. They refused to join us in Atlantos. Remember?"

"I remember," he said. His lips were set in a grim line. "That river. It has terrible floods. Villagers are swept away. You took them *there*."

"Maybe I wish them to be washed away."

"Cleatah!"

Her face remained hard but she managed to look at him, hold his eye. "I cut the hub out of her wrist."

The sound Boah made was more a shout than a groan.

"You want to know how I could have done such a thing."

Now his gaze was as furious as hers.

"People fight fist to fist. They war with their neighbors. Even murder. But for Talya, with her terrible powers, to take all the girls from my body…forever…"

"But Poseidon…"

"Poseidon is helpless against his own technos! He says he cannot restore what was growing *here*." She clutched her belly and let out a wail. "Seeds of my daughters! She stole my daughters. And Great Mother stood by watching. Let her do it. She is dead to me."

"No!" Boah grabbed her shoulders and shook her, searching for words to shut out the blasphemy.

But Cleatah wriggled out of his grasp.

"Why did you tell me where they are?"

"Because you deserve to know."

"You're certain I won't go after them?"

Her look was so fierce, so terrible that they were both sure of the answer.

"I don't remember the words she used. I'd drunk too much." Boah's shoulders slumped, and his arms hung down like broken tree limbs. Maybe she never said the child was mine. Perhaps I only assumed it. Then it would not be a lie."

"She did nothing to correct you," Cleatah added in a hoarse whisper. "That made it a lie. She extracted Poseidon's seed while he slept. That is worse than a lie."

"I've been such a fool!"

Cleatah laid a gentle hand on his arm. "How could anyone have foreseen so horrible an act? I believed she was my friend. Poseidon's too."

"Please," he said. "Let them come back."

"Boah," she said, "if I'd had to look at her for one more moment…I might have killed her." An icy tone crept into her voice, and he thought he saw a hint of a dark smile. "So I devised a 'protocol' to rid us of her."

Boah startled at this. Here was a Cleatah he had never known in all his life. Like the wolf she'd brought into the Shore Village those many years before, his friend was utterly fearless, strong and ferocious.

"I'm sad that it's come to this," she said, "but I'm not sorry."

He turned to his horse and laid his head on its broad flank, as though he might find comfort there. Courage. But his voice when it came was weak and helpless. "For a long time I saw Talya as my woman, but never my mate…not until she conceived the child. She bore her as if she was mine." He hoped he did not sound pitiful. "Everyone believes this child is mine."

"Isis," Cleatah said in a whisper. "Her name is Isis."

Boah rubbed his hands over his face. "Isis…" He tested the name on his tongue. "She may not be the seed of my body. But she *is* my daughter." He looked pleadingly at Cleatah. "My heart tells me she's mine."

Cleatah's face prickled with tears and the brisk breeze.

"They cannot come home?" he said pleadingly.

"No," she said. "They cannot come home."

She wrapped her arms around him and held him as he shook. In weary silence they contemplated what these strange and beloved creatures from another world had wrought upon their own, how they had changed the Erthe forever…and wept.

SEVENTY-SEVEN

FOR ALL OF Cleatah's absence the boys had fussed and cried, even rejecting the breast of the two young mothers kind enough to share their milk. He could hear Sanja now, trying to sing Atlas one of Cleatah's lullabies, but nothing was quieting the wails. Then Geo joined in.

Poseidon found the three of them in the gathering room. The woman's own infant lay contentedly in the pillows while Geo, sitting up beside the baby girl, was squalling. His face was an alarming shade of crimson that matched the tear-streaked cheeks of Atlas who was cradled in Sanja's arms. She just shook her head helplessly. Poseidon swept his young son up and slung him onto his shoulder, nearly deafened by the screams in his ear.

Then all at once the crying stopped. In an instant. Both boys at once. There was nothing from them, not even a whimper. Poseidon could see their heads swiveling slowly from side-to-side, as though they were looking for something. Sanja gazed at Poseidon, puzzled. Then her own child began to bawl, and they laughed at the strangeness of it all.

"Take her," he said of Sanja's daughter. "I'll hold the boys." He lowered himself into the cushions setting Geo onto one knee. Then Sanja handed Atlas down onto the other.

Their silence continued. They uttered none of the new words

they had recently learned and loved to repeat endlessly. Then one at a time Poseidon turned them to his chest and held one on each shoulder near to his heart, and closed his eyes.

"What is it?" he whispered. "What do you hear?"

He thought how he missed their mother's voice, both words and songs, and the voice that was unspoken.

Then, with the merest shimmer behind Poseidon's eyes a vision began to materialize. It was so clear it might have been a diffracted image. *Cleatah alone, sitting straight-backed on the seat of their wagon traversing the Great Plateau. She was wearing skins, and her dark hair was loose about her shoulders.*

Is this what had quieted the boys? Bloody stars, she was thinking of them! *I hear you, love. I see you! We all see you coming!*

Now Poseidon noticed Manya far in the distance, and before the cart Cleatah's destination. He thought his heart would burst with the relief of it – just a few miles ahead were the headlands of High Atlantos.

✍

On foot Poseidon traversed the bridges and ring isles, never stopping for the many greetings, nor to admire the gorgeously carved stone pillars of the city's newest bath house or accept the warm meat pies held out to him by vendors in the South Market Square. His sights were set squarely on the South Ramp – the gracefully curved roadway running from the market to the High Atlantos Stables. But when a crone with a bright toothless smile waved her arm above a great bucket of tall-stemmed flowers in whites and yellows and purples he slowed, turned and backtracked.

Recognizing the urgency on his face she wordlessly scooped an armload of her beautiful bounty and laid it in Poseidon's arms, whispering, "She will like them."

He nodded his thanks and ran the rest of the way to the base of the ramp where he stopped, feeling suddenly foolish. *What*

*made him so sure she was coming? A mysterious vision he had con-
jured in the gathering room?* It was just as likely wishful thinking
as anything. But the boys had stopped their crying so suddenly.
He wasn't imagining it. Even Cleatah's protracted silence couldn't
last forever. *She is thinking of me... and she is near!*

But what if his fears were real? What if she could never
forgive him for what he'd allowed to happen? It had been his
leniency with Talya that encouraged such audacity in the first
place. Against Cleatah's wishes she had meddled with nature and
altered the course of a great river. Now Talya had tampered with
Cleatah's very body and changed the course of her life. Much as
she loved him, surely some part of Cleatah's affection had been
sullied forever. He was almost afraid to look up at the curving
roadway. Afraid that she'd not be coming. Afraid that she would.
He lifted his eyes and prepared to wait. Forever if he had to.

There, halfway to the bottom...was that the side of their cart?
Was it a woman in profile? *Cleatah!* His heart leapt to his throat,
nearly choking him, and he forced himself to breathe. She had
not seen him yet. There was more of the curved ramp to descend.
Poseidon felt the weight of his future in the next moments – endless pain...or forgiveness.

The clopping of the hooves on the cobbles was louder now.
The horses' heads emerged first, and finally the whole team and
cart and the driver were before him. He was stuck to the ground,
feet made of stone. His voice caught in his throat, dry and
rasping. All he could do was lift his arms high in a wild waved
greeting. The forgotten flowers were falling in a shower around
him at the instant Cleatah clapped eyes on him.

In the next moment she was running down the curved ramp,
her hair flying behind her. Their collision was sudden and shocking and sweet. His raised arms lowered slowly down around her
pulling her into him, closer and tighter, and tighter still.

"You heard me calling you," she whispered.

"No. I *saw* you. Our sons heard you."

"And you brought me flowers."

"Yes."

He began to laugh at the thought of it and bent to gather them. She stooped and took some up in her arms as well. The horses and their driverless cart clopped to a halt beside them.

"Shall we go see the boys, Love?" she said.

He nodded, unable to utter a sound.

Side-touching-side, blossoms festooning her lap, they drove through their city of circles, marveling at all they had conjured out of thin air, with countless shouted blessings and the cries of seabirds following them all the way home.

ATHENS, 399 BC

WITH THESE LAST words uttered, Solon's image – so steadfast over the countless hours of storytelling – slowly dissolved.

"Wait!" Xanthippe cried, reaching out her hand.

Plato sprang to his feet and moved to the place his great-great uncle's facsimile had stood. He looked at Xan. "He can't be finished. He's only just begun."

He helped her off the couch. She groaned to move muscles stiff from not moving for what? Half a day? A day? More?

Together they stood above the table looking down at the volumes of Giza's Chronicles, and at the strange device that had summoned Solon – the dynamo called a "phaetron." Its functions were known to them now, as were those who had wielded it for good and for evil. He held onto her hand as they ascended the torchlit steps.

Always sure-footed, Xan stumbled on his villa doorstop. He caught her fall and she smiled gratefully, but Plato could see she was shaken. For himself, he was as raw as freshly plowed earth after a rain. All was laid bare. Love. Jealousy. Loathing. Fear. And monsters.

Monsters!

"You won't go back down there without me," she said.

"Of course I won't. We'll do this together."

"But what *is* this?"

He smiled. "Just like old Socrates. The clearest way to truth is through questioning."

"I already have a thousand."

"This story puts the *Epic of Gilgamesh* to shame," Plato said as he shut the front door behind them. He stopped and gazed back at Solon's villa, its crumbling, vine-bedecked wall, remembering the wonders of its library and glorious mysteries of the secret alcove.

The dark hid their shadowed eyes as they walked the narrow streets shoulder-to-shoulder, too overcome to speak. They'd gone the length of two entire blocks before they said, in perfect unison, "I've been thinking…"

Of course they laughed.

"You first," he said.

"Who *is* this Poseidon?" she demanded with irritation. "He's no Poseidon we've ever heard of."

"Certainly not Homer's 'Storm Bringer,'" Plato agreed, "whipping up such a hurricane that Odysseus is nearly drowned."

"His father is not Cronus, and Zeus and Hades are not his brothers," she added. "And his lovers…well, there were a lot of them, but I've never heard of Talya or Cleatah."

"He does wield a trident," said Plato. "That is the same as the Olympian Poseidon. And there were two quakes in the story – one of which he caused."

"'Earth Shaker.' He's well known that way."

"But 'God of the Horse?'"

"Well, the Arcadians – not that we should ever believe anything the Arcadians say – told a fanciful story of him striking a rock, and the rock becoming a horse," Plato offered. "Older stories say he *was* a horse."

"Nonsense!" Xan snapped. "And tell me again why we're taking the word of Egyptian priests reading stories off their stone stelae about *our* gods?"

"Don't you remember Socrates telling us that our gods may have once been Egyptian?"

"No, I do not!"

"He did. And Xan, if Solon believed the priests at Neith, and on their words he found the *Chronicles* and the device between the stone lion's paws…"

"Then we must believe the Egyptians," she relented.

"Pure Socratic logic," Plato said.

"This is a tragedy," Xan added mournfully.

"Tragedy? This is the great miracle of our lives."

"Only that Soc did not live to meet Solon."

"But he'd have met him on the other side!" Plato argued, partly to cheer her, partly because he believed it to be true. "In that 'Place of Judgement' he always talked about. The place we all visit after death, the one with a personal guide to the next world. Solon is surely his. This story is being told to him…" Plato said with all his mustered confidence, "…from one great storyteller to another."

Xan seemed pleased at the thought. "He's hearing it along with us."

"Without question."

"Without question," she said, and smiled.

The *Gods of Atlantos Saga* continues…

Enjoy an excerpt from Book III

Enjoy an excerpt from

CHRONICLES
OF
GIZA

THE GODS OF ATLANTOS SAGA

BOOK III

Four decades later. The planet Mars has been devastated by a trio of comets, and the colonists have escaped their world on a fleet of transports to find a new home on Erthe. They were relieved to be leaving behind the monstrous phibions and grey interdimensional, mind-invading aliens called the "Zozen," but as they fled, most of their precious stores of titanum and gold were lost as parts of Mars's mantle were blown into space, smashing into the escape fleet.

*The people of Atlantos, standing together on the Great Plateau
under a blue bowl of sky, have been warned of both the terror
and beauty of what they are about to witness – the arrival of
colonists from Mars. It will be a surpassing spectacle, one as
naturally mighty as the Great Quake and sea wave of fifty
years ago, and as miraculous as Poseidon's building of the
ringed canals and Seawall.*

But now the Marsean fleet simply appears from nothing-
ness *before our eyes, full-blown in its metallic glory – the crafts
hovering steadily and soundlessly as though such heavy, solid
objects have every right to float in the air with no effort, like
a puff of clouds on a windless day. And despite the warnings,
there are howls of outrage from the people on the ground,
moans of fear and dread.*

*We watch as Poseidon, Cleatah and Atlas step forward
deliberately, unflinchingly, till they stand underneath the
loveliest of the fleet's vessels – a silvery disc, massive in circumference, simple and elegant in design. There they wait, Cleatah
finding Poseidon's hand hidden in the folds of his tunic. Talya,
sister of Poseidon, and her husband Boah, shield their eyes
against the blinding sun-shards glancing off the flying machine
as they step forward to join them. The Atlans press forward,
eager to witness this meeting of two brothers separated by time
and fathomless space, and to welcome their "cousins" from
another world.*

*The Marseans' history is tragic and terrifying. Their home
has been visited by three great "Serpents From the Sky "crashing down upon land and sea, flooding it and setting its very
air afire. Who are these strangers hidden behind the walls of*

the dark, boxy airships casting giant shadows on the grass-lands? Who are the people who will henceforth share the Erthe with us?

And then, like nothing we have ever seen or imagined in our wildest dreams, a sudden shimmering column of blue light shoots from the bottom center of the silvery disc.

From *The Chronicles of Giza*

The crew on the bridge – even Persus and Athena – had fallen into shocked silence at the sight of their new home planet below. Athens wondered if the viewing decks of the three transports had been similarly soundless during the Gaian Approach. Colonists with eyes wide, jaws slack. Guilty comparisons with Mars crashing around in their heads. They'd loved their mono-forests of giant tree ferns, their inland water parks, city gardens. But here was something far more splendid in its infinite variety. Vast rolling plains, jagged snow and tree-crowded peaks, broad rushing rivers, cloud-shrouded jungles. And the sea. A sparkling ocean that stretched endlessly to the curving blue horizon.

Earlier, coming out of his sleep pod, Athens's head had begun to clear of the sticky webs that blanketed his brain. There was once again an edge to everything he saw. *And the voices were gone.* That sensation alone was cause for a small celebration. Still, his legs were rubbery and the olfactory sense was dull. No, he thought, he could smell nothing at all.

"Are you ready to go down?" Persus said behind him.

"No," he answered, with his last shred of combativeness.

"How long, sir? They're all waiting down there."

"I can see that."

"It looks as though the whole population's come out to welcome us," she said.

"Ogle us, you mean."

Athena came to his side and gave Persus a half-smile.

"Let's be optimistic," said Persus, placing a light hand on Athens's arm.

"Our host is your brother, after all," Athena added.

"And they've found us a wonderful place to settle." Persus fixed Athens with her eyes. "Don't you agree?"

"I do agree. We're all going to live there happily in the sun forever," he said.

"And.." Athena prodded him.

"…and we'll have everything we need to rebuild the colony," Athens intoned like a schoolboy.

"That wasn't very convincing," said Persus.

"So much was lost…" Athens said, some threads of dark web threatening to pierce his embryonic cheerfulness…*the last titanum barge floating away into space.* "So much…"

"Sir, stop. This is a rich planet. We'll find what we need. I promise."

Athena came and stood directly before him. His daughter's lovely face did soothe him, he thought. The sight of her banished the bleak image, and when she smiled he was able to smile back.

"Good," she said. "And you're going to be very cordial to my Aunt Cleatah," Athena continued.

Athens inhaled, the breath straightening his back. "I'll be the *picture* of cordiality."

She grinned. "I think the protocol worked, Persus." She neatened Athens's collar. "But if you act up, I promise we're putting you back in your pod."

"Sir?" Persus urged. "They're waiting."

"Tell them I'm ready," he said.

⤸

With the Marsean Fleet hovering overhead, thoughts crashed wildly around in Poseidon's brain. He loved his brother, he supposed, as well as any Terresian-born man could do. He and Athens had been born of the same mother and father, neither of them gestated in womb factories. And their mother had laid a rich foundation of affection for them both. But Athens had been hard to love, even as a child. Angry, jealous, prone to tantrums. They'd steered parallel courses at Academy, and then Federation, never having to mingle in each other's cultures. In truth, Poseidon's nomination of Athens as Colonial Governor instead of himself had been more selfish than most believed. That his brother had, at first, flourished on Mars was to his own credit. Honestly, Poseidon had been relieved to have him millions of miles away. That way he'd been mostly spared the embarrassment of voicing his sometimes harsh judgments of weak or flawed decisions and character.

But now Athens was here. suspended a thousand feet above the Great Plateau in a ship identical to the *Atlantos*. The five retractable legs had yet to be extended, as though a firm landing on the surface was still in question. Of course Athens would be dreading this encounter as much as he was.

More, Poseidon expected.

He could feel Cleatah beside him, exuding a forced grace. This was rare with her. Next to nothing on Erthe made her uncomfortable. But Athens was not of the Erthe. He was soon to be its adoptive son, but she dreaded his coming. Dreaded his disregard of Great Mother. *If he did not feel the Goddess's body, did not care for her,* she agonized, *how could he live well on this planet? How could the Marseans live? Would they take from her, insult her, harm her?*

These were Poseidon's own fears – what had lost him years of sleep, caused him to tremble now as he gazed at the familiar Terresian vessel hovering before them. He loved the Erthe with a passion equal to his love of the woman beside him. In his most primitive instincts he knew that Athens's coming meant danger for them both. But there was nothing to be done. There was nowhere else for these people to go. This invitation had been a gift, in Poseidon's eyes. But it was a punishment in his brother's. A humbling.

A failure.

The sudden shock of the blue elevator beam shooting down from the center of the ship wrenched Poseidon from his thoughts and set him back on his heels. Cleatah put a steadying hand on his arm.

"Great Mother protect us," he had heard Cleatah saying as she'd knelt at her altar this morning. "Protect us all from my beloved's brother." He had wondered whether her Goddess wielded a kind of natural contour dome, a protective shield that could keep Erthe's "fabric" intact despite alien disturbances. He had never wished to believe in Great Mother's existence and omnipotence more than he did at this moment.

Then Athens appeared floating at the top of the beam, a woman on either arm. As they began their descent Poseidon linked fingers with Cleatah, taking a step forward. Another, then another.

Athens stepped first out of the glowing blue cylinder of light. To see him this way, without the distance of space or vibral aura between them revealed him to be softer, less frightening than imagined. But oh, what Poseidon did see before him! It clawed at his belly. Cleatah's fingers tightened around his. She'd seen it, too. Desperation. Unspeakable sadness. The barely hidden old jealousies.

Enough! Poseidon thought. *Go to him now!*

Poseidon strode three steps forward, and Athens did the same. Their arms clapped around one another's and they hung there for a single moment together, passionate and unguarded.

"Brother," they both said simultaneously, then laughed at themselves. They pushed to arm's length to take each other's measure... and there was nothing to see in Athens's eyes except weariness. *Maybe my fears are unfounded,* Poseidon thought. *Maybe he will be all right.*

Destiny hung between them, for better or worse. The future had arrived.

"Welcome home," Poseidon said.

∽

Athens had tried to be agreeable, even ingratiating. He really had. But every word, every gesture, every sight was borne as a new cut. How fine and healthy Poseidon had looked when he'd come and embraced him. The real warmth and welcome in his voice when he'd whispered, "Brother." Cleatah – she wore her years lightly on her long frame. They hadn't any right to be so perfectly happy when his world had died that terrible death. Even this horse-drawn conveyance brought to ferry Persus and him back to their city boiled his blood. *To revel in backwardness like this!* Wouldn't one's brain atrophy? No wonder Talya had been driven to the edge of insanity.

And Persus – was she genuinely *enjoying* herself? She sat next to Cleatah on cushions laid down on hard wooden seats, and took the jouncing carriage with ripples of laughter, pointing here and there so her hostess could tell her what they were seeing. The "South Ramp" was a broad curving thoroughfare that swept down from their "Great Plateau" into the heart of the city. Surrounding them on the ramp were hundreds of simple wagons carting the colonists down to their new guest quarters – family homes happily thrown open to "their cousins from Mars."

Atlantos City was, he had to admit, a remarkable sight – a metropolis of concentric circles – canals and ring-shaped islands, and as prosperous looking as it was pretty. He could see from above that the market at the base of the ramp on the outermost island was busy and vibrant. The waters teemed with sailing vessels, rowed boats, and barges piled with goods. The horse racing Stadium, docks and harbor were, by any standards, magnificent feats of engineering.

"You're quiet," Poseidon finally said. "Are you all right?"

Athens could see Persus turn her head slightly and lower her voice to hear this exchange, even as she continued in unbroken conversation with Cleatah. He was unready to admit to his misery. "I'm fine," he said. "Fine." He watched Persus's shoulders soften slightly. Her voice rose again – immediate disaster averted.

Poseidon leaned in to his brother and spoke quietly. "I can't imagine what you must be feeling."

"No, no you cannot. Not even *begin* to understand." Athens gulped a sharp breath of air for strength, but suddenly the yeasty-sweet aroma of fresh baked bread rising from the market assailed his nostrils. He felt undone. Weak as a child. He grimaced and Poseidon saw it. *Damn him!*

"What is it?" he asked, alarmed.

"Nothing, Poseidon," Athens said with a petulant gaze. "Nothing a new planet of our own wouldn't fix."

"You'll share Erthe with us," Poseidon said slowly, clearly embarrassed by the implication. *Share the Erthe but obey my rules* was what he really meant.

"How do you expect us to survive without ore?" Athens said, forgetting to keep his voice low.

Persus and Cleatah turned to listen.

"Come look at our city," Poseidon urged. "You'll build a similar one on the Middle Sea…You'll want for nothing."

"You expect us to live like *this*?" Athens snapped.

"You haven't seen it yet, Athens," Cleatah said. "Its comforts might surprise you."

"You have no idea what you're talking about!" he spat.

Everyone went still. They listened uncomfortably to the clop of echoing hooves and the gabble of many voices as the carriage descended into the marketplace.

"I think what he means…" Persus began.

"What I *mean*, Vice Governor, is that Cleatah has no right to comment on our circumstances – something she knows nothing whatsoever about. Less than nothing." Athens's smile to Poseidon was an ugly grimace. "Now how's *that* for our first family conversation on Uuuurth?"

"Not unexpected," Poseidon said, and heaved a long sigh.

Persus opened her mouth, probably to demand he apologize for his rudeness, but there was a sudden commotion around them.

"Poseidon! Poseidon!" Vendors and citizens had surrounded the carriage, waving and calling to their beloved leaders. "Mother Cleatah! Ask the Goddess for her blessings!" "Where is your brother?" shouted a butcher from his stall.

The hanging animal carcasses filled Athens's vision. The stench of bloody meat revolted him. Even Persus turned away, embarrassed by her disgust.

"Athens!" he heard. "Athens!" People were calling in friendly voices. He forced himself to look out at the bustling market rows. He saw the handsome faces, colorful garments, happy children chasing through the crowds. *Athens...Athens...* Who was calling him now? He couldn't see them. Everyone had gone back to their business. *Athens...Athens.* Were those sly voice *inside his head?*

"No!" he cried, clutching his skull with both hands.

"What is it, Sir?" Persus leaned in to him.

Athens listened carefully. It was whispered low, but he thought he heard, *We are here, Athens.*

"We are here on Erthe. We have followed you," he said aloud. "We will follow you wherever you go." He clutched Persus's hand. "Are they here?"

Her face was calm, composed. "No, Sir. Listen to me. The Zozen are not here. It's *not them* speaking to you."

"How do you know?" He held her eyes with his, the only anchor in this sudden storm.

"That's fear talking. They're your own voices. Nothing more. Listen carefully. Do they sound anything like the Zozen?"

Athens did listen. There were voices – fainter now – but Persus was right. They were not Zozen voices. He loosened his grip on her fingers and she gasped in relief. He'd been crushing them. He sat back in the cushions.

"What are you staring at?" he said to Poseidon. He glared defiantly at Cleatah. "I've had to live for years with those hideous creatures inside my head. Can you imagine? Can you?!"

"Perhaps the only blessing in having to leave Mars," Persus said," was leaving them behind."

He thought her smile at Poseidon and Cleatah was a bid for forgiveness on his behalf. They both smiled, forgiveness apparently granted.

He sat back as they crossed the broad bridge from the outermost ring of land to the Middle Ring Isle. Below them boatmen were waving merrily, calling up as though they didn't have a care in the world. *I hate them all,* Athens thought, and before he could stop himself, chuckled maniacally. *They must all think I'm mad. Maybe I am.*

The Middle Isle was, in fact, quite beautiful, if strangely antiquated. Graceful neighborhoods of modest red and white and black stone houses, each with a roof garden of flowers and trailing vines. On the main thoroughfares public buildings had been grandly enough designed, but there was something irritatingly primitive about them. It seemed there were as many public bath houses as small temples and city greens.

"Our Academy," Cleatah said, sweeping her hand before her at graceful, low-slung edifices, a grassy quadrangle, and a soaring stone obelisk. A scattering of students and teachers sat talking beneath ancient, heavy-boughed trees.

It was an impressive campus, even to Athens's eyes. It was… Terresian, he thought. "You designed this," he said to his brother.

"We did it together," Cleatah countered, smiling at Poseidon. "I'd diffractor-visited the Xenophon ScienTechnic Academy many times, and wanted to bring the best of your planet to ours."

She's bright, Athens thought, gazing back at the obelisk that so resembled their home academy. *And gracious. Why didn't he like her more?*

"Athens..." he heard a woman say.

"What?" He turned back to them all.

Persus looked blankly at him. No one here had said his name.

"Don't look at me that way." Athens squirmed in his seat.

Athens... The voice was tender, familiar.

He glared at Poseidon. "I know what you're thinking." Athens knew how shrill he sounded.

Poseidon put out a gentle hand to him. He slapped it away. This shocked them.

No one moved, nor spoke, nor met each other's eyes. They all looked down at the floor of the carriage.

Sandals, Athens thought, unable to tear his eyes from Cleatah's feet. *I'd like to wear sandals.* Eyes wide open, a vision burst suddenly upon him, blotting all else from his head – *the drone army in their underground quarters as heavy stone and girders crashed down around their heads. On their faces he recognized the same shrieking fear he'd seen in Praxis as crushing tentacles drew the Vice Governor into the phibion's razor-toothed maw.*

He had been responsible for both.

Praxis deserved it, Athens thought. *Did I say that aloud?* Then those boys filled his vision again... the pale-skinned slave miners danced before his eyes, their arms and legs flailing. Blood splashing. A glimpse of that triangular birthmark they all wore high on their right cheek. *They didn't feel a thing, Athens,* he heard a woman say. "That's right. They *couldn't* feel," he agreed. "Not pain. Not heat." *None of that,* the woman said. And suddenly he knew her. "Mother!" he cried out. He vaguely heard his brother groan. Athens closed his eyes, hoping to see her. Manya. And yes! The moment his lids had settled, her face was before him. She looked so beautiful. Her voice soothing. Not speaking words exactly. More like bird sounds muffled by powdery down feathers. Words did not matter. *She was forgiving him*! He turned his head to lay it on her soft, fragrant breast. He breathed in her mother scent and sighed, feeling his body sink bonelessly into her embrace. "Mmmmmmm…" was all he could manage. Moving his lips to form a word was too much. "Mmmmmmmm" was more of an expelled breath.

The change when it came was microscopically subtle. But a change it was. In the powdery fragrance a hint of burning rock. Mother's cupped hands and pillowy fingertips on his back now felt more like a hard bony grip on his ribcage. He inhaled the last remaining wisp of female perfume, leaving only the thin vacuum of deep space. He *knew* whose hands clutched him. Perhaps if he stayed very still, pretended to sleep, pretended *death*, it would leave him alone. Remove those grey spindly arms from around him and translocate back to its own dimension. *Didn't they miss home? Miss their hive?* He chuckled out loud at the thought. *The Zozen couldn't hurt him. They were mindless workers, not much smarter than his drones.* He would face this thing. Banish it from his vision. Its voice in his head. *Open your eyes,* he told himself. *Open your eyes.*

The curtain of his lids rose on the Zorn's looming face. Athens steeled himself against the sight of bulbous eyes so black his own reflection stared back at him. He saw the nearly invisible slash of a mouth. The sharply uptilted nostrils allowing an obscene view into the creature's head. He felt calm, near as he was to her, strangely fearless in her close presence. Her telepathic intrusions were silenced. There was no alien invasion of his brain. If he could withstand it for just a little longer…*a little longer*…he could conquer it forever! He felt strength stiffen his back. His lips began curling into a smile. The Zorn began to smile back. Athens saw the mouth, the lipless gash begin to deform, twisting so far upward that its two corners twined around its nose. Then before his eyes it distorted further, growing larger, longer, its nose and mouth protruding outward from the face, becoming a snout.

A scaled snout.

You know what this is, he thought, shrinking away, moaning. *You know what this is!* The phibion's dagger-toothed mouth yawed open, drooling viscous gel laced with bright red blood. *You won't feel a thing,* it whispered.

Athens began to scream.

AN ABRIDGED AUTHOR'S NOTE
AND ACKNOWLEDGEMENTS

The irony of writing about a civilization that destroyed itself 12,000 years in the past while watching it all happen again today is simply mind-shattering. Conflagrations in Siberia, the Pacific Northwest and Australia. Deadly floods in Europe and Asia. Killer heat domes and a thousand-year drought. Twenty-seven volcanoes going off at once with ten waiting to blow? Monster hurricanes. Millions dead in the first of many pandemics. Oceans, lakes, and rivers dying from pollution. Extinction of species on a grand scale. Glaciers and both polar ice caps melting under extreme heat waves. The Atlantic "Conveyor Belt" about to quit, threatening a "Day After Tomorrow" scenario. Mother nature is striking back, yet… a debacle at the 2021 Glasgow Climate Conference, and the leaders of the world floundering and paralyzed.

I find myself these days trembling with rage and despair watching our own brilliant, suicidal, technology-obsessed society – so spoiled and addictively entertained by its own jaw dropping talents – doing it all again, threatening nuclear war, and destroying the only planet in our solar system capable of supporting higher life forms. We are thwarted by governments, religions, corporate billionaires and oligarchs, and deceived by shortsighted, closed-minded scientists, mainstream academia and media that seek to hide some of our most important truths. Even our own history, the true chronology of our species and its civilization, is forbidden to the masses.

We've become a *juggernaut*, an overstuffed train of fools racing headlong down the tracks, toward the South Wall of the Great Unknown.

In this saga, one that has taken me more than two decades to write, I desperately wanted, once and for all, to give Plato his due. The few historians who deign to allude to the great Greek as the progenitor of the story of Atlantis might mention him as the original source, but few take the story seriously as he intended it to be – they call it "myth" or "allegory," and no one has ever taken the time to wonder why this philosopher – a man revered *in his own lifetime* – would write something so radical and outrageous. These were dialogues he *knew* would earn him ridicule, or perhaps death (as was the Fate of his teacher, Socrates) *for daring to tell the truth.*

My "Plato Bookends" were some of the most delightful and satisfying writing I've ever done, and I was thrilled to give the philosophy student an historically accurate "friend," Socrates's uppity young widow, Xanthippe…and the scripture-spouting "Master Grae," named after our genius African parrot, Mister Grey – significant roles in bringing the story to light.

I count four "Godfathers" of *The Gods of Atlantos Saga.*

The project's "*Great*-Godfather" – **Plato** – is, of course, the first.

Another Godfather of this project, whose non-fiction masterpieces were the foundation of my historical, archaeological and astronomical research, is **Graham Hancock** – *New York Times* mega-bestselling author, world authority, and exceptional lecturer on forbidden history, advocate of the *true* chronology of civilization, and champion of psychedelic research and therapies. His friendship – as much as his fortitude, encouragement and endorsements – have been an essential inspiration to me while writing on a subject derisively called "the 'A' word," one that is constantly battered by scathing ridicule and character assassination.

The original champion of the project and third Godfather – **Ronald Shusett** – is in fact the "Godfather of Hollywood Science Fiction." The monster-meister who literally dreamed up the stupefying chest-burster sequence in "Alien," has been my mentor, producer and story consultant since *before* the novel's first draft in the mid-90s. It was his influence that encouraged the hard science and science fiction elements in my storytelling. All three species of creatures – *Zozen, Phibions* and *Solies* – that inhabit my worlds were by-and-large Ron's inventions. Ron's wife, producer **Linda Shusett**, consulted on and proof-read the earliest drafts of the book.

The fourth Godfather, **Chris Vogler,** international bestselling author, writing teacher and the esteemed "Master of Mythical Storytelling" in Hollywood for three decades, has also been an editor and advisor since before *Gods of Atlantos* was even a book. He segued with me as the manuscript grew over the decades from 515 pages to nearly 2,000. Chris has read, commented on and edited every major draft I've written.

My dear friend **Suzan Crowley**, the literal voice of the *Poseidon in Love* audiobook, has given and given and given herself in more ways than I can count. A brilliant, classically trained British actress and *AudioFiles* "Earphones" winner who has given voice to three of my other novels, she is an entire repertory company rolled up into one person.

Wonderful friend, neighbor, and Emmy and Peabody Award-winning producer, **David S. Miller**, is not only *The Gods of Atlantos Saga's* greatest fan, but worked tirelessly and masterfully as the editor and sound designer for the audiobook of *Poseidon in Love*.

Luigi Maiello is the astonishing and prolific Italian composer whose *Hero's Journey Symphony* enriches and elevates the audiobook, lending it a gravitas I could never have dreamed of.

Over the course of more than twenty years, four individuals became my tireless and faithful editors and critics. To writing partner **Billie Morton, to Greg Blair**, my cousin **Iris Zweben**, and one of my oldest friends **Tom Ellis**, I owe the greatest debts of gratitude for their perseverance, honesty and good humor during what must have seemed like the "Ground Hog Day" of book projects. They read and gave notes on countless drafts and never failed to steer me towards clarity and simplicity, much needed in so complex a saga. Tom, a painter I consider the "American Leonardo," whose painting "*Poseidon*" graces the cover of *Poseidon in Love,* with an artist's eye is also a proof-reader extraordinaire.

Other valued readers are **Victor Megenes, Vincent Covello, David Cohen, Mac McIver** and **Ginny Higgins**. Every one of them brought important insights to the books.

Australian Graphic designer and new friend **Elissa O'Brien** created the stunning covers for all five *Gods of Atlantos* books as well as the audiobook, and Spanish illustrator Rocío Espín Piñar's title page spread of *The City of Atlantis* – found in all five books – simply made my day when she agreed to let me use it.

Harry Duran, acclaimed podcast strategist and producer, and my partner in "An Alien in Hollywood: The Life and Times of Ron Shusett" Podcast, has been an avid fan of *God's of Atlantos* since he first heard Suzan Crowley's audio performance of *Poseidon in Love,* and fell head-over-heels with the project. Since then he's brainstormed, networked and strategized with me on the myriad ways it could be brought to market.

But no one deserves more gratitude than my husband of forty years, **yogi Max Thomas.** We moved, on the eve of the Millennium from Topanga Canyon to a 22-acre tract of high desert wilderness, and together fell passionately in love with this magnificent planet. As Poseidon and Cleatah did, we became stewards and protectors of our own little piece of paradise. Besides his reading, re-reading and *re-re*-reading of the manuscripts, it was Max – an astute judge of the human condition – to whom

I turned whenever I was blocked with character, relationship or motivation. A lover of happy endings – from the first draft to the last – he kept doggedly asking me, "Does Atlantos really have to sink?" Max has been my inspiration for the romantic, planet-defending Poseidon…and is the person I love most in the world.

Believe it or not, this is a *brief* rendition of my "Author's Note and Acknowledgments." There are *many* more people whose help and fascinating research need enlarging upon and thanking, but this volume has gone on long enough already. The unabridged version can be found at the end of Book V in the Saga, GOD OF DESTRUCTION.

Robin Maxwell, Pioneertown, 2022

Please visit me at:
www.RobinMaxwell-GodsOfAtlantos.com
www.RobinMaxwell.com
Facebook: www.facebook.com/AuthorRobinMaxwell
Twitter: @TheRobinMaxwell

Made in the USA
Middletown, DE
25 November 2022

15961002R00364